WHAT HAPPENED AT LAKE TALLULAH?

NINA HANN

Brilliant Books Literary
137 Forest Park Lane Thomasville
North Carolina 27360 USA

"Skim the wide ocean; cut the deep sky
Relentlessly bound to a meeting with you…"

Uell S. Andersen, Author, *"Three Magic Words"*

Chapter 1

MARGAUX SLOWLY OPENED THE HEAVY, gray, steel door that lead from the women's locker room toward the Olympic-sized swimming pool and stood there transfixed, holding the door, her azure eyes scrutinizing the shiny, aquatic complex.

Two of the four lofty walls were comprised of towering glass-paned windows reaching from the floor towards the gray, steel-beamed cathedral ceiling. Soft light-blue canvas curtains were pulled up and secured near the ceiling. The other two walls were painted in ivory and were bounded on all four corner edges with the same light-blue patina. Close to the cathedral ceiling, a long line of massive piping in powder blue extended around all four sides of the complex like a sinuous snake. Vents that extended from the piping provided either hot or cool air inside the entire complex depending upon the season.

Today, the warm June sunshine streamed through the sparkling glass of the windows, its bright rays reflecting across the transparent, aqua-blue of the pool water.

It was Margaux's first day at the newly-built aquatic complex, dubbed the Yorkbury AquaClub. It was the pride of Mirrington Heights. Stationed around the pool were the white-and-blue folding bench seats for the fully clothed bystanders and spectators. Some read books and others played with their IPads and IPhones. A few tired swimmers lounged lazily on the benches, cooling down before heading for home.

Several blue-and-white mesh bins full of colorful arm and leg floaters, noodles, and balls were positioned against the two windowless white walls for all to use in the pool. A few adults and children huddled enthusiastically around the multicolored pool accessories, checking them out.

Sitting high above the pool on striped chairs, young, college-aged lifeguards maintained constant vigilance over the swimmers, ready to leap at the first sign of distress.

As she walked away from the locker room door, Margaux watched the die-hard athletes in the competition pool, vigorously swimming laps, splashing water all around, as they moved furiously back and forth. To her right, she saw several divers, young and old, waiting patiently in line as they practiced in the deep-diving well.

Bolstered by curiosity and excitement, Margaux looked to her left at the instructional pool. Today, in the adjoining guest room, a birthday party was in full swing with cakes, party favors, streamers, and colorful balloons. Adults and children laughed and splashed each other, as they celebrated the birthday child.

A swimmer in front of her lifted his body up from the pool, breathing heavily, as he picked up his towel from a bench nearby and walked tiredly towards the men's locker room.

Finally, a lap lane freed up.

After taking a deep breath, Margaux dove into the water and began her swim. Soon she was enjoying a "runner's high." Sheer happiness filled her as powerful endorphins flooded her brain.

After several years' hiatus, including a move back to her childhood home, Westbury Moor, she had been guided by her mysterious friend from long ago, who had suddenly appeared in her bathroom mirror, cryptically telling her to go back to the pool. She wasn't sure why it had been so important for her to go to that pool, but at least she wanted to try. She agreed to try. Her friend did say to "go to where it's white and blue".

Her friend also knew she loved to swim.

"How do you want to register?" a bored lifeguard asked sitting in front of a computer in the lobby station by the entrance door. "We have daily punch passes for a few weeks or months and we have one electronic pass for the entire year".

"I'll take the electronic pass." Margaux smiled back at the lifeguard. After punching a few keystrokes into the computer, he handed her the laminated bar code pass. "There you go, ma'am. Welcome to Yorkbury Aquaclub." Thanking him with a smile, Margaux clipped the pass into the ring that held the keys to her cherry-red Mazda Miata and her house. Although expensive, the pass was a well worth the investment. She planned to use the pool frequently and return to the form-fit swimmer's body she had lost over the years she was married to that jerk.

It was time to be at one with the water.

The last lap finished, Margaux paused at the curb of the deep end of the pool, breathing deeply, as she removed the swim goggles. She grabbed her right ankle and began stretching the tired quadriceps of her right thigh. She did the same with her left thigh. After a few seconds, she stretched out her body toward the bottom of the pool and bent backwards in the form of a dying swan, her arms fully outstretched.

She felt beautiful.

And yet, nothing happened today.

Brushing away disappointment, Margaux lifted herself out of the water, breathing deeply. As she headed towards the women's locker room, she felt her right foot land on something sharp. With a whimper, Margaux lifted her foot and bent over to see what she had stepped on. In an instant, she found herself sitting on the floor, startled, her hands automatically stabilizing her body.

Someone had pushed her!

Irritated, she looked up from the floor, ready to berate whoever had dared to push her down. Instead, she saw a handsome lifeguard towering over her, casting a looming shadow. He looked quite worried. Margaux was stunned.

He was incredibly tall, almost 6 feet tall, with broad, broad shoulders extending from his muscled neck in perfect swimmer's form. He was wearing an off-white t-shirt emblazoned in the front with the familiar burgundy-and-navy pool logo of Yorkbury AquaClub. A small black belt wrapped around his waist holding a two-way communication device. The navy swim shorts only served to emphasize his tanned, powerfully muscled thighs standing too close in front of her eyes. Margaux dared not breathe, her wide eyes staring at his legs in curious fascination, her heart beating in rapid staccatos.

He was so handsome, it hurt to see him.

"Hello," he said. "I seem to have accidentally knocked you down. Are you all right?" Margaux nodded quickly. "Okay, then." He extended his hand to help her get up.

Pushing herself up, Margaux looked closer at his face and was startled. He seemed so much older than all the younger lifeguards she had known over the years coming to the pool. Clearly, he must be their manager. And yet, she had never seen him before. She surveyed his face again. His thick, black, wavy hair gave him a distinguished look. His tanned face with a prominent 5 o'clock shadow at the lower half of his cheeks had all the right, rugged curves from his smooth, wide forehead to an aquiline, Roman nose and dimpled chin.

Wow! was all she could think at that moment.

Smiling quizzically at her, the handsome lifeguard bent forward to stabilize her, as she struggled to stand on her injured foot. With her hands firmly planted on his broad shoulders, Margaux hopped awkwardly on her stable foot to find her balance, embarrassment flooding her cheeks.

The lifeguard grinned at her frustration. "Just hold onto my shoulders and I will take a look at your foot."

"Okay." She replied.

Once again, she looked up at him, staring into his deep, brown eyes. In an instant, she felt jolted by several quick flashes of black-and-white images, memories lost in time. An image came to her of the two of them alone in the darkness somewhere far away and vague. She had felt safe in his arms.

Why was he holding her?

A blinding, white flash appeared from above and enveloped them tightly like a blanket. The light was so dazzling, she could barely see his face. After a few seconds, the enigmatic darkness once again engulfed them, and she realized that she was no longer in his arms. He was gone. Gone into the darkness and silence, and she had ended up somewhere else. Where? She couldn't remember. She could not even remember the exact place where all that happened—the streaming light, the darkness, the separation, the final landing she knew not where.

Margaux shook her head vigorously hoping the images would stop. But they didn't. She saw him again and again, this time with mysterious black, almond-shaped eyes. In one vision, he was wearing a military-issue, camouflage uniform and standing on an airport walkway, then moving away from her. In another vision, he was wearing a dark-green, military dress uniform and entering a yellow taxi, which also moved away from her. Those eyes, she thought now, they're not his eyes. They weren't even human eyes.

Finally, after what seemed a long pause, the visions dematerialized into a small, spiraling vortex that disappeared toward the back of her mind. Margaux suddenly found herself jolted into the present, still holding onto the shoulders of this handsome lifeguard. He was staring at her with a worried look on his face. Margaux cocked her head to one side, as she searched his face.

Who was he and why did he seem so familiar?

The lifeguard observed her, amused and puzzled at being examined so thoroughly. "Can you please hold still, so I can take a look at your foot, hmm?"

Margaux quickly nodded. "Oh, of course, sorry."

"Good. Now, let's see what you stepped on."

He searched along the sole of her foot slowly and gently from the heel to the toes. Margaux shivered at his touch. She was instantly aroused. It felt so good and yet, so frustrating. It felt so familiar and yet, he was a complete stranger to her. Or was he?

Where had he touched her like that? When?

"Ah, there it is." His hand reached out toward a small object deeply embedded inside the ball of her foot just near her big toe. She winced, but he quickly removed it with his deft fingers. He showed it to her. "It appears to be a splinter from something wooden." He shook his head reprovingly. "We need to cover the floor thoroughly. This shouldn't have happened. Can you walk now?"

A tiny trickle of blood came out from the wound, but that didn't matter to her. The pain was gone, thankfully. "Yes, I can walk now." Margaux nodded, slowly placing her right foot down on the floor. "Thank you so much."

He looked up at her and smiled. She gasped. On his face were the same large, almond-shaped eyes filled with the liquid blackness she had seen in her visions. And yet, as quickly as they had arrived, the mysteriously, creepy eyes disappeared, replaced by normal eyes. Leaving Margaux astounded and frustrated. She quickly stepped away from him. He blinked at her.

That was certainly a strange response to his help.

Lifting himself up from the floor, the lifeguard threw the wood splinter in the trash can nearby. "I think you will be fine as soon as we bandage that wound. It is bleeding." He pointed to the far end of the pool. "Come on with me to the lifeguard station over there, where we keep the emergency kit."

"Okay." Margaux agreed. They walked in silence. It seemed the wrong time to ask his name.

Once inside the station, a sense of normalcy returned. The strange eyes did not return. Margaux sighed in relief.

"Sorry, I didn't mean to stare at you like that back there." Margaux apologized sitting on the proffered chair. She lifted her foot towards him. "Thank you for doing this." He smiled nonchalantly as he placed the Band-Aid firmly on the wound. "No problem. I'm glad we found that splinter. You'll soon be as good as new." He crumpled the wrapping paper of the Band-Aid and deftly threw it into the nearby trash can.

Standing up from the floor, he stepped back, and presented his right hand to her. When she took hold of his hand, Margaux once again felt that burning ache of familiarity. Even as she stood up from the chair, she stubbornly held on to his hand, ardently staring at it, hoping to remember. He raised his eyebrows at her. This was certainly awkward.

"Hello?" he jiggled his hand slightly within her tight grip and bent down to look into her eyes. "Are you ok?"

Flustered, Margaux quickly released his hand. "Yes, yes, I'm ok. I'm so sorry"

He laughed at her softly and she saw the twinkle return in his eyes. He seemed to have noticed her cheeks hot and red with embarrassment. "Don't worry about it. You are all set to go now."

"Thank you." Margaux whispered softly. "Goodbye."

"Goodbye."

Margaux stopped by the exit door and stood for a moment, looking back at him one final time, her eyes squinted narrowly. She tried again to rustle a memory, but her mind remained blank. He cocked his head in curiosity, raising his eyebrows once again.

What?

"Oh!" Margaux quickly turned away and was gone through the door.

Taken aback, the lifeguard stood there momentarily, his one hand on his hip, the other scratching his head. "What a strange woman." Shaking his head briefly, he picked up the blue, regulation lifeguard float and walked out the door.

Chapter 2

AFTER CHANGING INTO HER STREET clothes, Margaux walked down the hallway away from the women's locker room with her sunshine-yellow, canvas swim bag slung lazily over her shoulder. She leisurely passed by the water coolers and headed straight towards the glass-covered rows of shelves a little further down. On them stood in full display of photographs and championship awards the young Yorkbury AquaClub swimmers and crew teams had won over the years. Margaux stopped briefly to admire the trophies, wistfully wishing she had been part of a swimming team during her high school years. It would have been wonderful to be recognized as a swimmer who won awards for her high school. She sighed as she straightened the strap of her canvas bag on her shoulder. It is the past now and apparently it wasn't meant to happen.

She walked towards the lobby station by the entrance door. She wished she had asked that handsome lifeguard for his name. It might have provided a clue. No use going back to him, but there is another way.

Standing in front of the station, Margaux adjusted her oversized sunglasses on her nose and hummed softly. A young female lifeguard sat in front of the computer terminal fervently clicking away on the keys. "Hi." Margaux smiled.

The lifeguard smiled back, her head raised from the computer terminal. She brushed back her auburn hair with her hands into an impromptu ponytail and arched her back. Letting go of her hair, she let the thick tresses slide back softly around her shoulders as she raised her arms outwards to stretch them.

Margaux smiled. It must be hard to sit in one place so long.

"Sorry. How can I help you?" The lifeguard asked placing her hands on her lap.

Margaux described the handsome older lifeguard she had just encountered and asked who he was.

"Oh, he is our new assistant manager. He just transferred from another aqua-center."

"I see." Margaux murmured. That explained why she'd never seen him before. That also explained his age. Margaux looked back at the lifeguard. "And what is his name, do you know?"

The young woman replied, "Byron O'Neill."

Byron O' Neill.

The name rang a familiar bell like a long-forgotten song. She repeated it inside her mind in a sing-song manner as she walked outside the building toward her car parked nearby. She had hoped that by repeating the name, a memory would manifest itself clearly to her and she would remember who he was.

But that did not happen.

Margaux sighed with frustration as she opened the door to her cherry red Mazda Miata and threw her canvas swim bag on the passenger seat. She slammed the door in frustration. "Byron O' Neill." Her mind sang out the name once again, as if daring her to remember, almost mocking her for her forgetfulness. Gritting her teeth, Margaux walked around the Miata toward the driver's side. Once inside, she clicked her seat belt on. "Byron O'Neill." The name rang out again. She shook her head, gripping the steering wheel tightly.

"Stop!" She begged plaintively. "Please stop!"

After checking the rear view mirror, Margaux quickly turned on the ignition key and the Miata with the top side down thrummed softly into life. Slowly, she backed away from the curb and drove through the exit, heading toward her home, a few minutes' drive away. "Byron O' Neill". The name returned as loud as before.

"Enough!" Margaux yelled out. "Please stop! I can't take this anymore."

The intonation stopped.

As she drove the Miata closer to the intersection that led to her neighborhood, she saw that it was blocked by the county's white utility vans. Numerous orange cones were placed strategically on the road blocking access to her home. There was a strong scent of hot, black asphalt and mixed gravel being smoothed on the road by the lumbering, construction rollers. The machines made an earsplitting whine. She could see that the county workers were busily repairing the gaping and dangerous potholes that had materialized on the road after that last awful thunderstorm just a few weeks before.

A single bow derecho.

Most storms came from the west and the north of Mirrington Heights, but they were normal thunderstorms and normal snowstorms appearing on a regular basis every year. But not this one.

This year, a straight-line derecho arrived from the west, a frightening weather monstrosity plowing through the bedroom community. Just about everything and anything that wasn't tied down or put away was scattered helter-skelter all over the community, including cars, SUVs, and trucks. It was a mess the next day. When the derecho passed through and the storms subsided, the sleep-deprived residents came out to assess the damage and begin the repairs to their homes and vehicles.

And yet, that one intersecting road that led to her home had been neglected for several weeks too long, and remained pockmarked with the gaping potholes. Finally, her neighbors complained. They needed to reach their homes. Even now, the repairs are clearly still not finished.

Abruptly, Margaux turned the steering wheel. The Miata purred and reverted back to the main road, heading toward a back road to her home on the other side of the town. The one she knew so well, but often tried to avoid. Soon she saw the overpass bridge and drove up the side ramp towards the back road. Casually leaning her left elbow on the open driver's side window ledge, Margaux stretched her neck and breathed in the fresh air, as the evening breeze brushed back her wet, golden-blonde hair.

Ahead, she saw a large white sign on the right side of the road, before the back road banked into a left downwards curve. The sign she had tried so hard to avoid. "Wildwood Tennis and Pool Club." The sign was beautifully engraved in dark-green and gold against the off-white background. Every time she passed by it, the sign always seemed to shout at her, as if trying to tell her a secret or a memory long past. And always she ignored its shout and the unsettled nauseous sense of doom. In time, she stopped driving past the sign.

But not today.

This time Margaux stopped the Miata by the curb adjacent to the sign. She shut off the engine. Taking off her sunglasses, she stared at the sign as if trying to listen to its shout, but she could not hear the message clearly. Worse still, it refused to stop shouting at her. Her eyes glanced beyond the sign where the tennis courts and pools stood adjacent to each other, separated by a long winding sidewalk leading downwards to the pools.

Soon the neighborhood families and pool members who owned exclusive memberships to the private pool club would gather in droves to enjoy picnics, parties, and swims. From the driver's seat of the Miata, Margaux stared at the pristine, aqua-blue water for what seemed a long time. Resting her head on the back of the driver's seat, she closed her eyes and felt her mind relax into a void as she tried to recall a place and a time long ago.

Nine years ago.

The fall of her senior year had just begun. It was her last year at Westbury Moor High. She had looked forward with excitement to her graduation the following summer with her friends. But suddenly, one night at the dinner table, her parents had dropped the bomb on her. They told her that they had found new jobs with better pay at another town 800 miles south of Westbury Moor. The only problem was they had to move immediately. She could not graduate with her friends at Westbury Moor High. It was a condition of their new jobs that they live nearby. Their new employers even assisted in finding a new home for them, furnished and ready to move in.

So yes, it was time to say goodbye to everyone they knew in Westbury Moor.

All in all, Margaux hardly had the chance to breathe. She quickly packed up and said goodbye to her old friends and finished her senior year at a new private school 800 miles away. The public schools in Mirrington Heights did not pass muster with her parents, who demanded quality education for their only daughter. It had been an abrupt change from the life she had known over the years at Westbury Moor High into the land of complete strangers at Crooked Oak High School. Her new classmates had stared at her sullenly when she entered the building. It was worse in the classrooms. Margaux had stared back at them feeling uncomfortably shy, awkward, and withdrawn.

She was in a hostile land with no friends.

Feeling unwelcome, Margaux had wandered around the school like an alien from another world. She did not belong there. For the entire senior year, she was often left on her own, burying herself in the school library to read her books or finish her homework. The Dominican sisters and Franciscan brothers there were nice, but they couldn't help her adjust. It was simply too hard to make new friends when it was your last year in high school and all of her classmates' thoughts and plans were excitedly focused towards the future.

At 19, Margaux had graduated with honors from Crooked Oak High School with all the pomp and circumstance befitting the graduation ceremony. Holding her diploma tightly to her breasts, she had smiled to herself contentedly, looking forward to leaving the loneliness and awkwardness behind and starting her future at university.

A new life and new friends along the way.

For now, it was the month of June and she was looking forward to the summer, her favorite season, and all that summer brings, especially the pool. Her parents had obtained prestigious membership at the popular Wildwood Tennis and Pool Club from another family moving away from the town. They did not even have to be on the waiting list.

For Margaux, with the new pool membership in hand, the summer could not get here fast enough. She had spent hours at Victory's Stand and Yvette's Boutique trying on new competition swimsuits and fashionable bikinis. She bought her favorite suntan lotions, super-sized beach towels, a brand new fuchsia canvas swim bag, and several books on historical romance.

She was more than ready for the summer at the pool.

"Sign in on this sheet, please." The lifeguard on duty at the registration booth of the Wildwood Tennis and Pool Club instructed her, pointing towards the clipboard on the booth counter. Wearing dark oversized sunglasses, Margaux shifted her brand new swim bag on her shoulder and smiled. She picked up the pen and signed her name. It had been that time in the 1980s, before the computers became widespread and one could electronically sign oneself in. Margaux looked up and out behind the lifeguard at the pools. It looked nearly empty.

Perfect.

It was early Sunday morning and the pool would be open for adults only for just a few hours. The summer café was open to provide an early brunch of coffee, juices, sandwiches, and pastries. The sky was a clear blue tint, not a cloud in sight, and the sun was shining. And it was hot, so very hot. Margaux could feel the sun's sizzling rays on her bare shoulders and head as she exited the women's locker room towards one of the colorful vinyl lounge chairs scattered around the pool area. There were only a few adults lounging lazily on the chairs, mostly seniors. Some were already in the pool enjoying the respite from the heat for a few minutes. Not seeing anyone her age, Margaux walked towards a lounge chair at the far corner of the competition pool. After rubbing suntan lotion all over her body and face, she brushed her soft golden hair back and put on her sunglasses. She picked a book from out of her swim bag and began to read.

After what seemed like an hour under the brilliant sun, Margaux woke up from her sleep. Feeling burned and restless, she turned around and put her legs down over the lounge chair, breathing in deeply. She stretched her back and arms. Time for a swim. As she got up from the chair, the book she had been reading slipped from her lap onto the ground. She picked it up and placed it inside the canvas swim bag along with her oversized sunglasses.

She tried to shake off the feeling that someone was watching her.

Picking up her swim goggles, Margaux quickly headed toward the competition pool and dove inside the water, splashing it out in sprays. Holding her breath, she glided forward underwater for a few feet more. How cool and refreshing the water had felt against her hot, sunburned skin. After a few seconds, Margaux finally broke into the surface to begin her swim. She barely noticed the changing of the lifeguards near her lap lane.

Chapter 3

THE FEMALE LIFEGUARD WITH A perky smile and strawberry blonde ponytail was already descending the steps of the chair, while a male lifeguard with black hair and handsome rugged face waited to ascend and take her place. He never took his eyes off the young, lissome swimmer in front of him.

He was intrigued. She was the only one swimming laps at this early hour of the morning. The only one who was so young, a teenager, in this panoply of seniors at the pool. Quite out of place.

He settled on the chair and watched her swim. "All by herself and yet, she is beautiful".

Earlier, he had noticed her reading her book from the silent enclosure of the lifeguard station not far from her. He had noticed her tall body relaxed and soft on the lounge chair and had moved his eyes towards the beautiful curves of her breasts, hips, and long, lean legs, her toes pointed like a ballerina. He had noticed how she stretched her body on the lounge chair comfortably to welcome the sun's rays with a peaceful smile on her face. How different she was. He had seen so many women, young and old, from time to time in his tenure at the pool every summer, their faces often slathered with voluminous amounts of sunscreen creams and lotions, their heads covered with oversized hats and scarves, their bodies hidden under the enveloping dark shade of the umbrellas. And, yet, this young woman adored the sun with her full open body and a smile of joy. He noted there was only golden brown tan on her skin and not a dark spot or sunburn scars visible anywhere.

What was her secret?

This beautiful woman, he thought, should have been surrounded by at least her friends and family, and yet, here she was all by herself. What was even more puzzling was she ignored everyone at the pool, preferring to intently focus on reading her book. Sitting on the lifeguard chair high up above the pool, he watched her swim her laps.

After an hour, Margaux reached the curb at the deep end of the lap lane where the lifeguard's chair stood and finished her swim. Placing her water soaked hands and arms on the curb, she deftly removed the swim goggles and blinked her eyes in the bright glare of the sun, letting her body stretch in the water. She breathed in deeply, feeling her heart beat in strong, regular rhythms. Closing her eyes, Margaux lifted her face towards the open blue sky to catch the warm rays of the shining sun.

She smiled.

But not for long. Someone was watching her. Someone close by.

Margaux opened her eyes and found herself looking into the twinkling deep brown eyes of the handsome lifeguard with the dark wavy hair and rugged face.

"Hi."

Margaux flushed, her cheeks burning hotly. "Hello," she responded awkwardly, riveted by his attention toward her. Margaux shifted her arms on the curb. She felt irritated. He was blocking the sun that had warmed her face just a few seconds earlier. And yet, she felt herself drawn into his deep brown eyes and wondered what to do next. It didn't help that he was so handsome. Only movie stars looked like that. He did not belong here at the pool club surrounded by mediocrity. Margaux found herself intently studying the rugged lines of his face.

"What's your name?" he said.

"Margaux. Margaux Martin."

"You swim really good. Strong strokes."

"Thanks." Margaux lifted herself up off the curb and faced him. "God, I love the water. It heals me."

Byron pressed on. "I get that. Are you in any swimming meets?"

"No. Not interested. I prefer my books."

"I see that. You've been reading for quite some time before your swim. Must be a good book. What's it called?"

"Rebecca. It was written by Daphne du Maurier. Don't bother asking, it's too complicated for you." Margaux declared haughtily as she brushed away the water droplets from her arms and shook her hair free of the water, completely oblivious to him. Byron watched with interest and amusement, a grin appearing at the corner of his mouth.

She turned and looked up at him again, her arms akimbo on her waist. "Well, it's been nice meeting you, but right now there is a chapter I need to finish. Goodbye!"

"Huh?" Perplexed by her behavior, Byron looked over his left shoulder and stared at her beautifully muscled back walking away from him. She was clearly not interested in having a conversation with him. What a snob. He shook his head. "Have a nice day, too."

For the rest of the day, Byron found himself discreetly watching her as she toweled herself dry and then lay in a full body stretch on the lounge chair facing the sun. Margaux squirmed uncomfortably. Raising her head, she locked her eyes with him.

The past zoomed and merged into the present.

Chapter 4

"No, it can't be!" Margaux opened her eyes, startled at the revelation from her dream. She shifted in her car seat and shook her head vigorously, her strands of wet hair flying about her face. She brushed her wet hair back with both hands and held it up, all the time staring in abject disbelief at the empty pool, its secret finally revealed to her. "Oh my god." she murmured releasing her hands from her hair and cupping her face, as she recalled the deep brown eyes from long ago. "Oh...my God, it's him. That's Byron O' Neill. Oh...my...God." Margaux sighed heavily as she vividly recalled the past few hours with that handsome lifeguard at the pool as he tended to her wounded foot, the one and the same person from her dream. Clearly, he did not remember her.

That night Margaux crept into her bed. She closed her eyes and tried to sleep, her body moving restlessly from side to side. Silently, from above the ceiling in her bedroom, two dark almond-shaped eyes of alien nature emerged from the darkness and stared at her sleeping body. Several seconds passed before the liquid black eyes disintegrated into the darkness of the room. Yawning, Margaux pulled up the covers to her neck and fell into a deep REM state of sleep.

She dreamed once again. This time taking her back to nine years ago.

It had been her senior year at Crooked Oak High. In one month she had been fully integrated into her lonely schedule at school. On a cool fall day, Margaux jumped off the school bus, ran home, and stood in front of the mirror suspended over the white marble countertop in her bathroom suite. An array of makeup, skin creams, hairbrushes, ponytail holders, and vitamin pill containers were scattered over the vanity.

Dinner with her parents was over and, as usual, it had been quiet. Her parents knew Margaux had been and still was upset at the abrupt move to their new home. Even after a month had passed, Margaux still could not forgive them, however hard she tried to rationalize the move and make her peace with it. The world did not feel kind to her, and that included her parents. She needed more time, her parents reasoned, as they settled into the normal routine of family life in their new home. Just a little more time and she would be back to being the Margaux they both knew and loved.

Inside the bathroom suite, Margaux rested her hands flat on the sink countertop and stared at her reflection. Her reflection stared back at her. Seconds passed as Margaux examined the mirror with desperate, searching eyes. She called out the name softly.

"Anastasia."

She kept her voice down as she called out the name, so her parents would not hear her. They couldn't possibly understand the enormity of what had just happened this past month, the sudden appearance of her doppelganger, Anastasia, from another world she knew not where. A little frantic, Margaux put her hand against the smooth, shiny surface of the mirror and whispered a little louder.

"Anastasia, where are you?"

Margaux felt frantic. What if Anastasia had been just an illusion all along? "No." She shook her head. No, she had to be real. She had to be real, because she wanted to believe Anastasia was real. Talking to her was like talking to a long lost friend.

Still searching into the mirror, Margaux remembered the night when Anastasia had first appeared to her one month ago. She had been by herself in the bathroom, alone with bloodshot eyes from all that crying, trying to clean her face with cold water. Bereft of her old friends and angry at her parents, she was particularly angry at her domineering mother, who constantly looked the other way, pretending that nothing was wrong. Her father was invisible day in and out, his job being the only momentum keeping him alive each day. And quiet too. Hardly one to even reach out and say hello, how was your day? She only saw him briefly at breakfast before he left for work and at dinner before he headed to the living room to watch TV with a glass of bourbon or whiskey, or whatever he had on hand that night. To all their questions on how her day was, Margaux simply gave them brief noncommittal responses, her mind blocked by the gnawing daily resentment that would probably never go away.

Because of that one specific day.

The year before the move to Mirrington Heights, a family had offered to host her for the senior year at Westbury Moor High. A family her parents had met at the awards dinner one evening when Margaux was there with them. Their daughter also attended Westbury Moor High, although Margaux hardly knew her. They moved in different circles, hardly crossing paths. Margaux among the geeks and nerds, and Tiffany among the cheerleaders and jocks. But the family had offered to host Margaux in their home for the last year and that was all that mattered to Margaux. It didn't matter that she and Tiffany barely knew each other.

Tiffany's mother, a soft-spoken and petite Southern belle with elegantly upswept dark brown hair had felt compassion for Margaux's sadness at leaving Westbury Moor High and her friends. She had dismissed Tiffany's reluctance at the proffered suggestion that Margaux stay with them for the year, sharing her bedroom. But Margaux's mother refused to hand over her daughter to another family, albeit one with generations that had attended Westbury Moor High with pride. A good Roman Catholic family, it would seem.

Chapter 5

UNBEKNOWNST TO MARGAUX HER ENTIRE life, the reason for her reluctance was a secret she'd strictly kept to herself since Margaux was born. Eighteen years ago, she had given birth to two daughters, twin daughters, but the nurse had refused to show her the other daughter and refused to tell her why. She simply took her other daughter away from the room as fast as she could. And the next day, the other baby was gone from her nursery crib, disappearing under the care of the nurse, who had adamantly protested she never left the neonatal suite all night.

Only Margaux was left behind, without her twin.

And that damned nurse had the gall to say it was all for the best and still wouldn't tell her why, only that before her disappearance, government officials had wanted her baby, which infuriated her even more. Even a request for police investigation had fallen on deaf ears. And for years that other daughter was listed as missing, never to be found.

Terrified that Margaux could disappear too, her mother had kept tight reins on her daughter all those years Margaux was growing up. It became a terrible, terrible secret. One only she knew and would not, could not, did not tell anyone else on earth, not even the man who had agreed to marry her and bring her and the infant Margaux to his home town in the United States. It was too unreal to wrap one's mind around it, even for herself, having had a prior enigmatic circumstance months ago, in which she was missing for 23 days and inexplicably returned, naked and pregnant, near a small village in Russia.

So yes, the world couldn't know the strange circumstance of Margaux's birth and not even Margaux herself must know. That was how it should be at all costs. Buried in the past. And thus, once again, her mother had simply put her foot down and refused to accept for Margaux that one last chance to stay at Westbury Moor and finish her senior year with her long time classmates and friends. No, she had declared stubbornly, Margaux must remain with her parents. No question about it.

All of Margaux's pleadings fell on deaf ears. Just one year was all she asked for. They could write to each other, phone each other, and even visit each other on holidays. Then she would come home and go to university. Only one year. How hard could that be? And still her mother refused, ever unrelentingly, even though, for a moment, it did seem a good idea to her, but no, she would not chance Margaux disappearing.

She would not reveal her terrible secret.

Chapter 6

Resigned, Margaux shut down that day. And each day thereafter, she nursed the festering wound in her heart. She wasn't certain she would ever forgive her parents for this. This was simply not fair.

Alone in her bedroom that same night with the door locked and the lights dimmed, Margaux had curled up into her bed and sobbed into her pillow. She turned around to stare at the ceiling and think. Resigned to her newfound unhappy life, she would throw herself into her studies. She resolved to do well at Crooked Oak High and then start her life at university. At which point, she reasoned, her mother could not argue with her choice to live away at a dorm and be with her peers. And even if her mother argued, she would be at an age where she didn't even have to comply with her mother's obstinate, irrational fears. That was her mother's past, her fears, not hers. Margaux could simply walk away.

With that thought in mind strengthening her resolve, Margaux breathed in and out softly, her coughing spasms lessening, her confidence returning. Soon the tears stopped flowing.

Her left hand reaching for the pink-and-purple gingham textured tissue box on the nightstand next to her bed, Margaux lifted a tissue to dry her eyes. She blew her nose into the tissue and breathed in again. Yes, that was a good plan. Throwing the tissue away into the small, braided wastebasket propped next to the nightstand, she got up from her bed and walked into the adjoining bathroom suite to wash her face. Standing in front of the vanity countertop, Margaux lifted her head and stared into the mirror. Her eyes were still bloodshot from all that crying. She waved her hand around in the air. She watched her reflection mimic her movements. She smiled. How nice it would be if her reflection could suddenly come into life and talk back to her, chat with her, laugh with her, and cry with her. A doppelganger. Almost like having a friend. Better yet, a twin sister exactly like her. To share secrets with.

Impulsively, she lifted her hand to touch her reflection in the mirror. The surface felt smooth and so cold. Margaux closed her eyes. After what seemed only a few seconds, she opened her eyes and noticed with alarm a subtle change occurring at the mirror where her hand pressed against it. That one small area was starting to feel warm like an iron slowly being turned on, the heat eventually spreading out in a ripple effect towards the entire perimeter of the mirror. She quickly let go of the mirror and stepped back, as she watched with bewilderment at the changes taking place.

Something was happening *inside the mirror.*

Her reflection in the mirror had disappeared and in its place was a group of tiny twinkling lights. The pinpoints of light moved outwards in a circular motion resembling a galaxy of stars, before bursting into shimmering white and gold that saturated the mirror. Margaux gasped as she watched the bright explosions converge into each other, becoming a solid figure staring at her from the other end of the mirror.

The figure looked exactly like her.

"Hi." Her living reflection smiled at Margaux. She spread her arms and hands toward Margaux from the other side of the mirror. "Here I am. Your doppelganger, as you so wished. You summoned me from my world. What can I do for you?" Tiny stars in her blue eyes gleamed with brightness as she smiled.

"Oh my God," declared Margaux. Hesitantly, she stepped back from the vanity countertop, both hands covering her mouth. "My doppelganger? In the mirror? And you are talking to me? But how is that possible?"

"Easy. You thought. You wished for me to come into being. In effect, you were speaking to me with your mind. I heard from my world and I simply complied with your wish. There is no mystery in that. You called and I came. I am so pleased to meet you, Margaux." The reflection placed her hand on the mirror's surface from the other end. "See I'm moving without you. It's me. I'm real, not your reflection."

"But that's not possible," Margaux shook her head. "You are but a reflection in the mirror. You aren't real." Margaux backed away a little further from the mirror and closed her eyes. She hoped that when she opened them, the doppelganger, or whatever that creature called herself, would no longer be there.

That it was just a figment of her overactive imagination.

She opened her eyes. Her doppelganger was still there behind the mirror, still smiling sweetly. Waiting patiently. Margaux sighed rubbing her eyes. She stood a healthy distance from the mirror.

"Not possible." She murmured again.

"Oh, but it is possible!" The doppelganger smiled, tilting her head to the right. "All things are possible to those who believe. You must have believed in spite of yourself, for here I am." Again, she spread her arms and hands out towards Margaux. "Look, you have no need to be afraid of me. I won't hurt you. That is not my intent. Come here closer to the mirror. Let me prove it to you. Put your hand on the mirror."

Slowly and hesitantly, completely mesmerized, Margaux stepped towards the mirror. Standing still, she put her right hand against the mirror. The mirror was now fully warmed and glowed with a soft, white light. Again, there was no reflection of her extended hand.

"Oh my God…" Margaux whispered both her hands cupping her face, her eyes wide as the realization fully hit her. It was true. "Can you really talk with me?" Margaux asked. "Really? Like a person? A mind of your own?"

"But of course, I have my own mind and therefore, I can talk to you. I can talk with you as surely as you can talk with the next person where you are at the other end of this mirror."

"But where are you from?" Margaux demanded.

The doppelganger in the mirror smiled secretively. She shook her head slightly. "Not now. You cannot know where I'm from yet." She lowered her voice in a whisper., "Were I to tell you where I came from now, you wouldn't understand, at least not yet. But I can tell you this. You have nothing to fear from me."

Margaux sighed. "Okay, I guess." She put both her hands on the vanity countertop and gazed at her doppelganger with newfound interest and curiosity, tilting her head sideways. "What's your name?"

"Anastasia, what's yours?"

"I'm Margaux. Gee, I do wish you could tell me where you came from. This is all so mysterious. I am quite curious now."

Anastasia laughed melodiously. "When you are ready, I will tell you. I promise, Margaux. All in its own time."

"Darn." Margaux sighed. "How will we know when I'm ready?"

"You will know." Anastasia said gravely. "It is a truth few people know and come to accept." She shrugged nonchalantly. "As for those who do not accept, they have their reasons, I suppose. I truly hope you will accept the truth with your whole heart when the time is right, Margaux, for that would be so wonderful for us both."

Gradually, Margaux accepted this strange beautiful creature inside her mirror, her doppelganger from another world. One she could share her joys and frustrations with, especially about her mother's strange, tight grip on her. She decided that no one needed to know about the existence of Anastasia.

From that day on for the entire year, her senior year at Crooked Oak High, whenever Margaux needed to talk or needed a shoulder to cry on, whenever she felt alone, she would summon Anastasia from within the mirror. Always Anastasia would arrive, shimmering into being from sparkling lights and white-gold bursts on the other side of the mirror. All through the year, alone in the bathroom suite, the bedroom door locked, the two improbable friends chatted and gossiped and cried.

Chapter 7

Two months after graduation.

It was a bright, sunny Sunday morning, truly hot in the middle of July, almost 100 degrees. It was adults only at the pool that morning and Byron was purposefully striding towards the lifeguard chair with his red regulation float under his arm. A few seniors lounged in the family pool, lazily enjoying the coolness of the water. The competition pool and the baby pool remained eerily empty and silent.

It had been two months since he met this mysterious beauty with golden tousled hair. He scanned the pool area briefly. Margaux hadn't arrived yet. He wondered if she would. She was usually prompt. Every Sunday from the day the pool opened on Memorial Day, Margaux would be there all by herself, swimming, basking in the sun, and reading her book. Every Sunday, that same routine. He shook his head. He wondered why she preferred to be alone. What made her different? Clutching the regulation float, he resolved to find out all about her, perhaps get closer to her.

If she would let him.

An hour passed. The sun was getting hotter. Byron's time was up at the chair and he prepared to descend for the changing of the lifeguards. The other lifeguard to replace him greeted him as usual. They chatted briefly. He jerked his head behind him prompting Byron to look at the corner of the pool grounds opposite the chair.

And there was Margaux.

Once again she was beautifully stretched out on the yellow, vinyl lounge chair, her swim canvas bag placed beside her. Her serene face worshipping the sun. Byron suddenly felt that familiar warmth in his body. He was so deeply affected by her gorgeous and mysterious presence, and yet frustrated at her reticence.

This was now or never.

He approached the lounge chair cautiously, effectively creating a looming dark shadow over her face. Startled, Margaux opened her eyes to find the tall, imposing stature of Byron standing over her. He smiled at her. "Sorry. It's me, Byron. I didn't mean to startle you. I was wondering if we can talk."

"About what?" Margaux asked as she lifted her body up on the lounge chair in a sitting position and put her arms around her knees. She looked up. She knew he was the pool's assistant manager. "Is something wrong?"

"No, nothing's wrong." Byron protested nervously. He shoved his hands in the pockets of his navy blue swim shorts that cut just down towards the middle of his powerfully muscled thighs. He sighed as he looked down at his feet, shuffling them on the concrete floor. "I was wondering if you'd like to go out with me."

"Okay."

"Okay?" Byron stared at her in disbelief. He had expected her to protest or even shy away, preferring to read her book. He was even prepared to swallow his pride at her rejection.

But he heard her say, "okay".

"Are you certain?" he asked again.

"Yes, I said okay." Margaux repeated, releasing her arms. She stretched out her long, tanned legs and lay back on the lounge chair, smiling at him seductively. "Don't knock yourself out. What are your plans for that date?"

Byron was thrilled. "How about this coming Saturday? I was thinking of picking you up from your home around 3:00AM in the morning and we head to Artemis' Realm. It's a two hour drive."

Taken aback, Margaux cocked her head curiously. "Artemis' Realm. What's that?"

"It's a national forest park, one I often go to."

Margaux was incredulous. "Wow. Our first date and you want to go on a ridiculously early morning jaunt to a national forest park of all places? Are you insane?"

Byron grinned.

"It's my favorite place to go and there's a reason for this ungodly hour I'm proposing to you. I hope you don't mind. Will your parents let you go?"

"They don't have to know. I am of age." Margaux said flipping her hand in the air, as if brushing away a bee. At this point, her relationship with her parents had become extremely strained. Margaux did not want to tell them what she was doing or where she was going. She didn't care. Not anymore.

In time, even her old friends from Westbury Moor all drifted away from her, all of them focusing on their own lives, forgetting their promise to keep in touch.

"So we have a date?" Byron asked once again. He wanted to make sure this was real and not an unpleasant retort from her. She wasn't exactly easy to approach to begin with.

"All right, I guess." Margaux nonchalantly shrugged her shoulders. "But, this is an awfully strange date, if you ask me. Anyways, here is my address." Margaux rifled a pen from her canvas swim bag and reached out for his hand.

After scribbling the address across his palm, she let go of his hand and gave him a seductive smile, the one side of her lips curving upwards. Byron's eyebrows arched in pleasant surprise at her gesture, but he quickly recovered his composure. He smiled down at Margaux, displaying that oft contagious twinkle in both his eyes. "Then we are set to go." He nodded. "Thanks for the address. I look forward to meeting with you then. Look for my Jeep Wrangler. It's forest-green, quite banged up." He turned around and headed back to the pool's lifeguard station, hands in his pockets.

He looked at the address in his hand and shook his head. He could not believe his luck.

Chapter 8

MARGAUX SAUNTERED INTO HER BEDROOM, locked the door, and threw her canvas swim bag on the bed. After placing her oversized glasses on the nightstand, she headed towards the adjoining bathroom suite. It was early evening and she had just come from the pool, having spent the whole day chatting with Byron on his breaks from lifeguard duty. Her eyes shining with happiness, she closed the double French doors and earnestly faced the large bathroom mirror above the vanity countertop.

"Anastasia." Margaux called out softly.

She waited a minute. Nothing happened.

"Come on, Anastasia." Margaux implored at the mirror. "Come on. I want to talk to you. I have news, Anastasia, exciting news. I can't wait to share it with you. Come on, where are you?" Impatiently pressing her hands against the vanity countertop with her head lowered and her eyes closed, Margaux thought of Anastasia, believed in Anastasia, and waited a minute more.

"Hi, Margaux. I'm here. I'm so sorry I took so long. Someone important contacted me. So, tell me, what's the exciting news today?"

"I'm going on a date this coming Saturday, can you believe it?" Margaux said excitedly suddenly feeling like she was going to burst with happiness. "No one has ever asked me for a date the entire year I was at Crooked Oak High. The kids didn't even want me around, you know, my being new and all that. But here at this pool, I got a date with the pool's assistant manager. I'm so excited, I can't stand it!"

"Oh, but, Margaux, that is too wonderful!" Anastasia clasped her hands, nodding happily. "Oh, yes, I agree, it's about time! You see, I had been waiting some time to hear about that. I knew it would happen. Oh, I am so happy for you, Margaux!"

"You knew about it, Anastasia? But how? Oh, never mind. I still can't believe it. He asked and I actually blurted out okay. I wonder what made me do that?"

Anastasia laughed knowingly. "That's not important. So, Margaux, tell me all about it."

"Like I said before, he's that lifeguard assistant manager I told you about who works at the pool club." Margaux twirled happily around holding her body with her arms. "He woke me up from my sleep on the lounge chair and asked me out just like that. I was so mad at him for waking me up, you know, ready to yell at him to leave me alone. I got to admit, though, he is quite handsome. You should have seen his face. He was in a state of shock."

"Naturally, Margaux, you had kept him at a hostile distance so long, he expected the worse. Anyways, what was his name?"

"Byron O' Neill."

"I like that name. I'm reminded of Lord Byron of time long past."

"Who?"

"Lord Byron, the Romantic poet who lived in England in the 1800s. This just came up in my mind's eye from the Amarnic Records that he could be a reincarnation of the poet, himself."

"Armanic Records? Reincarnation? What are you talking about, Anastasia?"

"Of course. Too complicated to explain." Anastasia said mysteriously. She smiled. "I promise you, though, he is definitely a romantic."

"Hmmmmm, okay, that sounds good. Then, Anastasia, tell me, with all your magic are you able to visualize my future with Byron? Can you see it? Is it all good?"

"No, I can't, Margaux." Anastasia shook her head. "I can't see it from my end and for good reason. It has to be a developing story from you with all your own choices and decisions, your free will. This is a planet of free will and it is our universal policy from where I come from. I cannot interfere at all. And what's more, Margaux, I would not tell you, even if I knew the possible outcome, be it good or bad, because the future is never set in stone. Never. Each step is ever changing, each direction leading somewhere else."

"I see. All right. Better this way, I guess." Margaux sighed.

Anastasia tried to distract Margaux. "So what's his plan for the date? I'm dying to know."

"Okay, well, the way he described it to me, our date is a two-hour drive toward Artemis' Realm. He said that there is this particular five-mile, off-road trail he wants to drive on with his jeep. Show it to me. I think it's called Gray Snake Trail that leads to the Quashone Meadows."

"What a strange date," Anastasia commented, a hint of a smile appearing in her face. It was exactly as she had hoped it would happen.

"I totally agree, Anastasia, but he did tell me it's his favorite place, so why not. I'm not averse to trying new things, but this is a first."

"Well, I am glad you feel that way." Anastasia declared with a knowing smile. She did not venture further. With this momentum already starting, she already knew the two possible outcomes. It all depended on Margaux. "Strange as it is, Margaux, you should definitely go."

"Oh, I will." Margaux nodded with a laugh. "And get this, he wants to leave at 3:00AM in the morning. That is when it is pitch black dark out there. My parents had they known would throw a fit."

"You don't have to tell them." Anastasia advised firmly. "Just go on and have fun." Suddenly she looked back over her shoulders. "I'm being summoned elsewhere, Margaux. An important contact, again. I must go now. Please do go to Artemis' Realm. It will all come together eventually. Goodbye for now."

Waving her hand at the mirror, Margaux watched Anastasia slowly dematerialize into a shimmering, translucent being, before exploding again into white-gold bursts. As the remnants of the explosion settled behind the mirror, a new figure emerged as a passive reflection of Margaux herself, waving her hand in exact synchronization. Margaux smiled at her reflection as she lifted up her bright orange sundress over her head, dropping it on the granite floor. She turned on the hot water in the Jacuzzi tub located just below the skylight window. She reached for the bottle of Neutrogena Sesame Oil.

It was time for her beauty spa beneath the soft glow of the twilight sky.

Chapter 9

MARGAUX CLOSED THE DOOR OF her house behind her. It was 2:45AM and the night sky was still velvety black with millions of glistening stars scattered from horizon to horizon. Turning around, she inserted the door key and locked the door. Her parents were still sound asleep, still oblivious to her planned date with Byron at this unearthly hour. It was easier this way to escape them and not have to tell them where she was going. There was no point in getting them all worked up and worried and then face a barrage of questionings.

She had had enough of that all year long.

Standing on the porch, she looked down at her gold, chain-linked bracelet watch, the clock face glowing softly in the dark. It was now 2:50AM and Byron would arrive in ten minutes. They had earlier agreed to meet two blocks away from her house, so her parents would not be awakened by the sound of his jeep. She must hurry. Looking up at the millions of twinkling stars, Margaux smiled at their beautiful mysteriousness and wondered what life, if any, was like way up there among these stars. She wondered where among the millions of these stars did Anastasia lived. One day she would find out. Anastasia promised.

With a contented sigh and looking forward to seeing Byron, Margaux quickly walked down the porch steps towards the adjoining sidewalk. She clutched her silvery-gray, leather handbag embossed with her initials in black cursive letters, *MIM*. Margaux Ishara Martin. Margaux, because her parents had told her they had stayed at the famed French castle converted into a hotel, L'Hotel de Margeaux, the night she was conceived, and Ishara, after her Russian grandmother. That was what her mother had told her, reminded her, every year on her birthday. Margaux sighed. That was nice, but really. When she reached the intersection, she made a left turn and hurried towards their meeting place under the soft, incandescent glare of the street lamps.

Chapter 10

AN HOUR INTO THE DRIVE along the main highway of the town, Route 585, heading toward the acceleration ramp of the superhighway, the forest-green Jeep Wrangler rolled over the dark, asphalt road. Byron rested his right hand on the 12:00 spot of the steering wheel, feeling relaxed and lulled by the powerful vibrations of the jeep's brand new engine.

He had bought the second-hand jeep a couple of years ago for a cheap price of $1,000 from the owner living far out in the mountains west of Mirrington Heights. Then he replaced the older noisy engine, which had hacked and choked with disjointed spasms of dirty air, spewing, dusty, malodorous smoke all around and out of the hood of the jeep. The updated engine thrummed powerfully and silently, akin to the soft whine of jet engines cruising the skies. All four Michelin tires were also brand new, bigger in size, and rugged as befitted the all-terrain vehicle he intended to use on several off-road trips. They had been enormously expensive, the engine and tires, but well worth the investment over the years and numerous off-road trips with friends. And today it was with Margaux. She had never been on a jeep before, she had told him earlier, which added to the excitement of the date for both of them.

Byron smiled contentedly, as the jeep cruised on. The night was still dark. Stars twinkled in a mass gathering above and beyond the windshields into the distant horizon. At this hour, the superhighway was stark and empty save for the lone Jeep Wrangler droning along purposefully against the night sky, the luminous, full moon watching benevolently over it. He looked to his right to check on Margaux. She was still asleep, her head turned towards him, limp and relaxed against the headrest of the passenger seat, her body buckled in. Her chin lay on her chest and she was breathing softly and regularly, still clutching the soft beige cashmere blanket Byron had offered when she got into his jeep at the meeting corner an hour ago.

"It will be a long ride," he said. "You can get some sleep for the next two hours while I drive towards Artemis' Realm. I will let you know when to wake up."

Margaux had complied with his request, settling in her seat with the blanket pulled up around her shoulders. She fell asleep instantly.

Taking the wheel with his left hand, Byron reached out with his right hand toward Margaux's exposed cheek, caressing the skin softly with the back of his hand. He smiled. She looked as beautiful and vulnerable in her sleep as he had imagined she would be. He felt a slight stirring in his loins. How badly he wanted to gather her in his arms right now and make love to her. Margaux's body shifted slightly at his touch, but she remained sound sleep. He removed his hand quickly from her face and turned his attention to the dark road before him, lighted only a few feet ahead from the jeep's powerful headlights. The half-moon, now closer to the horizon, still watched them benignly with its soft lunar light.

An hour and half later, Byron gripped Margaux on her shoulder, earnestly shaking her. She opened her eyes, startled awake from the long sleep. Yawning, she pushed herself up on her seat and rubbed her eyes. It still seemed dark outside as her eyes, bleary from the long sleep, glanced towards the windshield in front of her. She noticed that the sky ahead and above was now becoming a shadowy grey-blue color punctuated with small, linear patches here and there of soft pink and orange lights, announcing the impending dawn. She remembered somewhere that someone had called this color, sky blue and coral. It seemed fitting now. The moon and stars were still there, but were now becoming less and less noticeable.

Turning her head left, groggily, she looked up to find Byron watching her, his lips curved in an amused grin, the rugged features softened around his jawline and mouth, the dimple she loved prominent in his jutted chin. A five o' clock shadow now peppered the planes of his cheeks and chin, giving his face the mysteriously handsome aura she had not seen before. His face had always been shaved when she saw him. Byron grinned at how cute she looked just trying to stay awake from a long deep sleep with her blonde hair disheveled all around her face as he imagined it would. It had taken some time for him to compose himself during the long drive, mightily resisting the stirrings he had felt earlier when he touched her face. The wall was now up between them, securely in place the minute Margaux woke up.

"What's so funny?" she asked, staring at him in puzzlement as she settled herself once again on the passenger seat and shook her head to release the stiffness in her hair.

"Oh, nothing," he responded nonchalantly and turned his eyes to the road. "Nothing at all. We are almost there. You should wake up now." Her eyes narrowed at his response, not sure what to believe, but she was too groggy to argue with him. It seemed pointless now. They were so far away from home and heading towards what?

Having settled herself sitting upright on the passenger seat, Margaux arranged the soft blanket in a folded pile on her lap. She brushed through the strands of her tousled, blonde hair with her extended fingers and yawned once again. She closed her eyes. "What time is it now?" she asked Byron, her voice thick and her throat dry. "God, I'm in desperate need for coffee. Can we stop somewhere?"

Byron grinned keeping his eyes on the road. "It's almost 4:30AM. Nothing in sight for miles around, not even a gas station. So, no, no coffee yet, but we'll have some when we arrive at Quashone Meadows." He glanced at the mileage and time on the dashboard of the jeep and made a mental calculation. "Just relax now and be patient. We should be there soon." With a lift of his head towards the windshield, he added, "See, it is almost daybreak. In 30 minutes, we will be almost on that off-road trail I spoke about, the Gray Snake Trail. Then we'll have coffee at the Meadows, how's that?"

Coffee at Quashone Meadows? Margaux smirked silently to herself, wondering how in the world they'll obtain coffee if nothing was around to offer this much-needed replenishment at this early morning hour on a lone superhighway, let alone the Meadows. But he did promise there would be coffee. She would hold him to that.

"Fine, I'll be patient." She said, as she pulled the blanket back up around her shoulders, still feeling the chill of the early morning. She sighed. It would be interesting to see how he came up with that promised cup of coffee. Shaking her head in mild frustration, she settled back against her seat, leaning towards the passenger window, and watched the shadowy outlines of the passing farm fields and rolling, green meadows along the border of the superhighway.

"I still don't get it, this weird date," Margaux said as she folded the blanket once again into equal squares and put it on the back seat of the jeep behind her. "Normally, one goes to the movies and dinner afterwards and definitely not at this hour of the morning." Thirty more minutes had passed and still they were not at their destination.

Byron nodded humming softly. "Yes, I know. It's not a normal first date at all, but why not do things differently for a change, hmmmm. You will like it, I promise you. Now, look behind you."

"Ok." Margaux said. Stretching herself around behind her seat towards the back of the jeep, she glanced to the right and lifted her eyebrow. There was a brown cardboard storage box with a closed top placed on the back seat behind Byron. A red-and-white checkered blanket lay on top of the box. Her eyes traveled down towards the floor of the back seat just below the box. There she saw what looked like a small picnic grill stove and a container of propane oil beside it. So that's how they were having coffee.

She turned around and looked askance at Byron, her annoyance rising. "What, are we having a picnic breakfast at that park in this ungodly hour? Are you crazy?"

Amused at her reaction, Byron looked back at her with a secretive knowing smile. "No. I'm not crazy. Not at all. You'll see."

"What are you not telling me?" Margaux declared folding her arms against her chest. "I don't like the suspense."

"You'll find out when we get there." He turned towards her, almost letting out a shout. "Will you relax? It's supposed to be a surprise. Can you just be patient a little bit longer? That's all I'm asking. We are almost there."

Margaux shrugged, relaxing her arms. Her hands rested on her lap. She sighed. "I have no choice, do I?"

"Nope. No choice at all." He grinned at her. "Now, sit back and enjoy the ride."

Margaux secretly looked at Byron sideways admiring his dark, handsome profile as she watched him drive the jeep with a sense of self-assurance, almost an arrogance, that somehow made her heart beat faster every time he was near her. She did not like that he could affect her so deeply. She wanted to be mad at him, yell at him to take her home, to take her out on a real date to the movies and dinner, damn it, but she did not. They were too far away from home now. And what's more, she felt herself oddly pulled to him like bees drawn to flowers and moths to a flame. He exasperated her with his plans, yet his quiet self-assurance calmed her down. Just be patient, he kept saying all through the drive on the superhighway. Oh, how she hated that word. With a sigh, Margaux forced herself to relax against her seat staring ahead into the windshield of the jeep.

"See, there's the off-road trail I spoke about, coming up right about there." Byron gestured beyond the jeep's windshield toward the distant horizon, still bathed in charcoal gray with long, thin streaks of sky blue and coral.

Following his direction, Margaux could see that the left side of the superhighway extended for a half a mile up to where the rolling grasslands stopped abruptly and the adjoining land became thickly covered with dense verdant forest for miles on ahead, softly illuminated by the jeep's headlights into a ghostly montage, quiet and foreboding. Not unlike a haunted forest.

"Where? It's all forest from what I see." Margaux rolled her eyes as she peered into the windshield. Byron aimed his finger, again. "See that dark spot there between the trees? It's the opening to the trail. Pretty soon I'll change into second gear and we are off on a wild ride.

It's fun, you'll see. I've done it many times." He smiled at her, happy that they have finally arrived at their destination.

He could see she was getting cranky already from the desperate need for coffee.

"I should hope so." Margaux said, her mouth and throat tasting dry and bitter. She shifted in her seat to get a better view. "I'm not quite prepared for the wild ride you so describe in this early hour of the morning. It's not even light out there yet. And, God, I'm still trying to wake up." She had been terribly thirsty for the past 30 minutes and now terribly hungry just when the jeep pulled up at the mouth of the off-road trail. Her stomach grumbled painfully as Margaux bent her head and searched in her shoulder bag for a moist tissue to wipe her face. She whined. "I'm so glad we are here now. I can't stand the suspense anymore. I'm starved. Can we eat a little, please?"

Byron winked at her. "Not yet. We still have that five-mile off-road trail to tackle."

Margaux groaned.

A huge ornately-carved Victorian iron gate stood end to end at the mouth of the trail covered in shiny black sheen. The gate was clamped shut. A road sign was placed next to the gate embossed in bold black letters, "Gray Snake Trail – Enter at Your Own Risk". Below it, smaller embossed black letters recommended that the drivers please shut the gate behind them once they entered the trail. In addition, the sign emphatically declared that only all-terrain vehicles were strongly recommended for this trail. Byron stopped the jeep in front of the gate and put it in standing mode with the parking lever up and the engine purring softly. "Wait here. Do nothing," he instructed as Margaux watched him get out of the jeep to open the massive gate.

After shutting the iron gate behind them, Byron pulled down the parking lever and shifted the gears of the jeep to accommodate the primitive, dust-covered, gravel trail ahead of them. "Hang on tight, Margaux, I'm not kidding when I said a wild ride. Since it's your first try, you might want to hold onto the dashboard or the grip handle on your right by the door."

"Fine!" Margaux replied, choosing instead to place her left hand onto the passenger seat at her left. She held on tightly, her eyes closed, her body stiff with anticipation and uncertainty. Byron laughed quietly, amused at what seemed her determination to hang on for dear life. She took it that seriously.

"That's not the way to do it," he suggested softly. "You'll miss all the fun. Hold whatever you are holding onto, but please, relax and open your eyes. Look ahead of you. Isn't it beautiful?" He nodded his head towards the twisting sandy-colored dirt trail extending towards the furthest reaches of the shadowy forest. Only a few feet of the primordial trail in front of them were highlighted by the powerful halogen rays of the jeep's headlights in the murky light of daybreak.

Having opened her eyes in response to his suggestion, Margaux could see the shadowy outlines of different species of trees—tall oaks, maples, and birch trees, clustered on both sides of the 108-inch wide, grubby trail. Their thick russet trunks appeared to soar high into the heavens. In fact, it was hard to see the heavens as she peered up through the jeep's window. What's more, the early morning light made it hard to discern the various shades of green on the leaves. They all looked alike to her, a reflection of the morning's shadowy light. Even so, the jeep's powerful headlights outlined the magnificent tableau of the densely packed forest, expressing its intense strength, endless height, and ghostly beauty.

Anastasia was right. Byron was a quite a romantic.

"Oh, it is so beautiful." Margaux said. "I'm quite impressed. See, my eyes are open, but I'm not letting go of my hands!"

Byron grinned. "That's okay. That's good. I just don't want you to miss anything. Hang on, here we go." With a grunt, he firmly settled back in his seat, fully buckled, and shifted the gears once again. The jeep lurched forward abruptly, tires groaning and pushing against the gravelly sand, splattering forth tiny black, white, and gray stones and leaving a trail of dust spiraling into the air.

Byron was right. Margaux was definitely unprepared for the first four miles of the 5-mile trail, even though he had said it would be beautiful and fun. Yes, it was beautiful, but where was the fun? Margaux found herself constantly being jolted and jerked from her seat, even as she was restrained by the close-fitting seat belt. She turned to observe Byron, the intent to tell him to slow down the jeep, but he did not notice her at all. His attention was completely focused on driving the jeep along the convoluted trail in front of them. He grunted and groaned at each hairpin turn of the trail, and yet, he conveyed the utmost confidence from the years of experience, truly enjoying the ride.

At certain points along the trail, especially at the harrowing hairpin turns, they had to watch out for the big, sharp boulders, most of them jutting up bluntly from the sandy embankments. And then further down, they were faced with thick muddied water that splashed in an instant into the air, when the jeep entered the murky depths.

"Take a look around," he urged Margaux. "Get to know each and every tree and rock. Get to know them personally. Eventually you just ride along like one would on a boat coasting along the waves. You've been on boats, haven't you?"

"Oh, yes!" Margaux nodded. "But only on the long, smooth waves, not the choppy ones, heaven forbid. This ride would be close to choppy waves, I would gather. I will try to get used to it."

"Good. You'll find your balance eventually. Hang on now." Byron turned to face the trail, his hands gripped harder on the steering wheel, urging the jeep on.

"I should hope so," Margaux said, rolling her eyes up, her hands once again gripping the bottom left of her seat and the right handlebar. "Now I know why it's called Gray Snake Trail. How much longer do we have to go?"

"Three more miles judging from that boulder I see at that corner, the one with a sharp point jutting towards the sky. There are more of these boulders along the embankment. I must be careful not to topple this jeep."

"Three more? You're kidding me?" Margaux groaned. "I'm quite black and blue by now. This feels like riding a tsunami."

Byron laughed heartily. "You'll get used it. Hang on, now!"

Past yet another muddied shoal, they faced a split in the trail, dead ahead in the shadows. The left fork displayed the familiar, well-worn tire treads left behind by the multitudes of previous off-road vehicles, but that same trail had a very tight left hairpin turn, disappearing into the dense trees. Not much could be seen beyond that hairpin turn.

The right-forked section was a sudden stop blocked by an iron-grilled fence. A wooden sign hung in the middle loudly declaring to all in bold red letters, "DANGER. Do Not Enter". Byron applied the brakes to the jeep, shutting off the engines. Margaux could see that a thick carpet of grass covered what was once a trail filled with silt, dirt, and pebbles. She shivered at the eerie blackness extending into the depths of the forest behind the warning sign.

"I wonder what's out there." She turned to Byron. "Do you know?"

Byron nodded staring grimly at the forbidden forest. "I'll show you later. It's easier to show you than to explain. We should go. Hang on now." He started the ignition, pulled down the parking lever, and forcefully turned the steering wheel to the left, the jeep lurching forward to follow the tight 90-degree, hairpin turn.

"Ahhhh!" Margaux screamed, abruptly putting her hands on the dashboard, nearly hitting her head on the windshield.

"Dammit!" Byron swore under his breath as he struggled at the steering wheel.

Just past the turn, but before the trail leveled itself, the jeep unexpectedly ended up with its two massive front tires on top of the tallest embankment mound Margaux had so far seen on the trail. Almost as tall as the jeep itself. It felt as if they were hanging in midair sideways sitting almost upside down in their seats. Her heart beating fast, she looked at Byron, hoping he knew what to do. Byron looked back at her. He shook his head.

He was baffled at this juncture of the left hairpin. It was not familiar to him, although he was immediately prepared to deal with it. Quickly applying the accelerator, with both hands gripping the steering wheel, Byron forced the jeep to dive through the large, sandy mound, spraying silt and sand into the air. It didn't work. The tires had become stuck, running helplessly in place, unable to move forward. Grunting with frustration, Byron pulled up the parking brake and let the jeep settle for a moment.

Margaux pummeled his body with her fists. "Damn you, Byron! You nearly got us killed. The jeep could have rolled over."

"I know, I know! Just my luck." Byron shouted, restraining her. Small beads of sweat appeared in his forehead. "I honestly did not expect this. That mound has grown higher since I last used this trail, almost six months ago, in February." He looked out of the windshield. "It is very strange, this growth. Come to think of it, it's not the only place that's higher now than before. This entire forest is apparently changing. I only wish I knew why."

Margaux softened her stance, staring at him quizzically. He really meant what he said. She touched his shoulder. "Are you all right?' She wasn't quite sure what else to say.

"Yes, yes, I'm all right. We turned out okay, thankfully." Breathing deeply, Byron smiled at her. "I think we should go now. I will think about this anomaly later. We are losing time already." His right arm propped against the back of his seat, Byron looked behind the jeep and slowly maneuvered it backward and down the incline. Changing the gears into forward, he deftly pushed the jeep away from the mound and back on the hairpin turn towards the remainder of the 5-mile journey. All the while keeping his eye out for unexpected anomalies.

The last mile of the journey was quiet and uneventful. The jeep adeptly purred over the winding trail fenced in on both sides by more of the tight contingent of tall, brown trees, their leafy branches nodding softly as the jeep passed by beneath them.

Ten minutes later, Byron declared triumphantly, "We are almost at the Meadows!" With a whoop, he propelled the jeep into familiar terrain, the off-trail road still twisting here and there, true to its name, Gray Snake Trail, with nary a stone or boulder in sight at the last mile. He breathed a sigh of relief. "Now Margaux, there is one interesting geographical feature I want to show you that is located just before the trail ends into Quashone Meadows." He shook his head quickly. "Actually, not one, but rather three geographical features. The first one is nearby, the second one is a bit further down, and the third one is within the Meadows."

Margaux groaned, exhausted from the rough, bumpy ride. "What are they now? Am I to worry?" By now, her body ached from every jolt and jerk it had endured the last 4 miles of the drive. She was also very hungry and desperate for the comfort of a hot, frothy coffee to warm her hands and wake her up. She rolled her eyes up before settling back into her buckled seat, both hands holding firmly onto the jeep's dashboard. "Okay, then, here we go! I sincerely hope you have a first aid kit somewhere in this jeep."

Byron grinned at her attempt at sarcastic humor. "Hey, no need to do that." He reassured her trying hard to stifle a laugh that chortled in his throat. "Believe me, the worst is over. This is different and I know those three features very well. I call them jewels. They are interesting and quite harmless, and, in fact, two of them are quite beautiful. Why don't you do me a favor and just sit back, relax, and enjoy the scenery."

"Are you kidding me, after what we just went through back there? Just go!" Margaux yelled at him, hanging on for dear life, not sure whether to believe him or not. In the end, she decided to believe him. At least, if he was telling the truth, then the worst was over and she could look forward to a hot cup of coffee with hopefully toast and eggs or whatever he had brought for breakfast. As the jeep purred on ahead, she let go of the dashboard and settled back quietly into her seat, her hands relaxed on her lap. She gazed at more of the woodland scenery in front of her, grateful the trail was now level. In an hour, she knew, the sun's glistening rays would furtively peek through the dense trees, the dim early morning shadows giving way to the welcoming light of day.

Soon, Byron slowed the jeep to a stop and they both looked out from the windshield. Margaux's eyes widened. Oh shit, he promised! This time they were facing a gentle downwards sandy slope that led to a roaring creek ahead of the jeep. Slats of plywood were nailed to each other along the vertical line of the creek creating a makeshift bridge without, yikes, hand railings. The gray-and-brown muddied waters of the rushing creek had sloshed up the on the plywood boards for years creating permanent deep-rooted stains that made the bridge appear older and weaker.

Margaux stared at Byron. "Are we going over that thing?" It didn't look very strong from her perspective. "You promised!"

Byron grinned. "Relax, that bridge is actually stronger than it looks. I know it by heart. It'll hold."

"It better." Margaux said grimly, putting her hands back on the dashboard.

"Ah, Margaux, don't worry, sit back. The crossing is fun. In fact, the rushing water you see is actually shallow, so much so, you can practically walk over yourself on two feet, if you want. Do you want?" He looked at her with amusement in his eyes. "Go on. Walk over it."

"I think not!" Margaux shook her head, not relishing the thought of putting her two feet in that fast, roaring water, however shallow. Besides, she was tired and hungry and thirsty and, right now, wading in there did not look appealing. She let out a sigh. "Let's go," she announced as she firmly braced herself for the crossing.

"All right!" Byron turned on the ignition.

The jeep moved forwards cautiously. The four sturdy tires lumbered downwards on the sandy, stone-peppered slope ever so slowly and expertly as it headed towards the bridge. As they neared the plywood slats of the makeshift bridge, Byron deftly turned the steering wheel to the right. With his feet against the accelerator, he urged the jeep to a huge forward push. The left tires, front and back, landed on the wooden bridge, while the right tires, front and back, entered into the rushing torrents of the creek. The water forced the jeep to tilt over to the right throughout the crossing. Margaux' eyes widened ever more, as she felt her body sway to the far right, as the jeep crossed over, half in and half out of the water.

"Whoaaa…" She whispered softly, looking out and down from the open window of the jeep. She stared at the furious waters roaring below them with wide eyed curiosity, her throat tight with dread. Byron chuckled at her apprehension and yet he knew she was enjoying the ride.

"Like it?" he inquired as he deftly maneuvered the jeep away from the waters, the left front and back tires stumbling away from the platform bridge to settle into a level straight line on the trail. He stopped the jeep.

Margaux breathed a sigh of relief. She glared at him. "Believe me, I'm not looking forward to the next thing you want to show me."

Byron chuckled again. "No worries." Placing his foot back on the pedal, he started the ignition again and set the jeep in a forward cruising mode, leaving two, wet tire treads behind in its wake.

From her seat, Margaux looked back at the rushing creek, impressed at having crossed it unscathed. It actually was fun. She turned around to face him.

"Now what?"

"Ok. It's what I call the first beautiful jewel of the last length of this trail," Byron explained giving her a knowing smile. "Not too far along. I need you to close your eyes."

"Ok. But I'm not going to like this." Margaux wrapped her right hand over her eyes, while her left hand gripped the dashboard. The jeep rumbled on a few feet more, before veering off to the right and landing on a smooth dense surface. To Margaux, it felt like soft, thick sand beneath the jeep.

"Now open your eyes." Byron instructed as he slowed the jeep down and turned off the ignition. With a grin, he turned and watched Margaux's reaction, his right hand resting on the headrest of her seat, his left hand gesturing beyond the windshield.

"Behold Loch Tallulah."

Margaux slowly removed her right hand and looked ahead with dread. From their vantage point, the jeep's powerful headlights only served to enhance the evocative beauty and serenity of this most beautiful landscape in front of her, an enormous lake sitting at the end of the right-forked trail. The lake extended for miles beyond the horizon, its dark, blue-green water quietly shimmering in the powerful glare of the headlights.

"Oh, my God, Byron!" She gushed, her eyes wide with astonishment and wonder, her hands holding her face as she stared at the expansive quiet lake in front of her. "It's breathtaking! I'm almost tempted to jump in and swim in there."

"Huh, huh, not allowed." Byron shook his head grimly. "There's a sign out there saying "Swimming Strictly Forbidden", but for you, I would probably not worry too much." In his mind's eye, he could imagine her swimming within the serene cyan-green sheen of the lake, pushing the water aside in each strong stroke. All of a sudden he wished she would jump in there right now and swim. Just so he could watch her. The thought of her striding in the cavernous depth of the lake in her swimsuit, no, in her nakedness, brought strong stirrings inside his loins. He clamped it down quickly.

"Wow. That sounds harsh," Margaux commented, oblivious to his thoughts. "Is the lake dangerous?"

"It's just too deep, practically bottomless a couple of steps from the shore. Several people have drowned in the dark. Last year, after a third deep-dive rescue to retrieve a body, the park reserve put a stop to it."

"Oh, that's too bad," was all Margaux could say, feeling deflated. She looked longingly at the lake surrounded by lofty, brown trees embedded in the light, brown sand. "Yes, it would have been a lovely swim in there." It was still too early for the sun's rays to peek through the wooded flora and twinkle upon the lake, but she could see from the jeep's headlights how smooth and inviting the crystal water was, however deep. Inviting her to swim.

"But," Byron said, empathizing with her disappointment, "since we are both expert swimmers, why not? Hell, I'm a lifeguard. We could swim unbeknownst to anyone at this hour. But, see now, I am running out of time for the first and second jewels I want to show to you. That one is important to me." He glanced at his watch. "Look, we have to be there on time, seriously, and now we have only 20 minutes left. Can the swim wait?" He glanced towards her, his eyes beseeching, his smile imploring her to agree, his right hand reaching out to gently touch her left shoulder. "You'll like it. I promise you."

"Hah, you and your promises. How do I know I will like it?"

"You have my word this time, believe me. I hope." He smiled awkwardly.

"Oh, ok, then, let's swim another time. Go on. Show me." Margaux gestured towards the window.

She had to clamp down her disappointment to postpone the swim. And yet, she felt an undercurrent of warm shivers flow through her body at the touch of his strong, gentle hand on her shoulder. It felt fuzzy and warm and wonderful all at once, and she instantly regretted it when he removed his hand to clutch the steering wheel. She wanted more of his touch on her body. She wanted to say it out loud to him. Touch me again. Please. I like what I feel.

Instead, she looked up at Byron and smiled. "Can you at least give me a hint?"

"Nope, it's a surprise. You'll see," Byron promised as he switched on the ignition and turned the steering wheel to the left, the jeep rumbling away from the lake.

In a few seconds, they reached the main trail. He turned the jeep to the right, smiling at Margaux. "Actually, it's kind of hard to describe. Not many people have ever seen it. It's something you have to see for yourself. We need to hurry now. Time is of the utmost importance and you'll see why. It's guaranteed to astound you, I promise."

"Will you stop saying you promise!" Margaux protested with a sigh as she settled back on her seat. She glanced furtively at Byron, still longing for his electrifying touch on her body, still feeling the warmth, the need on her skin from before. No one had ever touched her like that.

"Oh God." She crossed her arms against her stomach. It was growling painfully.

"Me too, just hang in there. Only a few minutes more."

Seven minutes after leaving the magnificent Loch Tallulah behind them, the mud-splattered jeep arrived at the demarcation point of the grungy, off-road trail. The two tracks of dense forest on both sides of the trail abruptly ended at that point. Beyond the invisible open boundary, one could finally see a glimpse of the missing expanse of sky above the trees, still covered in the dusky, charcoal gray shadows of the early morning with streaks of sky blue and coral. And at each moment passing by, there were signs that the sky was slowly but deliberately changing into the brilliant hue of daylight.

"Oh great, we must hurry. It's almost daylight as you can see." Byron gestured at the sky. "That would certainly spoil the surprise." He urged the jeep ahead through the opening, its powerful headlights shining to reveal a vast open land in front of them.

A panoramic meadowland covered in masses of fresh, green grass and flamboyant wildflowers. Speechless, Margaux squinted her eyes to get a better view ahead. "Is that the jewel you were talking about? Wow. Look at all those flowers. So many colors, it hurts my eyes. It's incredibly beautiful."

"I knew you would like it." Byron responded with a grin and put the jeep in park, its engine idling, letting Margaux enjoy for the moment, the multicolored view of this remarkable landscape. "That's Quashone Meadows and we are just in time for the surprise, maybe a little bit late, but not by much."

Chapter 11

BYRON WAS RELIEVED. ANY MORE time and it would be getting much too late for the surprise and they needed to eat first. He realized just how hungry he was. He turned to smile at Margaux, taking her hand into his. Margaux gasped softly. There it is again, that warm, fuzzy feeling.

Byron apparently did not notice her reaction, focusing on his discourse. "The other jewel I wanted to show you. It's a little further on, through that little opening between the trees, but first, we need to eat. And you, of course, need your coffee. Shall we?" He extended his hand.

Margaux beamed at him, nodding vigorously. She grasped his hand. "Yes! My coffee! Finally!"

Byron grinned, releasing his hand. He took a deep breath as he maneuvered the jeep forwards a few feet to where it settled at the center of the vast, iridescent-colored meadow of grass and flowers. He switched the ignition off and relaxed, brushing his hair with his hands. Having let go of the intense mental focus driving on the rough 5-mile trail with a nervous Margaux beside him, he suddenly realized how tired he was. Bone tired. It would be good to have a hot breakfast. After all, the day has only just begun.

He opened the jeep's door to let himself out. Margaux followed suit. Standing by the jeep, surrounded by the wildflowers, she looked up to see the moon and stars slowly fade into oblivion.

It was nearly 6:00AM when Byron put the picnic basket and the red-and-white checkered blanket on the back seat, along with the small stove and propane bottle. Margaux stood beside him, as he leaned into the back seat from the driver's side jeep door arranging the picnic items in their places.

She found herself admiring the long, muscled length of his legs and firm bottom covered by the dark denim jeans. Earlier, sitting cross-legged on the checkered blanket, both hands holding the hot steaming, mug of coffee, she had watched him with admiration as he prepared the hot breakfast with the ease of a world class chef. The scrumptious aroma of sizzling eggs and toast and the heady scent of the fresh air had whetted her appetite. She had never felt so pampered, especially out in the wilds. Clearly, camping and cooking outdoors was yet another set of surprising talents Byron had about him. He was quite the outdoorsman, although she would never have guessed it in the first place.

She handed the empty coffee mug towards Byron, a warm smile curving in her mouth. Byron smiled back, puzzled, as he took the mug from her.

"What?"

"You. You never cease to amaze me with your talents."

"That's funny. Not long ago you were complaining about the rough drive on the trail. Change your mind already?"

"Now that I feel better and we are in this magnificent place, I would think so. I could get used to this."

"That's good. It's a huge of part of my life, this place and my jeep. Come, I think we should get going now."

"Okay." Margaux lifted herself up. She folded the blanket and handed it to Byron. "I can't wait to see it."

She watched him shut door of the jeep and put the keys in his pocket, her heart beating a little too fast. It was tantalizing to be so close to him, inhaling his male scent. Turning around, Byron smiled at her. He arched his eyebrow when she quickly looked away. "Ok, what's up now?"

"Oh, nothing. Nothing at all. Just getting impatient, you know." Margaux lowered her eyes, embarrassment flooding her cheeks. She quickly stepped away from him, her hands behind her back, not trusting her feelings for him at this moment. Her feelings bothered her. She wanted him to take her in his arms, and yet, did he want her, having whined and complained in this trip? Margaux dared not ask. Unsure of what to do next and hoping to distract him, Margaux forced herself to look back at him. "I'd like to see that mysterious jewel. Can we go now?"

Byron chuckled seeing her cheeks blaze, the red color showing up through her suntanned skin. Even while he was putting away the breakfast items, he had felt her eyes straying upon him from time to time. He had also felt her sense of longing. He knew at that moment that his frustration was now over and that she was falling in love with him. Yes, he had finally pierced the wall of resistance she had stubbornly raised for the past two months and now they were both alone in this vast clearing surrounded only by grass, wildflowers, forest, and sky.

"Come on." he reached out to Margaux, the crinkles around the corners of his eyes deepening with tenderness and warmth. "It's just a little way beyond on that small trail ahead of us over there." He pointed to the small opening in the thickly dense forest, hard to see, but he knew where to find it.

When they reached their destination, he touched a tree trunk at its base. "Look."

There was a small crudely-carved image of a hunting arrow on the gnarled, ancient tree trunk pointing towards the dark opening into the forest. Above the arrow was an image of a circle surrounded by wiggles of rays extending outwards. Perhaps the sun? Margaux peered into the gloomy opening. The trail in there was hardly discernible.

"Not many people know about this place," Byron said. "I found it by accident. I go there every time I lose faith in the world. Its remarkable beauty sustains me."

"Okay, you lost me now. I'm quite curious about it. Go on." Margaux grasped his hand into hers and silently followed him into the forest.

Byron trekked ahead armed with the unwavering confidence of a Native American scout furtively tracking the faint signs of life hidden upon the earthen ground. Margaux tightened her grip and followed closely behind him. Soon both of them came upon yet another clearing, a much smaller one, devoid of grass. Granted, it was not like the colorfully-panoramic meadow behind them that had so captivated her heart, but this small clearing revealed something the likes of which Margaux had never seen nor experienced before in her entire lifetime.

Hand in hand, Byron lead Margaux towards the biggest boulder standing upright just before what seemed to be a sheer cliff a few feet further. Even in the twilight shade of the early morning sky, she could see that the ground sharply cut off at the edge with only the open sky visible, extending far out into the horizon. Positioning himself next to the massive, standing sarsen that appeared almost 8 feet tall, the 6 feet tall Byron quickly released his grip on Margaux. With both hands, he touched the boulder, gazing at it with rapt admiration. Closing his eyes, Byron expertly and knowingly caressed the smooth, glossy surface as if it was his long lost lover. He smiled, his eyes still closed, his face emanating a sense of utter peace and relief.

Perplexed, Margaux stood behind him and waited. What was that all about?

"Come, feel it." He urged as he guided her hands slowly on the sleek surface of the stone in the same manner he had done earlier. "Feel how smooth it is. How heavy it is. And most importantly, feel it coming alive. Just close your eyes and feel the energy flow into you."

Stroking the giant boulder with her outstretched hands the same way Byron did, Margaux sensed the colossal stone vibrating and suddenly felt a small jolt of electricity jump and burn into her hands. She automatically tried to pull them away, but Byron kept a firm grip on her hands, rubbing them onto the stone. "Don't worry." He whispered. "Trust me." Margaux closed her eyes.

In a few seconds time, the fiery, electrical glow burrowed deeper into her hands and quickly coursed throughout her body. Oh, it felt so good, Margaux thought, so warm. So relaxing and yet, so energized. The emotional albatross of stress and depression that had haunted her the entire year evaporated in an instant, replaced by a renewed sense of hope and vigor.

She smiled, her face beaming from the lingering warm vibration exuded by the sarsen.

Byron released his grip. He turned to face her. "See, do you feel what I felt?"

"Wow! I feel so invigorated, so powerful, and yet, so peaceful. I'm not upset anymore, not angry at all. It's quite an awesome feeling. I can see why you love this place. Does it last, this energy?"

"It does last for some time. Until you get hit again by anxiety or trauma, you know, at least in my experience. That is why I come back time and again. It is better than therapy. It is therapy itself. I always find the strength to face whatever problems I had after I touch this stone. Always." He smiled at Margaux, placing his hand on her cheek. "This stone even gave me the strength to ask you out on a date. You are not exactly approachable, you know?" Margaux nodded her head, smiling weakly. Byron pressed on, caressing her cheek. "Why is that?"

Margaux shrugged her shoulders. "Hard to explain. Too complicated. A lot of it has to do with trust."

Byron nodded. He removed his hand. "Be that as it may, I'm here if you want to talk."

"Thanks. I just need more time."

Byron turned and patted the stone gently. "Of course. Well, anyways, you are the only other person who knows about this stone. I'm counting on you to keep it a secret."

"I'm impressed. Thank you. Of course, I'll keep your secret. I even have a secret of my own, but that is another story, another time." Margaux looked up at the gigantic rock, feeling small in light of its towering strength and power. She touched it lightly with her hand. "Gee, I wonder what it is and where it came from."

"It's a bluestone. I took photographs and did some research, because I've never seen this kind of stone before. And you know what? This kind of stone is very hard to find around here. The quarry itself is nonexistent in this country. What's more, this stone has got to be very, very hard to transport to this place. To date, no one knows who or what put it there or even why. I don't think many people know about its remarkable healing powers, this bluestone."

"I'll give you one guess. It's across the continent. Near a place called Avebury?"

"Oh, my God, of course!" She declared enthusiastically. "England. Bluestone is what made Stonehenge. How did you know all that? How did you know I'd know?"

"I figured you might know from all that reading you do," Byron explained. "Like I said before, for myself, I did a little research and it does appear to be bluestone. What boggles my mind is how it got here. Apparently it has been here for tens of thousands of years, about the same time as Stonehenge."

"No doubt." Margaux agreed patting the stone affectionately. "It had to have been transported from England or Ireland. You are correct. There are no places around here to quarry bluestones." She looked out towards the cliff, shaking her head. "And both countries are thousands of miles across the ocean."

"My sentiments exactly," Byron said. "So, Margaux, behold Quashone Henge. At least, based on my research, that's what I call it."

"I like the name. It fits perfectly, Byron. After all, we are in Quashone land."

"Anyway, there's more still to come. It's probably why the bluestone was erected here long ago." He gestured towards the overhang crag with the steep vertical drop. "Let's sit in front of this stone."

"Ok." Margaux lowered her body. She placed her back firmly against the sarsen and crossed one ankle over the other, her hands clasped together on her lap. She looked up at Byron and smiled. "So this is the jewel that is hard to describe, huh?"

"No, not really." Byron positioned himself next to her, his right leg bent upright at the knee. He placed his right arm on the upraised knee and pointed to the horizon. "It's hard to describe the jewel. We're a little late, but there it is." Languorously, he clasped both hands around his knees and watched with anticipation.

The sky was changing.

"Oh, my god, it's so beautiful!" Margaux stared in fascination.

As if an invisible hand was indolently painting onto a broad, blank canvas of the sky, the weak interplay of sky blue and coral streamers against the dusky, gray background morphed explosively into this gorgeous expansion of lavender, orange, and white-hot pink. Here and there several strands of soft, white clouds gracefully floated through the inflamed sky, exposing the nascent glare of the sun behind them, although the sun was nowhere to be seen, not yet.

Margaux blinked her eyes. She looked out again. It was quite mesmerizing in all its exquisite beauty. Not unlike a sparkling jewel the color of a rainbow. Byron was right. It was hard to describe it. She had to see it for herself.

"Like it?" Byron turned to face her, smiling at her upturned face expressing awe and wonder at the gorgeous dawn unfolding before them. "You kind of missed the sun appearing up there. At one time, it was moving up vertically from just below the horizons."

"Darn, is it because we're late?"

"No, you can't see it from here today going up like that. Today, it's scattered behind the clouds. See, a few years ago, quite by accident, I saw that sun coming up on the 21st of June from where we're sitting. God, it was mind blowing."

"The summer solstice? Really? And last month too?"

"Yes, really." Byron nodded. "And yes, last month too. Apparently it only shows up on the summer solstice."

"Ahhh…" Margaux murmured softly. "That explains it." She lifted both knees up towards her body and hugged them with her arms, her chin resting upon the kneecaps. "Just like Stonehenge."

"Huh, what do you mean just like Stonehenge?"

"Stonehenge is a calendar. Didn't you know that?

"No. I thought it was a ritual place for human sacrifice, you know, with the Druids running the place."

"No, you are wrong. The Druids never practiced human sacrifice. And yes, it was originally was built to be a calendar."

"Calendar for what?"

"Well, see, the sun shows up in there at summer solstice, too, through an opening between the rocks thousands of years ago. It still does. It's the only way for the ancient farmers to know that summer has arrived and it's time to plant the wheat and corn. And here, with this bluestone, you obviously have a calendar, too, for that same reason, I imagine." She turned to Byron. "Do you know who lived here that far back?"

"That far back? I'm only aware of the Quashone Indians, no other inhabitants, ancient or not. This Native American tribe has lived here at Artemis' Realm for eons of time, before they all disappeared."

"Disappeared? What happened?"

"No one knows. The entire tribe just disappeared in the middle of whatever they were doing, leaving behind a settlement in ruins, even half-cooked food. To this day, it is still an unsolved mystery."

"Well, this stone is much too heavy for them to carry, even on wooden rollers." She glanced towards the trees behind the stone.

"What's that supposed to mean?"

"It means, and you've got to keep an open mind, ok? Margaux said aiming directly into his questioning eyes. Byron nodded. "Sure."

"Ok. Well, do you know Sherlock Holmes by Conan Doyle?" Byron nodded again quizzically. Yes, he had read several books of the adventures of Sherlock Holmes. "What has that got to do with this bluestone and the Quashone Indians?"

"See, Sherlock Holmes, well actually Conan Doyle, has said— and I really love this—that if you eliminate the impossible, whatever remains, however, improbable, must be the truth."

"And?" Byron cocked his head curiously, his eyes narrowed.

"In my opinion, it can only be extraterrestrials. Alien visitors from the stars. From other worlds." Margaux watched him warily from the corner of her eye wondering if he was going to explode into laughter. Most people did. Few actually understood, much less believed in the possibility of extraterrestrials.

But he did not laugh.

"Extraterrestrials? Those little gray men with big eyes like those pictures I keep seeing in the news from time to time? You're kidding me? The ones that go around abducting people left and right?"

"They are not that bad, Byron. I'm willing to bet they are nice. There must be a reason for those abductions. None of them have ever been killed, only returned."

"True, so how come we don't have those gray bodies? We'd need proof, you know."

"I can't answer that one. I don't know, but the proof is all around you in this earth if you would just open your eyes and mind. The proof is in Stonehenge and in this beautiful boulder carried over thousands of miles across the ocean tens of thousands of years ago. Only extraterrestrials can possibly do that with their spaceships flying at the speed of light. Our ancestors did not have ships at that time, Byron, not even the Quashone Indians. Not possible. It's much too early in their evolution to even think of something as complicated as a flying machine, not to mention lifting massive stones."

"Oh, man, and you believe it? This theory of little gray men in flying spaceships? The UFOs?"

Margaux sighed patiently. "Well, I choose to believe it, Byron. You don't have to. To me, it's the only possible truth. They had the technology and what's more, I believe they shared the technology with our ancestors. The thought is incredible, isn't it?"

"I'll say. I hope you don't mind I'm still skeptical. I require hard proof."

"Suit yourself. But you'll see it clearly one day. Just stick with me. This time, it's my turn to show you." Margaux smiled mischievously, locking eyes with him. He had no idea of the proof out there she would show to him.

"Okay, then, I'm all for it. Just one more question, though." Byron grinned. "Why bluestone, do you know? We have all these buildings and structures made of steel and fiberglass and aluminum composite all over the world. Why did they use bluestones?"

"Eh, why do we have castles and Greco-Roman buildings and statues thousands of years old all made in stone and granite and marble? Why do we have our federal buildings, most of them, at least, made out of granite and marble? It's quite simple. They last forever," Margaux responded with unwavering conviction, hugging her knees tightly and staring out at the blue-tinted sky. "Somehow, we were meant to find them, these ancient stone structures all over the world and in the ocean. And in finding them, I believe we might find the truth of our origins, where we all came from, who knows. Did you know that right now there is already a huge gap between early man and Homo sapiens? Even now, we don't know what to make of it. Can you see, Byron? It makes perfect sense to me. The grays are the missing link."

"Now that is getting too complex for my head to wrap around, thank you. We can stop now." Byron shook his head, his fingers swiftly combing into his dark hair.

He was nervous. It was all too much for him to absorb, too incredulous, and yet, strangely enough, coming from Margaux herself in all her fluid logic using Sherlock Holmes' iconic quote, it did not seem highly illogical either. In fact, it could work.

It could be the truth.

But, he needed more time, more evidence, before he could let go of the diehard skepticism born of his own reality. For if it was true at all, that extraterrestrials existed, that they created modern man, and that they were the ancient stone builders, this would change his entire perception of history as he knew it. And the world as he knew it.

Yes, he needed for Margaux to show him some more.

He propped himself up against the standing bluestone once again and sighed in contentment, enjoying Margaux's close physical proximity and feminine scent. He even liked how she chattered on and on with all the excitement and conviction on this seemingly outlandish theory of the existence of extraterrestrials. Margaux certainly had very strange interests, but so far, she apparently had what seemed to be the right answers.

Finally, he understood her lonely life, unable to share her strange interests with anyone else. It took a lot of her courage to even confide in him, which is why he didn't laugh at her. But still, he needed more persuasion.

And then there was one more thing he needed to know. Did she like him? Oh well, only time will tell.

Breathing in the fresh morning air, he became calm and quiet, almost in a dream state. He leaned his body lazily against the bluestone and stared serenely at the white-gold morning sky.

Chapter 12

FEELING THE TANTALIZING NEARNESS OF his strong, male body sitting beside her, Margaux turned to stealthily glimpse at his rugged male profile, the minute he turned around to admire the morning sky. To Margaux, he looked so handsome and at peace, comfortable in his own skin and power, and was at one with nature. They were worlds apart, and yet, he continued to surprise her at how different he could be. He even patiently listened as she chattered about extraterrestrials, a subject she had been loathe to discuss with anyone, fearing ridicule.

She longed to put her hand on his cheek and stroke it, to feel the rough surface of that five-o'clock shadow, now so prominent, giving him the rugged look of a veteran mountaineer.

As if reading her thoughts, Byron turned his head slowly to meet her searching eyes. He smiled broadly, exposing the creases in the corners of his mouth, his eyes punctuated with tiny wrinkles. He looked down at her full, soft lips, almost open, his mind still intoxicated from the extraordinarily stunning beauty of the dawn's early light.

This time Margaux did not look away. She did not even resist him like she often had the past two months. This time she silently relinquished her power to him, revealing that she wanted him.

Once again he looked back into the depths of her deep indigo eyes and saw the longing there, a need, her head now nodding ever so slightly. With a raspy intake of his breath, Byron lowered down to meet her lips, holding her head firmly with both his hands, his fingers intertwined into her lush, golden hair. He lightly brushed her lips, feeling its soft, moist fullness, before swiftly locking his mouth into hers in a hard, driving kiss. He hungrily pushed his tongue into her wet, pliant mouth, exploring its inner, silky environs with a passion born of long resisted need, as his arms quickly encircled around her soft, yielding body.

Margaux leaned her trembling body against him, allowing herself to be swallowed entirely within his embrace, breathing in his heady, male scent. She moaned softly as his tongue passionately explored inside her mouth. She met his need with an equal driving force, her head pushed slightly back by the force of his kiss, allowing him to explore the silky, length of her neck and shoulders. Byron groaned thickly from his throat. His right hand slowly reached down towards the muscled curve of her lower back to slip inside her denim shorts. He found and cupped his hand against her smooth, naked bottom. Margaux gasped softly. Instinctively, she reached down to remove her denim shorts and threw them aside, moving her body closer to him, wrapping her legs around his hips.

He helped her by holding her against him. He could feel her chest heaving and the intoxicating sensation of her full breasts against him, as her throbbing body joined his pounding heart, their arms now fully encircled around each other in a tight embrace. He pulled away from her and proceeded to remove his jeans and checkered hiking shirt. Pulling her back towards him, he gasped with the heat now searing throughout his body, his heart beating ever faster, as his hand explored all the sensitive places of her body.

Margaux moaned softly.

Releasing his hand from her, he put both hands into her ruffled golden-blonde hair, pulling her head back tightly and looking deeply into her half-lidded, blue eyes.

Be mine?

Lost in her ecstasy, Margaux bobbed her head quickly, sat up, and smiled at him seductively. She reached down to lift her t-shirt up and out, revealing her pink-lace bra. Byron smiled, as his hands went around to unlock the clasp and deftly removed it off her shoulders. Cupping the underside of her right breast in his hand, he devoured the nipple with his wet mouth. Margaux moaned softly, her hands both holding his head tightly against her, pulling him down with her onto to the earthen ground.

The need between them was becoming unbearable, excruciatingly so. Byron groaned as he gently mounted his body onto hers. His searching hands fondled and kneaded at all the sensitive places he knew to find on her body, first to excite her, then to arouse her, and finally to take her to the soaring blissful heights of rapture.

"Margaux," he moaned thickly from his throat.

"My Byron," Margaux whispered huskily as she arched her back towards him and gasped as he entered fully inside her, his mouth still on her breast, inciting ever higher her desperate feelings for him, their bodies rushing headlong into an explosion of exquisite lust and love.

Above them, the massive bluestone henge stood in silent sentinel.

Chapter 13

MARGAUX SIGHED WITH CONTENTMENT, STRETCHING her naked body. She snuggled deeper into Byron's arms, their bodies leaning against bluestone behind them. Her head was propped up against his muscled chest.

He held her towards him and kissed the top of her yellow, tousled curls, a few strands flopping over her half-lidded eyes staring at the brightly, illuminated sky ahead.

Margaux looked up at him questioningly, embarrassment showing in her cheeks, "Do you think anyone saw us? Making love out here, I mean? God, we are so out in the open."

"Highly doubtful," Byron assured her. "Hardly anyone comes here this early in the morning. Most visitors normally show up past 9:00AM and hardly anyone knows about this trail and the bluestone. I wouldn't worry about it." He kissed her glistening forehead and stroked her hair as she rested her head back against his chest.

Margaux sighed lazily. This is perfect. This must be what being in love feels like. She stroked his strong arm holding her against him, trailing the prominent lines of his muscles with her finger.

Byron lifted her head towards him, smiling, "Margaux, my love, do you see that cliff drop ahead?"

"Hmm…mmm…" Margaux mumbled raising her head to view the overhang. "What about it?"

"These cliff edges extend all the way around to that place where we saw the sign on that one forked road. Remember? The sign that said 'DANGER. Do Not Enter.' That is why we could not go in there."

"Oh, geez." Margaux sat up. She peered at the crag-lined edges. "I hope no one fell in there. That would be awful."

"Well, one off-road vehicle did. And that was it. One was too much. And besides, it's too hard to drive against that cliff-edge, day or night. That is why the sign is put there. To warn us off. It's been like that for years, the grass now overgrown on that trail."

"That's good." Margaux said, relieved that they had not ventured into that area, even if it was tempting at that time. Just to take a peek. She was reminded of Bolivia where an even more dangerous cliff-road, the horribly narrow North Yungas Road, snaked perilously around the mountainsides. There, numerous, careless drivers had accidentally plummeted in their trucks, buses, and cars down the sheer cliffs.

Margaux shivered. It didn't even make sense that anyone would attempt that cliff-road at all. She lay back and snuggled ever deeper into Byron's strong body, feeling the warmth and safety of his arms around her. They lay together for a few minutes more.

"You know what, Byron?" Margaux declared as she quickly lifted up to prop her elbow on the ground. She looked up at him mischievously, the fullness of her breasts exposed. He stared at the protruding red-brown nipples, his fingers lazily rubbing the right tip to its taut firmness.

"What?" He enclosed his hand on the breast.

"Let's go for a swim in Loch Tallulah," Margaux suggested, her eyes gleaming with excitement. "Naked like we are now. I know it's crazy, even forbidden, but like you said before, who's to know?"

"Why not?" Byron smiled indolently. "Come on. We got to get dressed."

Within a few minutes, the forest-green jeep approached the shores of Loch Tallulah and Byron pulled it to a stop, applying the parking brake. He shut off the ignition and turned to look at Margaux. She was already removing her t-shirt, shorts and sandals.

He smiled at her eagerness and excitement, her beautiful nude body once again inciting the stirrings in his loins.

"Go on." He gestured to the lake. "I'll join you shortly. For now, I'd like to watch you dive into that lake from here. Naked." He winked at her wickedly as his hand reached to caress her cheek.

Margaux giggled softly, gave him a quick kiss in the mouth, and jumped out of the open jeep door to head into a running dive into the lake.

Soon Byron joined her in all his nakedness. Together, they waded into the deep, cool waters to the center of the lake. Blue jays, robins, and morning larks flew over the lake, as insects chirped their individual morning songs. Holding each other under the morning light, Byron and Margaux kissed with the white-hot passion born of their love. Skin against dripping skin, mouth inside yielding mouth, they were ready to once again reach the soaring heights of their passion, when suddenly, a piercing white beam of laser light shone upon them from far above the circle of dense, russet trees surrounding the lake. The solid sheen of the light beam shone brighter than the morning light, almost rendering the two of them invisible within its shimmering rays.

Startled by this intrusion, Margaux and Byron cautiously looked up towards the source, only to find themselves being roughly pulled upwards, the powerfully bright beam absorbing their wet, naked bodies, before it pulled away and swiftly vanished into the open blue sky.

Chapter 14

MARGAUX SLOWLY OPENED HER EYES and found herself looking upwards at a non-descript ceiling that was hard to discern in the hazy, gray light surrounding her. To her mind's eye, it looked simply like a misty, out-of-focus light, not unlike a foggy morning at sea. She carefully lifted her head, trying to get a better view of her surroundings, but found herself restrained from the shoulders down.

As she writhed in her struggle to make sense of her restraints, she looked down towards her legs and saw two metallic-silver clamps enclosed over her ankles, preventing her feet from moving. Looking sideways, she saw two similar, metallic-silver clamps over her wrists, handcuffing her hands to the long silvery-gray steel table where she lay. It didn't make sense. Where was she? And where was Byron?

Fear gripped her when she realized that she was alone on the table. Not long ago, she had been in Byron's passionate embrace in the lake, before that bizarre beam of light showed up and swallowed them. She remembered him being pulled upwards and away from her.

In her last glimpse of him, Margaux saw him staring at her in confusion and alarm. Hard as he tried, he couldn't hold onto her. When she faded into the light, she saw him struggling against a nameless force to no avail. His arms and legs kicked with a fierce resentment born of an inherent impulse to fight or flee.

But the light was too strong for either of them as Margaux and Byron disappeared from each other's locked arms. Pulled upwards into some kind of circular, black void above them in the sky. Margaux saw that Byron was gone towards that open void, having let go of his fighting instincts, his body overcome by utter fatigue. Her inner being railed with the intense fear of being snatched by what? By whom? And then darkness overwhelmed her, mercifully, as her exhausted body went limp.

And now in a nameless room she knew not where, Margaux struggled to find a way to release the metallic restraints on her ankles and wrists. They held her down tightly, locked, not even an entry point for a key. It was useless now, her body spent from the effort. As she once again looked around the room, she struggled to make sense of where she was, her vision impeded by the vague, smoky haze of light hanging above her and all around her. She couldn't see any walls or ceiling, and worse still, she couldn't see any floor. It was as if the uncomfortably rigid table she was lying on was suspended in the dark air. Time seemed to stand still. It was just so dark and ominous all around the mysteriously shadowy room that it only served to elevate her fears and quicken her heartbeats.

She screamed until she was exhausted.

Searching for her love, she turned her head frantically. She noticed a little further on to her right side, another long silvery -gray steel table, similar to hers, also suspended in this confusing vacuum and surrounded by the ambiguous, dusky mist. Blinking her eyes to see through the hazy, foggy light, she caught sight of a prone, male body, its wrists and ankles restrained like hers.

Byron! She called out to him.

The taut, muscular lines of his immobilized body did not move. His face was tense and inert, staring upwards lifelessly, the lines on his mouth as rigid as the hard planes of his cheeks. He wasn't responding. He wasn't moving. Was he even alive? Margaux became frantic with worry. She struggled with her restraints.

"Byron," she whispered, "come on, talk to me. Please tell me you are alive, please. I'm so scared." He still did not respond, his body remaining inert on the cold, steel table. And yet…Margaux peered closely. Yes, oh yes, he was still alive. Oh, thank God! She could see his chest heaving softly up and down in tandem with his breaths.

Turning around, Margaux sighed dejectedly, as she looked up towards a nameless ceiling. Where were they? Why had they been brought to this godforsaken place only to be restrained like this?

Margaux screamed. "Somebody help us! Please help us!"

Once again, Margaux thrashed against her tight restraints to no avail. Exhausted and spent, her body lay listless on the table, as darkness consumed her conscious mind.

Margaux opened her eyes. She wasn't sure how long she was out. A hand gently stroked her forehead, wiping away the sweat accumulated around her eyebrows and brushing back her tousled, blonde curls. Grateful for the kind gesture, Margaux glanced up to thank whoever it was, hoping he or she would also have the kindness to release her and Byron from their restraints. Instead, she was confronted with an alien being studying her face with enormously huge, almond-shaped eyes.

The eyes were completely black, liquid black, not a pupil in sight, not even eyelids and eyebrows. The skin on its face was gray and taut, and she noticed that the back of its head was unusually elongated. She opened her mouth in a scream of utter fright, but no sound came out. She was completely frozen as the six, long, gray fingers softly brushed back her disheveled hair.

Lifting her head for a better view, Margaux saw a second gray, alien being, exactly like the first, with what looked like a very long, medical syringe in his six-fingered hand.

"Oh, my god…" Margaux nervously stared at the syringe. The second gray alien approached the other side of the table and positioned itself just above her stomach. "What are you doing?" she whispered in frantic resistance, her body once again thrashing to release the restraints. "Let me out!"

The first gray alien held her down firmly at the shoulder with its other hand, saying nothing to her, only gazing at her with its huge dark eyes. At a closer look at its face, Margaux noted that the mouth was very small, almost a slit, at the lower end of its heart-shaped face. The nose was equally small and finely upturned. She wondered if it could talk, for nothing was being communicated to her for all her frantic protests against the procedure being done on her.

Held down by the firm hold of the first gray alien, Margaux could only watch helplessly as the second gray alien plunged the long, sharp needle of the syringe into her abdomen. She winced, gripping her hands at the edges of the table, as excruciating pain surged within her body, the needle digging deeper, drawing bright, red, liquid blood into the container of the syringe. This second gray alien noiselessly handed the syringe to the third gray alien standing at the foot of the table and, in turn, was given a second syringe filled with a clear liquid, she knew not what. Once again, Margaux felt the sting of the syringe and the liquid being forced this time into the nook of her arm where her elbow was. Almost immediately, she felt a sensation of calm and relaxation, a sense of grogginess. The liquid given her was obviously a sedative, but why?

And what did they do to Byron?

Were these the so-called extraterrestrials she had read about, the creators of humankind? The ancient stone builders?

She forced herself to remain awake, as she watched the second gray alien lift the syringe from the niche near her elbow and walk away from the table, followed noiselessly by the third gray alien. The first gray alien gently removed its firm hold on her, ignoring her completely, and noiselessly followed the other two. Slowly, Margaux turned her head to the right and saw that the other table was empty. Byron was gone. Her sleepy eyes closed as her valiant struggle to stay awake failed her.

Chapter 15

His head throbbing with intense pain, Byron shifted his body to sit on what felt like soft, grainy sand. He surveyed his surroundings, groggy from what felt like a long, deep slumber. Shaking his head to distract the pain, he looked behind him and noticed that he was sitting by a lake, an endless blue-green lake, its surface glimmering from the bright rays of sunshine. He looked up. The sun was not yet at noon.

Ahead, he saw a forest-green jeep standing alone on the grassy terrain adjacent to what looked like a trail pulverized with chalk-white dust and brown earth. Small gray and black rocks and stones littered the well-worn trail. Byron wished he could at least recognize the jeep, but for the moment the throbbing tension in his head had blocked any and all recollections of what had happened to him. He felt completely clueless and disoriented. Looking down at himself, he saw with a wry smile that he was also completely nude. A small incision was evident and he daintily touched it with his finger, eliciting a twinge of pain.

This was getting stranger and stranger.

Quite bizarre.

"What the hell happened here?" He wondered lifting himself up on the ground. He brushed the sand from his body and arms. Ignoring the pain of the throbbing headache, Byron quickly walked towards the jeep. He needed some help now. He needed some clothes to cover himself. Perhaps the owner of the jeep would be willing to help him, assuming he could find the owner.

He tried to open the door. It was not locked. He pushed the door aside and saw a pile of clothes neatly arranged on the driver's seat, including Levi jeans designed for men, but he did not have a glimmer of recognition for these clothes. They are his size, he noted, checking the label in the jeans. He reached out and opened the glove compartment, extracting a wallet sitting on a pile of maps and documents.

Closing the glove compartment, his eyes strayed to floor below and noticed an open shoulder bag. Clearly, it was a woman's shoulder bag, but it too was unrecognizable. Beside it, in scattered array, lay a pair of denim shorts, a white t-shirt, and pink lacy bra. So there was a woman, also? Without her clothes? Why would she do that? Even more to the point, why was he naked himself?

Not wanting to think too much, distracted by the pain in his head, he stepped out of the jeep and carefully opened the dark-brown, leather wallet for some sort of identification. There was a registration card, an insurance card, a few credit cards, some cash and coins, and finally he found what looked like a driver's license. He stared at it for some time not quite comprehending its significance. The picture on the driver's license was him, definitely, unarguably him, and it listed his name as Byron O' Neill.

He glanced back at the forest-green jeep. The driver's license stated he was the owner, although he clearly did not remember this jeep at all or even the past events, whatever had happened to him that had finally left him sitting on the sand by the lake alone, completely disoriented, and in pain. And obviously, judging by the feminine clothes strewn on the floor of the passenger side, a woman had accompanied him, but she was nowhere to be seen. He wasn't sure what to make of it all, but one thing was definite.

He needed to get out of here.

Looking back at the pile of clothing on the driver's seat, he surmised that they were evidently his and proceeded to dress himself. Feeling gravely responsible for the missing woman, he realized he could do nothing. He did not even know where to start to look for her, especially since he did not know what had happened to him. But one thing he knew. She would need her clothes if and when she showed up in this place. But he wasn't going to wait for her. Hell, no. Who knew if she would ever show up? And then how would he explain himself, waiting all day for a missing woman, whose only existence was supported by her clothes and shoulder bag sitting in his jeep.

After zipping up his jeans, he inserted his feet into his Teva sandals and walked around to the passenger side of the jeep. He opened the door and picked up the shoulder bag from the floor, depositing it on the seat. He rifled gently inside the bag and noted her house keys sitting in the small inner pouch of the bag. He lifted the keys and placed it on the palm of his hand. A small jeweled item was latched onto the ring of keys and he noted that it had a cursive inscription of her name in glittering faux gold: Margaux. A look into her burgundy, leather purse that he had found at the bottom of the shoulder bag revealed her last name and address, quite unfathomable to him. He had no idea who Margaux Ishara Martin was, although the picture on her driver's license showed a woman of indescribable beauty, her smiling face framed with tousled, golden hair. He scratched his head in confusion. He needed to leave now and see a doctor. He looked back at the lake. What if this woman showed up at the lake like him, suddenly sitting all by herself without any idea of what was happening to her and who, like him, had a throbbing pain in her head?

His plan set in motion, Byron placed the little purse back into the shoulder bag and zipped the bag closed. After collecting her clothes into his arms along with the shoulder bag, he walked towards the sandy boundary of the peaceful blue-green lake. He quietly placed Margaux's clothes and shoulder bag in a neat pile at the same location he had earlier found himself. After standing up straight, Byron faced the lake in silent contemplation, the headache slowly subsiding.

He took one last searching look around the lake's wide perimeter for the missing Margaux. He shouted out her name. An echo sounded out mournfully, but it was to no avail. The only other sounds were the morning larks singing melodiously among the silent, stoic trees.

Byron sighed. There was nothing more he could do. She would have to take care of herself. At least she had her clothes and bag at the ready.

He took one last look at the vast, shimmering lake, turned around, and ran towards the jeep.

Chapter 16

ONE HOUR LATER.

Having changed into the clothes that she had found nearby on the shore of the lake, Margaux picked up her shoulder bag. Soon, she started her long trek through the off-road trail adjacent to the lake.

Earlier she had suddenly found herself alone by the lake, hot, sweaty, and naked, her head throbbing painfully under the late, morning glare of the sun. All alone in her surroundings, Margaux had been gratified at the sight of casual, feminine clothes arranged in a neat pile along with a shoulder bag. She was even more delighted to find that those items were indeed her own as an investigation into the contents of the shoulder bag had indicated she was the owner of the bag propped up against the feminine attire, all carefully displayed on the ground. She wondered who placed them there. Was it someone she knew? And more importantly, why did this person leave her?

Facing the off-road trail, Margaux surveyed her surroundings, confused and disoriented. She was distracted by the stabbing knife pounding in her head. She had no idea and no remembrance of what had occurred to cause her to show up all alone near a lake, surrounded by a dense forest and quite naked, thank you. She shook her head weakly, clutching it tightly.

Why was her head in so much pain?

Willing herself to ignore the pain, Margaux looked around once more, checking out the forest. As far as she was aware of, there were no vehicles parked in the vicinity of the lake and there was no one around to whom she could ask for help. All around her, there was only the scattered flock of airborne birds, as if announcing an impending omen. Margaux shuddered. She must hasten now, not sure how long the sun would stay up.

It was imperative to find her way out before nightfall.

An hour passed. Stepping on stones, dirt, and mud, she moved along the rough trail, with still a long way to go. Margaux stopped, bending over sharply, her hands placed firmly on her knees. She took in long, gasping breaths, feeling her ribcage contract and expand. Her throbbing head had been quieted down by the ibuprofen pills she had found in her bag, thank God. Breathing in and out, she could feel the sweat collecting into small, wet beads on her forehead. She wiped away the sweat with the back of her hand and narrowly eyed the off-road trail at a distance. It was hard to see that far along, the trail disappearing into the dark recesses of the forest and shrubs.

Not much light in there, either.

She wondered how much longer the walk would take. She was getting so tired already. And thirsty and hungry. The scorching heat of the sun was slowly sapping her strength and stamina, already weakened from the lack of food and water. Her throat felt dry and scratchy and her stomach grumbled painfully. But she needed to move on. Time was of essence. There was no point in staying in this remote forest with not a sight of humanity thus far. She needed to find a way home, grateful that she at least remembered where she lived with her parents.

And then it hit her. Maybe her parents were clueless about her whereabouts. Otherwise, she would have been quickly found and brought home safely, considering her mother's tight, unyielding grip on her.

And still, 24 hours had to pass before she could be declared missing and a search party organized for her. Margaux sighed. For now, it was up to her to get home. Taking in a last deep breath, clutching her shoulder bag tightly, her face grim and determined, Margaux stepped forward and resumed the long, tiresome walk.

Several minutes later, Margaux was startled aside by an olive-drab Jeep Cherokee rolling unsteadily past her from the hairpin corner of the off-road trail. The jeep was terribly noisy, breaking the silence of the woods with its grumbling roar, its tires thrusting powdery dust into the air. Annoyed, Margaux brushed away the dust surrounding her. She looked back. Deeply embedded within the thick dirt and sand, the Jeep Cherokee continued to rumble away from her, apparently disregarding her. All of a sudden, there was more noise behind her. Margaux turned her head quickly and was once again startled into leaping sideways and out of the way of a Highlander, a Land Rover, a Jeep Sahara, an Outback, and several more trucks and SUVs in what looked like an endless convoy coming around that hairpin turn.

Margaux stared at each of the mud-splattered vehicles passing her by, completely baffled. Why were there so many of them? The passengers inside idly glanced through the windows at the tired Margaux leaning against the sandy embankment. Some even waved at her. To them, she was just a normal tourist hiking by herself on the trail.

This was after all, Artemis' Realm.

Suddenly, the convoy stopped in front of her in a domino effect. Nervously, Margaux moved her body back against the embankment, wondering why they all stopped. Perhaps a deer has crossed the path ahead. She waited for them to move on. Not far from her, a head stuck out of the window of the yellow Nissan Exterra.

"Hey, Gerald!" a shout burst forth. "What's up? Why'd you stop now? We're not even there yet." Margaux's eyes widened. She waited patiently as all the other passengers from the convoy yelled out in a loud cacophony of agreement for this Gerald to get a move on, wherever he was. There was no response from Gerald. Even now, Margaux realized that they all still ignored her, as if she was completely invisible to them.

She waited a bit longer, unsure of what to do in all this chaos. Studying the endless line of SUVs and trucks with their unhappy passengers yelling at each other, Margaux decided it would seem safer to wait it out, whatever was going on.

Obviously, the Jeep Cherokee that had passed her by so unexpectedly from that hairpin corner was the lead SUV. And that color and mud on the jeep. Why was it so vaguely familiar to her?

Grunting, Margaux lifted herself up from the embankment behind her and brushed the sand from her clothes and bag. She brushed back her mussed-up hair and glared. Ignoring the group of travelers, who were just now seeing her for the first time, she narrowed her eyes and searched for the lead vehicle.

There it was, not too far from her.

Suddenly, the driver-side door of the Jeep Cherokee opened. A young man clambered out to survey the back of his jeep and all along the convoy, a hint of concern in his brow. He ignored the discordant shouts aimed at him to get a move on.

"Shut your mouths, guys!" he yelled back. "I gotta check something out, all right!" The convoy settled into silence. Some of the riders stared at Margaux, who nervously stepped back into the embankment, hoping to hide herself.

Shutting the door of the jeep loudly, the young man ambled towards the back of the convoy, until he reached Margaux. She stared at him nervously.

"Hey!" He waved and smiled at her, showing the whites of his perfectly aligned teeth. Margaux could see he was very young, perhaps her age or younger, with a thick mop of disheveled strawberry-blonde hair, its strands almost covering his forehead and eyes. Tiny freckles dotted along the pale, white skin of his nose and cheeks. He looked quite the gamin from a J.R Tolkien novel, what was his name? Frodo! Margaux smiled inwardly, amused at the sight of him when he finally approached her. He offered his hand.

"Hello, there. Do you want a lift? You look awful, you know." He grinned sheepishly.

"Yes, I know." Margaux nodded, embarrassment flooding her cheeks. She covered her chest with her bag. "I'd like a ride, but is there room in your jeep?" She looked behind him towards the lead jeep, its passengers already observing her with interest. She noted they were also as young as the driver himself. "Plus I was heading that way." She pointed in the other direction.

"Well, then why don't you join us? We will all be heading back in your direction anyways in a few hours after our bash at the Meadows. Course, we'll make room for you. Come on with us."

"I don't know. There's a reason I have to go home quickly. I can't even explain."

The young man paused, his eyes narrowed, as he looked at Margaux's tired body, grimy and slumped from the long, hour walk in the hot sun.

"Look. This trail goes a long ways back to the front gate. It's a very long walk. It's even longer getting back to your home on the highway. But if that's what you want, I won't stop you."

"I'm thinking. I'm thinking." Margaux sighed. The offer was tempting. And yet, he was right. It did seem easier to get back home with them. At least she was not alone. "Ok, ok, I'll go with you guys. Thanks."

"All right!" He turned towards the convoy, his thumbs up in the air. "Guys! She's coming with us. Now we can hustle on!"

"Yeah, yeah, Gerald!" Several heads and arms were out of the windows, fists raised in the air, the convoy's inhabitants all yelling. "Let's get a move on! Time's a wasting! Look where that goddamn sun is!"

Gerald grinned. "My buddies. They're telling me it's almost noon. We had planned to be at Quashone Meadows before noon, you know, for our big bash there."

"Oh."

Margaux smiled as she walked in step beside him on their way towards his jeep. "You're Gerald, aren't you?"

"Yup, I'm Gerald" He grinned back at her, the one strand of strawberry-blonde hair flopping down his forehead to settle over his right eye. "And you are?"

"I'm Margaux Martin. Thanks again for taking me on."

"No problem. So, here we are. Hey guys! This here is Margaux." He raised his fingers in the air, pointing at her. "She's coming with us."

The lead jeep's open door was held in place by another young man, tall and muscular, his blond hair cropped in short military fashion. "Go on in." Gerald gestured to Margaux. "They made room for you."

Poking her head inside the jeep, Margaux could see a petite, raven-haired young woman with violet eyes covered in heavy makeup. She was sitting on the lap of a young man, whose dark-brown hair was cropped in a Mohawk down the middle of his bald head. He had two small earrings clipped on both his ears. His arms were wrapped around the waist of the petite, young woman, holding her tightly. Margaux observed the tattoos on their naked arms, each a name of the other.

Next to them sat a statuesque, blonde female with gray-blue eyes looking very much alike to the tall, young man with the military haircut. She had moved aside to make room for Margaux, patting the chair. "Hi, Margaux, come on it. Sit here with us."

Margaux stepped inside and seated herself. The tall young man clambered in.

They all smiled at Margaux.

Gerald slammed the back door. With a wave towards the convoy behind him, he yelled out loudly, his right finger twirling in the air. "Guys! Let's rumble!"

"Yeah, yeah! Right on! Let's rumble!" They all yelled back revving up their off-road vehicles, one by one, the heavy, rubber tires spewing dirty, grimy dust into the air. Soon, the collective roar of the entire convoy reverberated loudly in the air, sending birds flying off in all directions.

Gerald glanced at the rearview mirror towards Margaux, his hands gripped onto the steering wheel. "Time I introduced you to us and these clowns back there. See, back there to your right is Cesar Morata and this here is Marigold de la Fleur on his lap. She's his girlfriend."

"Hi!" Cesar and Marigold grinned, their cheeks glued to the other. Margaux smiled. They were obviously in love.

"And on either of you are Arnold and Annaliese Von Grappelin. They're twin brother and sister on vacation from Germany. I invited them here. Their family hosted me when I was a transfer student back there."

Margaux looked at each of them. Annaliese, seated on her right, was like her brother, big-boned with white-gold hair, hers streaming thickly over her shoulders like a waterfall in direct contrast to her brother's short military haircut. Both had blue eyes that gleamed when they smiled at her.

"My, but you are tall." Margaux said.

Gerald grinned. "They're training for the Olympics. Swimming for Germany."

"Wow! That's great. Good luck."

"Ya, we'll need it." Arnold grinned. "You Americans beat us last time."

Margaux nodded compassionately. The American swimming powerhouse of Matt Thorsen and Missy Yancigay had been more than anyone had hoped to beat.

"Ya, next time we'll be ready." Annaliese added grimly, slamming a fist into her other hand.

Margaux grinned. She wasn't going to argue with that.

"And this here…" Gerald interrupted nodding at the pretty, young woman seated next to him in the front passenger seat. "This here is my fiancé, Romy. She's the one that caused it all."

"Caused it all?" Margaux asked quizzically glancing at the pretty girl next to Gerald. Romy had flame-colored hair cut in a page boy style with straight bangs at her forehead, almost covering her eyebrows. A single, purple stripe swept down one side of her hair, adding to the dazzling rock-star effect. She had a wide heart-shaped face that exploded into a perky smile, revealing the dimples on both her cheeks.

"Yeah, she's the one that stopped the convoy behind us, yelling at me to go get you. Admittedly, though, I had to agree with her. No question about it."

"Oh, so it's it you I have to thank for rescuing me, not Gerald." Margaux edged closer to the front. She smiled at Romy, offering her hand. Romy grinned and clasped it. Confused, she turned to

Gerald. "What do you mean, you agreed with her, no question about it?"

"Oh, nothing. It's nothing. It's just something she knew and I had to agree with her. Let's leave it at that, shall we?"

"Well, okay...I guess." Margaux sat back against her seat, pushing her body between the two Olympic-bound giants. She folded her arms. "I'm curious, what is this big bash you mentioned a while back?"

"A party!" All six chimed in a chorus. "Barbecue, music, dancing, and booze!"

Margaux laughed.

"That's right." Romy added, turning to face Margaux, "It was supposed to be a camping trip at first, but some of these guys could not make it overnight, so we changed it into a daylong picnic bash. Should be fun!"

"It does sounds like fun." Margaux grinned. "Thanks for inviting me."

"And some of us will open up our trucks to check out the engine, transmission, carburetor, muffler, piping, et cetera, et cetera. Make sure they are all in working order and to just take a look see at how they work." Gerald patted the steering wheel affectionately. "We love fixing cars, the whole lot of us guys."

"And don't forget some of us girls." Romy pushed his shoulder.

"I can see that." Margaux turned and looked behind her at the back window. "There must close to twenty trucks back there?"

"Which is why Quashone Meadows is perfect for this setup," Gerald explained enthusiastically. "Who knows we might start a regular tradition from here on, all of us guys on this road trip."

"So." Romy turned towards Margaux, her arm hugging the back of her seat. "Why were you walking on that trail all alone?" The others nodded in unison, all of them, except Gerald, staring at her. Yes, why?

"I don't know, Romy. I really don't have the foggiest idea why." Margaux murmured, her eyes becoming vacant, her body still, as she stared out of the windshield at nothing. She shook her head mournfully. "It's like there's a gap of missing time that I can't even remember. I don't know what to tell you."

Romy lifted her eyebrows quizzically at Gerald, who shrugged his shoulders. He shook his head briefly. Let it go. Not a good idea to pursue this.

"Oh, by the way." Margaux rifled inside her shoulder bag. "Can I offer some cash for food? I'm terribly hungry right now. I haven't been able to find anything to eat."

"Oh, no, no, no, no." Romy pushed the money away. "No cash. No way. Nope. We are happy to share our food with you. I'm going get a ham-and-cheese sandwich and a bottle of water for you right now." She reached towards the picnic basket on the jeep floor between her legs. She unscrewed the cap on the water bottle and handed it to Margaux along with the sandwich. "Here, that should tide you over until the barbeque."

"Oh, thank you so much," Margaux whispered. She placed the water bottle between her knees, ripped off the waxed wrapper from the sandwich and proceeded to devour it, gulping the water from time to time. Gerald, Romy and their friends quietly watched with alarmed interest, wondering what the hell had happened to her?

Chapter 17

MARGAUX SETTLED BACK INTO HER assigned seat, 9C, the last seat available on the midnight flight, when she checked herself in at the registration desk at the airport. She buckled herself tightly. With a relieved sigh, she leaned back against her seat and looked out of the porthole window dejectedly, watching the contingent of empty baggage carriers drive away into the distance. It was dark outside, almost pitch black. Tears building up inside her eyes, Margaux listened to the melodious strains of a lonely electric guitar inside her mind accompanying a song that spoke volumes of love, pain, and loss.

Soon it would be time to depart. Turning away from the window, she waited for several seconds, her arms resting comfortably on each side of her seat, her hands softly gripping the underside of the armrests, the song still humming in her mind. At last, she began to feel the soft thrum-thrum vibrating throughout the fuselage of the airplane, the jet engines already set in motion by the captain and co-pilot behind the closed, cockpit door.

Closing her eyes, Margaux let herself feel the vibrations of the jet engines. The shuddering became stronger and stronger, intermixing with the haunting, guitar music in her mind, filling her body with a two-fold sense of sadness and excitement.

Soon, the BlueStar Express jerked and proceeded to glide backwards slowly, before the plane stopped briefly and turned around, heading towards the main runway for the takeoff.

Her eyes still closed, Margaux listened to the powerful jet engines whine in ever increasing crescendo, as the Boeing 737 quickly accelerated down the runway and, with a gentle thump of the landing wheels, lifted and soared into the far reaches of the night sky.

From out of the air, within the cabin, the captain's voice confidently announced that they were now cruising at 35,000 feet. His voice intermixed with the final stanza of the lyrical song in her mind reassuring her that she was flying the friendly skies.

Fighting back tears that only managed to drop onto her cheeks one by one, Margaux sighed with a mixed sense of victory and sorrow, releasing the buckle of her seatbelt. She was on her way, now. She was going back to Westbury Moor.

Margaux dabbed the last tear that fell from her eyes with a tissue. Just yesterday evening, she had had a horrible fight with her mother, who had demanded that she explain her whereabouts, when Gerald and Romy and their friends dropped her off at the end of the day.

She remembered Quashone Meadows. She remembered the long, bumpy ride on the off-road trail and the amazing convoy of 20 trucks, jeeps, and SUVs filled with the young, flamboyant party bums, herself becoming one of them. And what a party it was. There were food and drinks and music and dancing. Full of the joy of friends celebrating life and their trucks. It was their final bash, when all got together to party one last time, before heading back to the normal, boring life of universities and jobs. And she had immersed herself with them, drinking and dancing, as if there was no tomorrow.

Then finally, it was time to go home for all of them, the sky having changed into a shadow of the approaching nightfall. After another long, meandering convoy ride back to the entrance gate, all the SUVs, jeeps, and trucks then separated into their scattered individual directions home, all of the drivers and passengers yelling out their goodbyes and so longs and see ya laters, their hands waving, their faces poking out of the windows, all of them smiling and promising each other to keep in touch.

To always keep in touch.

But the fight that night she was dropped off was horrendous. Her parents, more her mother than her father, demanded to know why she'd disappeared that day and why she had left them distraught and worried. They had discovered her bed empty and found no message from her. They had waited and waited all day and was only beginning to call the police, when they heard the door slam and watched Margaux enter into the living room.

She had sat on the couch nervously, her mother sitting across from her, glaring with venom. Margaux's only response was that she didn't know anything. She couldn't even tell them anything, because she honestly didn't even understand what had happened to her when she found herself all alone in Artemis' Realm, two hours away from home. All she knew was that kind young strangers had picked her up, lost and tired and hungry, and had invited her to spend the day with them, which she did.

Her mother was not satisfied. "You could have disappeared." She declared angrily, slapping Margaux's cheek. "Gone just like that other one." There was silence.

Her mother gasped, covering her mouth with both hands. That wasn't meant to be said. Margaux looked at her father. There was no sound from him, standing a safe distance away by the kitchen door, a forlorn look in his face. He held a bottle of beer in his hand. He shook his head sadly at Margaux, not willing to challenge his irate wife.

"What other one?" Margaux demanded turning around to face her mother. "What are you talking about?"

"Never mind that. It's not important. You are now grounded for two months. This can never happen again. Never, you hear!" Her mother slapped at her again.

"That's it!" Margaux yelled and stood up from the couch, her hands desperately holding her head. She could still feel the stinging burn on her cheek, where her mother had slapped her twice. She was enraged and tired and unhappy, all at the same time. And now her mother had grounded her for no reason at all.

Margaux let go of her head. She smiled lovingly at her tired, drunken father. She turned and faced her mother, the anger seething in her voice. "That's it. I've had it. I have had it with your tight control on me all those years, Mother, and I don't even know why. And you know what? I've decided to leave this godforsaken town and your tight grip on me. I'm no longer putting up with you. It's ridiculous."

"That is not possible, Margaux," her mother said. "You haven't even started university."

"That's right. I'm not going to university."

"And what will you do with yourself, Margaux. You are too young to leave home."

"Oh, but I am so ready to leave home. And I will. Right now. It's what I should have done long ago. And guess what? I'm going back to Westbury Moor."

Her mother scowled at her father, beseeching him to intervene. He refused, staring silently at the shaggy, white carpet on the living room floor, the bottle of beer now empty in his hand.

Her mother turned back to Margaux and hollered. "How will you live, Margaux? You do not even have a job, much less any savings. We will not pay you for this, you know."

"Yes, I know, Mother." Margaux responded quietly, her eyes set in grim determination. "But no matter, I will figure it out. I do have some money saved and I really need to leave. I hate this town and the awful loneliness you had forced to me to endure the entire year."

Her mother started to protest, but Margaux held her ground.

"Yes, you. I will not be forced to stay here any longer. I don't have to. I don't even like you."

Her mother recoiled back in shock, silently staring at her daughter in wounded confusion and anger, unable to find the words to rebut her. Not without having to reveal her terrible secret.

Her mother tried again. "It's dark outside, Margaux, and very, very late. Can you at least wait until morning?" She hoped that Margaux would change her mind after a good night's sleep. This was after all a hasty, unexpected argument, soon to be forgotten in the morning.

"No, I'm not. I'm taking the midnight flight."

Having made her decision with renewed strength and confidence, Margaux turned away from her parents, both of them still in shock, entreating her silently to stay. Ignoring their pleas and tears, Margaux ran up the staircase into her bedroom.

Twenty-five minutes later, Margaux ran down the stairs, gripped by fear and terror, carrying her luggage and shoulder bag. She ignored her distraught parents, both of them sitting on the couch holding onto each other, as they watched her leave.

She slammed the front door behind her.

An hour later, at 35,000 feet, the BlueStar Express cruised harmoniously, the humming sound from the jet engines providing some measure of comfort. Margaux looked out through the porthole to admire the pale, crescent moon suspended against the backdrop of the velvety-black sky and surrounded by the sparkling stars.

"Coffee or tea?"

"What? Oh, water, please, if you have it."

"Certainly." The flight attendant smiled bending down to search for a bottle of water in the refreshment cart.

"Thanks." Margaux smiled accepting the proffered Evian water. She placed the bottle inside the pocket of the seat in front of her. Letting out a sigh, she settled back into her seat and closed her eyes. Thirty minutes passed. Sleep eluded her. The skin on her face felt damp and clammy. It would feel good to wash up. Clutching her shoulder bag, Margaux stood up from her seat. She carefully edged past her two seatmates, looking at them enviously, both of them in deep sleep. She walked towards the lavatory located at the rear of the plane. Locking the door, Margaux placed her shoulder bag on the sink counter and looked into the mirror. Her eyes looked sad, bleary, and tired. She had gone through a lot the past twenty-four hours. She turned on the faucet and placed her hands under the rush of cold water. She splashed the water on her face. It felt good.

Reaching out for a paper towel, Margaux found herself paralyzed with fear. The light inside the lavatory was slowly dimming. Soon, she found herself in total darkness, unable to see anything. Blind, frozen, and fearful, Margaux searched frantically in front of her for the sink counter. She gripped it tightly. It was so dark, nothing, not even her shoulder bag could be seen, only felt. And for some reason, she felt compelled to look up into the mirror in front of her covered in the opaque blackness. To her fear and dismay, a shadowy spray of smoke appeared, transforming into a white-blue phantasm, quite unclear to her, at the center of the mirror.

Anastasia?

She blinked her eyes and looked back. She gasped softly. The smoke was gone, but in its place were two huge, almond-shaped eyes, the liquid blackness of the pupils staring menacingly at her, not saying a word.

Seconds passed. The eyes still stared at her.

"Oh, no! Not again." Margaux had seen those eyes before, in the bathroom suite at home hours earlier. The eyes had disappeared as quickly as it came in front of her mirror.

And where was Anastasia?

Staring back at the malevolent eyes, Margaux shivered. Something was not right. She looked down at her arms.

They were disappearing.

She screamed inside her head.

Margaux found herself seated on the lavatory toilet, her head pounding, her legs extended, her arms drooping. She felt groggy and tired. Looking down, she pulled up her t-shirt. There was a red incision.

"Not again."

Grunting, Margaux pulled herself up from the lavatory seat and reached out for her shoulder bag, not wanting to stay in there a moment longer. She stepped out of the lavatory.

The flight attendant was approaching her, directing her to quickly seat herself and strap her seat belt in.

"Huh?"

"We are approaching Trurora City International Airport."

Margaux was incredulous. "Now?"

"Yes, quickly." She warned making sure Margaux was properly buckled with the seatbelt, before she headed to her own jump seat to strap herself in. The plane, which had banked deeply to the right when Margaux strapped her seatbelt in, leveled ahead, and was now descending in a rapid shift of motion. Soon, the landing gears thudded on the runway and the plane roared ahead briefly, before slowing down toward its final stop at the airport terminal gate.

Gripping the armrests on both sides, Margaux silently panicked, a sliver of sweat appearing on her forehead, as the headache relentlessly hammered her brain. She looked at her watch.

She had lost two hours of time.

Chapter 18

FORCING HERSELF TO STAY AWAKE and alert, Margaux gripped the side rail as she stood on the moving airport walkway, heading toward the taxi depot. She refused to even think about what had happened in that plane lavatory. What mattered was she was back where she should be. And that horrible headache was thankfully gone.

Margaux gazed through the glass-domed ceiling above her, lost in her thoughts. It was 3:00 in the morning, the night sky still dark, still peppered with myriads of twinkling stars. How comforting they seemed, so far away, and yet so bright. How many of them have planets just like earth?

Margaux looked away and stared ahead wordlessly. Right now, she needed to find a place to sleep for the night. Tomorrow she will decide what to do with the rest of her life.

And, yet, for some reason, she felt compelled to look towards her left. She turned her head to face another moving walkway heading in the opposite direction toward the airport terminal gates. And on that walkway was a lone soldier standing silently, oblivious towards her, his right hand gripped on the rail, his left hand clutching the strap of his heavy, military backpack. Margaux observed him. He was tall, nearly 6 feet tall, big-boned with dark, military-cropped hair that revealed the muscled form of his neck and shoulders. He was wearing the standard-issued, camouflage uniform and thick, tan, leather, combat boots.

Margaux narrowed her eyes, trying to make out the outlines of his face from a distance. It was difficult to see him that far and he was slowly, unavoidably, moving away from her.

But then, she noticed something strange happening, even bizarre, and yet so familiar. The soldier was now staring at her. Margaux gasped loudly, her hand covering her mouth. They were no longer his eyes. They had changed into the huge liquid-black, almond-shaped eyes, not unlike the ones she had encountered in the plane's lavatory and in her bathroom hours ago.

Margaux gripped the rail, paralyzed by fear, her heart beating in rapid staccatos. She wanted to run away from those eyes, afraid she would disappear once again. And yet, she had nowhere to go on this moving walkway, the exit to the taxis still quite a distance away.

She closed her eyes and surrendered herself.

In an instant, she found herself naked and moaning lying on the ground near a massive upright boulder. Looking down, she saw that she was locked in the hot embrace of a tall, handsome man with dark hair, who was making passionate love to her. He called out her name as he entered her. Margaux shook her head at the image, feeling aroused and confused. The man in her visions looked just like that soldier moving away from her.

But why?

She closed her eyes again.

This time, she found herself half-submerged in the center of a large, blue-green lake surrounded by a lush forest. Again she was naked. Her arms and legs were entwined around the naked form of the same handsome, dark-haired man, before they both were pulled up and away by a mysterious light beam coming down from the sky.

The visions stopped abruptly.

Margaux opened her eyes, terrified and confused. Did they really happen, and if so, where and why? Who was her lover in there? And what did that soldier have anything to do with these visions? Margaux sighed. It all seemed pointless to pursue it. It would be difficult to explain it to the soldier himself. She did not even know where to begin.

"Enough!" Margaux chastised to herself. "Get a grip or you will go crazy."

She looked back at the soldier again. He was now far away on the moving walkway. He turned around and looked back at her, the bulbous, black eyes no longer there. Margaux shivered. Having reached the taxi depot, Margaux quickly hopped off and headed towards the revolving door. She needed to escape to the outside world, where everything seemed normal.

Where she could breathe in the cool, fresh air and try to calm down her frantic, beating heart.

Chapter 19

IT WAS DARK OUTSIDE. BYRON clutched the reins attached to his parachute backpack, his heart racing. He moved towards the open door of the Army AH-Zephyr helicopter hovering above the war-infested country of El Ahraira in the Middle East. He wasn't sure why that one day he had impulsively entered a non-descript building at Mirrington Heights and joined the U.S. Army, volunteering to serve multiple tours fighting fundamentalist Arab insurgents, the Bakhabar.

The United States was now in its fourth year of war with the insurgents, fueled by the horrific bombing of the U.S. Embassy at Farizal, Al Ahraira's capital. One hundred and fifty Americans were dead. Furious at the blatant disregard for human life, the President had declared war immediately, Congress not even arguing with him. And now, Byron was among the thousands of American men and women, who volunteered to avenge the murdered Ambassador and his staff. The Army had assigned him to special operations as a paratrooper, the Delta Force.

Byron gripped the edges of the open door of the helicopter and stared out into the blackness of the night, scoping the dangerous, enemy territory below him. Two of his paratrooper buddies, Charlie and Jimmy, had already hopped out, their canopies blown open. Now it was his turn, albeit too late. The enemy had already detected them.

"Go, go, go, go, go!" the Nightstalker pilot yelled from the cockpit, as he struggled mightily to keep the helicopter flying in place, amid the constant strafe of bullets and explosives.

Byron quickly jumped out and moments later, his canopy was released. Clutching the nylon ropes, he whispered a prayer as he began his slow descent, barely missing the shots aimed at the helicopter.

Looking up, Byron watched the AH-Zephyr zig-zag one last time, before it quickly banked away to disappear into the night.

The strafing suddenly stopped.

He breathed in deeply. That was close.

He landed with a bump and rolled his body against the ground, his full blown canopy being dragged by the prevailing desert wind. He struggled on the ground, pulling the parachute ropes towards him. The canopy had attached itself to the prickly thorns of a desert bush, effectively stopping his body.

He surveyed his surroundings. So far, so good.

Suddenly, not far from him, the silent, nocturnal air roared and exploded into a fiery mass of rock-and-sand debris, white-hot flames, and burning smoke. Byron groaned as he picked up a small knife from within his specially-designed, stealth outfit. He proceeded to cut off the nylon ropes. He was lucky this time.

He hoped his buddies were okay.

He huddled deeper into the ground, keeping his head low. Once again, he carefully surveyed his surroundings through the ghostly-green reflection coming from his night goggles. Not a sound was heard nor a person in sight, not even Charlie and Jimmy.

Byron shivered. He wondered if they survived the IEDs.

Rustling up his courage, Byron paid attention to the task at hand, as he adjusted the night goggles and checked the grenades, the GPS device, and military-issued rifle. He groaned softly. The GPS device wasn't working. He was now on his own. He had hoped to be able to hook up at some point with Jimmy and Charlie, although right now he could see that seemed highly unlikely, as the dust from the recent explosion settled into the ground. Peering into the blackness of the night, he found himself facing the northwest side.

He decided to take a chance and head that way.

Byron hunkered down on the rough, sandy ground and began a slow, vigilant crawl in that direction. Somewhere in this bone-dry wasteland lie a hidden, underground enemy bunker, hiding massive quantities of explosive bomblets and stolen assault rifles. His mission was to get inside that bunker and destroy it.

As he diligently and carefully edged forward, keeping his head down towards the ground, his arm suddenly brushed a soft mass to his right. It was a body. Scrambling to his knees, Byron removed his night goggles and bent down to feel the throat with his fingers. There was no pulse. He sighed and lifted the military, head armor from the body. It was Charlie. The IED got to him. The Army would need to send a backup now. He turned on the silent, homing device attached to Charlie. Soon, the Army would find and retrieve the body in the night. He hoped his other buddy, Jimmy, survived, but right now he had to move quickly to complete his mission.

From above the night sky inside the vastness of the universe, Anastasia closed her eyes and waved her hand.

As if compelled by unseen forces, Byron picked up the night goggles and adjusted it on his head. He could see small pinpoints of lights arranged on two sides in his range of vision, blinking on and off, as they moved towards a diminishing point. Byron was puzzled. He slapped at his head gear. What in the world was that, those lights inside his binoculars? They stopped blinking when he moved his head away. And blinked back on when his eyes returned to that particular northwest direction.

"Go there, Byron, go there." Anastasia's voice urged inside his mind. Byron shook his head. No way he was going to go crazy with a voice in his head right now.

No way.

But what if the lights were telling him where the bunker was? He had no other way of knowing, the GPS being broken. It was a chance he had to take. There was no time to waste. Byron cowered down into the ground and followed the direction of the lights through his goggles, trusting the voice in his mind completely.

He groped ahead on the ground for a few minutes more, until the lights suddenly stopped blinking and the voice was gone. He waited, unsure what to do. A hand reached out in the dark, flailing about in the air. Still crouched into the ground, Byron grabbed the flailing hand and felt himself being pulled in. He looked up. To his enormous relief, it was Jimmy. Alive.

"Where's Charlie?"

"Dead. I just passed him by. I activated the signal. They should pick him up soon."

"Roger. It's out of our hands now. We gotta move quickly. We have already used up one hour."

Byron nodded in agreement. "My GPS is broken. What about yours?"

"It's working, but I found the bunker door without even using it." Jimmy pointed to the ground a few feet in front of him, still hidden in the darkness. "For some strange reason, I was led here by a voice in my head and lights blinking in my goggles."

"You too?"

"What do you mean, you too?"

"Never mind. Go on."

"Well, like I was saying, I found the door bunker like that and all of a sudden this same voice told me to look for you this way."

Byron nodded grimly. "It looks like we were both saved by an unseen force out there. I'm actually thankful for it."

"Me, too. But man, that was strange." Jimmy declared, staring at Byron in confusion. "Anyways, here we are."

"Yup, here we are." Byron took charge immediately. "No time now. We'll worry about our strange experiences later. Let's get down in there and destroy that bunker, Private."

"Aye, aye, Lieutenant." Jimmy quickly saluted. Both men positioned themselves at opposite ends of the trap door. With a slight, muffled groan, they both opened it and quickly disappeared into the shallow black pit.

Up above, far out in the universe, Anastasia smiled, her arms folded against her chest. It worked beautifully. She would let her assistants take over now.

It was time to check on Margaux.

The two men groveled stealthily in the darkness of the hidden, underground cavern. Each step of the way, they treaded carefully through a twisting maze of passageways. As they moved forward slowly, Byron unrolled the white, nylon rope behind him. It would guide them back to the trap door at the end of their mission.

The Bakhabar was clever. This cave had been hard to find and it was intentional. At the briefing before the mission, the team had been given only two hours to find the cavern, bomb it, and hustle out to safety.

At last, the two men found the cavern where the weapons were stockpiled in the wooden pallets. It was hot and damp in there. The smell of gunpowder lead and rotting wood hung heavily in the air, causing them to cough and hack from time to time. They needed to move quickly. It was getting hard to breathe. Byron and Jimmy hurriedly went through the motions they had been instructed to follow in their training. Fifteen minutes later, gasping for air, Jimmy placed the last, timed grenade on the last wooden pallet.

He looked at his watch.

They now had only 30 minutes left.

Jimmy looked back at Byron in anticipation, his eyes grim and focused. Their jobs done, they were both tensed, ready to spring into action. Byron nodded.

Now!

In an instant, they both broke into a run back into the twisting passageways and rocky antechambers, guided only by the white rope that lead back towards the trap door.

At the midpoint of the escape, Byron suddenly stopped running and looked around in confusion and fear. Jimmy bumped up behind him. Byron grabbed onto his buddy to keep him from falling to the ground.

"Move, Move!" Jimmy pushed Byron forward. "Are you crazy?? We're running outta time. This place's gonna blow!"

"Yeah, where?" Byron looked around him fearfully. He pointed at the broken end of the nylon rope, neatly slashed off. "The rope's gone."

Jimmy picked up the tattered end of the rope. Someone had cut it intentionally. They were now hopelessly lost.

"Oh, God," Jimmy groaned softly. "What do we do now?"

Byron looked down at his watch. Only eighteen minutes left.

"If they were here already, why the hell did they not finish us off at the cave back there?" Jimmy asked, his irritation rising. It did not make sense.

"I suspect they knew it was too late and it was easier to just cut the rope," Byron responded calmly. "We were already made a while back at the desert landing. It was just a matter of time for them to find us and follow us into this maze, even late as they are."

"Oh, great. Now what do we do? Sit down and wait to die?" Jimmy yelled out. He grabbed at Byron in desperation. "I don't wanna die!"

Byron gripped his frantic buddy's arm and shook him. "Stand down, Private. Calm down. Nothing we can do now, except to keep running one way or the other. Keep running. Ok? It's our only option. Do you want to lead or shall I? We have to try. Remember the Ranger Creed?"

Jimmy nodded in agreement. "Go further, go faster, fight harder. Go on, Lieutenant. I'll follow."

As time ticked off slowly, Jimmy and Byron became increasingly anxious and agitated, driven by fear and terror to keep on running, even as they were out of breath and overcome with exhaustion.

They were not giving up. They were trained not to give up.

8 minutes passed.

Suddenly, Byron felt a sense of clarity envelope him.

"There! Over there!" he yelled, pointing his finger. He stopped and bent over, his hands on his knees, breathing heavily. Jimmy stumbled behind him, breathless, looking at him in anticipation.

"What? Where?"

Byron pointed towards the wooden covering embedded on the rocky ceiling a few feet ahead of them. It was the trap door. Both men wasted no time running towards it.

Hard as they tried, no amount of pushing by the two of them would budge the door open. Clearly, they were blocked from the outside.

"Jesus, Byron, now what?" Jimmy gripped Byron frantically. "In five minutes, we are dead, man! Five minutes!"

Seeing how hopeless it was, Byron suddenly felt unnaturally calm, accepting of their fate. He looked grimly into Jimmy's frightened eyes. "Right now, we can only pray, Jimmy. We should pray. We've done what we were supposed to do. Now, we go with God." He grabbed Jimmy's left shoulder and offered his right hand. "Private, it has been a pleasure to serve with you. We did good."

"Likewise here, Lieutenant." Jimmy declared smiling back at Byron. He was calmly facing death, too, but he was not alone. There was no point in getting upset right now. They were clearly doomed. He gripped Byron's hand. "Yeah, we did good. See you at the other side."

The trap door room exploded in multiple, fiery bursts of white light, debris, and deafening roar.

"Now!" Anastasia ordered.

A steady beam of white, opaque light appeared from above the night sky, and enveloped Byron and Jimmy. The two men stared at the other in abject terror, before they both lost consciousness, their limp bodies swiftly pulled upwards into the abyss of the mothership.

Chapter 20

Margaux opened the door into her grey-and-pink Cape Cod house and tossed the mail on the mahogany table in the foyer. She picked up the cell phone from her shoulder bag and placed it next to the mail. Removing the woolen, lavender beanie from her head, she brushed her static-frizzled hair and stared into the crystal-studded oval mirror above the table. She sighed. Her face was ghostly-white and her eyes drooped sadly.

Having just arrived home late in the evening, she felt herself suddenly overcome with the weight of depression, fatigue, and stress, altogether. She was desperate for a hot bath, a hot meal, and sleep.

It didn't help that the weather outside was freezing.

She quickly unbuttoned the red, woolen winter coat and placed it on the hanger. Her mind was still going over the details of the past few hours. She had just come home from a four-hour long meeting she had attended with her divorce attorney, Mr. Gianni Pastorini, Esq. Together, they had sat down and discussed the terms of the divorce settlement with Michel, her soon-to-be ex-husband, and his divorce attorney, Mr. Benjamin Bonewyn, Esq. The question was should she finally agree to these terms adjusted by her ex-husband for the last time? Margaux still wasn't sure.

In fact, she needed something much more concrete to make it a sure thing. There was no going back, once it became final. And Michel, dear, angry Michel, was getting impatient, even annoyed. He wanted to settle the divorce once and for all and be done with it, so he could move on and return to Paris. He could not stand the sight of her. And neither did she, him. The negotiations had been going on for a year and a half, and they had been so close to finalizing it. The only problem was what to do with their fairytale Cape Cod house at Westbury Moor.

Worse still, Margaux couldn't see what to do with herself going forward and the house she had decorated so lovingly over the years was a big part of that problem. It bothered her. Should she keep it or should they both sell it? By all rights, splitting the profits seemed fair, since they had bought the house together in the early years of their now broken marriage.

How long ago it seemed. How unreal. Margaux stared at the foyer mirror, letting her mind drift away into the past.

Seven years ago.

Margaux had set her life in motion the minute her midnight flight landed at Trurora City International Airport and she spent the night in a nondescript motel by a roadside at Westbury Moor.

She had already shrugged off two hours of lost time and the strange encounter with the soldier in the airport. There were bigger things to worry about now that she had returned to her childhood hometown.

But this time, she was all alone.

"Thank you, Daddy." Margaux whispered, when, unbeknownst to her mother, he had discreetly wired a significant sum of funds to her bank. It was more than enough to help her get started.

After finding a suitable apartment to rent for herself, Margaux had registered at the Academy of Culinary Arts, patterned after the famed Sorbonne in Paris. She had decided she wanted to be a chef. Probably the only good memories she had of her mother, the both of them cooking delicious meals together all those years, especially during the holidays. What better way to make use of all that experience and be paid for it.

On her first day at class, she had been running late. After a moment of hesitation, she quickly entered the classroom. All eyes were on her, but the instructor was nowhere to be seen. What a relief.

Margaux grinned sheepishly. "Sorry," she said. "I was held up by traffic." The class laughed. It was too cliché.

She surveyed the classroom. There were seven adults in the classroom built to resemble a large commercial kitchen one normally finds at restaurants. Only one countertop table had a space left to claim and Margaux trotted towards it, stashing her handbag inside it.

Turning around, she faced her partner and offered her hand. "I'm Margaux Martin."

He was an African-American with a benign smile and dark hair fluffed up in an Afro style. He shook her hand. "Welcome. I'm Deshaun Lavelle. We are still waiting for our instructor to show up."

"And here I am." A gruff male voice boomed. All eyes turned towards the newcomer at the door. He was expertly outfitted in the standard-issued master chef's white apparel and white cap. He was now establishing himself at the head of the class with the supreme arrogance born of his title.

He surveyed his new students with critical interest. "The name's Michel Ragnarowski and I will be teaching this class for the next two years. When I am done with you all, you will be master chefs ready to take on the world."

The students clapped enthusiastically.

He glanced at Margaux and grinned knowingly. "I believe we have met before, have we not, Ms. Martin?" Margaux nodded, at a loss for words. It was true. They had already met in the midnight flight plane. After that terrible episode with the alien eyes, he had asked if she was all right, as she hurriedly passed over his aisle seat.

She had basically ignored him.

And now, there he was standing in front of her, her culinary arts instructor, of all people. Margaux shifted awkwardly, not sure what to say. Michel smiled at her broadly, revealing the perfectly aligned, white teeth against the tanned, olive skin of his round Slavic face. His mahogany-brown hair was loosely ruffled around his head, as if he never brushed them. He did not seem the ideal image of a master chef and yet, he was quite intimidating.

Margaux wished she hadn't ignored him in the plane.

Michel scrutinized her with narrowed eyes, wondering what had happened to her in the plane.

She had been clearly terrified, even speechless. But no matter. She was his student, now. They would have to get along, awkward as it was.

He bowed his head towards Margaux. "Well, it would appear you have recovered now. Welcome to my class, Miss Martin."

The class stared at Margaux. Recovered? Margaux kept her eyes down, blushing furiously.

"Are you all right?" Deshaun asked curiously. "Is there anything I can do to help?"

Margaux quickly shook her head.

Michel clapped his hands abruptly, breaking the awkward silence in the room. "Attention, please!"

The class turned towards him. Margaux breathed a sigh of relief.

"Good. Good. So now, class, shall we begin our lessons with preparing beef bourguignon, no?"

Two years later.

It was graduation time. Margaux was at the top of her class, as usual. She would soon graduate with honors, but no one from her family would be there to congratulate her or see her receive her diploma.

She wasn't sure whether to be happy or sad.

The day before her graduation, she had received a letter from her parents wishing her the best on her success, but would she please come home, now? Margaux smirked. That message could only have come from her mother. She rolled her eyes up, ripping the letter into pieces and throwing them in the trash. She still could not figure out what made her mother so fearful, checking on her time and again for the past two years, just to make sure she was still alive and safe. Alive and safe? From what? Try hard as she could, she never could get a satisfactory answer to that question. And, besides, it was getting tiresome.

In time, she chalked it off to her mother just being an overprotective, overbearing mother bear.

"Beautiful ceremony, wasn't it?"

The gruff voice was familiar, and yet, it was disquieting to hear it so near her. Frozen to the ground, Margaux's eyes warily turned to face the speaker of the voice. It was Michel. He had quietly snuck up beside her, while she was deeply engrossed admiring the vibrant beauty of the rose garden, where the graduation ceremony had taken place.

The garden was the pride of the town's local nature conservancy and a perfect venue for the ceremony. And it was Michel who was responsible for this arrangement, endearing him to Margaux. Yet, standing so close beside him, she wasn't sure what kind of mood he was in right now. He had a very unpredictable personality, constantly at one mood or another in a short flash of time. Not one to get along easily. For all she had known him the past two years, he had surpassed himself in teaching his art, but lacked the grace to bond with his students. He often dismissed them as mere trivialities not to be bothered with. They were simply below his stature. Not surprisingly, the entire class all kept their distance from him, even Margaux herself.

Margaux steeled herself, unsure of the mood he was in, but he stood beside her quietly, staring at the garden with her. "Beautiful, isn't it?" had been his only words so far. She wasn't sure whether he meant the graduation ceremony or the rose garden.

Or why he bothered to stand beside her, a mere student.

Mustering up her courage to face him, Margaux studied his arrogant profile. Today, he looked quite dashing, with long, tan Docker slacks, a silky light-green shirt, and a tan tuxedo. The shirt was open at the neckline, revealing the equally tanned skin and hairs of his chest. Today, he was tantalizing and attractive to her. Blushing hotly, Margaux turned around to admire the garden.

"Yes, it's beautiful, I agree. Thank you for choosing this place for the ceremony."

"You're welcome."

Margaux smiled inwardly. Today he was in a good mood.

"Mr. Ragnarowski, I want to thank you for the honor of being number one in your class. I didn't think I was that good, but thank you."

Michel grunted briefly and shifted his foot. He turned around to face her. He smiled. "The honor was mine, Margaux, but of course, you should know you earned it. I can only suspect you were not exactly a novice in this field, when you started my class."

"You are correct. I assisted my mother for several years as a little girl. I just needed the diploma to get started."

"Naturally. Still, I was quite surprised at your level of expertise compared to my other students." There was pride in his voice, which startled Margaux. This was the second time she realized of his attraction to her.

The first time was at the ceremony itself. She had sat at her place among her fellow graduates, her hands on her lap, looking serenely at the audience in front of her. To her great surprise, Michel had stood up and applauded loudly, when she accepted the diploma from the Director of the Institute. People had stared at him and then at her and then back at him. She had blushed terribly, as she shook hands with the Director and resumed her seat, clutching the diploma on her lap. Equally surprised, her classmates all had grinned at her and whispered into each other's ears.

"Why did you do that?" Margaux asked suddenly feeling irritated, her eyes staring at the resplendent beauty of red, orange, and yellow roses, not wanting to look at him. She knew she ran the risk of inciting his temperament.

"Do what?" He inquired curiously, keeping his hands inside the pockets, staring straight ahead.

He was unnaturally docile today, it would seem. Margaux took a leap of faith.

"Embarrass me up there, Mr. Ragnarowski. You were so loud, I wanted to hide. Was that even necessary?"

Michel laughed out loud, his eyes reflecting a gleam of wickedness. "Ah, Margaux, my dear! But, of course, I was so very happy for you, I couldn't help myself! You were my best student. Everyone knew that."

"But…but, what about the others? What about their feelings?
Michel sighed.

"Again, my dear Margaux, I am rightfully applauding the success of my best student in class. I am not worried at all. It's past graduation now. We all move on, including you and me." Michel paused briefly. He turned and looked down into her sapphire eyes, his brown eyes becoming dark with need. "What will you do now, Margaux, my dear? Do you have plans?"

Margaux shook her head. "I don't know. It's too early now. I'll think about it later."

"Ok, then. Don't take too long to think." Stepping closer next to her, Michel took her hand into both of his and held it tightly. Margaux blushed hotly. It felt warm and inviting in his hands. He cupped her chin and lifted her face towards his, his dark, smoldering eyes boring into her own.

"How about we have dinner tonight, hmmm, my dear? It is my treat. I wish to celebrate your success and your bright future."

"Are you asking me out for a date?"

"If you would like to call it that."

Margaux stared into his eyes, inflamed with need and affection and pride. Inwardly, she ached for him. She couldn't help but like him, in spite of the surly and cold distance he had maintained during her two years of training with him. And yet, that one inauspicious day, he had been there for her, when her mother called yet once again, rudely interrupting her class. She had been forced to apologize profusely, as she headed out of the classroom with her cell phone. Again, her mother was checking on her and demanded that she come home. And again, her pleas for answers were ignored.

"Please go away!" she had yelled out as she smashed the cell phone across the hall, sliding her body towards the floor. She sobbed and sobbed, hugging her knees against her body.

It was bad enough that for the past two years, Margaux had had bizarre episodes of missing time. It was something she could not explain to anyone, not even to herself. It had seemed easier to lie about her whereabouts than to say "I disappeared for an hour or so, I know not where."

The classroom door opened silently.

Michel had quietly sat down beside her and tried to comfort her. She decided to confide in him, hoping he would not think that she was crazy. Listening to her story, Michel had thought that it was strange indeed, this persistent, alarming request coming from her mother and not even a reason why. And surprisingly, he had agreed with her. It was not fair to Margaux. It was distracting her in class, perhaps her life. "Best to ignore your mother." He had consoled her at that time, putting his arms around her shoulders. "You cannot let her run your life."

Margaux had nodded in agreement, and settled against his chest. The sobs had subsided by now.

"She may be losing her mind, who knows," he had whispered into her ear. Margaux smiled weakly.

She never forgot his kindness that day. And from that day thereon, she stopped being afraid of him, in spite of his volatile nature. It was something she felt she could handle once she got used to him. He had proven he cared for her.

"Ok, I guess. It's a date. What time?"

"Eight o'clock. I shall stop by your home to pick you up. I know your address. Until then, ciao, my dear, and please call me Michel." He softly kissed the top of her hand.

Margaux smiled. Bowing his head, he turned around crisply and walked away towards his car in the parking lot beyond the rose garden.

From far, far away in the universe, an otherworldly being watched the scene unfold before her.

"Not good." Anastasia shook her elegantly-coiffed, elongated head covered with thick, shiny, golden hair flowing down her back. Frustrated, she paced back and forth along the invisible floor, her long, silky, empire-waist toga swishing softly behind her. She raised her arms in frustration. "Not good at all. I did not anticipate this ridiculous union. He is all wrong for her."

A gray-skinned alien being tentatively approached her, his huge, black, almond-shaped eyes not revealing any emotions. He had been summoned to explain the situation.

"High Priestess, she is but one of many we select for our work. A most viable human test subject, true, but nothing more."

"Not anymore." Anastasia scoffed. "You must be very careful with her. She is important to me. Are you monitoring her as I wished?"

"Yes, High Priestess, we are still monitoring her."

Anastasia sighed deeply, crossing her arms, as she watched Margaux enter into her car and drive away. She quickly turned around to face her minion, pointing her long, blood-orange fingernail. "Go! Bring her other life back. But carefully, my vices, carefully. I don't care how long it takes. We must not violate the Primary Principle."

"Agreed, High Priestess, so shall it be." The gray-skinned underling bowed down slowly, before he joined his compatriots standing discreetly at a distance behind him. Together the three alien beings with the large, menacing eyes disappeared into the mists.

Chapter 21

FIVE YEARS LATER.

A marriage that should have been made in heaven, considering their exalted status as master chef and sous chef, both husband and wife, instead became tumultuous and ugly. The relationship was fraught with fights and disagreements, even insults, between Margaux and Michel Ragnarowski.

All it took was a careful nudge from high above.

The first two years of their five year marriage that took place after graduation had been magnificent with a promise of a forever and always, two hearts interlocked in a passionate embrace. A small, intimate wedding took place at that same rose garden, surrounded by flowers. Just the two of them and family as they were joined in marriage by a civic marshal of the town hall. Her parents attended the wedding and proudly remarked what a wonderful couple they made. And this time, her mother did not pressure Margaux to come home. There really was no need to. Margaux's ultimate safety was now in the hands of her new husband.

A mother and son dance was in full swing.

"Never let her out of your sight." Her mother said, a sinister whisper into the groom's ear. "Or I will make you pay."

Startled, Michel stepped back slightly and narrowed his eyes, his anger kept at bay. He did not like being threatened at all. He wanted to quickly return his mother-in-law to her husband, but it was too late. She had locked eyes with him, her dark, pupils glaring with venom.

Perfect. From his otherworldly perch, the gray assistant went to work, closing his eyes and focusing his thoughts.

From out of his wife's mother sinister stare into his wide, open eyes, the floating seeds of animosity had begun to trickle into in his brain, igniting multitudes of tiny sparks among the synapses of the nerve cells.

Michel had only been too glad once her parents boarded a flight for home. "Crazy bitch," he sneered, holding Margaux's hand in a possessive manner as they both watched her parents board their flight. "I'm only too glad to get my wife away from you. You do not scare me at all."

"Goodbye!" Margaux had waved at her parents, as she watched them disappear through the terminal gate. Michel held her closer to him. His eyes narrowed in suspicion at the empty terminal gate. He had hoped nothing would go wrong for her mother seemed so sure of it. Something that happened in the past could happen again, she had whispered to him menacingly, adding to the vagueness and confusion of her threats. He was relieved when she announced this would be the last time and Margaux was now his responsibility.

He didn't like the sound of that. Still, her mother was gone, thankfully. There was so much to do with Margaux.

Together, Margaux and Michel had exploded into fame and fortune, propelled by a tantalizing offer from a close friend of Michel's, Javier Enrique de Ortiz, who owned The Culinary Channel, a reality show that was broadcast every Thursday nights on TV. It had been a wedding present from him, providing the newlyweds let the TV cameras follow their work as they traveled far and wide around the world showing off their combined culinary expertise. The couple sampled various exotic foods of each country they visited. For the first year, they traveled from Beijing to Mumbai to London to Paris to Glasgow, to Athens, and finally, to Rome. By the end of the second tour, they had traveled to Rio de Janeiro, Singapore, Dubai, Sidney, and finally their home country, the United States, including New

York, San Francisco, Chicago, Las Vegas, and New Orleans. In every prominent and illustrious city, each day of the week, Margaux and Michel together had hosted high-class gourmet culinary seminars to the thrill of throngs of adoring fans.

In time, the famous culinary duo of Margaux and Michel Ragnarowski became prosperous and wealthy, counting themselves among the jet setters and elite.

And now it was time to go home to Westbury Moor and settle down to raise a family.

They had bought a charming, Cape Cod house at Westbury Moor in a well-to-do neighborhood. In fact, so happy was she, Margaux took the liberty and had their dainty, cottage house painted in light gray with bright, pink window shutters, and a lime-green roof. The front door was painted in sunshine yellow. A flowering assemblage of hydrangeas, hyacinths, narcissus, and hibiscus peppered their front yard with an explosion of vibrant colors and scents. Margaux loved bright colors and Michel wasn't going to stand in the way of his adoring wife's happiness, even fighting the urge to destroy the pesky flowers with all his might. In his opinion, the flower arrangement was quite too opulent, too grandiose, and not his taste at all. Even the news media were unabashedly critical of their colorful, fairytale house, much to his dismay.

He chose to ignore their remarks. And for a time life was good, even great for the two of them.

All the while being oblivious to the silent hidden scourge that had already taken over Margaux, promising to destroy her future, even cause her death. Bending the Primary Principle to save her charge, Anastasia instantly ordered her vices into action, instructing them to be careful each step of the way. The time must be right and no one must be the wiser. Margaux must never know what was happening to her. She must always feel happy and normal.

In time, the memory of those frightening alien eyes had finally receded into the dim corners of Margaux's mind. She did not even think about them, anymore. But unbeknownst to her, her periods have stopped. And yet, it did not bother her at all.

By the third anniversary of their marriage, Margaux was like a beautifully-tousled, blonde-haired doll enjoying the beauty of life and love and worshipped by her adoring fans. Every man wanted her to grace his arms. And yet, behind her beauty and grace, there lay an unpleasant surprise her husband had only just found out. In point of fact, they had tried several times to conceive a child to no avail. Finally, the couple saw a fertility specialist, who provided the earth-shattering diagnosis. Margaux simply could not produce a child in any way at all. Her ovaries were gone.

And all of a sudden, Margaux came to this awful realization.

"It' true. I don't have my periods anymore, Michel. Not for a while. I actually thought it would pass, you know, and now I'm frightened." She pleaded to her husband in desperation. "I don't know what to do, now, Michel. God, I am too young for this."

Instead, he pushed her away from him.

Michel had been livid at what seemed to be an apparent duplicity. Questions rolled around his mind like a raging tornado. How could she not have known about her problem for months? And if she had known how dare she duped him into this marriage. She had to have known he wanted a family to call his own. Only a vengeful, selfish bitch would do this.

From up above in the cosmos, the gray assistants nudged him ahead with their thoughts. It was going in the right direction now.

Michel slapped her face in fury. Margaux recoiled in fear, tears flowing down her cheeks. He slapped her hard again causing her to crumple onto the floor. She dragged herself away from him. He followed her slowly, his face seething with anger.

"And why the hell did you not get yourself checked out before we married? Do something about it? How could you not have known you were missing your periods?"

"I didn't think it was necessary." Margaux sobbed bitterly. "I didn't even realize what was happening inside me all those years. I did not even think about it, all right! I was so busy with us and our lives and career. I'm so sorry, Michel, please don't hate me for that. Please."

"I don't just hate you." He spat vehemently at Margaux. "I am disgusted with you. Furious with you."

"Listen to me, Michel. If you want a child so badly, we can always adopt, maybe two or three."

Michel slammed a fist into the wall, creating a gaping hole. He winced in pain, holding his wounded hand. "Get away from me, you lying bitch, before I slap you again! Leave me alone to think."

With a groan, Margaux lifted herself up from the floor and, with both hands covering her tear-stained face, disappeared upstairs into their bedroom.

The bedroom door slammed.

Michel poured a glass of Wild Turkey bourbon. He gulped down the burning, amber liquid. He poured himself another glass, picked up the bottle with his other hand, and slumped in exhaustion against the sofa.

He felt utterly betrayed.

By midnight, he had become quite inebriated. What to do was all he could think of. Margaux was beloved by her fans more than him, and therefore, leaving her was non-negotiable. He would be at risk of becoming a pariah. He would have to accept his dismal fate with Margaux.

And then he smiled.

There was another way. Had been for years. And he could have it both ways and no one would be the wiser.

After downing the last drop of the bourbon, he went to bed.

The three gray-skinned assistants murmured among each other. It did not work. But they had a backup plan this time, fully approved by their High Priestess.

Chapter 22

IT WAS JUST ONE MINUTE past 3:00AM. Margaux was fast asleep with her back towards Michel in their king-sized, four-poster bed. Michel slept soundly, his back also towards Margaux.

A grating whine resounded inside his ears and vibrated throughout his body. Michel quickly covered his ears, pressing his head against the pillow in pain. The noise and vibration was loud and irritating, preventing him from going back to sleep. He looked behind at Margaux, who was still sleeping soundly and peacefully. How odd. Whatever that was that bothered him seemed to have no effect on her.

He tried to go back to sleep to no avail.

"That's it!" He threw away the covers and stood up ramrod straight. He got out of the bed and walked towards the large, bedroom window adjacent to their bed. He angrily pulled back the drapes. "What the hell is out there keeping me awake at this ungodly hour? I've a mind to report to the police." He yelled out the open window.

In an instant, he froze in his place, his hands gripping the ledge, his eyes staring dead ahead.

Chapter 23

FEELING A COLD DRAFT BRUSHING against her back, Margaux shivered and turned around, wondering why the blanket was thrown aside letting in the frosty air. She saw that Michel's side of the bed was empty. She looked at the alarm clock on her bed stand. It was 3:45AM, still too early in the morning. Groaning softly, Margaux sat up and surveyed the front of the dimly-lit bedroom, where the door was left open.

"Michel, where are you?" She called out tentatively. There was no response. Another cold draft hit her from the left.

Turning to her left, she finally sighted the dark outline of Michel standing in front of the open bedroom window, his back towards her, his hands tightly clutching the window ledge. He stood frozen solid. The only sound coming from him was his slow rasping breaths.

Margaux felt irritated. "What's wrong, Michel." She called out. "Why are you standing there looking out the window like an idiot? It's freezing out there. Shut the window and come back to bed. Please."

Michel turned around and looked at Margaux. She could see that his eyes were vacant and unresponsive, wholly unfamiliar to her. Alarmed, Margaux gasped. His eyes had changed. The pupils had morphed into a liquid-black sheen covering the entire eyes. He looked quite evil.

Turning back towards the window, Michel pushed his head out as far as he could, as if he was searching for something in the night skies. The wintry night air wafted into the room. Shivering with the bitter cold, Margaux pulled the covers up towards her neck and stared at Michel in alarm, her heart beating fast. What was happening with him? Why was he looking out the window like that?

She wondered if the eyes of her past had gotten to him.

In a swift sudden flash, a straight beam of light appeared from the dark backdrop of the night sky and hit Michel, paralyzing him in an instant. He grimaced in pain and screamed.

Margaux's eyes grew wider as she watched the piercing bright light glow on his face for several seconds, before quickly disappearing back into the dark night. At that instant, Michel's body slumped forward against the windowsill, his head precariously bent down out of the window.

"Oh, my God! Michel!" Margaux pulled the covers off and quickly got out of the bed. She rushed to his limp body and put both of her arms around his waist, pulling him in. She laid him on the floor with a grunt. He was very heavy. Leaning over him, she stroked his face with a worried look in her eyes. "Michel, darling. Wake up, Michel. Are you all right? What just happened here?"

For several seconds, Michel did not respond.

"Come on, Michel, wake up," Margaux begged. "Are you all right?"

In an instant, his eyes were wide open. Margaux gasped. They were still pools of liquid black. Abruptly, she could feel the eyes boring into hers and they were evil and angry. It was as if he was possessed.

Margaux quickly removed his head from her lap and backed away, staring at him fearfully. "My God, who are you? What have you done to Michel?"

His mouth opened slightly and a loud, raspy growl manifested itself, pushing the frightened Margaux back further from him. She was backed up against the wall. She watched him nervously, wondering what he would do now and who was controlling him.

Seconds passed.

Finally, Michel lifted himself up with a grunt in his throat. Ignoring Margaux, he walked towards the bed and got in, forcefully pulling the covers. Still sitting speechless against the wall, Margaux could hear him growling from his throat, his face contorted malevolently, as he succumbed into a fitful sleep.

She dared not go back to bed.

The room became dark and quiet, as if nothing had happened in there the past hour and half. The velvety drapes shuffled from the push of the strong, night breeze still wafting in.

Warily, Margaux lifted herself up and walked towards the open window. She stared out into the dusky skies towards the horizon. All she could see was millions of twinkling stars. And yet, Michel saw something out there. She gasped.

Two dark, almond-shaped, alien eyes appeared before her, suspended in the night sky. The same eyes she had seen before. Only this time they were larger than life. The menacing eyes looked directly at her, as if imparting some sort of message. A low humming voice whispered inside her mind, chanting two words she had never heard of.

"Alaku Seru. Alaku Seru. Alaku Seru."

For several terrifying seconds, Margaux stood transfixed, becoming irritated by the droning voice inside her head. It was getting louder and louder. Painfully loud.

"Alaku Seru. Alaku Seru. Alaku Seru."

"What?" She yelled out towards the open sky, holding her head in frustration. "What is Alaku Seru? Why am I hearing this? What do you want from me?"

The unswerving alien eyes did not respond, slowly fading into invisibility, the low, pulsating alien voice trailing behind faintly.

"Alaku Seru."

Exasperated, Margaux slammed down the windows and quickly closed the drapes. None of this made sense to her. Instead of losing time, as she had so often in the past when those strange eyes appeared, she was now hearing those two peculiar words in her mind. Alaku Seru. No spoken foreign language had these words in its vocabulary, as far as she was aware.

She slipped under the bed covers wearily and closed her eyes. Perhaps tomorrow she would think better with a clearer head and try to find their etiology. Or simply forget about it. There were more important matters to deal with, most specifically her marriage.

The next morning, Margaux knocked at the closed bedroom door. "Michel? Are you awake? I have brought you a hot cup of coffee. We need to talk."

There was no answer. Perhaps he was still asleep. Margaux opened the door and entered. She saw that Michel was busily packing his clothes into a luggage. Margaux became alarmed.

"What are you doing?"

"What do you think, my dear Margaux?" Michel sneered, as he picked up more of his clothes from a drawer. He slammed the drawer. "I'm leaving you, of course."

"But....but....but, what about us? What about our careers? I wanted us to talk about adopting."

Michel furiously zipped the luggage and threw it on the floor. He glared at Margaux. "You don't seem to understand. One, I cannot stand the sight of you. Two, as a matter of fact, there is someone else. Has been for a quite a while. She lives in Paris and is already pregnant with my child. I was going to keep it quiet, a double life with her and with you, but after what you have done to me recently, I see no reason to stay with you. No reason at all. I have perfect grounds for a divorce from you. I want to move to Paris and marry my mistress."

"Oh, my God." Margaux slumped against the wall, small drops of tears flowing down her cheeks. "This cannot be true. This is all an awful dream. Don't you know that last night, you might have been possessed by something out there and it's already warping your mind right now. Don't you remember what happened last night? You would have fallen out of that window, if not for me."

"Now you are talking nonsense. As usual." Michel jeered. "Nothing happened last night. I slept like a baby, now that I've made this crucial decision to leave you. It wasn't that hard at all, my dear, because every time I look at you I see that act of betrayal. Now step aside, Margaux. You will be hearing from my lawyer soon."

Without bothering to look at her, Michel swiftly walked past her and out the door, pulling the mobile luggage behind him. A minute later, Margaux heard the front door slam. Dejected and heartbroken, she crumpled down onto the floor and covered her face with her hands, sobbing wretchedly.

Chapter 24

In the conference room of his attorney's office building, Michel waited another minute, impatience showing in his face, as he sat opposite Margaux and her attorney. Once again, Margaux was being irrational and indecisive. He hated that. He hated the sight of her. He wasn't sure exactly when and how it happened, but he knew he was a changed man. He growled softly, his eyes still dark with anger and hatred. He was desperate to leave for Paris with his long-time love and a baby on the way. And yet, this divorce from that conniving bitch must be done with first. And it was taking too long. Much too long.

Mr. Bonewyn subtly placed his hand on Michel's arm, restraining him, as he patiently went through the motions once again.

"My client would like to know if Mrs. Ragnarowski plans on selling their house? Of course, if she continues to keep the house and live in it, she will have to buy it from my client. He has no intention of being co-owner of the house any longer, much less help her pay the mortgage. He is adamant that your client is financially well-off on her own. Finally, my client wants his name off the deed of the house. Or, should your client decide to sell the house, my client rightfully demands his half the proceeds from the sale."

Margaux shook her head. "I don't know. I don't know what to do right now. I'm tempted to sell the house and yet, at the same time, I have nowhere else to go. I don't even understand what is happening to me. I keep hearing this strange, hissing voice inside me constantly repeating "Alaku Seru", day after day after day, even now. It's disrupting my chain of thoughts. Really I can't decide."

Both attorneys stared at her, mystified at the turn of events. Mr. Bonewyn's eyes narrowed. Michel uttered a malevolent chuckle.

"What is Alaku Seru?" Mr. Pastorini inquired. "I have never heard of it. Are you certain about that voice in your head? Are you aware how this puzzling turn of events would impact the negotiations?"

Margaux nodded quickly, shrugging her shoulders. "I know. I know. And yet, I can't decide. That voice is in the way. Has been for quite some time. I should have told you. I'm sorry."

"See she is crazy!" Michel fumed loudly, pointing his finger at Margaux. "I can't believe I'm hearing this utter nonsense. It's no excuse at all." He stood up, placed his hands on the conference table, and growled. He turned to his lawyer. "No more excuses from her. Get her declared mentally incompetent." He leaned forward against the table, ominously staring at Margaux. "For the last time, Margaux, get rid of that house or buy it from me."

"Sit down!" Mr. Bonewyn ordered, pushing Michel towards his chair. He glanced at Margaux's lawyer.

"I must apologize for my client's harsh reaction. This episode coming from your client is wholly unexpected and, frankly, we are quite puzzled at her reaction. It does not make sense to prolong the negotiations. You must understand that my client is anxious to complete the divorce proceedings in a fair manner and return to Paris as soon as possible."

Margaux whispered into her attorney's ear. He let out a sigh of frustration.

"We respectfully request a little more time. She is disoriented and not feeling well."

"More time?" Michel snarled, pounding his fist on the table. "This is insane! Can you imagine the distress caused me by that conniving bitch each time I'm forced to stay here longer against my will? This marriage had been false from the start. Three years of lies. Lies!" He roared, raising his fist in the air.

"Yeah, well, you lied to me, Michel." Margaux raised her chin defensively, tentatively rising from her chair. "You had a mistress all along and I was completely, utterly clueless." Mr. Pastorini placed his hand on Margaux's arm.

"Sit down!" Mr. Bonewyn ordered Michel. "Their request is legitimate in light of this inexplicable circumstance and the law. We cannot, must not work with her, if she is considered mentally impaired at this moment. The law is clear in this context."

Michel grunted in acknowledgment, angrily crossing his arms. He glared at Margaux. Margaux glared back.

Mr. Bonewyn addressed her attorney.

"We will give her one more week to think about it. If she is still indecisive, my client will have no choice but stop the mortgage payments and have his name removed from the deed. He is anxious to leave for Paris. Your client will have to assume the financial burden of the house, in addition to waiving her right to a financial settlement from him. He will, of course, not request any monies from your client except the proceeds from the sale of the house. It is a conclusive and final offer on this."

"Margaux?" Mr. Pastorini inquired.

She nodded wearily. "One more week is fine."

Ten minutes later, Mr. Bonewyn shook hands with Michel at the elevator lobby. He assured him that all would work out soon and he could finally leave for Paris. In fact, he was absolutely certain of that. "Goodbye for now. I will see you next week."

The elevator door shut. Mr. Bonewyn leaned against the wall, crossing his arms. And waited.

Chapter 25

MARGAUX ARRIVED AT THE ELEVATOR lobby. Her attorney had left earlier without her. She had told him she wanted to spend some time in the ladies' restroom, hoping a splash of cold water would restore her jagged nerves.

The elevator door opened the moment she arrived. Mr. Bonewyn entered it. He held the door open for Margaux.

"Thank you," Margaux whispered warily, as she stepped inside, clutching her shoulder bag. "G2, please." The elevator door closed. He pushed the requested button for Margaux and his destination also. The elevator sprang into action moving downwards. Mr. Bonewyn turned towards Margaux, smiling compassionately. Margaux lifted her eyebrows. He wasn't supposed to be talking to her.

"My client is an exceedingly difficult man, I must admit. And technically, I am not supposed to talk with you at all."

"Indeed." Margaux nodded warily. "And yet here you are attempting to talk to me. Why is that?"

"I want to help you."

"Help me? With what? You are not supposed to help me, you know."

"Of course, I know. This would have to be a clandestine effort, mind you. Not one word to anyone. I believe my help would hasten the divorce proceedings in favor of both my client and you."

"That's interesting. How?"

"Back there you had mentioned a voice repeating two words inside your head, impacting your ability to decide what to do with your house. I believe you said, "Alaku Seru. Am I right?""

"That's right. I hear those two words many times. But it's stopped now. Regardless, I know that voice will come back later. Always seems to come at the most inopportune time."

Mr. Bonewyn nodded gravely. He narrowed his eyes at Margaux. She wasn't stupid after all, merely confused at what she could not comprehend. All she needed was guidance in hopefully the right direction. Guidance from an expert.

"First of all, I can't determine why are you are having these hissing voices in your head, as you so described, but perhaps there is a reason for it. Unlike the majority of the populace, I'm not averse to strange occurrences. I even find myself investigating them."

Margaux lifted her eyebrows in surprise. "What are you talking about?"

Mr. Bonewyn ignored her reaction. "Regardless, I am quite familiar with the intonations of those two words you had uttered back there, Mrs. Ragnarowski. I may be able to determine what they mean and help you."

"Really? You know what they mean? But how?"

"Archaeology is my hobby, my passion outside of my work as an attorney. It relaxes me. Recently, I have been dabbling with Sumerian cuneiforms with a buddy of mine, a professional archaeologist from Stanford University. And believe me, those two words are unquestionably Sumerian in origin."

Margaux stared at him perplexed. "Sumerian?"

"An ancient civilization lost to time. It existed tens of thousands of years ago near the Middle East. There had been an advanced race that perfected the art of symbolic writing. Unfortunately, the people mysteriously disappeared without a trace, leaving those cuneiforms behind. We have only begun to understand their meanings."

"Huh? But why me? Do you know what those words mean?"

"Not yet, but I intend to find out tonight. You will need to give me your contact number." He reached inside his business jacket and offered a small notebook and a pen.

Margaux hastily scribbled her phone number. "But...but... why me?"

"Not sure exactly, but like you said the voice shows up at the most inopportune moments. Perhaps you should look into that carefully. I do not think there is anything wrong with you, as my client so insisted. This may be the sign you need."

Margaux narrowed her eyes. How did he know she was looking for a sign?

The elevator stopped abruptly. The door slid open. Mr. Bonewyn stepped out onto the lobby floor. He turned and nodded at Margaux and smiled. "Remember, we never spoke. Goodbye."

Chapter 26

MARGAUX BLINKED HER EYES AT the mirror, the memories of the past seven years fading into that one significant turning point in her life, the dissolution of her marriage. She breathed in deeply, feeling a sense of purpose coming back. Tonight she would learn what the voice in her mind was trying to tell her, assuming that lawyer knew what he was doing.

Margaux picked up the mail from the foyer table and rifled through the envelopes. There were several bills and a couple of real estate advertisements. An envelope without a return address contained an offer from a stranger in a distant location, who appealed to her once again to sell the fairytale house to him. He had tried to contact her several times before, even offering his phone number. He had promised millions of dollars for the house, way above its market value, but she must contact him immediately. And this letter was the last warning. Margaux rolled her eyes in disgust. *They are certainly tiresome, these scavengers. Thank God this is the last one.* She ripped up the letter and dumped the torn pieces into the trash can.

Letting out a breath, Margaux returned to scrutinizing the remaining mail. The last envelope caught her attention. It was from her parents' lawyer. Her heart skipped a beat as she opened the envelope and pulled out the letter. She began to read. In a few seconds, tears streamed down her cheeks. She did not bother to wipe them. She placed the letter gently back on the foyer table. Still crying, she headed towards the glass cabinet in the living room that housed several bottles of bourbon, gin, and whiskey.

Margaux gulped the remainder of the whiskey from the bottle and placed it on the mahogany side table. Her emotions exhausted and slightly drunk, she slumped on the armchair facing the dark, empty fireplace. She blinked her bloodshot eyes several times, but it was no use. There were no more tears to cry.

Her right hand gripped the letter from her parents' lawyer, unable to finish reading it. Her beloved father had just passed away. Cirrhosis of the liver, the letter said. All that heavy drinking over the years since she had left them five years ago. He had been terribly sick and she didn't know, because she didn't want to know. She had been so busy with her life with Michel and their successful careers as world-renowned chefs, that she had never bothered to check in on her aging parents, particularly her father. And besides, going back to Mirrington Heights would only fuel her mother's paranoia. It was all her fault.

What was worse, Michel had left her for a frivolous French harlot carrying his child and living in Paris at his expense. He would soon join them and marry her. All Margaux had to do was produce a child, but she couldn't. And Michel didn't want adoption. He wanted a child of his own flesh and blood, and he had constantly been adamant about it. Of course, she had to let him go.

And now she had no idea what to do with her life and their fairytale house. How much more bad luck could she bear? And why was that pesky voice still whispering those ridiculous two words inside her head?

Alaku Seru. Alaku Seru.

She screamed. "Leave me alone, all right!"

Overcome with fatigue and weariness, having finished off the bottle of Jack Daniel whiskey, Margaux mercifully succumbed to a deep, dreamless sleep in her armchair. The tear-stained letter slowly slipped from her hand to softly land upon the carpeted floor.

The cell phone rang inside the foyer room. Margaux barely heard it.

Five hours later, Margaux blinked her tired eyes open to find the living room in total darkness. Margaux tried to ignore the throbbing knives of pain inside her head, as she rolled onto her side and fumbled for the switch to the Tiffany lamp. She noticed the empty bottle of Jack Daniel whiskey sitting on the side table. The source of her pain, of course.

Margaux glanced at the antique clock above the fireplace. It was now past midnight. Lifting her body upright on the armchair, she suddenly remembered the letter and searched for it. She found it crumpled on the floor nearby. It was time to finish reading the rest of that letter.

The letter had been written in her mother's distinctive handwriting only she and her father could read. Having buried her father, her mother declared she was now preparing to leave Mirrington Heights to go back to Russia, her birthplace. Her grandmother was now very old and in need of her care.

She wanted to apologize to Margaux. It had been a mistake to move to Mirrington Heights, her mother realized that, but she was grateful a marriage had taken place for it removed her grave responsibility to protect her. She hoped the letter would find her well, safe, and alive with Michel, her beloved husband. They had been following the news of their travels around their world via newspapers, internet, and the nightly TV newscasts.

The letter was signed, "With all my love and affection, Your Mother."

Margaux laughed weakly. Here we go again, Mother dear. Always safe and alive. And now I have to deal with Alaku Seru on top of your paranoia for my safety. Thank God you are going back to Russia. She sighed. God knows she wasn't going to let her mother know that her marriage with Michel was officially over and she would be all alone. There was absolutely no point. It would only upset her and cause her to worry all over again. Not worth it.

Margaux gently placed the letter on the side table. This personal letter from her mother had been wholly unexpected. Just yesterday, she had received a registered letter from her parents' lawyer. In crisp businesslike manner, the lawyer informed her that her parents' house in Mirrington Heights was already paid for and they had both willed it to her. It was hers now to do as she wished.

A gift from them both.

Margaux was stunned. After all those years, when she had failed to check on them, preferring to focus on her career and marriage, they both unhesitatingly and lovingly gave her their house. They could have easily given it to another relative, there were several on both sides, but it was to her they willed it to. The letter did not even mention her father's death, deferring to her mother's wish to personally announce it in her letter.

Feeling horribly guilty, Margaux sighed and fell back against the armchair. She stretched her head upwards, her eyes staring blankly at the stark, empty ceiling above, silently railing at the injustice of it all. It was her all fault. She should have checked in. God, she should have. And now it was too late. Her father was gone and now, her mother was mercifully returning to Russia.

Their house was now hers, whether she liked it or not.

Margaux grimaced. What was she to do now with that house in Mirrington Heights? She hadn't even decided what to do with the fairytale house she was still living in, courtesy of her soon to be ex-husband. He had promptly moved into an apartment the morning after their fight, promising to promptly start the divorce proceedings. It had been very odd that he did not remember his shocking behavior the night before, growling at her like a possessed entity from hell.

And now she felt trapped with two houses, unable to move forward with her life.

Wearily, Margaux got up from the armchair and headed towards the kitchen, the crumpled letter falling softly to the floor. She was hungry now. Too hungry to think and so very tired. It was almost 2:00AM. She would think about everything tomorrow.

Hopefully she would get a sign.

But wait. The cell phone! What if?

Margaux quickly headed towards the foyer. She picked up her cell phone. A lone message was embedded inside it. It was from Michel's lawyer, as he had promised. He had found the meaning to the mysterious Sumerian words. The rest was up to her. Be careful, he warned. There was always a reason for the most inopportune time, he reminded her.

Margaux rolled her eyes and sighed. She deleted the message. According to Mr. Bonewyn's research, *Alaku Seru* meant "to go back." She laughed weakly. Go back where?

Chapter 27

THE SOFT, GLOWING RAYS OF dawn penetrated the slit between the closed velvet drapes, caressing her face with its warmth. Margaux yawned. She looked at the alarm clock.

It was 6:20 AM.

She bolted upright in bed, suddenly realizing that she was due at Mr. Bonewyn's office in two hours. Her attorney and Michel would also be there. The problem was a week had passed and she was still undecided. Knowing that Alaku Seru meant "to go back" was not helpful, either. What was worse, the one problem had now become two. There were now two houses to deal with, in towns hundreds of miles apart. And there was no sense in keeping both of them.

So, which one should she live in for the rest of her life?

The voices whispered inside her head. "Alaku Seru. Alaku Seru." "Go back."

"Oh, I would if I could." Margaux grinned as she poured hot coffee into a white, porcelain mug decorated with wildflowers. "I have no idea where to go back to, and you are not helping. Be nice if you'd give me a sign. Any sign."

An hour later, Margaux parked her car in the underground garage beneath the lawyers' offices. On the 5th floor, she left the elevator and walked across the hall, approaching her attorney, who had been waiting for her. He had his hand on the doorknob.

"Ready?"

Margaux shrugged her shoulders. "Not really, but I don't have a choice today, do I?"

Mr. Pastorini shook his head slightly, his mouth set in a grim line. "Let's hope it all works out today."

They entered into the conference room. Michel was already seated at the table with his attorney. Mr. Bonewyn stood up and smiled. He gestured towards the chairs at the opposite end of the table.

"Welcome. Please be seated." He winked at Margaux ever so subtly. Mr. Pastorini raised his eyebrows.

Margaux prayed silently for a sign. Any sign.

"Now, shall we proceed?" Mr. Bonewyn asked. He arranged the divorce papers in a systematic order on the table.

Mr. Pastorini nodded, glancing at Margaux. Today is the day. What will it be?

"I'm still undecided unfortunately. New developments had occurred that only made matters worse for me." Margaux said bluntly, not even worrying about her husband's temper. "My father just died and was buried without my presence. My mother is gone to Russia. They willed their house to me. I am not only stuck with two houses to deal with, I'm also grieving the death of my father and dealing with a new problem. I think it I am entitled to more time."

Both lawyers nodded. It seemed a reasonable request.

"Jesus Christ, Margaux!" Michel yelled angrily. "You can have the damn house once and for all! But if you sell it, I promise you I will come after you for my share!"

"Enough!" Mr. Bonewyn ordered. "Sit down." He looked at Margaux with compassion in his eyes. "Our deepest condolences, Mrs. Ragnarowski. It is indeed a terrible loss. Of course, it is reasonable to ask for more time. Isn't it, Michel?"

"And what is this new problem, may I ask?" Michel demanded ignoring his attorney.

"You do not have to respond, Margaux." Mr. Pastorini put his hand on Margaux's arm. "This is not his concern, except to grant you more time."

"That's ok, Mr. Pastorini, he deserves to know. I am keeping him from his new wife and baby."

"Well?" Michel growled, crossing his arms, his head cocked to the side.

"Screw you, Michel." Margaux hissed. "I have my rights. My parents gave me responsibility for their house. I'm stuck with both houses now, miles apart."

"Who cares?" Michel snarled, crossing his arms.

Mr. Bonewyn rested his hand on Michel's arm. He turned towards Margaux. "Where is this other house?"

"Mirrington Heights."

In an instant, the voices in her head grew louder and louder. "Alaku Seru...Alaku Seru...Alaku Seru..." Margaux grabbed her temples and doubled down in pain.

Mr. Pastorini looked aghast. "Are you all right, Mrs. Ragnarowski? Is there anything we can do for you?"

Michel grinned. "See. She is crazy. Call 911 and please get her out of my life."

"Michel, for the last time. Enough. This is serious. Something is wrong with her and we are obligated to help her." Mr. Bonewyn walked around the table towards Margaux. He rested his hand on her shoulder. His voice was gentle. "Mrs. Ragnarowski, is something wrong? Can we help?"

Margaux suddenly stood up from her chair, her eyes wide in frenzy. "Of course, that's it! I have to go back!" She yelled out loud. "I have to go back now!" All eyes descended on Margaux, mystified at her sudden reaction. Margaux laughed out loud, clapping her hands. "I should have known all along. Oh, it does make sense." Mr. Bonewyn placed his hands around Margaux's shoulders, gently guiding her back to her seat. She was still laughing. "Oh, God. I should have known! Alaku Seru!" She raised her hands in the air.

Mr. Pastorini stared at her. He was utterly speechless. What was this Alaku Seru all about and why didn't she tell him? He worried that she might be losing her mind at this most critical moment of her life, her divorce. Some women had been known to do just that.

Mr. Bonewyn pressed on gently. "Mrs. Ragnarowski? Go back where, do you know?"

Margaux nodded and laughed. "Oh, yes, I know. Finally, I know. Don't you see? The voice got louder and louder the minute I mentioned Mirrington Heights. Clearly, that was the sign. I must go back to Mirrington Heights."

Michel growled impatiently. "She is worse than crazy. She is insane. As her husband not-yet-divorced, I would like to have her incarcerated in a mental institution and be done with this divorce, once and for all. I am appalled at the length of time wasted to finish all this. It's all her fault. She is not of sound mind."

"Oh no, Michel, you will not." Margaux hissed quietly. "I am most certainly of sound mind. I have always been." She paused for a moment and laid back into her chair. "The voices are gone now. I can see it clearly. You see, I had a little help."

"What are you talking about?" Michel sputtered.

"Doesn't matter right now." Margaux spat at him. "Finally, I have control of this. I have made my decision. As of now, I agree to sell our fairytale house. You shall receive your share of the proceeds, but only through my attorney. Do not ever contact me, you bastard."

"No problem. I am thoroughly delighted to get rid of you once and for all." Michel growled impatiently.

"Actually, I'm the one that's delighted to be rid of you! Alaku Seru!" Margaux sang out, picking up a pen. "Now, where do I sign the papers?"

Chapter 28

BYRON STOOD IN FRONT OF the desk of the Aide to the Commander and saluted crisply. In a strong clear voice, he explained to the Aide that he had been ordered to arrive at the Office of the Commander promptly. No further explanation was provided. He had assumed it would be yet another secret mission.

It was 3:00 PM in the afternoon and a week had passed since his team of Special Forces paratroopers, comprised of Charlie, Jimmy, and himself, had successfully bombed the underground enemy bunker in the dark of night at Al Ahraira. Charlie did not make it, and he wasn't exactly sure what happened to Jimmy, but he had come home alive.

Byron barely remembered what had happened to Jimmy. They both knew they were going to die any moment and surrendered themselves to God, but something utterly strange and unexpected had happened. At the instant of the explosion, he had seen Jimmy being pulled up by a mysterious light beam coming through the trap door. A second later, he found himself being transported upwards into an unknown entity in the dark night.

Mercifully, he had been rendered unconscious.

Three days later, Byron had found himself spread-eagled in the desert zone not far from the Battalion 109 encampment near the city of Farizal. A battered M1A1 Abrams army tanker was lumbering across a desert trail on its way back to the base station, after a successful bombing run in the city of Farizal.

Standing guard on top of the tanker, his assault rifle at the ready, a lone, battle-weary soldier had noticed from a distance an anomalous shape lying motionless on the desert floor. The powerful army tank slowly lumbered closer towards the inert object and stopped. It was a body of an American soldier. After carefully scrutinizing the surrounding area for the enemy, the lone soldier leaped out from the tanker to inspect the body.

The man was still alive, barely breathing. But how in hell did it get there?

He quickly waved his arm towards the tanker. I need some help here! A second-battle weary soldier leaped out from the tank with his massive rifle. The two of them carefully lifted the limp body by the shoulders and quickly dragged him towards the waiting tanker. It sprang into action, rumbling over the desert trail.

The headache throbbing in his head, Byron groaned unsteadily and awoke to see two soot-covered faces staring down at him. They were the friendlies. And they were worried. How had he gotten to where he was in the enemy desert all alone, barely alive? He could have been killed. And where were his buddies at arms? Byron shook his head. He had no answer. He put his hand on his forehead. Pinpoints of white hot daggers were stinging in the frontal lobe of his brain.

The soot-covered soldiers looked at each other, mystified. There were no battle wounds on Byron's body, only a painful headache. Byron groaned and tried to lift himself up.

One of the soldiers restrained him. "Relax, buddy. We are taking you to our medic."

"You were damned lucky," the other soldier said. "Not a shred of shrapnel or bullet in you. What the hell happened to you?"

Byron shook his head wearily. He did not know. He could not remember anything.

"Maybe later you'll remember. Our base commander will no doubt want to know how you ended up there all by yourself without any backup."

"Big time." The other soldier declared. "I wouldn't want to be in your shoes."

But Byron never did remember. He never could. It would remain a mystery in his file and in his life.

What was worse, the base's resident physician could not determine the cause of his headache. He gave him a bottle of ibuprofen to relieve the pain before releasing him. And yet, something did show in the X-ray of his brain that greatly puzzled the physician.

Something that could kill him.

The base commander eventually found out that Byron was one of the three Special Forces paratroopers sent out on a night mission to bomb a critical enemy bunker. He was identified as the leader, Lieutenant Byron O' Neill. The base commander's search squadron eventually found the other one, Private First Class Jimmy Malone, who was also barely alive, his body abandoned not far from where Byron was found. And like Byron, mysteriously, not a shred of bullet wounds were found on his body. Only a painful, pounding headache on the frontal lobe of the brain.

Jimmy had no idea what had happened to him, either. What was so mystifying was this soldier did not even remember the other two members of his team, Byron and Charlie.

The body of the third paratrooper, Private First Class Charlie Bonsoirre, was already interred inside a flag-draped coffin. The coffin was held in the hangar, waiting to be placed in the cargo hold of the C-130 military aircraft bound for the United States.

All in all, it was a miracle Byron appeared in good health, given that he had lost three days of his life. Unaware of the recent development found by the resident physician, Byron mentally prepared himself for yet another dangerous stealth mission.

Instead, he found himself being summoned to meet with the base station Commander.

"Lieutenant Byron O' Neill reporting to the Commander!" He saluted sharply.

The Aide, a bespectacled female Army lieutenant dressed in green and gray regulation camouflage uniform, looked up at him curiously, looked down at her book of appointments, and quickly stood up to salute him.

Without a word, she opened the massive timber door behind her desk and gestured Byron to enter. The Commander was expecting him.

Soon, Byron realized he was going home. The X-ray scan had revealed a tiny, obscure anomaly inside his brain that should not be there at all. It may or may not be the source of the mysterious, pounding headache. However, it was clearly imperative that Byron undergo an MRI scan to identify this irregularity and get the necessary medical treatment, perhaps surgery.

The base resident physician was emphatic that this anomaly could kill him at any moment. He was useless to them at the base.

"As you can see now, Lieutenant O' Neill, we cannot keep you here." The base Commander explained gravely. "You will be put on permanent medical discharge and return to the United States."

Byron nodded wordlessly. There was nothing he could do about it. He had to go home. He stood up, clicked his heels, and sharply saluted. The base Commander shook his head. He raised his hand. "No, not yet." He said. "There is one last mission you must complete for us. A special mission requested by his family."

Byron lifted his eyebrows. "Whose family?" He listened intently as the base Commander read the new orders from behind his imposing desk.

Lieutenant Byron O'Neill, in his dress uniform, was to escort the body of Private First Class Charlie Bonsoirre, by air to Montgomery Air Force Base in Trurora City to catch a flight on the Bluestar Express, which would deliver the special cargo to his grieving family.

The mission would begin at 1800 hours that evening.

Byron accepted it with a heavy heart.

Chapter 29

"EXCUSE ME." MARGAUX STOOD IN front of the handsome stranger in dark-green, military-regulation, dress uniform. He was sitting on the aisle seat, 11A, his head leaning towards the porthole window at his left. "I need to get into my seat over there by the window." Irritated, the stranger turned to look at Margaux and instantly smiled. The woman was definitely curvaceous in every sense of the word. Her beautiful face radiated with a glow he hadn't seen for a long time, even during his tenure in the Middle East. She was a welcome respite from the melancholy that had consumed him since he was honorably discharged from his tour of duty. It didn't help that he was escorting a dead compatriot to his grieving family.

Sizing her up for a moment, he admired the sexy, feminine curves of her hourglass figure, which were emphasized starkly by the tight lines of the dark-blue Calvin Klein denim jeans and the bright, fuschia Donna Karan woolen sweater top. The plunging V-neck of the sweater revealed a hint of the full swell of her bosom. He could smell the scent of chamomile tea and roses wafting from her body at close range.

She smelled so good. So feminine.

Margaux lifted her eyes at him quizzically. "Hello? Could you please let me pass by?"

"Of course!"

Quickly, he lifted his military cover in deference to her and held it against his chest, standing up to let her move across him to reach her seat by the window. With a small gasp in his throat, he could feel the soft, intimate swell of her covered breasts as she brushed against his body in close proximity. He was instantly aroused, feeling hot with desire for this gorgeous, sensual creature sitting next to him. He couldn't help feeling that he knew her from somewhere else.

And yet, she was a total stranger.

Margaux thanked him with a smile and propped herself onto her window seat. She quickly buckled her seatbelt, obliviously lost in her own world as she looked out of the porthole window. Resigned, Byron breathed in deeply, clamping down the rising heat of sexual tension inside him and resumed his seat, buckling his seatbelt. He rested his head against the back of the chair.

In two hours, he would be in his home town away from the horrors of the war.

The flight captain's crisp, self-assured voice reverberated throughout the cabin, welcoming the passengers to his domain. He announced that they will be flying through pleasant weather and to please enjoy the flight.

In fifteen minutes, the BlueStar Express reached 35,000 feet in the air, cruising steadily among the mass of fluffy, white cumulus clouds nestled against the blue, morning sky.

Margaux sighed and relaxed against the pillow propped up against the back of her window seat. She glanced furtively at the handsome, well-groomed military officer sitting next to her, intently reading the flight emergency manual. There was no ring on his finger, but then again, not all men wore wedding rings. He didn't look exactly happy, either. She wondered what his story was.

"Excuse me." Byron gently nudged Margaux sometime later.

Startled, Margaux opened her eyes and looked at him quizzically. "Is something wrong?"

"Well, I thought you might like to know that we are now being served drinks and snacks."

"Oh, of course! Thank you." Margaux lifted herself up on her seat, releasing her seat buckle. She vigorously shook her head to release the stiffness in her neck. "I must have fallen asleep. How long was I gone?"

"Just twenty-five minutes," Byron responded, his smile crinkling at the corners. Margaux looked even more gorgeous with her indolent, blue eyes and fluffy, tousled-blonde hair framed in a halo around her head.

From time to time, he had watched her sleep peacefully, as if without a care in the world. It was as if he had known her before somewhere in the vast reaches of time. An intimacy he could not explain. He simply enjoyed being near her. Her presence had somehow calmed him, inspired him, and made him feel strangely protective of her. And last, but not the least, her radiant beauty somehow restored his faith in this convoluted world, leaving behind the rampant ugliness and terror of the war. People called it post-traumatic, stress disorder. PTSD. He would need to get help for that. He smiled warmly, as he looked at the sleeping goddess on his left one last time, before deciding to wake her up. He also wanted to know her story.

The flight attendant poured hot, espresso coffee into the white, foam cup and handed it to Margaux, along with several small, containers of sugar and cream. Byron shook his head briefly at the flight attendant. He did not want anything to drink or eat. Margaux thanked the flight attendant and placed the cup and containers on the tray in front of her. A couple of white, paper napkins filled the corner of her tray. Byron grinned inwardly as she poured the several containers of cream and sugar into her coffee, stirring briskly. Obviously, she liked her coffee with lots of cream and sugar.

And yet, they had no effect on her fabulous figure.

Placing the small wooden stirrer on the tray, Margaux slowly sipped the hot, fragrant coffee. The strong espresso flavor flowed inside her throat instantly waking her up. She sighed.

"That was a sad sigh," Byron remarked looking at her with a small, sympathetic grin. "I can't imagine you being sad. You looked like you are on your way to a happy place, I hope?"

"Oh, but I am sad." Margaux responded in a low voice, as she took another sip of the hot, steaming liquid, both hands hugging the white, foam cup for warmth. She placed the cup on the tray and turned to face her seatmate. "It's true. See, I just got divorced. It was a nasty divorce. And my Dad's passed away. I'm eternally pissed off with my Mom and thankfully, she's now gone overseas, back to her home in Russia. I have no siblings nor friends, and no family to call my own. At this point in my life, I'm indeed all alone and believe me, it's not a happy place to be."

"I'm terribly sorry to hear that. What will you do now?"

"In all honesty, I have no idea what I'm going to do now. No idea at all, other than getting settled at home after a long hiatus away. What could be sadder than that?"

"Well, a war buddy of mine died during a special operations mission," Byron whispered softly, his eyes darkening, his face grim and tight. "I'm bringing him home to his family. The funny thing is that I was told there was a third member of the team and the search squadron had found him lost and alone in a desert area, but strangely, I do not remember him and neither does he remember me. I still don't know what to make of that."

"I agree, that's obviously very odd. Do you care to tell me what happened to all three of you, assuming the third one you don't remember actually participated?"

"Charlie, Jimmy, and me, I'm told, were on a secret special operations mission that took place close to midnight. The three of us were a team. We were paratroopers. Our mission was to bomb an enemy bunker in a desert that was filled with dangerous explosive weapons. Charlie landed directly on a mine and died instantly. Jimmy and I had to keep going and we did in very strange circumstances. Unfortunately, the bunker itself was located deep inside a hidden cavern. The only way to get there was to traverse the endless maze of passageways surrounding it. Of course, I had placed a rope on the ground to guide us back, but in the end, the insurgents cut it off and we got hopelessly lost."

"Oh, that's terrible. What happened next?"

"Jimmy and me, we did find our way back to that trap door eventually, but it was too late to open it. It was purposefully stuck with the intent to keep us trapped in there. The bombs we placed in the cavern were going to off any minute, killing us instantly."

"And yet, here you are. How did you both survive?"

"That was the strange part even I can't figure out to this day. I don't know about Jimmy, who I'm told was there with me at the last minute, but I remember I got beamed out of there by this strange, bright light coming down through the closed trap door. After that, I don't remember anything. I was told I had been missing for three days. Same thing with Jimmy, who also doesn't remember anything."

"What a confusing conundrum. You both remember what happened at the last minute, but you both don't remember anything after that, not even your names. It must be unnerving."

"You have no idea."

"So what happened next?"

"Well, after supposedly three missing days, I found myself spread-eagled on a desert zone near my station. All alone, which was against Army regulations, you know. It was late afternoon. Again, I have no idea how I got there, but some buddies in a passing Army tanker picked me up and dropped me off to the medic."

"Wow, you were lucky they found you. Did the medic find anything wrong? Especially considering you lost three days."

"Well, the base doctor did find something wrong that apparently had nothing to do with the war, which is why I'm being sent home for good." Byron shook his head forlornly. Suddenly he looked up. "But wait, I did have something else wrong. A painful headache. It was hitting me like daggers at the front of my head."

Margaux narrowed her eyes. That sounded familiar. She was instantly curious. She wondered if, like her, he saw those strange, dark, alien eyes.

"Did anything else happen when you got those headaches?" She asked carefully. It was not an easy subject to broach. It was too strange to even speculate.

"No. Why?"

"Oh, nothing, just wondering. Sometimes headaches are activated by something else. Yours are probably just a remnant of your grueling experience in the desert. War does that to one, I would think. I hope they gave you something for it."

"Just some ibuprofen." Byron shrugged his shoulders. "The headaches are gone now."

"But how strange that you lost three days." Margaux declared as she finished her coffee and wiped her lips. "It would have been nice to know what happened in those three days, I would think."

"I agree. But right now I have a bigger commitment to worry about. I'm bringing Charlie back home to his family."

"Of course." Margaux whispered apologetically. "But, where is Charlie, if I may ask?"

"In his coffin in the cargo hold of the plane." Byron looked down sadly at his hands holding the head cover on his lap. "I have been tasked to escort his coffin to Mirrington Heights Airport, where I get off. There I have to hand over his coffin to a Lieutenant Colonel. He will accompany Charlie's body in the final leg of the connecting flight. I feel privileged to have known Charlie, you know, however briefly." The tears already welled up in his eyes slowly traveled down the rugged planes of his cheeks to splatter onto the cover on his lap. Impulsively, Margaux took his hands into hers and held them tightly. Her eyes filling with tears, she gently smiled at him. "I'm so sorry you lost your friend, Byron." Margaux whispered. "I'm so sorry you had to go through so much in that stupid war. I can't imagine what you're going through right now. You know, you are definitely right, my own sadness is quite pathetic compared to your terrible story."

"Thank you, Margaux, but I would not dismiss your sadness, either. I know it isn't easy being divorced and alone, trying to figure out what to do with the rest of your life."

For several seconds, their eyes locked deeply into each other as if they had known each other forever. Byron desperately wanted to take her into his arms and kiss her passionately. She was so beautiful, so kind, and for the moment, in her company, he had briefly forgotten the ravages of war.

The flight attendant's melodious voice broke through the silence of the cabin, announcing that the plane would soon land and to please buckle the seatbelts.

Byron and Margaux hastily let go of their hands, embarrassed at their brief moment of passion.

The plane finally braked to a stop by the terminal gate. In her clear, crisp voice, the flight attendant instructed the passengers to remain seated a few minutes more. Something special was about to happen. The passengers murmured and mumbled unhappily among themselves. This was highly irregular. There were those who needed to debark right away. And yet, as if compelled by some unseen force, they all remained in their seats, their heads straining above as they looked towards the front of the plane.

"Excuse me." Byron turned and bowed in deference to Margaux. He lifted his military cover from his lap and released the buckle of his seatbelt. "I must go now."

"Oh, of course." Margaux quickly nodded and smiled, offering her hand. "Goodbye, Byron. It was a pleasure meeting you."

"Goodbye, Margaux. The pleasure had been mine. I hope we meet again."

Margaux and the other passengers watched with heightened curiosity, as Byron walked down the aisle towards the flight attendant patiently waiting next to the open door of the plane. The flight captain and co-pilot stood quietly behind her, all three of them waiting with hushed anticipation. Margaux felt irritated and restless like all the other passengers forced to wait in their seats. How much longer would they all have to wait?

Finally approaching the open door of the plane, Byron nodded at the flight attendant. In an instant, he stood ramrod straight, clicked his heels, and slowly turned left in military fashion. He slowly brought his right hand up into a salute and waited. A collective hush fell among the passengers and Margaux.

That was certainly odd. What was going on, they murmured among themselves?

At that same moment, a Lieutenant Colonel dressed in dark-green, regulation, dress uniform entered the door of the plane from the terminal to stand ramrod-straight in front of Byron, saluting him slowly. For a brief few seconds, the two military peers locked eyes at each other, as they followed the protocol of the transfer of escort.

All the passengers, including Margaux, remained frozen in their seats, each of them enthralled by the surreal event unfolding before them. Something powerful was about to happen.

Byron slowly and methodically put his right hand inside his dress jacket and pulled out an envelope. He handed the envelope to the waiting, outstretched hand of his compatriot, who carefully took it from him and placed it inside his dress jacket. Their faces remained emotionless. The audience waited in hushed silence. What was that all about? A passenger crossed herself and prayed.

Another passenger, a burly overweight businessman, had had enough of this. He unbuckled his seatbelt and stood up quickly, raising his fist in the air. "I resent being restrained in this manner. This is uncalled for." The captain quickly moved towards the aggrieved businessman. "A minute of your time is all I ask, sir. Please either stand where you are or sit down in your seat. What you are seeing right now is very important. An American soldier gave up his life for us, all of us and our freedom. We are bringing him home to his grieving family. The respect bequeathed to him right now is non-negotiable. Just one minute is all I ask. Will you do that?" He looked around at all the other passengers. "Will you all do that?" The passengers nodded. But, of course, they could wait, all of them glaring at the offended businessman, who had no choice but to sit down. He grumbled angrily. "That's fine. A minute and no more."

"Thank you very much, sir. You won't be sorry." The captain responded and turned towards the waiting military officers. He nodded for them to continue.

With hands now resting on their sides, the two Lieutenants looked at each other with once again. Byron bent down to reach into his military satchel and pulled out a round, jangling object. They were Charlie's dog tags. They were not part of the protocol of transfer, but Byron felt that Charlie's family would want them. Byron handed the dog tags over to his compatriot, who clutched them tightly in his hands and nodded. He would make sure that

Charlie's family received the dog tags. Together the two Lieutenants crisply saluted each other one final time. With his satchel in hand, Byron quickly sprinted out through the open door of the plane and disappeared into the terminal. His replacement turned around and methodically marched down the aisle towards the empty seat next to the mesmerized Margaux.

The flight captain's commanding voice broke through the silence.

"What you just saw was the protocol of the transfer of escort. These two men, Lieutenant Colonels, were performing a transfer of authority to escort the body of our dead American soldier home to his family. But first, let me say this to all of you." The Captain stared at the disgruntled businessman. "We all of us here were honorary escorts to our American soldier's journey home for his final rest." The businessman flushed with embarrassment.

A hushed silence settled for the moment among the passengers.

"Captain!" A young male passenger shouted, breaking the silence. He waved his hand in confusion. "Where is this dead soldier we all were considered escorts for?"

"In the cargo hold." The captain responded grimly. "In his coffin, which is covered with the American flag. The BlueStar Express offered to bring his coffin home free of charge." He looked around the passengers. "Now, are there any more questions?"

The passengers all shook their heads.

"No questions? Then, you may all disembark immediately." He extended his hand towards the crusty businessman, who was first to leave the cabin. The sarcasm was not lost in his voice. "Thank you very much for your patience and for your patriotism."

Having left the boarding gate where the plane was parked, Margaux trotted towards the baggage terminal. She noted with interest the crowded throngs of people heading one way towards their assigned flight gates and, also, the other way towards the baggage terminal, the plaza of boutique stores, and the food court.

Eight years ago, the airport had been a massive, nondescript brick building covered in grey and black with no personality and no architectural structure and form. Just a boring building hastily put together to serve its purpose. And now it has changed and what a change it was. Margaux marveled with interest, as she gazed up at the cathedral ceiling of the airport building showing various works of art by the master artists of the town.

In one section of the ceiling, there were cottony clouds draped against the azure color of the sky. A collection of songbirds, blue jays, and robin redbreasts were flying among the maple and oak trees, resplendent with the green leaves of spring. In another section, there was a babbling brook meandering against the rocky cliffs of a canyon to tumble out as a waterfall, creating bursts of white foam and bubbles at the bottom of a pristine lake. Above them all, the bright glow of the golden sun stood out in all its glory.

What a magnificent sight to behold. The town has certainly changed. Perhaps returning to Mirrington Heights was not so bad after all.

Margaux pushed through the revolving door at the airport that lead toward the taxi depot. Her eyes settled on a lone figure standing not too far from her, his back to her. He was wearing the familiar dark-green, army dress uniform. Margaux instantly brightened up. Byron. Perhaps they could share a ride. Margaux quickly stepped forward dragging the mobile luggage behind her.

"Byron!" shouted Margaux, eagerly waving her hand above her head, hoping he would recognize her from the plane. Byron turned around slowly. Margaux froze instantly.

On his face were the dark, almond-shaped, alien eyes that were now staring at her. Margaux gasped. Why was this happening now? What did any of this have to do with him?

"Yes, can I help you?" Byron asked, puzzled at her behavior. Clearly he did not remember her from the plane. Margaux sighed in frustration. She wasn't sure what to do just now.

A yellow taxi stopped in front of Byron. The sullen, dark eyes faded away, as Byron bent down to enter the taxi. Soon, the yellow taxi sped away, leaving Margaux still frozen from where she stood.

From up above, the three gray assistants shook their heads at each other. That did not work. They would try again. Carefully.

Chapter 30

SHE WAS HOME NOW, THE home she had lived in for only one year in Mirrington Heights. But home was different now with her parents gone. The specter of unhappy memories permeated in each and every room like faint, white dust hovering around the long neglected furniture covered in linen. It felt nauseating in light of the abrupt way she had moved out of the house eight years ago. Margaux took a deep breath as she placed her fuschia mobile luggage in the foyer, gripped her shoulder bag, and headed towards the stairs.

Opening the door to her bedroom, she noticed nothing had changed since her departure eight years ago. Her bed was perfectly made and her books were in their proper places on the shelves. There was no dust or grime, only dead silence, as if the room was intentionally preserved to last forever like a shrine to her memory.

Margaux shivered. It had been so long ago, the last time she slept in this room.

Throwing her shoulder bag on the queen-sized bed, Margaux walked towards the adjoining bathroom suite. She opened the double French doors and looked in. Again, nothing changed in this room either. The toiletries she had left behind still standing in their proper places on the vanity countertop.

Margaux removed her clothes and threw them on the floor. It would be good to take a long, hot bath. The plane trip had been quite remarkable, and yet, unexpected and unnerving. She had spent hours conversing with the military officer and yet, in the end, he had acted like he had never seen her before. It didn't help that she saw those awful dark eyes on him triggering a memory that made no sense to her still.

And now he was gone and she did not know where he lived. She did not know how to reach him. There seemed no point in even contacting him if he did not remember her or their conversations on the plane.

"Oh, God" Margaux stared at the bathroom mirror towards a reflection of her naked, curvaceous body. Blah, it was disgusting. "How did I end up looking like that the past eight years? I'm all flabbiness. God."

A lilting, melodious voice came out from nowhere, sternly reproving her. "Do not deceive yourself, Margaux. There is nothing wrong with your physical form. Please stop it."

At that moment, the mirror shimmered, a small dot expanding into sparkles of white and gold lights obscuring Margaux's reflection. The sparkling lights exploded and finally settled into a living form.

Margaux gasped. "Anastasia?"

"Greetings, Margaux. I am delighted you remember me."

"Oh, Anastasia," Margaux exclaimed with joy. "I am so happy to see you. I have missed you the past eight years. Where were you?"

"I was always with you, Margaux. But there was a time where I had to be summoned to complete my destiny, before returning to my dimensional vicinity with a new mission."

"That's not fair, Anastasia. You are talking riddles. I only felt that you had left me rather abruptly. You really hurt me back then."

Anastasia sighed, placing her hand against the mirror.

"Oh, Margaux, believe me, it was never my intention to hurt you and no, I have never left you. However, please know that it was necessary for you to experience your life's journey all on your own. I merely stood by to observe."

Margaux narrowed her eyes. That was too creepy. "But I thought you were my friend, Anastasia. I don't like the idea that you were somewhere out there observing me when you were supposed to be there to help me."

"Ah, but that's where it became complicated the minute I found out the truth about you."

"Oh, I got all that from my crazy mother for years and years. And now you too?" Margaux scoffed disdainfully. "So, tell me, what did you find out about me?"

Anastasia shook her head. "I cannot tell you. From where I am, the Primary Principle strictly constrains me with absolute supremacy."

"Oh God, another riddle?" Margaux snapped back. "I've never heard of the Primary Principle. I suppose you are not "allowed" to tell me what that is."

Anastasia smiled. She nodded patiently. "Indeed, I'm allowed to tell you what it is. In its basic concept, it is a powerful universal paradigm. It demands with absolute certainty that your life is your own to make. Neither I nor any other can ever intervene."

"Not even as my friend?" Margaux was aghast.

"To a larger context, no, dear Margaux. I am forbidden by—"

"The Primary Principle, whatever it is." Margaux rolled her eyes. "Well, then, given all that, Anastasia, why the hell are you here in front of my mirror? Pretending to be my friend?"

Anastasia sternly shook her finger. "I am genuinely your friend, believe me. Like I said, dear Margaux, in a much smaller context, I can provide the comfort of my presence. Remember, in the beginning, many years ago, you called out for me. Of course, I complied with your wish to a limited extent and you benefited from my presence. But there was a time I had to leave to fulfill my destiny. And now, I am here again for you, but only through this mirror. For it has been especially configured for my appearance."

"That's great, Anastasia. That's just great. How was I supposed to know that you can only show up in this mirror? I could have sent for it when I left home."

"It doesn't matter now, Margaux. And rest assured, in all the years you were gone, I have never left your side."

"But, I still don't get it. Wasn't there a way you could have helped me through the hell I went through? You said you watched me?"

"Oh, but I did help you, in a manner of speaking. I did the only thing I could to bypass the authority of the Principle. I nudged you from time to time in what I felt was the right direction."

"What do you mean—nudge me in the right direction?" Suddenly, Margaux covered her mouth with her hands, as she realized what was happening. "Oh my God, Anastasia, were you that mysterious voice that kept repeating 'Alaku Seru' over and over in my head and I ended up here? Did you do something to my husband, Michel, that awful night when the dark eyes changed him into a vile man? And those were the nudges? But why, Anastasia, why?"

"It's too complicated to explain, Margaux, and it had to be done, trust me. Let's just leave it at that for now, shall we? Aren't you glad to be home at last? Aren't you glad you can see me now in this only place I can show up? Isn't that what you wanted?"

For several seconds, Margaux stared ruefully. "Heh, I would not exactly call this place home, Anastasia, and I'm not even sure if it's what I wanted to come back to, especially since its seems that you "nudged me back to here."

Anastasia did not respond.

With a sigh, Margaux placed her hand against the mirror and smiled. "But, you know, you're right. I'm awfully glad to see you again."

Anastasia responded in kind placing her hand softly against the mirror towards Margaux's. A faint white light briefly glowed from their touch.

Anastasia nodded gravely. The light proved the truth. "Be not afraid, Margaux. You are very special to me, and I will help you the only way I can." Anastasia stepped back and waved. "Farewell, I must go now. I am summoned to my higher duties. And you must find your true path in life by yourself. A little word of advice, though. Go to where it's white and blue and find three friends who will help you, too."

Anastasia shimmered in white and gold sparkles for several seconds.

"Wait, Anastasia!" Margaux yelled out. "What about those eyes showing up on the soldier? I don't get it."

"You will in time. Just trust me, Margaux. Go to where it's white and blue." Anastasia's melodious voice trailed before the white and gold sparkles diminished through the infinite distance of the mirror into a singularity.

Margaux watched her friend leave. She felt frustrated. Look for a place all white and blue? And find three friends who will help me, too? This is crazy. I cannot be spending an inordinate amount of time trying to figure out her riddles. I can't do this. I need to get on with my life.

As the shadowy twilight changed into the blackness of the night, Margaux slipped on her red, silk nightgown and tucked herself inside her bed. She closed her eyes. A good night's sleep was all she needed right now. And yet, it was a restless night.

Margaux wearily stood up from her kitchen chair and took one last sip of the strong French Roast coffee, sweetened with sugar and cream. Setting down the light-blue porcelain mug on the table, she walked toward the back door and stepped outside. She squinted her eyes. The sun's golden rays shone brightly, infusing its life-giving warmth into her body. Lifting her head towards the sun, Margaux smiled gratefully.

The sun always had this incredible power to restore her listless soul.

Margaux surveyed her fenced backyard from end to end. A wooden gate led towards a forest trail, where she had taken many a walk in her first lonely year at Mirrington Heights. The animals in the forest became her friends and she had reveled in watching them scamper here and there, playing hide and seek with her. Squirrels would sit on their feet staring at her with curiosity, as they munched on their favorite nut. At one time, she had seen a deer pass across the oft-worn trail. They had stopped in the middle of the trail and stared at her with their big, doe eyes, before disappearing into the forest.

She had forgotten about that forest trail. But there it was, all stones and dirt and gravel, beckoning to her to come. Yes, it would be good to take a walk.

As she stepped out onto the grass, Margaux glanced at a scrap of paper caught by the thorns of a rosebush that was tucked in the far corner of the wooden fence. The wind must have dislodged the paper from somewhere and it got trapped in the thorns. Right now, it looked like trash sitting among the blooming, red roses. Margaux plucked the paper from the thorns, being careful not to prick herself. Curious, she turned it over, smoothing out the wrinkled patch where the hole was. Her eyebrows lifted. It was an advertisement to join a pool club. The county had built a brand new pool facility and dubbed it the Yorkbury AquaClub. The wrinkled paper announced the pool's opening day, which was, of course, today.

Margaux smiled thoughtfully. She wouldn't have known it, but for this chance encounter with this wrinkled piece of paper that ended up in her rosebush of all places. And yet, what struck Margaux the most was the photograph of Yorkbury Aquaclub. The entire pool facility had been painted in vibrant colors of white and blue right down to the lounge chairs.

"Go to where it's white and blue." Those had been Anastasia's last words to her. Was that where she would find three friends who would help her?

Chapter 31

A FEW DAYS PASSED. NOTHING happened at the pool. Perhaps Anastasia was mistaken.

Until that day.

That one day, when Margaux was there and stepped on a sharp object, which was deftly removed by a handsome, dark-haired lifeguard she did not recognize at first. She had stood in front of him, holding onto his shoulders, and felt his deft hand probe her wounded foot, arousing her latent feelings. And all of a sudden, from just one look at his face, visions poured from her like a movie trailer. And it was all about that lifeguard tending to her bruised foot. She saw them together in a strange country pasture and then in a blue-green lake and then, all of a sudden, the both of them were quickly pulled up to the sky by a mysterious light beam. Finally, she saw him again, twice, at the same airport years apart. What was Anastasia trying to tell her? Margaux blinked her eyes. The visions were gone now.

"Are you all right?" The lifeguard looked at her quizzically. "Believe me, the wound is not as bad as it looks. We can fix it."

"Yes, yes, I'm all right. Sorry."

Later she found out his name was Byron O'Neill.

As soon as Margaux had left the pool building, Byron entered the lifeguard station in the lobby. Resting his elbow on the counter, he checked the daily incident report. All seemed well and in order. He looked up toward the staff lifeguard with the auburn hair. "Stephanie, who was that woman who just left here? The blonde with the yellow swim bag and sunglasses."

"Oh, her. She's new. Just registered a few days ago."

"What's her name?"

"Margaux Martin."

Byron shook his head as he placed the report on the counter. "Doesn't register."

"Pardon me?"

"Never mind. It's not important." He gave her the report. "Please file this report. Thanks."

"Sure."

Byron turned around and headed toward the glass door leading into the pool complex. He put his hand on the door latch and stopped for moment. "Is this woman a resident or guest?"

"Resident, why?"

"Oh, nothing important. Thanks." He nodded, walking into the pool complex. There was chance she would return. A chance to speak to her again.

Stephanie narrowed her eyes and puckered nose watching him walking away. That was strange. First Margaux had asked about him and now he asked about her. What was going on?

Stephanie shrugged and turned her attention toward an incoming swim patron.

By the time Margaux woke up inside her cherry-red Miata, parked across from the Wildwood Tennis and Pool Club, she suddenly realized to her amazement that Byron in her dreams and Byron at the Yorkbury AquaClub were one and the same man, albeit much older. Clearly, he was connected to her. But how? And why?

"Please stop with the riddles, Anastasia," Margaux pleaded and turned on the ignition. "This is getting ridiculous. I have no idea who that man is."

"You will know in time, Margaux. I promise," Anastasia whispered from the vast reaches of space and time, as she watched Margaux drive away. "Just wait a little longer."

"Just wait a little longer." Margaux found herself repeating, as the Miata banked into the right toward home. "Just wait a little longer."

A week later Margaux was on her way to her physician. The elevator reached the 4th floor and Margaux stepped out. She looked at the directional sign before her. Suite 508 was to the right, just down the hall, perhaps the last door. It was now 2:30 PM. She was half an hour early, but no matter. This would be just enough time to fill out the necessary insurance paperwork, before meeting with the new obstetrics-gynecologist, Dr. Lilliana Morena. She needed a second opinion.

Margaux grasped the door knob and entered.

"Hi, may I help you?" The desk receptionist inquired from behind an open window.

Margaux extended her hand. "My name is Margaux Martin. I have an appointment with Dr. Lilliana Morena at 3:00 PM. I'm her new patient. Just moved into town."

"Okay, then, please fill out the insurance paperwork, clip your insurance card with it, and have a seat. Dr. Morena will be with you shortly. She is with a patient right now."

"No problem." Margaux took the clipboard and walked towards a seat in the waiting lounge. She was the only one there for now. Hanging on the wall across from her, she saw a heavily-framed award plaque that announced the doctor as one of the best in town. Margaux smiled, silently applauding herself for making a good choice for that much needed second opinion. She briskly filled out the insurance form and signed if off, clipping her insurance card. She waited.

A few minutes later the door next to the receptionist's desk window opened and Dr. Morena's voice rang out. "You will be just fine. See you in six months, Romy." She turned towards Margaux. "Margaux Martin, correct?"

"Yes." Margaux stood up from the chair, walking steadily toward the doctor. She placed the clipboard on the receptionist's desk.

"Wait!" A high-pitched voice rang out. The two women turned around. A thin, dark-haired young woman suddenly appeared in front of Margaux, extending her hand. Her eyes were wide with desperation. "You must take this. Please," she pleaded. Margaux looked down at the young woman's hand. She saw what looked like a business card. She looked back at the young woman. "Huh?"

"Just take it, please." The young woman pleaded. "Something back there just told me to give you this. It wants me to give you this." She sighed in frustration. "Look, it's just a business card. You can always throw it away. Just please take it or this voice is not going to let go of me."

Margaux stared at her. A voice in her head had told her to do this? Give her a business card? Was it the same cryptic voice that had told Margaux to go back home? Anastasia's voice? If so, why?

"Please?" The young woman was begging her. "Just take it."

"Of course." Margaux quickly accepted the business card from the young woman, who immediately bolted from the waiting room, startled and embarrassed at her own inexplicable behavior. The door slammed behind her.

Dr. Morena stared in confusion. She had just completed a normal, routine appointment with this young woman, who had now exhibited a bizarre behavior.

"Who was that?" Margaux asked shoving the business card into her shoulder bag. She would deal with the mystery of the business card later. Away from the medical office. It would seem that the card was yet another annoying riddle she must unravel.

"Oh, she is one of my regular patients. Her name is Romy Roundtree." Dr. Morena turned towards Margaux. I'm quite surprised and dismayed at what just happened. Highly unusual and quite rude. My apologies for her behavior. I will speak with her about it."

"Oh, no, no, no, no." Margaux brushed away the apology. "Don't worry about it. I'll probably end up throwing it away. No harm done."

"Well, in that case, let's take a look at you." Dr. Morena opened the examining room door.

After the exam was complete, Margaux waited patiently inside the doctor's office, sitting comfortably in one of the two orange-and-white suede armchairs facing the doctor's desk. She stared out toward the large, glass-paned window behind the mahogany desk littered with papers. Time seemed to tick by slowly. Margaux wondered why it was taking so long. Two hours ago, she had been questioned and prodded and poked by the doctor, who finally insisted she take a MRI scan in the next room. And then she waited an hour more.

So, where was the doctor?

A blue jay with a white, ruffled mane on its back flew toward and settled on the window ledge, peeking inside and chirping happily. Margaux impulsively smiled. She hoped it meant good luck for her, especially now, when, after asking her several questions on her personal health and checking the previous doctor's recorded assessment, Dr. Morena had strongly recommended a MRI scan on her abdomen. It was the only way to make sure. Something was just not right, especially at her age. Margaux was only 24, but her periods were permanently gone. Her previous doctor had declared it a rare case of early menopause and to just live with it. That perhaps she had inherited it from her mother.

The one gene she had to inherit from her crazy mother that finally destroyed her marriage.

As if on cue, the blue jay decided to leave its perch and sail away. Margaux sighed. Once again, she looked at her watch. Immediately, the door opened and Dr. Morena entered. Margaux could see that she was confused. The doctor settled in her chair behind her mahogany desk. Clasping her hands together, she faced Margaux gravely. "My apologies for having kept you waiting for so long, but I needed to consult with a couple of my medical colleagues on this most unusual finding."

Margaux became alarmed. "What is it, Dr. Morena? Do you know what is wrong with me? You must tell me."

"Margaux, I regret to inform that you have no ovaries. The MRI scan shows the area completely devoid where your ovaries should have been. That is why you no longer have your periods. Are you certain a hysterectomy had never been performed on you?"

"Yes, I'm certain!" Margaux exclaimed vehemently standing up from her chair. "Yes. No, wait. I...I don't know. Oh my God, Dr. Morena, I just don't know." She sat back on her chair, frozen in disbelief. She had almost let the cat out of the bag. This can't go any further.

Dr. Morena was baffled at her reaction. "So *you don't know* if you had a hysterectomy performed on your womb? Why is that, Margaux?"

"I can't answer, Dr. Morena. I really, really can't. Things have happened to me that I don't even want to talk about. Not to you. Not to anyone."

Dr. Morena lifted her eyebrows. She sat back on her chair. "Well, in that case, when you are ready to talk about it, I will be here. The fact remains, though, you are, in a manner of speaking, post-menopausal. And my colleagues and I, we have not been able to come to a definite, medical conclusion, only plausible theories. We would know better, if you would only talk to me about "things that had happened to you.""

Margaux shook her head vehemently, her mouth set in a grim line.

"Well, then, I'm sorry, but the fact is you can never have children. Otherwise, you are in perfect health."

Margaux stood up from the armchair, calm and collected. She quickly arranged the straps of her shoulder bag and smiled weakly. That was close. No one, not even Dr. Morena, could ever comprehend the enormity of the "things that had happened to her." She extended her hand towards the doctor. "Thank you so much, Dr. Morena. I am definitely relieved to know I am otherwise in good health. That's important to me."

"Well, then, goodbye, Margaux." Dr. Morena smiled warmly, grasping Margaux's hand in both of hers. "I'm sorry this has happened to you. It is highly irregular and most unusual. I would have liked to pursue this further, at least to find out why it happened in the first place." The doctor gestured toward the door. "Please know I want to help you. Just give me a call, anytime."

"Oh, I will, Dr. Morena. I will." Margaux said. "Thanks again. Goodbye."

The elevator door opened to the first of the three, underground parking levels. Clutching her shoulder bag tightly, Margaux breathed in and fought back tears welling up inside her eyes. She quickly trotted to her Miata parked at a distant corner away from the dimly-lit elevator suite. Feeling claustrophic, she worried that the alien eyes would show up and pursue her. She finally reached her Miata and quickly inserted the key.

A movement brushed against her ankle. Startled, Margaux looked down. A bedraggled, dirty puppy leaned against her ankle, refusing to leave the spot. It seemed terribly nervous.

"Oh, you poor little baby." Margaux bent down and picked up the scruffy pooch. She cradled it in her arms, crooning softly. "Where are your owners, little puppy? Are you all by yourself? Oh, you must be so hungry." The puppy eagerly licked her face.

"Okay, okay!" Margaux giggled and petted her head. "You can come home with me. Let's get you cleaned up and fed. You want to stay with me, right?" The homeless puppy burrowed deeper inside her arms.

"Yes, you do."

Margaux threw her shoulder bag onto the floor in the car. She gently placed the wiggling puppy on the passenger seat, where it quickly settled itself into a ball of fur. Margaux smiled. She would keep the puppy.

Having settled into her seat, she slammed the door forcefully, locking it. The puppy looked up at her. "Sorry, puppy. I just found out I can't ever have children. But then there you are. You are so cute, you know, like a doll. Shall I call you Dolly?" The wide-eyed puppy stared at her, wagging it tail eagerly.

"Dolly it is, then. Let's go home now."

Margaux took a quick survey of the garage around and behind her. No one was around, not even those horrible alien eyes, thank god. Unable to rein in her emotions any longer, she leaned against the steering wheel and cried.

Dolly stretched out and laid her head on Margaux's lap.

From high above, Anastasia nodded, satisfied with the outcome. That puppy was just what Margaux needed in light of the bad news that only she, Anastasia, knew why.

Chapter 32

AT THE OTHER END OF the town far, far away, a young woman with flame-colored hair and a single, purple stripe jumped out of the Jeep Cherokee and ran upstairs in a two-story, garden apartment complex. She quickly headed toward a door at the end of the hall. She slammed the door behind her and leaned back, searching around the living room. It was silent and empty in the darkness.

"Gerald!" She yelled at the top of her lungs. "Where are you, Gerald!?"

"In here!" Gerald appeared out of a door from a hallway and switched on the lights. He looked disheveled and tired. He removed his glasses and rubbed his eyes. "I was just checking my instruments. Why are you yelling at me, Romy? And why are you crying?"

Romy stumbled into his outstretched arms. "Oh, God! I just came back from the doctor and something awfully weird happened in there. It scared me to no end. Too damn scary." Tears spilled from her eyes, as she buried her face into his chest.

Holding her close to him, Gerald felt protective and worried. He brushed his hand softly through her hair. Clutching him hard, Romy breathed in and out rapidly, trying to talk between the gasps and tears. He looked down. The tears were staining his shirt.

He sighed. "What happened, Romy?" he asked, as he lifted her face towards him and looked into her eyes. It was a frightened look the likes in which he had never seen before in her. Clearly she was spooked.

"Oh, Gerald, I saw creepy eyes coming out of nowhere in a hall at the doctor's office building. Big, black eyes surrounded by a hazy, gray mist. I was just walking to the elevator when those eyes appeared. And they just hung there and stared at me. I was totally frozen on the spot. Then all of a sudden I heard this hissing, low voice speaking inside my head. Telling me, no, forcing me to go into my backpack, pick up our business card, and hand it to this woman. Whatever it was pushed me to this woman."

Gerald narrowed his eyes. "What woman? Where?"

"At the doctor's office. She had the appointment after me. I was pushed there against my will to go to her. The doctor was with her. I'm pretty sure they both thought I had lost my mind."

"Strange, indeed." Gerald nodded. "Do you know this woman, Romy? Did you recognize her with your powers?"

"No, I couldn't even use my powers to figure her out. That force overpowered my mind putting some sort of shield in there to prevent me from figuring out who she was. And then, my hand was somehow pushed into my backpack to get our business card and forced me to give it to her."

"How did she react?" Gerald asked.

"At first, she was baffled and then she stared at me for a second or so, as if she knew something about it herself. Really spooked me out when she did that. But thankfully, she took that card. It was then the force dropped its hold on me. Oh, god, I was so embarrassed, Gerald. I left as fast as I could."

Romy gasped as a fresh burst of tears appeared.

"Take it easy, Romy." Gerald whispered, holding her tightly in his arms. He brushed back her hair and kissed the top of her head, trying to calm her down. He was the more pragmatic of the two. Romy had always been driven by her volatile emotions, a trait which somehow attracted him to her, as opposites tend to do that. He whispered gently in her ear. "Let's talk about this, shall we?"

"Hmmm, mmmm, sure." Romy gulped. She was in a safe place in his arms. The tears ceased to flow. She rubbed her reddened eyes.

Gerald offered her a napkin. She blew her nose and threw the napkin away. "I'm okay now."

"Good. First of all, I wonder why this entity told you that this woman needed our business card." Gerald asked thoughtfully, scratching his head. "What does it have to do with QET and our work?"

"It's crazy, if you ask me." Romy declared looking up at him with wild eyes. The purple stripe in her flame-red hair only added to the dramatic effect. She placed her hand under her chin thoughtfully. "Those eyes looked so malevolent, and yet, so familiar."

"Familiar, Romy?" Gerald lifted his eyebrows. "How so?"

"As if I'd seen them somewhere." Romy looked around. "Here in this room."

Gerald moved closer to Romy, placing his hands on her shoulders. "Here? How? Try to remember, Romy. This could be important."

Romy shook her head. It was all a blur in her mind from all that crying. She rubbed her eyes again and looked back at Gerald. All of a sudden, she wanted to know too. Like he said, it could be important. But where did she see them, those eyes? Romy closed her eyes. She probed inside her mind for anything that could lead to where she remembered those eyes. Perhaps the clue lay in their work. In this room. She furtively looked around the living room. There were stacks of books of all sizes sitting on the floor and table. Several more of those books lined the shelves against a wall. Her searching eyes finally rested on a thick, leather-bound book. She pointed at it.

"That's it. Over there, Gerald. That book. I'm sure of it."

Gerald gave her a quick nod and sprinted towards the dust-covered book. He picked it up from the stack and wiped it clean with his shirt sleeve. It was titled: "The Gods of Earth's Mysterious Past".

He looked questioningly back at Romy, his eyes narrowed. His curiosity was instantly piqued. Nodding excitedly, her confidence all but returned, Romy jogged towards him and took the book into her hands. "I think I know where it is." She said, as she flipped the pages across. Finally, she saw the page she had been thinking of.

"There!" She thrust the book back to Gerald, holding the page in full view. "Right there. Those are the eyes I had seen back there at the doctor's building, exactly like those eyes in this page. Only they were eyes in a mist. I have not seen any bodies."

Gerald swore softly. He took the book and smoothed the page for a clearer view. He adjusted his glasses and examined the illustration. There were two, large heads with elongated skulls the color of gray and on their faces were huge, black, almond-shaped eyes extending back toward their small pointed ears. These were artistic renderings based on the examination of several prehistoric skulls found in the near and far reaches of the earth. South America. India. China. Antarctica. Even Europe and the American Southwest.

Extraterrestrials.

Ancient astronauts that visited earth in the in the distant past. Age-old tales of their visitations had been passed down from generation to generation over tens of thousands of years. These were positive beings helping the human race advance, but there were also negative beings bent on utter destruction to mankind. Even in this day and age, a number of people still worshipped them, performing sacred rituals.

Gerald looked up at Romy, squinting through his glasses. If those were the same eyes that Romy had seen at the doctor's building, they were obviously contacting her with a purpose. It was hard to tell if their end goal was evil or good. Especially since they had apparently forced Romy to behave in a most, puzzling manner with a stranger at the doctor's office, a woman neither of them knew. They had forcefully blocked Romy's ability to read her and find out who she was.

Gerald and Romy stared at each other in utter silence, as they absorbed the gravity of the situation. They could only whisper to each other in alarm.

What was their agenda?

Chapter 33

LEAVING THE GARAGE OF THE medical building behind her, Dolly at rest on the passenger seat, Margaux turned into the main road. A few miles downtown, the main road split into two, three-lane roadways heading in opposite directions. A wide grassy median nestled in between them. Just before the split, a traffic light changed from yellow into red. Margaux slowed her Miata and stopped in front of a white, utility van. She smiled and petted Dolly, who was snoring softly, oblivious to the world.

It was early afternoon and the August sky was a glorious aquamarine with nary a cloud in sight. The blazing sun had settled closer to the horizon.

As she waited for the light to change, Margaux switched on the control in her Miata that activated the car roof. Dolly quickly looked up, her curiosity aroused. She growled softly. The car roof slowly disengaged and folded itself like an accordion at the back of the Miata.

Satisfied that there was no danger, Dolly settled back to sleep, snoring softly. Margaux chuckled, rubbing her furry head. She glanced at her shoulder bag. The business card was still in there. What a bizarre encounter it had been. But she would at least read it, before throwing it away.

The traffic light finally changed to green. Margaux sat up and focused in front of her. It was time to move on. But the white, utility van in front her did not budge an inch. It stood in front of the green light, silent and unmoving. Margaux hit the horn loudly. Dolly woke up, barking furiously.

"Move, damn it, move!" Margaux yelled to the driver of the van. "That green light is not going to wait for you!" She hit the horn again. Dolly barked some more, her front paws on the panel, helping Margaux.

Margaux yelled out again, this time giving a finger. "What's wrong with you out there?"

No response. Except for Dolly's excessive barking. Frustrated and irritated at the van driver's seemingly lack of cooperation, Margaux put the Miata in park. "Wait here, Dolly," she instructed the dog sternly, unbuckling her seatbelt.

From high above, Anastasia waved her hand. "Do not get out of the car."

Margaux automatically turned and buckled her seatbelt. She picked up Dolly and held her close. A heavy thump from behind rattled the Miata, jolting her from her seat. Only her seatbelt prevented her from hitting the front windshield. She held onto Dolly tighter and turned to look behind her. Another car had forcefully hit the back of her Miata. It now stood broken, its front bumper damaged significantly.

"Thank you." Margaux whispered gratefully to Anastasia.

Dolly wiggled in her arms. She placed the restless puppy back on the passenger seat. Dolly barked nervously.

"Easy does it, girl. Easy," Margaux crooned softly. "Everything is going to be ok and we'll soon be home. Just stay where you are now, ok?"

Dolly sat down and whined.

Margaux got out of the Miata and looked around, assessing her present situation. She felt irritated. First the disobliging van driver, who refused to move at the green light, and now this.

Both hands on her hips akimbo, she glared at the white, utility van in front of her, the driver still not even bothering to show himself.

She turned and glared at the other driver who had hit her Miata from behind.

"Stupid. Stupid. Stupid." Margaux cursed, shaking her head in frustration. "I'd really like to give you all a piece of my mind for putting me through all this trouble."

At that point, Margaux finally noticed that the car that had hit her Miata was a silver Ford Focus. Two occupants sat inside, both of them women, and both were staring at Margaux through the windshield. Margaux waited for them to come out of their car to no avail.

"What's wrong with you?" she called out. The Ford Focus driver nervously pointed behind her.

Margaux looked in the direction the driver had pointed. There, she could see another car, very old and rusted. It was a Honda Civic, the color of taupe, its front end horribly smashed. She could see the driver, also a woman, slumped against the steering wheel, apparently unconscious.

"Oh great." Margaux groaned. "Now we have to get help for her."

Suddenly Margaux heard an ear-splitting whining sound, not too far from where she stood. She winced and turned towards the direction of the noise. It was coming from a dark-blue and white Crown Victoria moving in the opposite direction across from the median. Blue, red, and white lights flashed from the car roof of the sedan.

Police.

The fast-moving police car headed towards a break at the median, a crossing reserved only for authorized vehicles. It made a turn.

Margaux breathed a sigh of relief, looking up at the sky. "Just in time. Thank you." She checked the back of her Miata, brushing her hand against the strong, rubber fender. It did not appear damaged at all, just a slight nick here and a scratch there.

"Are you all right?" a frightened voice called out, as Margaux bent down to check the undercarriage of her car. No damage in there either. She stood up and slapped her hands to remove the stones and dirt.

"Yes. Yes, I'm fine." Margaux responded taking a good look at the stranger in front of her. It was the driver of the second car, the Ford Focus. Apparently, she had decided it was a good time to get out of the car. The police were already on their way. Her companion, however, chose to stay inside, wide eyed and frozen.

"Sorry for my friend," the woman apologized, noting Margaux's glance at the passenger of her car. "She's a nervous wreck right now."

"I see."

"So, is your car ok? Are you ok?"

"Yes, of course. What about yours? What about you? What about her?" Margaux pointed at the unconscious driver in the third, badly-damaged car. "Obviously she caused it. I'm afraid to touch her for fear of making her injuries worse."

"Oh, yeah, I would agree with that and yeah, she did. She hit my car, which caused me to bump into you. You see, I had to slow down at the green light, because you weren't moving, and then she just went ahead and slammed into the back of my car."

"She must have been distracted."

"Definitely distracted. How come that white van didn't move?" The Ford Focus driver looked behind Margaux.

"I don't know." Margaux responded, as she herself looked behind at the van. It was still there, the driver still had not made any effort to come outside. "I'm not comfortable approaching that van, believe me. Let's let the police handle this."

"And there they are, coming towards us. That was fast. I wonder who called?"

"I'm just glad they're here."

"Lucky us." The Ford Focus driver shielded her eyes against the glare of the sun. "Look, there's the fire truck, too, and the EMT truck behind it. Yay!"

Margaux chuckled. "Not that we need the fire truck. More of like a tow truck."

"Ha ha, I agree, thankfully. No fire, as far as I can see." The Ford Focus driver offered her hand. "By the way, I'm Deiondra. I'm glad you're okay."

"Margaux. Same with you. I hope the other driver is okay."

"We'll find out soon enough. It's in their hands now."

Margaux sighed, as she surveyed the area of the accident. "This is quite a mess. I hope it doesn't take too long to process it."

Deiondra looked at Margaux. She grinned. "Let's see. Two stranded drivers. My paralyzed friend. A horribly, disfigured car with an unconscious driver. I have a feeling it will take some time, at least an hour or so."

Margaux groaned inwardly. Was there even a reason for all this chaos and time delay?

The two women watched the police car pull to a stop behind the damaged Honda Civic. Two burly officers, both wearing bulletproof, Kevlar vests, came out of the blue-and-white Crown Victoria. The firemen had already parked alongside the broken car and proceeded to check for fire and help the EMT remove the injured driver.

One of the two police officers approached to check on Deiondra's hyper-anxious friend. She willingly got out of the car at his urging.

The other police officer approached Margaux and Deiondra, who had been patiently waiting together near the Miata. Margaux stared at him, noting his thick, black hair, tousled and shiny against the blazing sun. The aviator sunglasses only added to his self-assured appearance. Her heart skipped a beat. As he got closer towards them, Margaux couldn't help but admire the rugged features of his handsome, tanned face.

He reminded her of someone. But who? And where?

The officer grinned at Margaux's puzzled stare. "Hello, ladies. Are either of you injured?"

"No!" was the simultaneous reply. They shook their heads.

"Okay. How about filling out these forms in your own words about what happened?" He handed out the forms, along with a couple of pens.

"Sure." Deiondra took the form and pen, gazing at the officer with a sigh. "I'd be glad to. Could somebody please call my boyfriend and let him know I'm all right and will be coming home late?"

"Of course. My partner over there will take care of it. Now, take your time with your testimony. Tell us what happened step by step." the officer sternly advised. Deiondra nodded in agreement and quickly headed towards the Ford Focus. She placed the form on the hood and bent down to write.

The officer turned to Margaux. Their eyes met and locked. He grinned, showing the small creases in the corners of his eyes and mouth. Margaux simply stared at the eyes. They were the same deep, brown eyes she had seen before.

"Hello?" The police officer asked quizzically. "Are you certain you are all right? Perhaps we can have our EMT check you out just to be sure?"

Margaux was jolted back into reality. She shook her head fervently. "Oh, no, no, no, no, please, I'm fine. I'll take the form now and fill it out for you."

Watching the scene from high above, Anastasia waved her hand.

As Margaux reached out to take the form, her hand brushed against the police officer's hand. The brief intimate touch startled her. Visions poured out in front of her eyes again like scenes from a movie trailer. The same visions she'd had not too long ago at the pool. Only this time they were clearly connected to this officer.

Then the visions faded back into a small singularity.

Margaux fainted.

3 hours later.

Margaux slowly opened her eyes. All around her was the blinding color of white. White walls, white table, white door, even a white armchair. Only the floor differed in color being slate-gray and very shiny. The room she was in spoke volumes of sterility and hygiene.

It even smelled of antiseptic.

Margaux groaned softly, placing her hand on her forehead. "Where on earth am I?"

"In a hospital," a voice gently informed her. It was a male voice, a soft baritone that sounded familiar. She looked up. It was the police officer from the accident, the one with the tousled, black hair and deep brown eyes. The last thing she remembered was reaching out to take a piece of paper from him, accidentally touching his hand.

"Oh my God, Dolly!" Margaux yelled, pulling the covers away. "Where's my puppy, Dolly? I must find her."

The police officer restrained her, pulling the covers back on her shoulders. "Don't move. I found your puppy in your jeep. She has been fed and is resting in my apartment. I'm not allowed to bring her in here, you know."

"Oh, thank you. Thank you so much." Margaux sighed in relief, leaning her head back against the pillow. Dolly was all right.

"How are you feeling now?"

"I don't know." Margaux looked around her. She was tucked in a hospital bed covered in white sheets and a blanket. An IV tube was hooked up inside the crook of her elbow. She raised her head. There was a TV attached to the wall above, but it wasn't turned on.

Margaux looked back at the deep, brown eyes of the police officer. "Who are you?"

The police officer smiled gently. He had been informed by the doctor earlier that Margaux might not remember anything upon waking. She had been rendered unconscious temporarily, although the doctor couldn't find the cause.

The police officer reached out to touch her hand.

Margaux snatched it away, startling him.

"I'm sorry. I'm so sorry," he apologized quickly. "I didn't mean to frighten you. I just wanted to comfort you. You fainted at the accident scene. Of course, the EMT had to bring you here."

"Oh, no, no, no, it's not you," Margaux stammered hastily, trying to explain. "At least not entirely you. I just would rather not be touched by anyone for now." She didn't want more visions or the subsequent blackout that had landed her in the hospital. How was she going to explain all that to anyone, least of all a police officer? "Just not now. It's kind of tough to explain."

"No problem." He smiled agreeably, stepping back from the bed. He clasped both his hands behind his back.

Margaux smiled weakly. "Thank you."

"Is there anyone I can call for you? Family?" he asked.

"No, no one. I'm basically all alone, except for Dolly. My father passed away recently, and my mother is gone to Russia. We don't get along."

"I'm sorry. Is there anything I can do for you?"

"Yes, I'd like to get out of here. I'd like to pick up Dolly and go home. Please," she begged.

The officer shook his head. "I'm afraid that's not possible. Given the strange circumstance of your fainting at the accident scene, the doctor would like to keep you here overnight for observation. You can leave in the morning. I'll make sure Dolly is returned to you."

"I suppose I have no choice." Margaux sighed. "Okay, then, what's your name?"

The police officer laughed softly, his deep, brown eyes crinkling. He bowed at her. "Officer Byron O'Neill, at your service."

"Byron O'Neill?" Margaux whispered. "That's interesting."

"Why is that?"

"You seemed familiar to me, somehow. I was hoping your name would a trigger a memory."

"And did it?"

"Not entirely, but I do remember you from the Yorkbury Aquaclub. I go there regularly. You even took care of my wounded foot, remember?"

"Wounded foot?" Byron said. "What wounded foot?"

"You pulled something sharp from my foot at one time. And then you had me follow you into the lifeguard station, so you could put a dressing on it. Remember, I hung onto your hand too long." Margaux smiled.

Byron stepped back, thunderstruck. "That was you? You are that crazy woman?"

"Yes, it was me." Margaux felt deeply offended. "And why are you calling me crazy?"

Byron grinned mischievously. "You keep running away from me. Every attempt I made to approach you caused you to run away from me. How crazy is that? I wasn't planning to hurt you, merely introduce myself. I finally gave up."

Margaux chuckled. "Sorry. Yes, I guess I was running away from you."

"But why?"

"Well, it's a long story, really. I just came out a bad marriage and wasn't ready for anything, I guess."

"Well, here we are again." Byron grinned. "Would you like me to leave?"

"Oh, no, no, please, don't. For some strange reason, I'm compelled to connect with you. I'm Margaux Martin, by the way. I didn't know you were a police officer, also. Is that why you left the pool?"

"It's my full time job. When I was in police training, I worked part-time as assistant manager at the Yorkbury Aquaclub for a couple of years. It paid the bills."

Margaux nodded. She stared thoughtfully at Byron for several seconds. She remembered the words, "Go to where it's white and blue." Perhaps he was the reason. But why, she wondered. Why, Anastasia?

"Pardon me?" Byron asked perplexed. "Who's Anastasia?"

She hadn't realized she'd spoken out loud. "Oh, it's nothing. Nothing at all." Margaux said. "I really appreciate all you've done for me and for Dolly. I don't know how to thank you."

"Well, you can thank me by not running away from me this time. How about I take you out to dinner?" Byron grinned. "But only if you want."

"Oh, I would like that very much."

"Great. I'll pick you up the day after tomorrow. I have your phone number. I'll keep in touch."

Margaux nodded. Feeling courageous, she extended her hand towards him. Byron grasped and held it for a moment, before placing it back on the bed. He lifted the blanket and gently wrapped it around her shoulders.

"I must go now. Duty calls. I will see you later."

As he approached the door to leave the room, Margaux called out. "Byron!"

He turned around. "Yes?"

"That man in the white utility van. What happened to him?"

"Dead. He had a heart attack caused by a blood clot. Nothing anyone could have prevented. He had been dead for quite some time, according to our medical coroner."

"Oh, no. No wonder he didn't get out of that van. And that other driver? The unconscious one?"

"We don't know, yet. She's in a coma. She's being taken care of in the ICU wing. She appeared to have been distracted by something, which caused the accident. We are still investigating."

"Oh, wow." Margaux breathed out, putting her hand on her forehead. "Somehow, I feel responsible."

"Get some rest, Margaux. None of this is your fault." Byron glanced at her quizzically. His hand reached for the light switch by the door. "I'll see you the day after tomorrow."

"Good night, Byron, see you then." Margaux burrowed into the blanket as the darkness enveloped her room.

Chapter 34

MARGAUX STARED INTENTLY AT THE large bathroom mirror in front of her. She had been staring at it for the past hour, as she diligently applied her makeup. Her tousled, blonde hair had been brushed thoroughly and elegantly swept up in a ponytail hairdo, revealing a striking profile of her neck and face. She turned her head each side admiring her visage. She felt as beautiful as she looked. The mirror told her so. Dolly barked, happily waving her tail. Margaux bent down and rubbed her furry neck. "Why thank you, Dolly! Now if only Anastasia would show up and tell me how I look for my date. I wonder where she is now." Margaux said. She sighed. "Well, she did say she had higher obligations, and that I probably won't see her much."

Dolly barked once again, tilting her head to the side. She offered her paw.

Margaux smiled, tears brimming inside her eyes. She missed her friend from long ago.

The doorbell rang. Dolly barked and scrambled down the stairs. Byron! Oh, no! Margaux quickly snatched white tissue from the pink-and -gray striped box tucked in the corner of the sink counter. She carefully dabbed her eyes with the tissue. It would not do to ruin her expertly-applied makeup and then have to start all over again, keeping Byron waiting.

She glanced at her gold-chained loop watch. It was almost 7:30PM. Margaux picked up the gold-loop earrings and fastened them into her ears. Stepping back, she took one last look at her reflection in the mirror and brushed down her Giorgio Missoni evening, cocktail dress.

Perfect.

The doorbell rang again. Dolly barked louder.

"Coming!" Margaux ran downstairs being careful not to slip on the stairs in her Enzio Verucio high-heeled sandals. Dolly was already pawing the door, whining plaintively.

"Okay! Okay!"

Margaux opened the door to find Byron holding a large bouquet of lilacs the color of wisteria and ruby red. Their exquisite scent wafted into the air. Dolly was already rubbing herself against his leg. She whined happily.

"Oh, hello, knucklehead." Byron grinned, bending down to pet her furry gray-white head. "You do remember me, huh?"

Dolly wagged her tail furiously.

"She certainly does, Byron. Thank you so much for taking good care of her."

"No problem. Ah, Margaux, I don't have to tell you, you look incredibly beautiful," Byron murmured at the sight of Margaux bathed in the glow of the lights from her house. He was mesmerized. Her smile was radiant and her makeup and hair, impeccable. She had on a velvety-soft, red dress that hugged the voluptuous curves of her body and showed the gorgeous lines of her long legs. A deep v-neckline exposed the promise of a full bosom. A gold choker wrapped itself snugly around her slender smooth neck. Two gold loop earrings put the finishing touch on her beautifully, made-up face.

"How did I get so lucky?" he whispered to himself.

"Are you ok?" Margaux asked.

"Yes, I'm fine, no worries." He handed her the bouquet of lilacs, embarrassment flooding his face.

"Oh, thank you." Margaux whispered, cradling the long-stemmed flowers against her face and inhaling their sweet, aromatic scent.

Dolly settled on the floor near his leg, resting her furry face on his shoe. She whined softly.

"Oh, look at Dolly. She doesn't want to leave you." Margaux smiled. "Should I be jealous?"

Byron picked up Dolly and rubbed her neck. "Ah, that's too bad. I made reservations at the Trattoria Bella Italia. We need to leave. We have only thirty minutes to get there." He whispered into her ear. "What shall we do with you now, knucklehead?"

Dolly wagged her tail. Margaux giggled softly.

"Just put her on the armchair, before the fireplace. She will settle down. I need to go upstairs and get my evening clutch."

Byron parked the car in the lot behind a quaint restaurant made up of blocks of stones fitted together and topped with a red, terracotta roof. A tall, stone fireplace was attached to the side of the house. Windows wrapped around the two-story building, each framed with beautifully-designed, green shutters. Wrought-iron flower boxes built into each window displayed exquisite flowers of red, yellow, white, and blue, lending an aura of a world presided by fairies and gnomes. A heavy, red antique door was centered in the middle of the building with a white sign above it.

"Trattoria Bella Italia".

It had been a long drive far out of the environs of the town into the rural woodland area beyond it. The picturesque, old-world restaurant stood alone and isolated, surrounded by an enchanted forest of oak and maple. The only way to get to it was through a grubby driveway that meandered just off the superhighway.

"Wow. It's quite far from town." Margaux commented, as Byron put the car in park. He shut off the ignition. "But, oh, it's simply adorable. However did you find it?"

Byron gazed at the restaurant building with tenderness in his eyes. "It's my favorite place. I happened on it one night on the way home from the airport in a cab, a few years ago. I had returned from my last tour in the Middle East. You see, I was in very bad shape and very hungry. The owner and his wife kindly invited me in, offering me hot Italian meals and their companionship. I have been coming here from time to time since then, especially when I have nightmares. They are like parents to me."

"Nightmares?" Margaux glanced at him warily. "You were military?"

"Yes. I had several tours at Al Ahraira. I was honorably discharged on medical leave."

Margaux was startled. Where had she seen him before?

"Did you escort a dead compatriot named Charlie that day you returned from your tour?"

Byron looked at her quickly, narrowing his eyes. "Yes, I did. How did you know that?"

"Well, gee, Byron, I'm the woman you sat next to on that plane. Do you not remember me? First the pool and now this."

"That was you? Oh my God. I didn't think I would ever see you again. I had completely forgotten about you. Even at the pool you were a stranger to me. That was you?" He stared at her for several seconds.

"Yes, it's me." Margaux smiled. She took a deep breath. "Well, here we are, together again. Seems fate has a way of getting stubborn with us."

"Indeed."

"So, tell me again, what was wrong with you that they had to discharge you like that."

Byron sighed. "Some sort of problem in my brain. I had forgotten all about it. I was supposed to have it checked."

"And did you?"

"I had a bigger problem to deal with. Post-traumatic stress disorder. I wouldn't have survived, if not for this kind, generous couple you will soon meet. They are Mario and Calandra Feruzioni, proprietors of this amazing restaurant." He gestured at the building.

"It was good of them to help you out." Margaux smiled. "And yes, Byron, I would certainly like to meet them."

"And you shall," Byron promised.

He stepped from the car. Margaux waited for him to open the door for her. She slowly put her foot onto the ground, revealing her shapely calf and ankle. Byron whistled. He extended his hand towards her and shut the door, when she finally stood beside him, holding the evening clutch. The sensuous scent of Forever Marilyn floated in the air around him, smelling sweetly of rose petals and lemons. Byron groaned softly.

"Byron?" Margaux looked at him, wondering why he was taking so long.

He quickly took her arm into his. "Let's go now, Margaux. I want to introduce you to my adopted parents."

Chapter 35

"Mio paisano!" boomed the tall, rotund Mario Feruzioni, ambling towards Byron and Margaux the minute they entered the restaurant together. Mario had extended his arms high in the air, as if welcoming home a long, lost son. His wife, Calandra, a petite, plump, dark-haired woman, followed behind him with a beaming smile. They had been surprised and, yet very pleased, that their paisano was bringing a date this time. She hadn't been easy to approach, he had pointed out, but he wasn't going to give up. They had thought that was very funny and told him to bring her over one night, if he got lucky. And he did. Calandra was overjoyed. He was like a son to her and often she wagged her finger at him, complaining he needed a woman to take care of him. Mio figlio she would call him and hugged affectionately, whenever he came to visit them.

"Mio figlio!" she called out coming from behind Mario, extending her chubby arms towards him. The husband and wife both hugged Byron, as Margaux watched from a distance. How sweet they seemed.

"Ah, but we are rude." Calandra pushed Byron and Mario away from her. She walked towards Margaux and placed two kisses, one on each of Margaux's cheeks. She stepped back and clapped her hands in wonder, looking at Margaux with admiration. "Molto bellissima! Perfetto for our Byron."

Margaux blushed.

"Come, come," Mario urged, gesturing Byron and Margaux to follow him towards the outdoor dining area. "Go, go." Calandra pushed them towards Mario. She wiped her hands on her apron. "I now finish spectacular Italian dinner for you both. Go. Have some good wine."

Margaux and Byron stepped out into the trattoria. The ground was covered with gray flagstones creating a large, square dining area. Several dining tables were scattered around, all covered in burgundy tablecloths. At the center of each table was a lighted candle. Above them, the velvety-black sky was sprinkled with bright twinkling stars, as the mellow moon gently beamed. Summer was winding down, but it was still warm outside with a hint of romance in the air.

Mario led the couple to a table prepared for them. "Sit, sit!" he ordered, "I will bring our most popular red wine. Imported directly from Italy. Home of romance, no?"

"He's talking about the Renaissance," Byron joked, grinning mischievously. "You know, Italy was home to the most explosive creation of arts, music, and literature. Leonardo Da Vinci, Michelangelo, Botticelli, Caruso, Palestrina, et cetera, et cetera." He bowed his head haughtily. "I learned it all from those two."

"Oh!" Margaux smiled impressed at him. "You know the masters of the Renaissance."

Mario twisted Byron's cheek in a gesture of dismay. He shook his head. "Renaissance, indeed? No, no, no, no, no! I meant una cenetta intima with this molto bellisima signorina! Per sempre insieme!" He added pointing at Margaux. Byron grinned. "No offense, Mario, but I would agree with you. Molto apologies."

Margaux stared at them wide-eyed.

Mario slapped Byron's cheek with his hand. "Now, now, that is better. Much, much better. I bring you wine soon. Please enjoy the beauty of the night sky. We will be expecting the Rafaella Diamonds tonight, you know." Mario exclaimed joyfully, gesturing towards the sky with his hands.

Margaux covered her mouth and giggled, as Mario proudly strutted towards the restaurant, leaving them both alone in the trattoria. They were the only ones there.

Chapter 36

"ARE YOU ALL RIGHT?" SHE chuckled and finally burst out laughing, as she watched Byron turn red in embarrassment. "Oh, but they are so sweet. Do you know what he just said?"

"No, not really. I'm sorry. It is all Greek me." Byron smiled ruefully. "I have not yet mastered their language to their utter dismay. At least, though, I'm familiar with molto bellisima."

"Well, then, tell me, what does molto bellissima mean? I seem to keep hearing those two words thrown at me."

Byron stared at her, his eyes darkening. Margaux quieted down.

"It means very beautiful," he whispered, as his hand reached over the table. "And they are right, of course. You are very beautiful, Margaux."

Margaux smiled. A warmth spread over her body as his hand enclosed into hers. She shook her head. "My, but you are full of surprises tonight, Byron. So tell me, what are the Rafaella Diamonds?"

"Ah, the Rafaella Diamonds. This I learned from them, also." He smiled. "Actually, they are a shower of meteors at night around this time of the year. They come every year and are a quite remarkable sight to behold."

"A meteor shower? But why call them Rafaella Diamonds?"

Byron leaned forward. "Ah, that name is from afar on the shores of Italy, only they know. Mario and Calandra used to live there. Here, we know it as the Leonid Meteorites."

"Indeed." Margaux said. "So, how did that name come about?"

"There is a legend among the villagers in Saramaggiore, Italy, passed on for generations. It is said one of the two brothers, both mortals, spurned a goddess of love and beauty. Her name was Rafaella. She was once mortal and loved a man in her village, but found him in the arms of another woman. Unable to bear the pain and humiliation, she escaped into the forest to die of a broken heart. As she lay dying, the other brother happened upon her and placed a kiss on her lips, confessing his love for her. Rafaella woke up briefly to see the man who offered her his abiding love and softened her angry heart. Her one true love more so than the brother that spurned her."

"Oh, how sad." Margaux whispered. "Go on, what happened? How did the diamonds come to be?"

"Well, the other brother held her in his arms, as she lay dying. He was inconsolable. The villagers surrounded them and prayed for her recovery. And that is when an amazing revelation occurred, according to their legend. Rafaella changed into a shining form dressed in a white, flowing robe with her upswept golden blonde hair held in place by a tiara of olive tree leaves. She revealed that she was a goddess, who had changed into a mortal to experience life in the village, including falling in love. That the pain of rejection and scorn had caused her to forget her true existence, believing it was better to die than live in abject humiliation. Only the love of this brother holding her in his arms changed her mind. It was time for her to return to Mount Olympus and reclaim her place among the gods.

"However, Rafaella had promised that because of this brother's true feelings, she would throw diamonds in the sky from her realm every year at this time, in memory of his love for her. And every year, couples from all over the world come together to watch the sky for those diamonds and make a wish, hoping her magic brings lifelong happiness to them." Byron leaned back in his chair. He smiled. "Heh, I hope I'm not boring you. It's just a myth, you know."

"Hardly." Margaux shook her head. She held his hand tightly. "That is such a beautiful story. I'm quite enchanted."

Byron stood up from his seat. "Come, Margaux. Let's dance before dinner arrives."

"No music?" Margaux asked.

Byron shook his head. "Not necessary. We are our own music." Margaux nodded, following him to the center of the trattoria.

Chapter 37

MARIO ARRIVED WITH A SILVER wine bucket filled with ice encased around the bottle of Vino della Ciara. He placed the bucket on their table and wiped his hands in his apron. His face beaming with delight, Mario clasped both hands towards his heart, as he watched Byron and Margaux dance slowly around the candle-topped tables.

It was exactly as he hoped for Byron.

Calandra appeared from the door. "Mario!" She called out, impetuously walking towards him, hands on her hips. She wagged her finger at him. "Come, I need your help to bring the food out. Oh!" She stopped herself, putting both hands on her mouth, as Mario shushed her with a finger. He whispered into Calandra's ear. She nodded vigorously, yes, yes, yes. Together, they held hands. Soon the air in the trattoria was filled with the melodious harmony of Calandra's mezzo soprano and Mario's baritone, as they sang together an aria from one of their favorite movies. An aria that told a story of a love spoken softly between two hearts beating as one.

Margaux looked up into Byron's eyes as the song was sung. Her heart was beating fast as the music entered her ears in all its promise and truth.

"What are you thinking?" Byron gazed darkly into Margaux's eyes. The refrain from the song intoxicated his mind and his heart with a strong desire for Margaux.

"I'm thinking…I don't know. But this feels so right, as if I've known you forever, and yet, I've only just met you," Margaux put her head softly against his chest.

Byron held her tightly, a soft groan coming from his throat. He felt the fullness of her breasts and her rapidly beating heart against his chest. He bent down to kiss her cheek and whispered into her ears. "I feel the same. It's very strange. It was as if I had to reach out to you."

"You had to?"

Byron looked back at her and nodded seriously. "Yes, it felt like I had to. It's like you were a part of me before. And you know what? I'm glad I did. I'm not questioning the powers that be anymore, whatever prompted me to do this."

"Oh, Byron…" Margaux murmured, as she lifted her face towards his, her feet dancing in slow motion to his leading steps. Her eyes searched for his and found them gazing at her with a smoldering need. Byron lowered his face to kiss her. Margaux responded by softly opening her mouth.

Emboldened and hot, Byron held her in a tight embrace and locked his mouth into hers, their tongues exploring, their arms around each other in a tighter embrace, as the final, haunting strains of the aria faded into the stillness of the night.

Above them, as promised, the Rafaella Diamonds tumbled down among the scattered, blinking stars and the genial moon.

From high above far, far away, in the infinite universe, Anastasia smiled from her gilded chair. Together at last. Thunder boomed ominously from a distance. Anastasia frowned. Change was coming bringing death and destruction. But, still, there was a way of last resort to deal with the Primary Principle. With a smile of satisfaction, Anastasia got up from the chair and walked away into the darkness. It was time to contact the One Most High.

Chapter 38

IT BEGAN AROUND 1:00AM. FIRST, it was a brief shudder that Margaux had often dismissed as coming from perhaps a heavy vehicle passing through her neighborhood at this strange hour of the night. After all, the town was still building 25-story apartments, even during the nights. And they were not supposed to work at night. The town apparently had a deadline to meet. How else?

Minutes later, another shudder, and this time it was stronger and lasted longer. Eventually, it subsided, but tonight it ended with a resounding thump on the ground, shaking the bed slightly. Margaux breathed in, annoyed at their appearance. Deeply sensitive, she hated the nightly reverberations and jolting thuds that kept her awake. It would take some hours, before the noise and vibrations subsided and she finally fell into a deep sleep.

She glanced at Dolly lying on her doggie bed nearby. It would seem that Dolly had gotten used to it, sleeping soundly like a baby, oblivious to the world around her.

And yet, tonight, something felt awfully wrong.

Feeling chilly and nervous, Margaux reached for the down covers and instantly felt the warm, skin of a muscular arm stretched out over her stomach, holding her to him. She softly caressed the arm. She turned her head around to see the sleeping form of Byron right next to her in bed. He was sound asleep, not even awakened by the unsettling roars of the night that bothered her so much. Unlike her, he and Dolly apparently could not feel nor hear them.

Lucky you, Byron. You and Dolly.

The night had been so wonderful. A night of intense lovemaking that had culminated in an explosive, passionate, burst of love and lust, when the two became one. Then they slept, his arm possessively enfolded around her.

Thirty minutes later, the earth clattered again beneath her bed waking Margaux up. Dolly whined, nervously clambering onto the queen-sized bed. Margaux held her to her bosom and waited for the upheaval to subside.

But, this time the commotion was greater than before, the blaring noise louder than ever, as if something had unleashed a power that caused the ground to shake and bend and twist with an unearthly, groaning sound.

Suddenly, the bed was shaking violently, too violently.

"What the hell?" Byron muttered, as he lifted himself up on the bed.

Dolly whined again. She burrowed her head inside Margaux's arm.

"I don't know, Byron. I've never felt this before in my entire life."

The rumblings only got worse. Inside the bedroom, Margaux and Byron watched in horror, as books, glasses, and her desktop computer all spilled over from a desk across the room.

The mirrors cracked loudly.

"Oh my God, what is happening?" Margaux cried out. She watched the rocking chair crash, throwing her shoulder bag onto the floor, spilling its contents. She fearfully held on to Dolly and leaned over to Byron, who was wide awake by now.

He glanced at the alarm clock behind Margaux. It was three o'clock in the morning, not yet dawn.

"It's probably an earthquake or a tornado. It certainly feels like one or the other." Byron tried to calm her down, holding her tightly against him. Dolly whined softly in her arms. He brushed her furry head.

"But we don't get earthquakes in this town." Margaux declared emphatically. "That can't be an earthquake. We're nowhere near a fault line."

"We don't know that. But we are in tornado country. We have to move quickly. Do you have a basement in this house?"

"Yes, I do. It's more of like a basement suite. I had hoped to rent it out."

"Even better. We should go in there and hope for the best. Come on, let's move quickly."

By the time, his feet hit the ground, the rumblings had subsided. Margaux screamed. Dolly growled. Two large, almond-shaped, black eyes were materializing slowly in the faintly, dark room, wrapped around by shadowy mists. The eyes finally stood suspended in the air above them. Following her gaze, Byron saw nothing. Puzzled, he looked at Margaux, but she did not respond. Ignoring him, Margaux remained transfixed, her eyes locked onto that one place on the ceiling. For several seconds, the lingering, menacing eyes silently stared at Margaux. They had returned.

But why?

Dolly growled, wiggling herself from Margaux's arms. She wanted to reach that ceiling.

"No. No. No. No," Margaux shouted, holding Dolly back. She wasn't going to let them hurt her puppy girl.

Suddenly knifelike stabs of pain materialized inside her head. Letting go of Dolly, she grabbed at her temples, crying out in agony. Dolly ran towards the edge of the bed and tried to jump up at the ceiling. She growled.

Mystified, Byron tried to calm Margaux, as he held her agonized face in his hands. And there was Dolly behaving bizarrely. And yet, he could see nothing at the ceiling. What was going on?

"Calm down, Margaux, calm down, darling, what is it? Why are you terrified?" He brushed her hair and held her head close to his chest. "Be quiet, girl." he shouted at Dolly.

But, Dolly would not listen.

Margaux looked up at Byron in surprise. Clearly, he could not see them, those eerie eyes. She shook her head quickly, saying nothing, and nestled deeply against his chest, letting him brush her hair. How could she explain those eyes that had haunted her most of her life? How could she explain the headaches that sometimes came with their appearance and she had no idea why.

Margaux lifted her head from his chest and looked back at the ceiling, but the preternatural eyes were still there, bobbing in the air and boring into her head with a strength of force.

In awful pain, she held on tightly to Byron, gripping her fingernails into his arms.

Frustrated, Dolly ran around and around her space and tried to jump up at the ceiling again, still growling from her throat. Byron gave up trying to quiet her.

"Margaux, what are you seeing up there? What is Dolly seeing up there? I see nothing. Nothing at all." Byron grasped her arms, shaking her body, trying to instill some sense of reality into her terrified mind. "What is up there, tell me! What the hell do you see?"

"Those awful eyes," Margaux whispered. "Those big, black eyes. I have seen them before…many, many times. They're back."

"Big, black eyes? What glaring eyes? I don't see anything, Margaux." He searched around the room again. Dolly was still barking at the ceiling. Byron groaned in frustration. He was getting upset at not being able to control the situation. He wished he had his police-issued revolver with him.

"Where exactly are those eyes, Margaux, where?"

Margaux pointed at the ceiling.

"But there's nothing there." Byron insisted in frustration. He was getting worried. Was Margaux losing her mind? "Wait here. I'm going get something for your headaches. Perhaps it's all in your imagination."

"No!" Margaux shouted, shaking her head. She grabbed Byron's arm. "Wait. Something's happening, now. Someone's trying to talk to me. Oh my God, I can hear them talking in my head."

Byron sighed wearily. "Ok, then, what are they saying?"

"I don't know. It's like some kind of foreign language." Margaux stood still and listened, still staring at the ceiling. "The voice keeps saying 'Alaku Asru' over and over." She looked at Byron. "At least, I know what alaku means."

"You do? Well, what does it mean?"

"I remember from way back someone told me it means "to go" in an ancient language. Sumerian, I think. It means 'to go.' Back then, it was 'alaku seru', to go.... back, meaning for me to come home here in this town."

"Interesting. And now?"

"I have no idea what asru means, Byron, assuming it's from the same language. But I might have a theory."

"Go on. I'm listening."

"If alaku seru means to go back, what if alaku asru is its exact opposite. Meaning to go forward?"

Byron smiled. "That is quite brilliant, I think, Margaux, darling. But, assuming you are right, what or where is forward?"

Margaux did not respond. She stared back at the eyes for several seconds, listening to the voice in her head. Curiously, the headaches throbbed less and less, the more the voice spoke to her. By then, Dolly had tired of growling and jumping.

Byron waited. If Margaux was acting like some sort of raving somnambulist, it would be dangerous to wake her up. Better to follow her lead.

Margaux nodded and slowly turned her head towards the floor beside her bed.

From the depths of the shadowy mists, a sharp ray of light shot out from an eye. Margaux watched as the beam landed on the small, white square, among the scattered contents spilled from her shoulder bag. The laser light just stayed there, as if pointing to it, not even burning the paper. At that moment, a sudden calm washed over her.

"Alaku Asru".

Margaux firmly removed Byron's arm from her body. "It's ok, Byron. I know what they want me to do. Alaku Asru is definitely tied to this piece of paper on the floor. Perhaps that's our answer." She bent down to pick up the small, white square. She looked back at the ceiling. "I know, now."

The sharp, beam of light quickly dissolved into the mists. In a second, the eyes were gone.

Margaux walked towards the bed. "It would seem I have to go to this address on the card." She held it out towards Byron. "I wonder what QET means?"

As Byron reached out to take the card, a thunderous boom resonated in the room. Margaux stumbled violently against the bed. Byron caught her and gathered her in his arms. Dolly barked loudly. Her sense of danger was heightened.

"It's an earthquake, definitely. Come on. It's getting worse now," Byron yelled out. "We need to get out of the house." He placed Dolly on the floor and bent down to pick up his clothes and shoes, dressing quickly. Dolly tensed, ready to bolt.

"In a minute!" Margaux yelled back and quickly dressed herself. Fully attired, she grabbed Byron's hand and together, with Dolly behind them, they ran downstairs through the living room towards the front door. All around them, the furniture was thrown into disarray. Glasses, books, and chinaware fell down on the floor, breaking into pieces.

When they reached the door, the earth suddenly and inexplicably quieted down.

Byron and Margaux looked at each other in amazement. The house was still standing. "Let's wait a bit more," Byron suggested.

Several tense minutes passed. The earth remained still and quiet. The house was still standing. Vastly relieved, Margaux and Byron scanned around in front of them. The entire living room was in shambles.

"Come on. Let's get out of there." Byron grabbed Margaux's hand. Dolly got up and followed them, her tail wagging.

"Wait, Byron." Margaux pulled her hand back. She pulled out the business card from shoulder bag. "Before I forget, there is something I must do. You don't have to come with me, if you don't want to."

"What do you mean, you must do?" Byron asked puzzled.

"I have to go to this place, Byron. This address on the card. I don't know why, but clearly it is a sign.

"Indeed?" Byron stared at the card. "I wonder why?"

Margaux slapped her head. "Oh my God, now I remember. There was this strange woman who pushed this card into my hand at my ob/gyn's office a few days ago. She said something forced her to do this. I was going to throw it away, but somehow I forgot about it."

Byron sighed deeply. It was getting more and more confusing, albeit alarming. Who are these people on the card, Gerald and Romy Roundtree? What is QET? How are they related to the strange occurrence upstairs, which he could not see himself? And yet, it seemed there was only one way to find out, since Margaux was so adamant about it. He wished he had his revolver with him.

"Well, then, Margaux, darling, come hell and high water, I will go with you. I'm not letting you and Dolly out of my sight."

Margaux smiled at him and bent down to pick up Dolly. She reached out for his hand and squeezed it. "Come on, Byron, let's go there now."

Chapter 39

"SO THIS IS WHERE THEY live?" Byron stared out of the windshield in utter shock and amazement.

He was staring at what looked like a lone, garden apartment in the middle of a vast, desert plain. They were hundreds of miles away from the town that had just experienced the devastating earthquake.

All through the breaking hours of the dawn, Byron and Margaux, with Dolly at the back seat, had driven for five hours on a superhighway already heavily packed with vehicles of all kinds and sizes, the remnants of the earthquake. Normally, it would have taken only two hours to arrive at their destination.

In time, Byron turned right and decelerated away from the superhighway. Several seconds later, the Miata entered a sandy trail covered with worn, tire treads and a half-broken street sign bent down at corner.

The apartment building itself looked eerily decrepit and abandoned against the bright morning sky. They had parked the Miata next to the olive-drab Jeep Cherokee and electric-blue Mitsubishi Mirage in front of the building. Obviously, people lived in there.

But what caught Byron's attention was the massive, white, radio telescope behind the apartment complex. He could only guess it was at least 50 meters tall and wide, eclipsing everything around it. He shook his head in disbelief. An astronomical radio dish behind an ordinary apartment complex, however abandoned it looked, made no sense to him.

But he was too tired now to argue the sheer illogic of the scene before him. This area they had arrived after 5 hours of driving was the exact address as documented on the card.

Alaku Asru.

The place where Margaux was supposed to go forward. But, why?

For the third time in the past twelve hours, he wished he had his revolver with him.

Margaux grinned at Byron. "Yup, this appears to be the address." She stepped out of the Miata. "I'm going in there now. Come on, Dolly." She picked up the wiggling puppy from the back seat. Margaux poked her head back inside the Miata. "Are you coming?"

"Do I have a choice?"

"Not really. Come on, Byron. It can't be that bad. Let's go find them." She slammed the passenger door shut and steadfastly walked towards the building with Dolly in her arms.

Byron promptly followed her, his senses in high alert.

Margaux rapped on the door of an apartment at the end of the hall, No.29.

"Who is it?" A female voice called out from behind the door.

"I'm Margaux Martin!" Margaux shouted through the door. "We have come here from a long way off. May we come in?"

The door slowly opened into a small gap at first, then creaked wider, revealing a striking, young woman with flame-colored hair and bangs on her smiling, heart-shaped face. A striking, purple stripe adorned one side her hair. Her violet eyes looked at Margaux and Byron questioningly for a moment. She gasped. "Oh! It's you!"

"I'm sorry?" Margaux inquired, puzzled at her reaction. "Have we met before?"

"Yes, yes, you did! At the doctor's, remember?" the young woman declared, her eyes blazing in excitement. "It's where I gave you that card. You found me!"

"It's you?" Margaux was taken aback. "You're Romy Roundtree?" She looked at the card. "As in Gerald and Romy Roundtree, QET?"

"Oh, yes, I'm Romy Roundtree. Gerald is my husband. QET stands for Quest for Extraterrestrials, our pet project." Romy held the door wide open and motioned to Margaux and Byron to enter. "Please do come in. I apologize for the mess in the living room. We just had a mild earthquake a few hours ago."

Romy gestured towards the living room, its furniture scattered in disarray. Margaux and Byron walked cautiously through the door into the living room. Romy shut the door behind them setting the deadbolt lock firmly in place.

Her back against the door, Romy chattered in nervous excitement, clapping her hands with glee. "Oh, this is too, too marvelous. I didn't think you would come. I did tell you to rip it up, didn't I? Oh, I am so, so sorry if I had upset you back then. I just couldn't stop myself, you know. Something was forcing my hand. It was all so strange. Oh, wow, you did come after all!"

Margaux placed Dolly on the floor. The puppy immediately set about to check the room with her nose.

"Yes, I did come. I had to. We had to." Margaux gestured towards Byron. "It was very strange. It would seem I am also being inexplicably forced to find you and your husband. Do you know why?" She looked at Romy with apprehension.

"Excuse me, but I'm curious." Byron quickly interjected. "What is that giant machinery doing at the back of this building?"

Romy turned towards Byron. She grinned excitedly. "Oh, of course, it's our very own radio telescope. Gerald and I, we use it to search for extraterrestrials on our own time, away from the scrutiny of the public, including his colleagues, who, you know, do not approve of his methods. My husband Gerald is an ardent astronomer, quite eccentric, you know, but very smart. I'm so proud of him."

"That's interesting." Byron said. He looked around the room. It was a humble abode with comfortable furnishings and thousands of books on shelves, floor, and a table. "This must have been quite an expensive undertaking."

Romy chattered excitedly. "Oh, no, no, no, no. We did not pay for it. The radio dish was paid for by our wealthy benefactor from another country," Romy explained. "He prefers to remain anonymous, but he liked our work. He's been looking around for people like us to do some work for him searching for extraterrestrials, you know. The money comes in every month to support us and our work. Our secret benefactor also owns this abandoned apartment building and offered it to us. You must admit it is quite an ideal location. No one around for miles."

Byron nodded in understanding. "I'd be curious to know what you have found in your work. Don't you agree, Margaux?"

"Hmm, "Margaux said. She was looking around for Dolly, who had disappeared into the hallway to check out the other rooms.

An open book lay on the table not far from where she was standing. She could see the pages. The second page was an illustration by an artist. Margaux gasped silently. The drawing depicted the eyes; the ones that had relentlessly pursued her all of her life and now she was here because of them. And there they were on the book owned by this unknown, eccentric astronomer and his equally eccentric wife.

But what did the eyes have to do with them?

Margaux glanced at Romy, who was still excitedly explaining the technology of their enormous radio telescope to Byron.

"Romy, I'm asking you again. Do you know why I had to come here?" She pointed at the open book on the table. "Do you know anything about those eyes I see on the page of that book over there?"

"Eyes?" Byron remarked quizzically. "What eyes? Where?"

At that moment, the ground suddenly lurched up, forcing the living room to sway and buckle. Dolly quickly appeared from the hallway, nervously settling herself between Margaux and Byron. Margaux picked up the scared puppy.

Margaux and Byron held on to each other. Romy fastened herself onto a Doric column at the center of the living room.

"Come on, everyone. We need to get out of this building." Byron ordered.

"Not again." Margaux groaned. "I thought we had gotten away from it back there."

Byron shook his head grimly. "Apparently not. This earthquake seems to spread out for hundreds of miles." Finally, the shakings subsided. "Let's go find your husband and leave this building."

Romy was thrilled. She clapped her hands gleefully. "You've had this earthquake before where you came from? That far away? Amazing! Gerald and Arnold would be so thrilled to hear that!"

Margaux and Byron stared at her. Had the woman lost her mind? There was nothing thrilling about the devastation the previous earthquake left behind at Mirrington Heights, where several homes and buildings were destroyed. And who was Arnold?

The hallway buckled and swayed, this time stronger than before. Dolly barked loudly.

A thunderous crash resounded at the far end of the hallway, before the earthquake subsided. All was quiet, as the dust spiraled up and settled on the floor around them.

Margaux and Byron looked at each other in alarm and then at Romy. Margaux set Dolly on the ground. The puppy promptly disappeared into the last room at the end of the hallway.

"What the hell was that?" Byron demanded brushing the dirt from his clothes.

"I don't know, but my husband's in there and also our friend," Romy cried out. "I must go to see if they need help."

"We're coming with you." Margaux said and grabbed Byron's hand.

"What happened?" Romy poked inside the door first. Margaux and Byron quickly entered in behind her. They found Dolly barking at the center of the room with everything in total disarray.

"Oh my god, Gerald!" Romy ran to her husband. He lay on the floor in a stupor, moaning with pain. She looked around the room in dismay. Books were scattered around the room, having been shoved off their shelves, when the heavy, mahogany bookcase fell, dislodged from the wall during the earthquake. His right leg was pinned under it. It was bleeding.

"I'm all right, Romy, just my leg is under there. This thing is too heavy for Arnold to lift. Go help him." Romy ran around to the other end of the antique, ornate bookcase and prepared to lift it. She groaned at the effort.

It was still too heavy.

"Let us help." Margaux and Byron dashed towards the bookcase, one at each end, bending down to lift it.

Dolly barked helpfully.

Chapter 40

"1...2....3....Now!" ARNOLD YELLED OUT LOUD. The four of them groaned, as they heaved and huffed. Finally, after several tries, the four of them lifted the heavy, dark-brown bookshelf altogether, gasping and panting with all their might. Finally, the bookcase moved up just high enough, enabling Arnold to quickly let go of it and pull Gerald away, his leg finally free. It was bleeding profusely at the thigh.

Gerald groaned painfully.

The other three let go of the bookcase and backed away. The bookshelf landed with a massive roar, breaking apart.

Romy sat on the floor, holding Gerald's head on her lap. "Do something!" she cried. "He's bleeding badly."

Arnold bent down and ripped the material from Gerald's pants, exposing a deep wound at the thigh. He folded the ripped material and pressed it on the wound.

"We need to put pressure on it or he will lose a lot of blood. Let's hope it did not hit the femoral artery."

"Oh God," Romy moaned. "What are we going to do? We are miles away from the nearest hospital."

Byron quickly assessed the room, his lifeguard training at the ready. There were books of all sizes and weight in assorted disarray all over the floor. On the gray, steel table nearby, albeit scattered, were what looked like scientific instruments, perhaps used to measure and collect information from the radio telescope. Quite useless.

"I need towels and a belt, also a needle and thread." He instructed. "A bottle of hydrogen peroxide. Quick, where are they?" He glanced at Romy.

"Bedroom." Romy pointed at the door. "Right across the hall. There is an adjoining bathroom. You'll find a Red Cross kit under the sink."

"Good. Any chance you have whiskey in this house?"

"No, not whiskey, but we do have bourbon."

"Get that, Margaux and some hot water," Byron ordered, as they both left the room to collect the necessary items. Dolly followed them.

"Oh, thank you so much," Romy crooned, cradling Gerald's head on her lap. The first aid procedures had taken two hours but Gerald looked as though he'd survive now.

Byron was drying his hands with a towel and Margaux stood by beaming with pride. He constantly surprised her.

Arnold leaned by the window and looked out at the desert panorama, grateful the ordeal was over. The wound had been carefully cleaned up and sutured, before wrapping it around with a clean towel. A belt was tied above the wound to prevent further blood loss. Arnold was altogether impressed and relieved. They had been lucky to have Byron there; the nearest hospital was 100 miles away.

Gerald weakly extended his hand to Byron. "Thank you, ummm…"

"Byron. I'm Byron O'Neill. Just doing my job. You need to rest now."

Romy gushed profusely, gratitude pouring from her voice.

"Oh, thank you, thank you, thank you so much, Byron!" She exclaimed, hugging Gerald. "We are so lucky you were here when all this happened. Aren't we, Gerald?"

"I would agree so." Gerald responded. "Although Arnold would not have done a bad job himself." He tried to lift himself and gave up, groaning in pain. "Looks too hard to get up now. So, tell me,

Romy, darling, aside from the luck itself, why are these people here and where did that dog come from?"

"Dolly belongs to me!" Margaux picked the wagging puppy up.

"Oh, Gerald!" Romy said, her face beaming. "Remember that incident a few days ago. The one I told you about something forcing me to give this woman our business card. How it had upset me so much. I had forgotten all about it, but that's why they are here. They found us!"

"You gave our card to her?" He glanced at Margaux, who shrugged her shoulders.

"Yes. I didn't think she would come, but she did. It's her."

Gerald let out a breath of annoyance. "Oh, great! Now why would she come? I thought you had told her to rip it up?"

"I did! I really did! And well, obviously, she didn't rip it up. She said she had been given a strange message through her mind to come to the address on the card. To us! She brought her friend with her." Romy looked at Byron with a sigh. "Oh and I'm so, so glad she did. Be grateful, Gerald. He saved your life."

"Of course I'm grateful. Where's Arnold? Is he all right?" Gerald asked trying to lift himself once again to no avail. He was still too weak.

"I'm here, Gerald". The big–boned, tall man with the white-gold hair turned away from the window. "Relax, I'm fine. I agree with Romy entirely. We were lucky to have them both here. I could not have lifted this monstrosity all by myself, even with Romy's help." He extended his hand to Byron. "Many thanks, man."

"No problem." Byron shook his hand. "Looks like we are stranded, now." He glanced at the window behind Arnold. "There's very little chance to get an ambulance for Gerald in all this damage outside."

"I agree," Arnold replied, as he looked back out the window. "No telling whether there might be more quakes coming. We would all need to stay put and hunker down here for the moment. At least we have food and water. And you for our medic." He slapped at Byron.

Byron grinned.

"More quakes coming? What are you talking about?" Margaux protested. "We aren't even on a fault line. The Jezebel fault line is on the other side of this country. Under the ocean, actually. What are you talking about?"

Arnold took a deep breath. He turned around to face them. "You are correct, Margaux. We are not on a fault line. But we are on top of something much, much bigger than a fault line. We are on Vulculcan's Folly, what's known as a supervolcano. We all of us here are but a small speck in a huge caldera stretching out for hundreds of miles around. So, in essence, what we had gone through with the earthquakes, one after another the past several hours, were likely the result of a mantle uprising from within the earth."

"But, how would you know all that?" Byron asked in amazement.

"He's a geologist specializing in volcanoes," Gerald explained, once again lifting his body up on Romy's lap, this time successfully. "Meet our good friend, Arnold von Grappelin. From Germany. He now works for the USGS. He's done research on the mantle below the earth on his own, which is why he is here with us. Arnold also shares our philosophy."

"Oh, what philosophy is that?" Margaux asked. Byron nodded in agreement. He was interested, too.

"Extraterrestrials and their history on earth." Gerald smiled. "We believe that extraterrestrials had been here on earth for millennia. The evidence is all around us and we are working to prove it. No easy task, you know. And it seems like they were responsible for creating Vulculcan's Folly, hence the name."

"No kidding?" Byron said. "All kidding set aside, extraterrestrials created a supervolcano? And how on earth did they do that?"

"Simple. According to Quashone legend, a sky being came down from the heavens in a roaring dragon, spewing fire and smoke from its mouth. Ultimately the dragon stood suspended in the sky above the ground not too far from here in Artemis' Realm."

"Oh great, a fairytale story." Byron rolled his eyes.

Margaux shushed him. "Let him finish."

"Suddenly, according to the legend, a strong beam of light shot out from the dragon's mouth and hit the earth, burning the ground around it. The light stayed there for quite some time before disappearing back into the dragon's mouth. What's remarkable is the mention of a whine that accompanied the light beam. The native Quashone tribe, who lived in the area at that time, thousands of years ago, declared it was quite loud and hurt their ears."

"Still, it doesn't tell me how the supervolcano was created." Byron pressed on. He wasn't convinced.

"I'm getting there." Gerald patiently raised his hand. He nodded at Arnold. "Arnold, it's actually your specialty. So, why don't you finish up this 'fairytale'?" Arnold grinned. Crossing his arms defiantly, he turned to Margaux and Byron.

"Well, between Gerald and me, our work and expertise, our fervent belief in the QET philosophy, we came to this conclusion, mind you, our own conclusion, that the dragon was actually a spaceship, to which the ancient Quashone had no reference for in their time frame. To them this spaceship largely resembled the image of an iconic dragon breathing fire and smoke. Does that make sense?"

Margaux nodded. Somehow, it did make sense. Still unconvinced, Byron eyed him skeptically. "Go on."

"Well, we also came to this conclusion, again, our conclusion, that this spaceship must have had extraterrestrials inside it working with technology far superior to ours, even at this time period. We believe the extraterrestrials were trying to create a hollow earth for themselves, whether to examine and monitor the Quashone people or for personal habitation away from the curious eyes of the primitive inhabitants. We do not know. We can only speculate that somehow the light beam hit a mantle. Not once, not twice, but several times with each return of the spaceship for who knows how long." Arnold breathed out slowly. "Remember, at that time, thousands of years ago, it was a dormant supervolcano, the mantle just slowly moving around in response to the earth's rotation. No one at that time, not even the Quashone was aware of its existence."

Gerald excitedly entered the conversation. "Now, my turn!"

"And so it goes, see, the light beam activated the mantle below, heating the molten rock up to enormous proportions for miles around underground. The gas and steam activated by the heat had no place to escape, so it pushed up, causing the ground to swell. It pushed and pushed up, until the entire supervolcano exploded outwards, obliterating everything in its surroundings, including the original Quashone tribe that were living there at that time. It took thousands of years for the land to recover. Eventually, a new group of Quashone from the southwest arrived to encamp in that same area where their ancestors lived."

"Something's missing. How was the legend formed if the original Quashone tribe was destroyed by the supervolcano?" Margaux pointed out. Byron nodded. It didn't make sense.

Romy burst out excitedly. "Let me tell them!"

"See, we found stone runes with hieroglyphs carefully carved and buried in Artemis' Realm near Chaparral Sky, and ancient Quashone civilization now in ruins. Anyways, we had to bring in an expert familiar with the ancient Quashone language. We were fortunate to find one with the help of our benefactor."

"That's right!" Gerald interrupted, nodding in agreement. "It was the messages in those runes and the drawings in a cave at Chaparral Sky that enabled us to come to this awful conclusion that perhaps the extraterrestrials did something either utterly stupid, that is, they had to know a powerful stream of hot mantle was underground in that area they were focusing the light beam, or they were being utterly reckless, killing the original Quashone tribe, as a result. The name, Vulculcan's Folly is right there in the stone runes written in their ancient language."

"What's Vulculcan's Folly?" Byron asked. It was an unusual name.

"It's a Quashone's derivative of the name Vulcan, the Greek god of fire and ironsmithing. They called the flying dragon by that name." Gerald explained. "I believe that's it, right, Arnold?"

Arnold nodded. "That's it. I agree with Gerald. There could be good and bad extraterrestrials, just like us. We think they were probably the bad ones."

Gerald nodded. "But again, they are only theories based on circumstantial evidence like the stone runes. We need more proof."

"No need to convince me." Margaux smiled. "I'm quite taken in." She turned to Byron. "What do you think, Byron?"

"Well, in my opinion, it's still a fairytale story." Byron scratched his head. "Okay, then. Here's my question. How does all this relate to what is happening right now with the earthquakes?"

"Your turn." Gerald grinned at Arnold.

"Well, right now the mantle is heating up and forcing the ground to rise, releasing energy and thereby causing the earthquakes. See, irrespective of extraterrestrials, let's focus on the geology of the earth itself. The mantle had been heating up for a long, long time, you know, the gases and steam rising towards the ground up, pushing the land up." Arnold demonstrated the effect with his hands. "You can probably see some changes already in certain places at Artemis' Realm. Like more steam coming up in the hot springs. The mud pots bubbling more and more. If you look carefully, you can probably see a rise in the ground here and there. Things like that."

"Good lord!" Byron exclaimed slapping his head. "That explains the sand embankments on the trails at Artemis' Realm and the land around Loch Tallulah. They have gotten bigger over time, at least to my observation."

The others and Margaux looked at Byron questioningly. Dolly barked helpfully.

He grinned. "I like to drive my banged-up jeep on the trails there."

"Oh. Us, too!" Gerald grinned slapping Byron's hand.

"So, in your opinion, Arnold, the ground is rising more and more and we are getting earthquakes, as a result. Where is all this leading to?" Margaux asked crossing her arms.

The others looked at Arnold, hopefully. Dolly barked again.

"I'm not quite sure." Arnold declared gravely, putting a hand on his chin. "Basically, we are overdue for a major explosion at Vulculcan's Folly, we just don't know when. The last one that obliterated the Quashone tribe happened 820,000 years ago. We might or might not get another one right now. We just don't know."

Gerald and Romy nodded together.

Margaux said nothing. She didn't like the response. And all this information was too much to absorb all at once. She did not know what to make of it now. First, the mysterious, dark eyes had sent her here and that had been her primary focus. And now, it was getting stranger by the minute with all this new information on a supervolcano she wasn't even aware of.

"Guys, help me onto that sofa over there!" Gerald pointed to the dark-green, suede loveseat nestled at the far corner of the room. "I'm feeling much better now, thanks to you, Byron."

"Ah, that's better." Gerald sighed, as Romy tucked a woolen Quashone blanket on his body. "Now, let's find out why you two are really here." He looked at Margaux and Byron pointedly. "I'm still curious about it. It all seems so strange what happened between you and Romy back then at the doctor's office. Let me ask you again, why did you come here?"

"Well, apparently Margaux had an experience with a paranormal phenomena in her home," Byron said. "Something about the dark, almond-shaped eyes showing up and a voice in her mind telling her to come here based on an address she had with her. I'm not able to confirm anything, because I couldn't see the eyes or hear the voice. Correct, Margaux?"

Margaux nodded. "The eyes made me come here. The eyes won't tell me why. Do you know why?"

Gerald looked at Romy. Romy nodded at him gravely.

"Well, we think we know why, but there is only one way to find out." Gerald looked directly at Margaux. "We would need to put you under."

Arnold nodded, crossing his arms. "Yes, that is a good solution to a mystery."

Romy clapped her hands. "I will put you under!"

Margaux's eyes widened. Dolly lifted her head.

"What?" Byron became alarmed. He put his arms around Margaux protectively. "What the hell are you talking about?"

Gerald raised his hand. "No worries, Byron. Relax. My wife is a hypnotist. She can help us find out why the eyes sent you here. That is, if you want to know why."

"How?"

"It's called regression. It is a complicated process, but Romy has done this hundreds of times. It's the only way we can find out about the eyes. We have to go through her subconscious."

Romy nodded, bursting with confidence. "That's right, Byron! That's how I can find the information about the eyes. It's all in there, her subconscious."

"But how?" Margaux interrupted. "Why is it in my subconscious?"

Romy chattered excitedly, moving about the room. "It would seem that someone, something, put the information in there. See, the information is safer in your subconscious. Perhaps all along, the extraterrestrials, that's what I call the eyes, do not want you to know their agenda, at least not yet. So, the logical place would be to put the information in the subconscious." She reached out for Margaux's hands. "See, Margaux, they sent you here, because I'm the only one that can help you find the answer."

Margaux was stunned. Anastasia had said something to that effect. Find three friends who will help you. Gerald, Romy, and Arnold.

"Extraterrestrials again?" Byron lifted his eyebrows, not hiding the sarcasm in his voice. "More fairytales?" It was getting worse than weird. It was getting too spooky for his taste. He wasn't going to subject Margaux to this regression, whatever that was. "What if something goes wrong?"

"It won't." Gerald reassured them. "Like I said, Romy has done it many times. Mostly related to people wanting to know their past lives, which has helped them tremendously to resolve the problems in their current lives." Gerald breathed in slowly. "But, in this case, we need to find out about the eyes. Again, the information is definitely in her subconscious and the regression is the only way to find out."

Arnold nodded. He walked towards Byron and placed his hand on his shoulder. "I understand. I used to be a skeptic, until I had it done on me. And Gerald's absolutely right. It's nothing to be afraid of. You need to keep an open mind."

Byron shook his head. "I really don't get it. Why don't the eyes tell her what they want her to know?"

Gerald lifted his eyebrows. "You're right. Perhaps something is preventing them from communicating with her directly, and they are pushing her to us. To Romy. We can help."

"I'll do it!" Margaux declared, pushing herself away from Byron's grip. She looked at Romy pointedly. "And Romy knows what to do. You guys wouldn't do this if it wasn't safe, right?"

Romy, Gerald, and Arnold nodded in agreement.

"Every regression has its risks, but yes, for the most part, it is quite safe," Gerald replied. "All Romy has to do is put you into a deep state of sleep, so that we can disconnect your conscious mind and call upon the subconscious mind."

"Don't worry, Margaux," Romy said. "We will be keeping an eye on you at all times, while we access your subconscious. Byron can watch if he wants."

"I most certainly will watch." Byron declared. "I still don't like this."

Margaux smiled at him. "Byron, darling, I'm not afraid. I want to do this. And, you know what? If I do this, then maybe, just maybe, the eyes will leave me alone."

Byron nodded. He still felt uneasy about it.

Margaux turned towards Romy. "Okay, I'm ready. What now?"

"I need you to lie down and be comfortable, Margaux," Romy said, placing her arm under Margaux's. "This process could take a while. The large bed in our bedroom would be ideal. Let's go there. Arnold, can you and Byron bring Gerald into the bedroom? There's an armchair in there for him."

Dolly followed behind, wagging her tail.

Chapter 41

MARGAUX FELT SLEEPY, VERY SLEEPY. She was stretched out comfortably on the bed. In a few seconds, her body felt limp as she entered the deep REM state of sleep. Sitting on the edge of the bed, Romy gave her firm instructions to withdraw her fully conscious mind and let the subconscious appear.

"You understand you will have no control, once your subconscious takes over. It will tell you where to go. You must follow its direction. You will not be harmed, Margaux, I will make sure of that."

Margaux nodded. She grasped Romy's hand and squeezed it. "Let's do this."

Byron watched with apprehension from the far end of the bedroom, where he had a full view of Margaux on the bed. Dolly sat obediently by his foot. The fiercely loyal puppy had seemed loathe to leave Margaux's side, adamantly refusing to get off the bed, threatening to nip anyone who dared touch her.

From the other end of the bedroom, Arnold quietly stood next to the armchair, where the men had deposited the wounded Gerald.

"Now. Go back in time, Margaux, back to where the subconscious wants you to see," Romy said. "You will know what you are looking for when you fly into the air and look down upon the earth."

Margaux nodded obediently. Her eyes closed, as the wispy, white clouds filled the inner chambers of her mind like a veil. She felt herself leave her body and fly away.

After a few seconds passed, Margaux found herself lying naked on the ground. A man was on top of her, making love to her. She reached out with her hand and felt a cold, hard boulder embedded on the ground beside her. She looked up and saw that it was early morning, the sky just changing from the bold orange-purple-pink sheen into the bright white-and-blue patina typical of the breaking daylight.

She was obviously outside somewhere, but she could not yet identify the place. And yet it was so beautiful. So peaceful. So romantic.

Margaux looked over in front of herself. Her arms were around this muscled, male stranger and together they were making passionate love. Then this stranger relaxed, his head resting on her shoulder, his arms around her body, breathing softly. Margaux noted he had dark, curly hair. She softly brushed her hand through the thick locks. He lifted his head.

"Oh my god, BYRON!"

Her stunned scream echoed around the room, startling all who watched patiently. Dolly quickly lifted her head, growling. All eyes were on Margaux wondering what she had seen. No one was allowed to touch her, only Romy with her vast experience with regression.

"Romy?" Byron demanded. He was becoming very worried.

Margaux's body sprang up from the bed, her eyes wide open, as if in shock.

Byron made a move towards Margaux. Dolly followed suit.

"No, Byron." Gerald commanded from the far corner of the room. "Your interference will harm the process. We could even lose Margaux. Please stand by and let my wife do her work."

"Oh," Margaux sighed deeply, as her body reclined back onto the bed. Her body started to twitch and she called out Byron's name, once again.

"What's happening?" Byron insisted. "I must know, please. Can't you see, she is calling out for me."

Romy raised her hand, silencing him. "This is normal, Byron. It's all part of her discovery process under regression. Trust me, she is fine, but if we interrupt her now without coalescing back her conscious personality, we will surely lose her."

"Pull him back." Gerald ordered his friend. "He must not break Romy's control."

Arnold reached out for Byron's arm. Byron stepped back, almost tripping over Dolly, who promptly headed to the armchair and lay down.

Romy caressed Margaux's forehead and instructed her to relax and let her subconscious lead her.

Margaux closed her eyes. This time she found herself again in Byron's arm, in yet another place unknown to her, their naked bodies entwined once again and they were kissing passionately. All around them was a very wide lake of blue-green water and rows upon rows of thick, leafy trees along its perimeter. And then suddenly a bright light beam came upon them, enclosing them completely. The starry-eyed couple looked up above them first and then at each other in utter alarm. At that moment, Margaux felt herself being pulled away from Byron's arms, quickly floating upwards towards an open, black void.

Then darkness fell over her. Margaux moaned softly, shaking her head, side by side, on the bed. It was becoming a nightmare.

Romy caressed Margaux's forehead, hoping to lend some form of comfort. She called upon the subconscious.

"What are you showing Margaux now?" Romy whispered softly. "What do you see, Margaux?"

"Light. I see light. Blinding, white light pulling me up into a dark hole in the sky. I don't know what that is. I can't see Byron anymore. I'm scared. So scared." Margaux whispered frantically, her body tense with fright, as she tried to get out of the bed.

Romy restrained her, carefully placing Margaux's head against the pillow. "Relax, Margaux. I would not put you in danger. The subconscious will not do that to you."

Margaux nodded.

"Follow its lead. What do you see, now?" Romy asked her, her curiosity fully aroused. Clearly, this was the mark of an abduction. By extraterrestrials. In her past.

Romy glanced at Gerald, who urged her to keep going. This was important for their work.

"Where are you, now, Margaux? What is your subconscious showing you?"

"Cold. So cold. So hard. So dark. I...don't know where I am."

Margaux found herself lying on a cold, steel table, her wrists and ankles handcuffed with cold, steel clamps. She lifted her head and saw that she was naked and all around her was a vacuum of nothingness infused with a strange, shadowy mist. No walls and, horrors of horrors, no floor either.

Margaux looked to her right. She could see Byron clearly now. He was lying still on the same cold, steel table, his wrists and ankles also locked by the clamps. She wasn't sure if he was breathing. She tried to call out his name, but her instincts told her to keep quiet.

Something or somebody was coming.

With a pained effort, she lifted her head and looked ahead in front of her. She could see a lone figure slowly approach her table. It wasn't human. Standing almost 4 feet tall, it was naked with gray skin and almost seemed to glide in the air, as it came closer and closer to her. Once over her table, she had a better look at it. This strange being looking over her had a large elongated head with bulbous, liquid, dark eyes stretched out towards the ears.

"Oh my God, the eyes! The eyes!"

Margaux struggled to move out of the bed. Romy attempted to restrain her, holding her shoulders down, but Margaux was too strong for her.

"Byron!" Romy pleaded urgently. "Right now, I do need your help to hold her down. The subconscious is not finished with her, yet. We are getting closer to its message, but the process is clearly frightening her. She needs to relax, so I can pull her out in time. Please help me."

Gerald nodded at Arnold, who let go of Byron's arm.

Byron firmly put his hands on Margaux's resistant shoulders. For some time, she fought his hold against her, yelling out, "No, no, no, the eyes, let me out of there, please!"

Dolly looked up and growled. Arnold picked her up and stood beside Gerald. It would not do for Dolly to interrupt the process, now in its deepest, most vulnerable stage.

Romy once again stroked Margaux's hair and sweat-soaked forehead, chanting soft words of encouragement to keep going, wherever she was in this process. They were almost there. She had found the eyes. Keep going. She must trust her subconscious, for it will not allow her to be hurt. And neither would Romy.

Margaux nodded and once again, her body went limp. Byron slowly removed his hands from her shoulders and sat in tense anticipation by her side, ready to restrain her, if necessary.

Gerald and Arnold waited, nodding at each other in approval at the progress of the regression. She found the eyes. She would soon find her message. They were anxious to know what the message was.

"Arnold, please go make some chamomile tea for Margaux," Romy instructed. "She will need it when she wakes up. We are almost there."

Placing the squirming Dolly in Gerald's arm, Arnold left the bedroom.

For a time, Margaux stayed under, moving her head back and forth, clearly distraught. Byron put his hand softly against her left shoulder, hoping his familiar touch would comfort her, wherever she was in her regression journey.

He looked at Romy, who shook her head slightly. Mustn't touch her, now, not yet. It would be dangerous to wake her up so soon.

Byron sat by helplessly, as he watched Margaux mumble unintelligible words. It was as if she was talking to someone else in a different language, a foreign language, albeit one he was not familiar with.

Again, he looked at Romy, who shook her head. She didn't know the language, either, but they had to keep going or they will never get the message from the eyes. Byron nodded, but he was not convinced.

He wondered if the information Margaux was gathering was causing her suffering, because the information was so terrible. He wanted so badly to wake her up and hold her against him and tell her that he loved her and that this was all crazy and it was not worth the effort. But he also knew that they needed to know the information or the eyes would never leave Margaux alone.

Another half hour passed. Romy worried. Never before had she performed a regression that took this long. They could lose Margaux.

Suddenly, Margaux lifted her head from the pillow. She smiled and called out, "Goodbye!" She waved at the ceiling.

Byron looked up. There was nothing on the ceiling.

At that moment, Romy knew it was time. Time for the subconscious to leave. Time to integrate Margaux's full consciousness and wake her up. "One…, two…, three!"

Margaux's eyes opened instantly. She turned to see Byron sitting on the edge of the bed, clearly worried. She smiled at him knowingly, placing her hand on his cheek. Byron looked at her questioningly. She had been distressed for some time under regression and now she was happy. What had happened in there?

"Help me lift her up, Byron," Romy instructed. Byron did so. She placed more pillows behind Margaux and he laid her back.

Margaux sighed, snuggling her head against the pillows. She was so tired. She smiled lovingly at Byron. He lifted his eyebrow at her. What?

Arnold entered the bedroom carrying a silver tray containing a porcelain blue mug of steaming chamomile tea. He placed the tray carefully on Margaux's lap. She thanked him. He smiled warmly at her. "Welcome back, Margaux. It wasn't so bad, was it?"

Margaux shook her head. No, it wasn't that bad, although she did have some moments that scared her shitless. But, in point of fact, with all that she had encountered in her regression, she had managed to collect more information than she had bargained for.

And it was incredible news, even to her.

Margaux picked up the porcelain mug and sipped the hot calming tea. She breathed in deeply, inhaling the tea's fragrant essence.

The others waited patiently, holding their breaths. Margaux placed the steaming mug onto the tray and looked around the room. She smiled joyfully.

"I have a child," she announced, her eyes brimming with tears of happiness. "My own flesh and blood child."

Romy, Gerald, and Arnold were mesmerized.

Byron was terribly confused. Earlier, she had told him only that she was divorced with no children. And worse still, she had no ovaries, so she could never have children. She didn't even know why they were gone. She didn't want to find out, either. Her adamant response to keep it under wraps had been strange, but he ultimately made peace with it himself, only because he loved Margaux, her beauty, compassion, and strength of will. Not to mention her intelligence. And yet, coming from her, this news was entirely startling. Incomprehensible, largely because he was the only love in her life after the divorce.

He was at a loss for words.

"Go on, Margaux." Romy encouraged her. "We're all listening. Remember, you are in a safe place with us. The child you gave birth to. Is that what they told you when you were under? Is that what they wanted you to know?"

"Not they." Margaux shook her head. "*It*. There was only one being in that dark, unfamiliar place. It didn't give me a name. It only talked to me in my mind in an ancient language. You probably heard me saying the words." She looked around.

"Yes, we heard you, Margaux." Romy declared excitedly. "And what's more, we now know the language."

"It's ancient Sumerian." Gerald nodded. "But you spoke so fast we could not catch the words properly, much less interpret them."

"So, what did it look like?" Arnold asked. Byron nodded in agreement. He was not happy with the outcome, but damned if he was going to go away without knowing who impregnated his beloved Margaux with a child. It felt like an outright violation to his senses.

Margaux's eyes became vacant, as if she was in a world of her own. For a moment, she did not utter a word. The others waited patiently. It had to be done at her pace. She had gone through a lot in the process.

Margaux sighed and sipped her tea. She looked up and smiled. "From what I remember, the being didn't look human to me. What's more it had those eyes I kept seeing all my life. Huge, dark, almond-shaped eyes with an elongated head."

"Go get that book, Romy, darling, in the living room," Gerald said. "We have something to show you, Margaux."

In a few seconds, Romy appeared with the book. She placed it on Margaux's lap and opened it to a bookmarked page.

"Is that it, Margaux?" Romy asked, pointing to an illustration. "Are those the eyes that followed you all of your life?"

Margaux nodded. "Oh, yes, yes, yes. That's what I saw. She looked up at Romy. "What are they?"

"What you saw, Margaux." Gerald interrupted. "Was what we call "The Grays". You are not the only one who has seen them. But you are definitely the only one we know of so far who has managed to at least communicate with one of them, face to face, in a language no one knows today. About a child, no less. Amazing."

Arnold nodded gravely.

"The Grays?" Byron asked. He reached out for the book. "Let me see." He stared at the page for a moment trying to wrap his mind around what Margaux had just communicated. "I still don't get it. This 'It' told her she had a child? This doesn't make any sense at all. Did any of you know she can't have a child?"

Perplexed, Romy, Gerald, and Arnold stared at Margaux.

"It's true." Margaux explained sadly. "I don't have any ovaries. They disappeared just like that one day in my twenties. My doctor thinks it's genetic. I never bothered to follow up on it. I didn't want to."

Romy clapped her hands excitedly. She and Gerald nodded. Somehow the Grays had a hand in this. It was the only obvious conclusion. But how? And why?

"Go on." Romy urged Margaux. "What else did this being say to you?"

"Well, it said the child was born of a love between myself and someone else. A human being."

"Someone else? Human?" Byron felt his stomach churn with the pangs of jealousy. He needed to know who had been fucking with his beloved Margaux. He had thought he was the only one. "Was there someone else?" He was becoming enraged at Margaux.

Margaux slowly turned towards Byron. She shook her head and reached out for his hand, grasping it tightly.

"Darling Byron, that stranger, that human being that made love to me… it was you."

The room suddenly became deathly quiet. Dolly laid down her head and whined. All eyes turned towards Byron, holding hands with Margaux, his entire being in utter shock. He quickly let go of Margaux and stood up from the bed, backing away.

He shook his head in disbelief. "Not possible!" He protested. "We've only just met, Margaux and I. And yes, last night, we did have sex admittedly. But no. No way there is a child. Like I said before, it's impossible."

He leaned heavily against the wall, at a loss for words. If it was true what Margaux had just revealed, then a child existed somewhere. His child. But how?

"Oh, but there is a child, Byron. You and I, we made a child." Margaux smiled warmly. She reached out to him again, but he did not take her hand. It was getting too creepy for him. "Apparently, you and I go way back, Byron. All the way back to my senior year at Crooked Oak High School."

"What? Senior year? But that's too long ago. Almost ten years ago," Byron replied aghast. "Impossible. I would have remembered it. I would have remembered you. "He pressed his hand on his forehead. "I just don't remember anything that far back."

Margaux smiled with compassion. "It's true, Byron. The Grays erased your memories of me. They had to."

She gestured him to come to her. "See, It told me to lock eyes with you and your memories will come back. They will reach you through my eyes. Just please come here and look into my eyes."

Byron stood still against the wall, hesitant to comply. This was worse than creepy. It was truly bizarre.

"Please, Byron, please. At least, do this for me."

"Jesus Christ!" Byron declared, his eyes locked into hers for several long seconds. Images of Margaux appeared in his mind. A teenage Margaux at the pool. The same Margaux riding the jeep with him at Artemis' Realm and both of them making love by a cliffside near a tall, standing bluestone. Margaux and he sucked up into the sky by a strange, light beam. And the last image he saw was finding himself lost near Loch Tallulah, naked and confused, with no memory of his time with Margaux or her existence at all, just a bunch of clothes he had found in his jeep.

Margaux blinked her eyes and pulled away. Byron was jolted back into reality. "Now, do you believe me?"

"But why?" Byron demanded gripping her shoulders. He needed answers. "Why abduct us? And more importantly, why erase our memories? I had no idea I knew you that far back."

Arnold stepped forward.

Margaux raised her hand to stop him. She shook her head. "Let me deal with him." She grasped Byron's hands, removing them forcibly from her shoulders. "Stop it, Byron. You're hurting me. I can explain."

"Explain away!" Byron exclaimed. "Why did they take our child away from us, if it is true at all?"

"It was necessary to take the child away and to make sure we didn't remember being abducted by them or even each other after they brought us back to earth. They do that to everyone they abduct, not only us."

"Fine. So they deliberately erased our memories from that far back. Why the hell did they not at least leave our child with you?"

"Because then I would be forced to find you, the child's father. How in the world am I going to convince you about what happened to us with your memories erased. You would have condemned me as insane."

"That's true." Byron admitted, scratching his head. He calmed down. "And now? Why are we being given all this astounding information."

Margaux sighed wearily. "I really don't know why, Byron. It didn't say why exactly, just that it was following orders from a higher power. It told me we needed to go to Loch Tallulah and wait for them there. Tonight."

"What? You've got to be kidding me?" Byron jumped up from the bed in surprise. "Tell me, you're joking, Margaux, because it is not funny. And no, I'm not listening to this drivel anymore. I'm not going anywhere with It or the Grays, or whatever they are called, and for that matter, neither are you."

He backed away staring at Margaux in confusion.

"Is any of this real?" he demanded of Margaux. "Do you realize how crazy stupid all this sounds?"

Romy, Gerald, and Arnold said nothing, letting the fight play out on its own. Dolly lay down and whimpered.

Margaux fought back. "Yes, Byron, I do realize how crazy stupid it sounds, but believe me, it was real, at least to me. Whatever I went through in this regression, it was real. All of it." Margaux implored with firm conviction. "It was as real back there then all those years ago as where I am right now. And so yes, I believe it. And them."

She pointed at Romy, Gerald, and Arnold.

Byron was astounded. "You believe all this malarkey?"

Margaux lifted her chin determinedly. "Yes, I do." She looked at Byron with stubborn determination in her eyes. "What's more, Byron, I do believe we had a child and they have our child. And we are supposed to go meet them tonight at Loch Tallulah. If you do not want to come with me, I can't help that, but I am definitely going to go and find my child."

Margaux smiled. "There's one more thing I need to tell you. It's important."

"What?" Byron asked bracing himself for the news.

"I saw those eyes on your face, not once, but twice. Both times at Mirrington County Airport. It explained that it was the only way to communicate to me and let me know you had a significant part in my life. The only way to do that without violating their Primary Principle."

Byron groaned, grabbing his temples with his hands. This was too fantastic to wrap his mind around. He did not even know where to begin.

"So, the eyes were trying to communicate with you all these years? It seemed more like scaring the hell out of you. Why and what the hell is the Primary Principle?"

Margaux shook her head wearily. "I don't know, Byron. It keeps telling me they were under orders from a higher power. You're right, they were frustrated because instead of communicating with me, they ended up scaring me over and over. But they had to try to get us back together one way or another. That's what it was all about all those years."

"Jesus H. Christ," Byron groaned.

"Wow!" Romy whispered softly. Gerald and Arnold nodded in agreement. It was indeed stunning news.

Margaux turned towards Romy, Gerald, and Arnold. She smiled knowingly. "There is something you guys should know, but there is no time to talk about it now. We, too, go way back."

Romy, Gerald, and Arnold simply stared at her dumbstruck at the news.

She turned towards Byron, reaching out for his hand. "So, are you coming with me?"

Byron nodded. "Only way to find out if it's real. Let's go, Margaux. Loch Tallulah is a full two hours' drive south."

Margaux removed the tray from her lap. "Help me out of this bed, Byron. I want to thank our friends before we leave. None of this would have happened if not for their help. Anastasia was right after all."

"Who's Anastasia?" Byron demanded confounded. Not another mystery to deal with.

"Another time, Byron. I promise you. Too complicated to explain now. Help me get up."

But it was too late. The floor started to move. Dolly barked and growled, her instincts on high alert. Margaux stumbled back onto the bed, pulling Byron down with her.

"Hang on!" Arnold shouted, as he gripped one arm of the chair where Gerald was seated. Romy hung on to the other arm. "The earthquake. It's coming back. Hang on to something."

Dolly barked furiously at the doorway. "Come on, let's get out of here."

The earth rumbled and shook. The floor rolled up and down in waves. The bed, armchair, and furniture perilously snaked around the room, in response to the rapidly shifting floor. The teacup clattered around the tray, before it fell on the floor in several, broken pieces.

Byron reached for Margaux and held her tightly to him. Dolly gave up barking and joined the couple on the bed. Romy and Arnold held on for dear life at each side of the seated Gerald. But the earthquake would not die down.

"Come on!" Gerald shouted at the others. "Let's get to my jeep and on the road. No telling how long this shaking will last. Dolly is right, you know. I'm not staying put. It's too dangerous. And besides, we need to get Margaux and Byron to Artemis' Realm by day's end. The Grays are waiting for them." He pointed to the ceiling.

"Are you crazy, Gerald? On the road like this?" Romy yelled at him. "No telling if the road will open up and swallow us."

"At least, we'll be out there and moving." Gerald yelled back. "We could get lucky and find safe ground somehow, somewhere, even at Artemis' Realm. Staying here like this is really not safe, Romy. The whole building could crumble down upon us."

"I vote to leave." Arnold yelled. "It's better to move, if we are careful about it, if we are three steps ahead of the earthquake. Like Gerald said, we could get lucky."

Margaux and Byron nodded in agreement. They both struggled to get up from the shuddering bed.

Romy shrugged her shoulders. Why not?

Dolly jumped down helpfully and headed towards the door.

Chapter 42

By EARLY EVENING, JUST AS the blue sky slowly transformed into the charcoal shade of twilight, the battered olive-drab Jeep Cherokee finally veered right into Grey Snake Trail. The motley group of Margaux, Byron, Dolly, and their newly-found eccentric friends had driven the past two hours towards Loch Tallulah. Time after time, the tenacious jeep narrowly escaped giant cracks that appeared on the asphalt surface of the superhighway. The earth seemed to bellow in all its anger, causing trees to topple and structures to disintegrate before their very eyes.

"What about the Grenoble Dam that powers the city?" Romy screamed in alarm, looking around in terror for a monstrous wall of water. "It might burst anytime! What are we gonna do?"

"Will you shut up, Romy!" Gerald yelled at his wife sitting next to him. "Try not to think about it. We gotta keep moving."

"I agree!" Arnold shouted out, as the jeep dodged several more cracks along the superhighway. "Let's focus on getting Margaux to Loch Tallulah. The aliens obviously want her badly. And I for one want to know why she is so important to them."

"God! Is that all Margaux is to you?" Romy spat at him, hitting his shoulder with her fist in disgust. "I'm actually afraid for her."

"Sorry." Arnold apologized, glancing at Byron, who was still struggling at the wheel of the jeep, lost in his own thoughts.

Arnold looked back at the others. "I didn't mean it that way, you know. But you got to admit it. This is big news for our QET work. First contact."

"He's right," Gerald added solemnly. "I too want to know where all this is leading. But don't worry, Margaux, your safety is paramount with us."

"Thank you, Gerald, that means a lot to me. Before I forget, do you remember the young woman you picked up on a road trip many years ago in this very trail?" He nodded.

"Well, that woman was me."

"Shit, Margaux! You came back to us! We are all together again!" Romy squealed.

"Amazing." Gerald said. "Romy's right. We are all together again."

"Full circle." Arnold added with a punch from his fist. "It must be some sort of karma to bring us all together like this. I wonder why."

"A friend from long ago said something to this effect," Margaux replied mysteriously. "She said 'Find three friends who will help you.'"

"Find three friends who will help you?" Gerald repeated carefully. "Is there more to it? I'm just curious."

Margaux laughed. "She told me to go where it's white and blue, which happened to be a swimming pool complex. It's where I somehow got back together with Byron. Don't ask how. It's too complicated to explain."

Margaux quickly glanced at Byron. His face was grim and contorted, drenched with sweat from the stress of the drive the past 2 hours. He was completely oblivious to the conversations. Only one thing mattered to him. They needed to get there on time.

Byron felt for the gun securely strapped within his belt. The Beretta M9 had been offered by Gerald when they were running from the crumbling apartment building. He had gratefully accepted the gun, a much-needed weapon for this mystifying escapade. He might need to use it to retrieve their child.

After making that right turn, Byron stopped the jeep in front of the gate, shutting the ignition off. He grasped the steering wheel and sighed dejectedly in front of him. The beautiful, black Victorian gate was broken from its foundation. It was twisted halfway towards the ground, blocking their way into the trail. To his left, the wooden sign lay shattered on the pulverized earth.

He smiled grimly at the irony of the words at the bottom of the sign: *Enter at Your Own Risk.*

"Arnold, I need your help to push the gate away."

"Sure." Arnold opened the door to let himself out.

"I'm coming!" Margaux offered.

"Me too!" Romy added, leaving Gerald all by himself with Dolly. "You'll be okay by yourself, won't you, Gerald?"

Gerald pushed her out of the door. "Don't worry, Romy, darling. Go on. Dolly here will keep me company." He rubbed Dolly's furry head. "Right, Dolly?"

Dolly barked and settled onto his lap.

Suddenly the earthquake stopped and all was quiet. The earth no longer rumbled and groaned. Dust settled towards the ground. The sky was still a haunting gray patina, but the group of friends could see a flock of birds flying across the twilight sky.

"It's over?" Margaux whispered by the open jeep door, her eyes searching the forest area.

"Oh, I hope so!" Romy said, shutting the jeep's door behind her. She was so happy to put her feet on solid ground, she even jumped up and down on it and kissed the earth.

"I don't want to ruin your good mood, my friends, but this respite might only be temporary," Arnold yelled, as he bent down to pick up the broken iron-wrought gate. "The pattern tells me it will happen again and the next one will be even worse, not to mention that potential giant wall of water from the dam nearby. Not sure when it's coming. We must hurry."

Byron nodded in agreement. "Let's go."

Even with all the effort of the four of them, it was hard work moving the massive, heavy gate away from the post. They needed to open it wide enough to allow the jeep to go through. Fifteen minutes of hard work, sweat, and tears. Seated at the back of the jeep, nursing his wound, Dolly on his lap, Gerald felt horribly guilty that he was too injured to help them out. He cheered them on as they mightily pushed and pushed the iron gate away from the trail.

Time seemed to move so slowly.

Finally, all four stood back and yelled in exultation, jumping up and down, their hands raised and clapping high-fives all around. Margaux and Byron embraced and kissed. From inside the jeep, Gerald raised his fist into the air, beaming with pride, yelling "All right! You guys did it! Let's go now! We have fifty-five minutes of this crazy trail to get through to the lake. Let's hustle on!"

Ten minutes later, the jeep was racing through the meandering, dirt trail. Rocks and stones were scattered pell-mell, the remnants of the last upheaval.

"Hang on!" Byron shouted, as he floored the accelerator. The jeep leapt forward, its engine roaring loudly. They were now entering the flooded creek below them, the wooden, half-bridge already disintegrated into the rushing waters.

Waves of dirty water splashed all over, as the jeep struggled to move forward against the strong, rising currents. "Come on," Byron urged the jeep. "Come on. We're almost there."

Behind him, Romy, Gerald, and Arnold silently prayed for success. Dolly whined, snuggling closer to Gerald. Margaux closed her eyes and gripped the door's handle. Finally, the jeep's front tires touched the muddy trail at the other side and, with a deafening roar, all four tires landed on the ground, rapidly leaving behind the creek.

"All right!" Byron exclaimed, raising his fist in the air.

"Yay!" The chorus of triumph resounded from the back of the jeep.

Margaux smiled with relief. She placed her hand on Byron's thigh and squeezed it gratefully.

"We're almost there," Byron announced, placing his hand on Margaux's.

In fifteen minutes, Byron slowed the jeep and peered through the grimy windshield. He pointed at the large, pristine circle of blue green water, surrounded by tall trees.

"See, there, to the right? That's Loch Tallulah." He turned to Margaux and smiled, his eyes darkening at their shared memories. He gripped Margaux's hand, his throat tight with emotion.

"Remember our lake? Swimming without our clothes in there."

The three passengers behind them pretended mightily not to hear. Arnold coughed loudly. Romy glared at him. Gerald grinned awkwardly, rubbing Dolly's head vigorously. Dolly whined.

Margaux smiled and nodded. "Only the good part, Byron, just before the abduction. Not after."

Byron did not answer. In an instant, his body slumped against the back of his seat, restrained by his seatbelt. His hands had gone limp and now lay at each side of his inert body, his head leaning downwards against his chest. His foot had dislodged itself from the pedal, leaving the jeep to slow down, moving erratically on its path to the lake.

"Oh my god, Byron!" Margaux shouted in terror. "What's happening?"

Arnold gripped Byron's shoulders from behind. "Pull up that parking brake, Margaux, and grab hold of that steering wheel. We'll end up in that lake, for Christ's sakes!"

Margaux quickly took action, pulling up the parking brake and hitting the brake with left foot, her left hand controlling the steering wheel. The jeep finally stopped at the water's edge.

Arnold let go of Byron's shoulders and slumped back onto his seat, breathing hard.

Romy silently shook her head in disbelief. She crossed herself and uttered a prayer of thanks. Gerald grinned at Margaux and gave her a thumbs up. Good work.

"Oh my God," She cried out. "What's wrong with Byron?"

"Take him outside, Arnold." Gerald instructed. "You know what to do."

Arnold lifted Byron out of the jeep. He dragged him a few feet away and laid him gently on the sandy ground. He quickly proceeded to loosen Byron's shirt. He put his hand on the neck. There was no pulse. He placed his head on Byron's chest. There was no heartbeat, either.

Arnold lifted his head and looked up. Margaux was staring down at them, her eyes beseeching him for news, any news.

He shook his head slowly.

"Noooooooooooooo!" Margaux cried, as she dropped to her knees, putting her arms around Byron, holding him tightly. "No, no, no, it can't be true. No. You can't be dead, Byron, my love! We've only just begun to live!"

Arnold placed his hand gently on Margaux. She shrugged it off, not wanting to let go of Byron. Tears brimmed in Arnold's eyes, as he nodded in understanding. He pulled himself up and walked towards the jeep, his hands in his pocket, his head hung down, leaving behind the weeping Margaux with Byron.

Dolly quickly lifted her head and jumped towards the side window of the jeep. She growled.

"Look!" Romy pointed out towards Margaux still weeping.

"Oh, shit!" Gerald exclaimed in surprise.

Puzzled, Arnold turned around and was immediately frozen in place.

All three waited with hushed breaths. Dolly barked furiously, her paws scraping on the glass.

Against the stark blackness of the night sky, coming out of nowhere near the grieving Margaux, a soft gold-white light appeared in a shimmering beam from above. Inside the light was a figure dressed in a flowing, empire-waist toga, reminiscent of the ancient Greek and Roman eras. A bright halo of light surrounded her beautiful face with high cheekbones, piercing blue eyes, and a tousle of golden hair. The shining figure looked down sadly.

Dolly barked louder and louder, refusing to leave her perch by the window.

"Oh, wow!" Romy exclaimed, placing her hands on her face in utter surprise. "She looks like Margaux. But how?" Gerald shook his head, staring in mystification at the glowing figure.

"What is she doing?" Arnold whispered, standing by the jeep. "Is this for real?"

Gerald shook his head. He did not know that, either. He had no idea what was happening. Nothing in all the years of their QET work mentioned this wondrous anomaly suspended in front of their very eyes; only gray aliens.

They could do nothing, but watch.

They dared not approach Margaux and Byron, despite the natural urge to get out of the jeep and help them, protect them. It was as if a force field had been erected around the jeep preventing them from moving forward. Even Dolly stopped barking.

Margaux looked up. "Anastasia!"

The apparition nodded and smiled gloriously at Margaux, extending her hands out toward her. All around her the warm, golden light brightened the darkness of the lake and forest, illuminating Margaux, Byron, and the jeep where Romy, Gerald, and Arnold waited. The light was so bright, it was as if the sun had returned to the sky.

But who was this strange apparition, the perfect image of Margaux herself? It was all too bizarre.

"Be not afraid, Margaux." Anastasia spoke in a soft soothing voice. "I was afraid this would happen. We know what's wrong with your love, Byron. It was too late to stop it but it is not too late to save him."

"Too late to stop what?" Margaux wailed through her tears. "What happened to him, Anastasia, and why the hell am I seeing you here just now?"

Romy, Gerald, and Arnold gasped in amazement. It was clear that Margaux knew who this apparition was, even called her by her name. Gerald wished he had his notebook and camera with him. He sighed in frustration. They were just going to have to rely on their memories when it came time to record this remarkable event. It was hard to tell whether it was supernatural or extraterrestrial or even both.

"Romy, Arnold." Gerald instructed firmly. "Focus on the interaction happening right now, all the little details too. I'm going to need your memories to record this incredibly significant incident in our QET archives, although I'm not even certain right now what the hell it is."

Romy and Arnold nodded in agreement, their eyes still fixed on the bright, gold-white light. Anastasia was talking to Margaux like a long-lost friend.

"God, I wonder who she is?" Gerald said. "I wonder what they are talking about."

"Yeah, well, I wonder why we are trapped in here." Arnold griped, pushing his hand against the air. The stiff invisible wall vehemently pushed his hand back.

"Look!" Romy declared pointing at Margaux. "She's smiling!"

Margaux nodded at Anastasia, waves of relief and happiness returning to her face. She kissed Byron's lips softly and pulled herself up.

"That's odd. I wonder what Anastasia said to her." Gerald said. "This is getting very interesting, now. We'll find out soon enough."

"I'm just as curious as you are," Arnold quipped.

Suddenly, Anastasia waved at Margaux, as she lifted her empire-waist toga and slowly dissipated into the gold-white light. In the next second, Margaux watched in astonishment as the light shot up towards the dark night sky.

Margaux stroked Byron's face with tenderness. "You are going to be all right, my love," she whispered.

"I'm getting out now," Romy declared, as she pushed open the door of the jeep. "I'm betting that force field, or whatever it is that's restraining us, is now gone with that light." Gerald nodded in affirmative. "I agree. Go on, Romy, go find out what's happening. Take Dolly with you. She's going crazy in here."

"I'm coming with you." Arnold offered.

Margaux heard footsteps approaching her. Something was rubbing against her leg. She looked down to find Dolly happily leaning against her. She picked Dolly up into her arms and held her tightly. "Byron's going to be all right, Dolly, isn't that wonderful?" Dolly licked her face happily.

"Are you all right, Margaux?" Romy asked, carefully approaching her. "Can you tell us what happened? We were worried sick back there."

"Seems your friend put some sort of force field around us," Arnold said. "It was pretty strong."

Margaux smiled radiantly. "It's going to be all right, now, Romy, Arnold. But we have to hurry. That wall of water is coming and we have to get to Anastasia's ship from another place." Startled, Romy and Arnold looked at each other and then at Margaux.

"Wall of water? You mean from that dam in the forest? It broke already?"

Margaux nodded. "What's more we have to get Byron to her quickly. She said she can bring him back to life. But there is only a one-hour window of time before his death becomes permanent."

Arnold was astounded. "Bring him back to life? But how?"

"I don't know, Arnold, and right now, I don't care." Margaux shook her head emphatically. "I just want him back alive. We must hurry now." She became frantic with worry. Dolly whimpered in her arms.

"But where?" Romy asked remaining steadfast in place. It could be a wild-goose chase for all they knew. "And who's Anastasia?"

"Yes, we watched you talk with her," Arnold added. "It's like you already knew her."

"Yes, oh, yes, I already knew her. I knew her way back when I first met Byron. We actually met through my mirror in the bathroom, imagine. And then later when I returned to Mirrington Heights after my divorce, I saw her again and again, always in that mirror. She was the one who told me to get together with Byron and find you three."

"Wow. That's amazing! Where is she from, Margaux?" Romy asked. "So, what was she, do you know?"

"Oh, Romy, I honestly don't know." Margaux smiled weakly, shrugging her shoulders. "She called herself my doppelganger when I first saw her in the mirror and said she lived in the far reaches of the universe. Light years away from us. That's all she told me. Wait, there's one more thing. She told me there is a secret that I will know when the time is right. *All in its own time,* those were her words. None of this made sense to me, so I don't know what to tell you. I only know that over the years, she was my friend, my secret friend. You three are the only ones who know right now. I know I sound crazy, but you have got to believe me."

"So that's why you are important to them," Arnold mused thoughtfully. "There is a secret affecting you. I can tell you right now this has increased my curiosity immensely."

Romy grimaced at him.

"Please, we must hurry, now!" Margaux pleaded, grabbing Romy's shoulders in desperation.

"Of course, Margaux! But hurry where?" Romy asked mystified. "Where do we go?"

"To the bluestone monument." Margaux pointed towards the trail behind her. "It's at Quashone Meadows, near a cliff. I know that place. Anastasia said today was the perfect day to create it. It won't last long, she said. And once we miss it, it's gone for another year."

"Huh?" Romy lifted her eyebrows. "Create what? What do you mean it's gone for another year?"

Margaux placed Dolly into Romy's arms.

"No time now. We really have to go. I'll explain in the jeep, I promise. Help me lift Byron." Margaux signaled to Arnold, who quickly bent down to pick up the body. "Can you drive the jeep, Arnold? Do you remember where Quashone Meadows is?" Arnold nodded, as both he and Margaux strained to place the body between them. "Yeah, I was there when we picked you up on that road trip many years ago. But I don't know where that cliff is. I've never seen it."

"Me, neither." Romy added.

"Doesn't matter." Margaux shook her head, as they dragged Byron to the jeep. "I know where that cliff is. Byron showed me long ago. Let's hurry now, please. We need to get there before it's gone."

Chapter 43

THE BATTERED JEEP CHEROKEE RUMBLED away from Loch Tallulah with Arnold at the steering wheel, nervously maneuvering it along the gravelly trail. By then, the sky was midnight black, ominously impeding a clear view of the trail, even with the jeep's weak headlights on.

Arnold peered through the windshield as he drove towards Quashone Meadows. He prayed they would get there in time. He hoped Margaux knew what she was doing. In any case, it was actually a no-win situation, as they were now faced with the grim reality of a giant wall of water coming from the broken dam. It would only be a matter of time before this monstrosity loomed over and consumed them to their deaths.

"Okay, Margaux, you promised." Romy leaned forward and put her hands on the back of the seat. "Go on, tell us some more. You promised!"

"Promised what?" Gerald asked, as he looked at Romy and then at Margaux. Arnold perked his ears and listened with interest from the driver's seat. There were two more miles to go.

Margaux smiled knowingly. "Of course, I promised you, Romy. And you should know too, Gerald, so I'm going to repeat some things." She sighed and settled back into her seat. "You see, I know that apparition you just saw out there at the lake. I know her very well. Her name is Anastasia. I encountered her in the mirror in my bathroom many years ago, actually the same year I met Byron."

"A mirror? But how?" Gerald was stunned. "Is she a ghost?"

"Yes, she came to me through the mirror and no, she's not a ghost. She says she's from another world and the mirror was the only place she could connect with me."

"And yet, here she was, in that bright, white, light, looking down at you. There was no mirror there." Gerald remarked confused.

"I know. I can't even explain that myself. I'm just as flummoxed as you." Margaux shrugged shoulders. "But see, she became my friend over the years and we chatted over the mirror like close friends many, many times. And then Byron and I got abducted by the Grays and we went our separate ways.

"Abducted by the Grays?" Romy was astounded. "What did they do to you and Byron?"

"A whole other story, Romy. No time now. Anyways, I lost Anastasia when I moved to Westbury Moor. After several years, I returned to Mirrington Heights and found her again in that mirror. And get this, she says I'm ready now, but that I must to go to where it is white and blue and then find three friends who will help me, all of which did come true, obviously, but why, I don't know. I still don't know."

"Wow," Romy declared.

Gerald nodded in agreement. He frowned. "I would be interested to know just what it is that you are ready for. It all sounds quite mysterious, even troubling. I'm guessing we'll find out soon enough."

Arnold nodded. That was the real question. Why her?

"I wish I had an answer for this, Romy, I really do. You know I would tell you if I could."

"Why not just pick us all up from where we were back there?" Gerald pointed out.

Margaux shook her head. "From what Anastasia told me back there, it was too late for the ship's shuttle to pick us up. The flood is coming quickly. But she said there was another way, a much faster way, but time is of essence and we must move quickly. It only lasts once a year."

Arnold perked his ears. "Once a year?"

"But how?" Gerald asked.

"And where?" Romy added. "Is that where we're going?"

Margaux sighed and collected herself. "Yes, that's where we are going, Romy. Anastasia said there's a point of electromagnetic upheaval near that bluestone monument. It is a naturally invisible earth phenomena that is at its strongest in the fall equinox, which is today. That bluestone monument was put there as a marker by her people, thousands of years ago."

"Whoa!" Romy murmured.

"Wow!" Gerald whispered.

"Oh boy," Arnold mumbled, narrowly avoiding a boulder in the middle of the trail. Only eight more minutes of driving. "Go on, what did your friend say about this once a year electromagnetic anomaly. What happens there at the bluestone?"

Margaux took in a deep breath. "Anastasia said we all are to go into that invisible vortex in front of the bluestone and we will all end up in a place where they can help Byron. The mothership, whatever that means."

Romy immediately lifted her arms in the air, upsetting Dolly who moved into Arnold's lap, placing her claws into his legs.

Arnold groaned painfully. "Just stay put, girl." he admonished the puppy. Dolly whined.

"Awesome, Margaux, it is so awesome!" Romy said. "The mothership! We are going to the mothership in outer space, Gerald. Oh I can't wait!"

"The mothership, of course. Directly from that vortex you just mentioned we are going to?"

Margaux nodded quickly.

"That can only mean one thing, Arnold," Gerald remarked.

Arnold nodded. "It's a wormhole."

Gerald solemnly turned to Margaux. "Margaux, this is incredible news, believe me. One question though, we are all curious here, did Anastasia say she knew what happened to Byron?"

Margaux nodded sadly. "She said he had an aneurysm hidden in a vein in his brain and it exploded just now."

"Oh man, why didn't he get a checkup? The docs would have found it earlier and done something?" Gerald asked.

"Yes, and then he would be alive right now, you know." Romy added. "Why didn't he?"

Margaux shook her head sadly. "I'm not sure, but I think I remember Byron telling me that he had a problem in his brain that caused him to be medically discharged from the army special forces, but that he wanted to focus on his PTSD problem first when he got home from the war." Tears brimmed in her eyes. "I think he eventually forgot all about it. Or didn't want to address it. I didn't realize it was so important."

"Yikes." Gerald remarked. "No wonder."

In 3 minutes, the jeep arrived at the wide mouth of the trail just before what used to be an expansive round clearing of green grass and wildflowers, now pulverized by the earthquake. Arnold stopped the jeep and shut the ignition off. He pushed Dolly off his lap and settled back on his chair, breathing a sigh of relief.

"Good job, buddy!" Gerald congratulated him. "You got us all here safely."

"Thanks, Gerald. Many thanks. I would rather not have to do this again, though." He grimaced, shaking his head at the view of the macerated meadow in front of him. He looked back at the others. "So, what now?"

"Now, we need to go find that bluestone monument." Margaux steeled herself for the unknown before her. There was no time panic. There was no room for uncertainty. "I know where it is. You guys, just follow me. Arnold, can you help me with Byron? Romy, you need to help Gerald. Just put Dolly down. She will follow us. Are you guys with me?"

Romy nodded. "Sure."

Gerald and Arnold each showed a thumbs up.

"Ok, then, Arnold, first drive down there and stop the jeep." Margaux pointed at the other end of the meadow from where they were at the mouth of the trail. Arnold groaned. Margaux ignored him.

"There's another trail in there, a much smaller one, hard to tell from here, unless you know what you are looking for. Byron showed it to me that one time we were together here in the meadow a long time ago. Just go where I'm pointing." Arnold nodded and quickly started the ignition. The jeep roared into life and groaned across the meadow fragmented with uprooted tree limbs and broken rocks.

The earth rumbled noisily beneath them. Dolly whined.

"Hurry!" Margaux shouted. "It's happening now. We have to get in there before it gets worse. And it will get worse. Anastasia said so."

"I'm hurrying as best as I can," Arnold shouted back, angrily maneuvering the steering wheel. "This jeep can only go so fast." He pushed his foot heavily down on the pedal. A crack showed up to their left, barely missing them.

"There!" Margaux shouted. "Stop the jeep now! We got to get out fast!"

Together Arnold and Margaux removed Byron's lifeless body from the jeep and settled it between them. Romy helped her husband get out of the jeep. He placed his arm around her shoulder.

The earth moved again. Dolly barked, trotting towards Margaux.

In an instant, they all disappeared into the darkened trail marked only by a tall ancient tree. Arnold noted the engraved image of what looked to be a circle with wiggling lines all around it. The sun, perhaps?

"There it is!" Margaux shouted in excitement and fatigue, all her efforts expended on bringing Byron's body to that most important place. Even with Arnold's help, he was heavy to carry, being a tall and muscular swimmer. "See that big gray stone just standing over there?"

Arnold nodded. So it was true, after all. There it was. The enigmatic bluestone monument put up by the ancients, thousands of years ago, still standing there.

"Okay, then, what do we do now, Margaux?" Arnold shouted back, holding onto Byron's limp body.

"Anastasia said to go to the front of that bluestone monument and to walk right in through the air. Exactly like that."

"Right." Arnold groaned, staring at Margaux. "Exactly like that. I only hope this wormhole is real and it works. This earthquake is getting stronger by the minute and no telling when that flood is coming by. Okay, then, let's walk right in!" He heaved forward with Byron's body.

"Come on, Romy, hurry!" Margaux looked back for her two friends still struggling behind them. "We're almost there. Remember. We will all walk right through in front of that stone, ok, you too, Dolly!"

Dolly barked and followed Margaux.

With a groaning heave coming out of the angry, rumbling earth, a large crack appeared behind Romy and Gerald, narrowly missing them.

"Oh my God! What's that noise?" Romy looked back behind her, her eyes frightened. "It's getting louder and louder!"

"The flood!" Gerald yelled pulling Romy with him. "Move!"

The five of them and Dolly quickly sprinted around the standing bluestone and, one by one, disappeared into the still night air.

Two seconds later, a mighty wall of water crashed onto the land, obliterating everything in its path.

Chapter 44

ALL FIVE AND THE PUPPY found themselves in a gray, nameless place.

"Come back here, Dolly!" Margaux yelled as she struggled to find her balance upon what appeared to be an invisible floor, if at all a floor. For in truth, there was no floor, only air beneath their feet. It was as if they were all standing on a smooth surface of glass below them and yet, there was no glass to be seen.

Margaux groaned as her curious puppy disappeared into the collection of mists beyond the group. "Damn you, Dolly! Now I have to go look for you and I have no idea where we are. You better come back!"

"I second the motion," Arnold commented, warily looking around him. "Where the hell are we?" He gingerly placed his feet upon the invisible floor. "I only hope we don't lose our footing and fall into whatever oblivion is below us. I can't see anything around us at all, except that mist and some sort of light."

"Me, neither." Romy added. She sighed. "I am getting tired of holding onto you, Gerald. Do you mind?"

"Nope." Gerald apologized, releasing his arm from her shoulder. "Just put me down. It feels kind of solid, and I trust that it is, even if we can't see what it is. I too would like to know where the hell we are. Any thoughts, Margaux?"

Margaux shook her head. "Anastasia did not tell me much." She suddenly felt tired. "Arnold, let's put Byron down on the floor. My arms hurt."

"Very helpful." Arnold remarked sarcastically. "Now what are we supposed to?"

"Maybe we're dead?" Romy suggested half-jokingly. "Maybe this is the heavens? Is Anastasia our guardian angel of sorts?"

"How should I know?" Margaux shrugged. She surveyed the surroundings, not knowing what to make of it. There was only that one time she had been in a place like this long ago, but it had been a terrifying experience. This place somehow felt peaceful, even welcoming. But, where was Anastasia?

"Look!" Romy pointed towards the thickening, white clouds that appeared among the gray mists. "Someone's coming. Dolly too!"

"Well, well, well, trust Dolly to find our Anastasia," Arnold remarked drily. "Here they come."

Sure enough, a beautiful female clad in a heavy, royal-purple, empire-waist toga appeared from the clouds, gliding effortlessly toward the waiting group. Dolly was trotting happily besides her. Several feet behind them, three gray figures, smaller in stature, appeared from the clouds and waited a distance away.

Margaux was startled at their appearance. She had seen them before. The Grays as Gerald had called them. And they had those eyes that had followed her all of her life.

And yet, here they were, following Anastasia, as if she was their supreme leader. Even Dolly was not afraid of them.

"Good Lord." Arnold remarked. "They're not walking. They are gliding."

"Indeed, they are." Gerald said. "Arnold, this is incredible. First contact with extraterrestrials. And I for one am glad to see them. Perhaps we will get our answers. Like, are we really in a mothership?"

"Hard to tell." Arnold agreed.

"Oh, but Anastasia is so pretty!" Romy gushed admiringly. "Like a glorious Greek goddess. How come she looks so much like you, Margaux?"

Margaux shrugged helplessly. "I have no idea. I'm just glad to see her, though."

Dolly broke into a run towards Margaux. She picked up the puppy, reveling in her wet kisses.

"Naughty girl, Dolly, naughty girl!" Margaux chided the puppy. "I thought I had lost you forever." She placed the wiggly puppy on the floor.

"She was with me the whole time." Anastasia smiled graciously. "What a darling little puppy. I quite like the name, Dolly." She extended her arms out towards the group, beaming brightly, the folds of her long royal-purple, toga sleeves spreading out behind her.

"Welcome to Star Centralia, my friends, and yes, you are indeed in a mothership, although it may not seem like it at first glance."

Romy, Gerald, and Arnold stared wordlessly. Not really.

Anastasia glided towards Margaux and wrapped her arms around her, hugging her tightly.

"Welcome home at last, my dear sister, Margaux."

Romy, Gerald, and Arnold looked at each other perplexed.

"Sister?" Romy whispered, her eyes becoming wide. "Wow."

"Does that make Margaux an extraterrestrial herself?" Gerald asked.

"Was that why they desperately wanted her?" Arnold pointed out.

The three friends turned towards Margaux staring at her in utter awe and confusion.

Margaux jerked away from Anastasia's arms, stumbling back in utter shock and surprise. She shook her head vehemently at this glorious, golden alien who had just called herself her sister.

"No, no, no, no, not possible. You can't be my sister. I have no sister and this place is certainly not my home. I grew up all alone. You were supposed to save Byron's life and give me back my child, that's all. That's what you told me back there at the lake, Anastasia."

Romy, Gerald, and Arnold directed their attention back to Anastasia. This was getting very, very interesting. Anastasia paused for a moment, adding drama to the already tense atmosphere. She beamed proudly.

"Oh, but I am truly your sister, Margaux, more to the point, I am your twin sister. It is time for the truth to come out, now more than ever." Anastasia lifted her head in an aristocratic manner. She clasped her hands. "And, yes, I do intend to uphold my promise to save Byron and bring you to your child." She turned around to face the three gray aliens, who had been standing solemnly a few feet behind the group, making themselves as quiet and obscure as possible.

She nodded graciously at them. They nodded deeply in return. Satisfied, Anastasia turned to face the group.

"All will be explained." Anastasia pronounced in a firm, strong voice. "But first we must attend to your Byron." She gestured at the still body lying on the floor. "Attend to it immediately, my vices."

As Margaux, Romy, Gerald, and Arnold watched in bewilderment. The three gray aliens surrounded the prostrate body of Byron and extended their arms on each side, their fingertips almost touching. A low, droning hum could be heard coming from their throats for several seconds, becoming louder and louder, as the three aliens raised their arms higher and higher.

The four friends backed away.

Byron's body was slowly levitating into the air and gently lay suspended above the heads of the three gray aliens, still humming loudly.

"Good lord," Gerald exclaimed. "How did they do that? Defy gravity?"

Arnold shook his in disbelief. "Remarkable."

Anastasia smiled at them. "It's quite simple, really. My assistants are using their mind powers, their inner energies. They are a highly, evolved, intelligent race."

"Your assistants?" Margaux asked confused and hurt. "But they abducted and poked at me and Byron a long time ago and left us without our memories. Why?" She found herself becoming angry. "Why did they separate Byron and me, Anastasia, why? And left us without our child? Why?"

"Like I said, Margaux, all will be explained." Anastasia replied, waving her hand in the air, the mark of a well-bred patrician. "We meant no harm to you and Byron. What's more, it all happened before I found out that you were my sister, believe me." She turned towards Gerald sitting awkwardly on the nameless floor and smiled.

"Would you like to accompany them, my friend? You look like you are in need of medical attention, also, am I correct?"

"By all means!" Gerald responded, eagerly trying to lift himself up. "I just can't get up and walk much though."

"That is no problem." She nodded towards her assistants, who proceeded to surround Gerald.

Gerald levitated and was suspended near Byron's body. He looked down in awe, placing a hand underneath him. There was nothing to hold him in the air and yet there he was, locked in place and secure. He looked back at the others behind him. "Now what?"

Anastasia smiled and nodded graciously. She pushed out her hand gracefully. "Now go."

The three gray assistants proceeded to glide towards the clouds, pulling the softly-floating bodies of Gerald and Byron along with them.

"Oh, my God," Romy was frantic, reaching out towards Gerald. "Where are they taking him? I'm not leaving him."

"Stay put." Arnold urged putting his arms around the worried Romy. "I'm not sure we are supposed to follow them."

Gerald turned around from his lofty, airborne position and waved excitedly with both hands.

"Look at me, guys! I'm flying in the air! Yeehah! See ya later!"

Dolly barked, wagging her tail.

Romy chuckled at the absurdity, shaking her head in disbelief, as she watched her husband enter into the clouds and disappear.

Arnold and Margaux laughed out loud. It was quite a relief to see an act of zaniness in this confusing, worrisome place.

Then silence settled all around them. Even Dolly lay down and sighed.

"Where did they go?" Margaux impulsively asked Anastasia. She still couldn't wrap her head around the sister part with this strange, beautiful alien. It was all too creepy for the moment. "What is going to happen to them?"

Anastasia smiled compassionately. "Do not worry, Margaux. They are both being taken to what is called the halls of healing. I can't tell you much more than that, I'm sorry. It is strictly forbidden by the higher powers, those beings higher than me."

"Halls of healing," Romy mused thoughtfully, placing a hand upon her face. "Gee, I like the sound of that. Halls of healing." She repeated. "It has a nice warm feeling to it."

"That is correct." Anastasia commented. "It is a nice, warm place, but again, strictly forbidden."

"What higher powers are you talking about?" Margaux demanded angrily. She didn't like it that they were not allowed in there. Not allowed to make sure that Byron and Gerald come back alive.

Arnold nodded in agreement. He too would like to know.

"That I cannot say." Anastasia responded firmly holding her ground even with her newly-found sister. "Only that I report to them, these higher beings. You see, the human race, including you all, are not yet at the level where you can access the powers higher than me, and even they remain mysterious to me. Believe me, I only have limited access to them."

"And yet, you report to them as you say. What are you, Anastasia?" Margaux demanded. "And how in the world am I your sister? I don't remember growing up with you. My mother never talked about you, much less having another child."

"Of course not, Margaux. Your mother, no, our mother had reason not to! Goodness, it is such a long story and terribly complicated. I feel it best to explain to you all sitting down and having tea around a warm, glowing fire, don't you think?" She extended her hand to Margaux, who refused to take it.

"Sure, but how?" Arnold looked around in mystification. "We can't see a floor, much less walls in here. It's all gray and white, not to mention the mists and clouds over there hiding secret places from us."

Margaux nodded in agreement, daring her sibling. "Yes, Anastasia, how are you going to build a fire in here?"

Anastasia smiled knowingly. "My dear sister, we at this point of our evolution do need not need walls and floors. You see, time and space do not exist at all with us. We do not even measure them like human beings do. We just are where we are." She waved her hand around the open gray-white space. "Do not worry, my friends. You are all most assuredly in Star Centralia, the mothership. However, if you want, we can summon up walls and floors to accommodate you."

Margaux, Romy, and Arnold said nothing. They really didn't know where to start. It was all too mystifying.

Anastasia turned to Margaux and took both hands into hers. "I know you want to know everything, my dear sister. Shall we sit by the fireside like I promised?"

Margaux nodded, grasping Anastasia's hand. Right now, she had no choice. She wanted to know the story behind the secret that just unveiled itself.

Because, right now, she wasn't even sure who she was herself.

Anastasia closed her eyes and raised her arms high into the air. A soaring melodious hum emanated from her vocal chords.

At that moment, the gray-white nothingness surrounding them slowly dissolved and changed its appearance in a dizzying transition of vibrations, waves, and colors. And suddenly, they were in a room, a real, living room with all the comforts of a sturdy log cabin with a fireplace in the winter. A real white, shaggy, carpeted floor appeared below their feet and followed by the four cornered walls of ponderosa pine.

Embedded in one of the walls was a real, red-and-brown, brick, mantle fireplace, replete with a roaring crackling, orange-red fire inside it. Two comfortable, suede sofas, the color of burnt copper, appeared opposite each other near the fireplace. Finally, a rectangular, glass coffee table appeared and it was followed by three golden, ceramic tea mugs and a golden ceramic teapot full of steaming hot water. A large tray of finger sandwiches and cookies appeared beside them.

Margaux, Romy, and Arnold stood speechless. Anastasia had thought of everything.

Unafraid, Dolly sprinted from Margaux's side and scrambled upon a sofa, grinning back at the group.

Anastasia picked up the teapot and poured the hot water into a mug. She handed it to Margaux. "Think of your favorite tea, my sister. I will do the rest."

Margaux accepted the mug and looked down at the hot water thoughtfully. The hot water began swirling clockwise, as if an invisible hand was stirring it. The water swirled and swirled for a few seconds before a light-green color emerged and saturated the water itself. Margaux sipped the hot steaming liquid carefully. She smiled. "It's good green tea, Anastasia, my favorite." She wrapped her hands around the cup, feeling its familiar warmth and comfort, and proceeded to sit down next to Dolly.

Romy and Arnold both picked up the remaining mugs, already filled with the hot water. Together, they both thought about their favorite tea and watched the waters swirl and change. Satisfied, they both settled down at the other sofa, sipping the hot tea and enjoying the sweet, strong flavor of orange-and-spice and earl grey, respectively. They hungrily helped themselves to the sandwiches and cookies.

"Wow, Anastasia, how do I get orange-and-spice tea while he has earl grey at the same time from this same teapot?" Romy asked.

"And I have green tea." Margaux added. "How do you do that, Anastasia?"

"It's all in your mind, you and your friends, individually. The hot water and your thoughts were all you needed. I merely took care of the manifestations with the powers of my mind."

"That is amazing!" Romy declared impressed. "This is incredible magic. You are quite a sorceress."

Anastasia shook her head knowingly.

"Not true, Romy. I am not a sorceress and there is no such thing as magic. What you just saw are all part of the energies coming together and being manipulated and controlled by our minds. Energy becoming matter. Matter becoming energy. And a scientist should know that." She glanced at Arnold, who said nothing, merely lifted an eyebrow, as he sipped his tea.

"Well, sure, but even so, we're not able to do what you just did," Romy protested.

"That's because your species simply have not reached those abilities yet," Anastasia explained, sipping her peppermint tea. She put down the mug. "Believe me, it will take many thousands of years of evolution before your species will have those abilities. What's more, it's all a matter of accepting your abilities, where right now you fear them, unfortunately."

"And it's not magic?" Arnold asked. "Well then, I'm curious, what do you call it, then?"

"Like I said, we simply call it abilities. It is a natural part of us. It is as simple to us as your ability to heat a teapot on the gas or electric stove. It just is."

Arnold shook his head. "I still don't get it, but why bother. It would be like grasping at straws. Too complicated, this realm of metaphysics."

"I would tend to agree with you, my friend. Perhaps we set it aside for now." Anastasia responded. "But rest assured, in time in the far, far future, your species will be able to access this vast region of the brain not currently used and then it will be as normal for you as it is for us." Lifting her royal-purple toga up over her ankles, she moved closer to Margaux and smiled. "Now shall I begin my story?"

Margaux nodded.

"Oh, yes, definitely!" Romy squealed, suddenly sitting upright. She was excited at the prospect of more out of this world information.

"I'm in, too." Arnold said in agreement. "It's too bad Gerald isn't around to hear all this. This is actually his specialty, not mine."

"Ah, but you all do have your memories." Anastasia explained. "You can always access your memories, when needed."

"Not if you erase them," Romy protested. This had often been true for her clients who had come for her help to remember the many alien abductions that had occurred to them. Their memories were always erased after their return from wherever they had been taken to. Arnold agreed. "It's like it never happened."

"Not necessarily this time." Anastasia responded. "I will, of course, allow you to retain your memories of this conversation, this place, and this time. Or if you wish, I could impart the necessary memories in your husband and friend with the powers of my mind."

"Sounds like a plan." Margaux interrupted impatiently, placing her mug of tea on the table. "Go on, Anastasia, how do I fit in all of this? Why am I here? And more importantly, how in the world am I your sister?"

Chapter 45

AND THUSLY ANASTASIA BEGAN HER story...

"Many, many years ago, Margaux, our human mother was taking a hike all by herself in the valleys near Mount Narodnaya."

"Where's that?" Romy interrupted.

"Russia," Arnold responded. He nodded at Anastasia. "Go on. Tell your story."

"Well, like I said, our mother was very beautiful and it had come to pass that a being higher than me was watching her from his ship above and fell in love with her. Of course, he took her away aboard his ship and disappeared into the far outer reaches of space. Twenty-three days of her life were missing. And you are correct, Arnold, it happened in Communist Russia many years before glasnost took place. When our mother was returned to her home, she was pregnant with us. Clearly, twins run in our mother's side of the family."

"So you are saying our father is an extraterrestrial, a being higher than you?" Margaux asked. "Why'd he return our mother, if he fell in love with her?"

"I agree with you, Margaux." Anastasia said unhappily. "That wasn't very nice to begin with, but it was typical of some of my people. They can be quite arrogant with your species if they want to. They've done it for thousands of years."

"Indeed." Margaux commented derisively. "Our father actually abandoned our mother? Thanks a lot!"

"I wouldn't say that, Margaux." Anastasia responded reprovingly. "I would not conclude that without just proof."

Margaux sighed in frustration. "Be that as it may. If there were the two of us in our mother's womb, then where the hell were you, while I was growing up all alone?"

Anastasia paused for a moment. She looked into Margaux's eyes with sorrow.

"I was taken away hours after I was born, Margaux. By our father in the dark of the night. It had been necessary."

"Necessary?" Margaux asked. "But why?"

"Because I was different. Too different. Uncomfortably different. We were twins, Margaux, but we did not really look alike. I looked more like our father and you, our mother. In point of fact, I was so different that I would have caused a massive state of alarm and fear among your people. We had to prevent that."

Margaux lifted her eyebrows. This did not make sense. "But Anastasia, look at you. You are the spitting image of me."

"Ah, but that was not the case when I was born, my dear sister."

"Of course, you were taken away." Romy remarked thoughtfully, fully understanding the dilemma posed by Anastasia's alien legacy. "If you lacked the normal human features we all of us have, of course that would raise alarms at your birth. What's more, you would not have been able to integrate with us in our world without explaining your alien features. It would have been difficult to hide you. Ultimately, you might always be on the run from the rest of us down there."

"Or worse, become some sort of government experiment, even prisoner." Arnold added solemnly.

"So, perhaps, it was better you were taken away." Romy nodded in agreement.

"Oh, God, so that's why Mom was nasty to me over the years on so many levels," Margaux murmured. "We were always fighting about my life and my safety, almost every day I was growing up. She wore me out constantly with her bizarre fear that I would be taken away from her. She never even wanted to talk about it. All she did was keep a huge grip on me every day of my life." Leaning forward, her hands on her chin, Margaux sighed. "You know, I grew up resenting her for all that and now, I understand."

"I'm truly sorry, Margaux. Truly." Anastasia consoled her human sibling. "But please realize that it must have been a terrible secret for her to carry all those years. You must understand she couldn't even talk about it. Who would believe her? Would you?"

"I don't know, Anastasia." Margaux replied, smiling weakly. "Perhaps not. I only have one question."

"Of course, what is it?"

"How come you showed up at my mirror? And why not tell me you were my sister then? Was that the truth I was supposed to know when the time came?"

Anastasia nodded. "Not entirely. But, yes, that was part of the whole truth for you to know. You were not ready then. You are now, Margaux. And I promise to reveal the other half of the truth, when that time comes." She brushed down the folds of her toga and paused for a second. "As for me, at first, I had thought you were just a byproduct of our abduction program, but later I discovered that you were my twin and I responded to your call." Anastasia said.

"Great, Anastasia, just great. Why did you leave me then?"

Anastasia sighed. "I had a greater responsibility to attend to, Margaux, that I am prevented from revealing to you. It would take away your perception of reality, which cannot happen, not yet." She smiled warmly. "Rest assured, my dear sister, I was always around, even if you were not aware of it, but I was."

"And now?"

"And now, the order of the universe where earth was concerned has changed significantly. I could not leave you behind when this unspeakable tragedy strikes and it will. Even if it means violating the very tenet we hold most sacred in the universe, the Primary Principle."

Arnold suddenly interrupted the conversation, grinning like a Cheshire cat. "Excuse me, Anastasia, but you know, like a scientist on a prowl, I'm indeed curious! What greater responsibility had been given to you that us mere mortals are not allowed to know?

And what unspeakable tragedy are you talking about? Is that on earth?"

"Me too, I would like to know." Romy added excitedly raising her hand in the air. "Me, too. What is the Primary Principle?"

Anastasia laughed melodiously, waving her hand gracefully in the air. "All in good time, my dear friends. All in good time." She adjusted her voluminous toga around her knees, clasped her hands on her lap, and took in a deep breath. "Well, you see, I was being trained for many years for I knew not what, until it was finally revealed to me, this greater responsibility, on the day your species might call 'graduation'. You see, Margaux, I finally found out that our father is one of the higher powers I report to and it was ordained that I become what was supposed to be my destiny, the moment I was taken away from you and our mother."

"Which is?" Romy, Arnold, and Margaux asked altogether, their eyes wide with wonder, their curiosity set at an all-time high.

"You see, my friends, I became High Priestess of my Council based near the blue star, Siriana, 9.3 light years away from earth in the Constellation Orion. My Council oversees three sun systems, each with their own revolving planets and earth is in my jurisdiction." Anastasia paused for a second. "Most often my Council tended to leave earth alone for the planet was too far out of the beaten path. What's more the human species had become too warlike for our comfort. It was better to monitor them from afar and use them only for our abduction program."

"Isn't that against the Primary Principle?" Romy asked. "Abducting us outright like that?"

"Indeed, it would appear to be a violation." Anastasia responded with approving smile. "Which is why it was imperative that we ask for permission from the higher power, which, of course, is my father and yours, Margaux." She slowly and deliberately placed her tea mug on the table. Margaux nodded involuntarily, unsure what to say. She still had a hard time wrapping her head around the fact that an extraterrestrial, and powerful one at that, was her real father.

Anastasia clasped her hands on her knees. "Our abduction program was designed with the goal to improve the disposition of the human species, which you all know now, has become extremely warlike."

"Hmmm, thanks a lot." Arnold smirked with a grin. "But then again, that would typically describe us now, I guess, whether we like it or not."

"Indubitably, Arnold." Romy added with emphasis. "There are too many wars going on in earth. Look at the Middle East and Africa and South America, the likes of which are spreading further out. I fear for us in the U.S. We are quite the warlike species, unfortunately."

Margaux nodded in agreement, smiling bleakly.

"Indeed." Anastasia murmured. "I am pleased that you all agree with our assessment. We were hoping to insert some genetic attributes that might hopefully improve the psychological, emotional, and intellectual makeup of your species for we fear you will end up destroying yourselves."

"We are doing a good job of destroying ourselves, anyways, Anastasia," Arnold remarked sarcastically. "In time, we might blow ourselves up to hell, who knows, so why waste your time with us?"

Anastasia shrugged helplessly. "I have no choice, my dear friend. Earth is my responsibility.

Margaux sighed. "I guess that's why I never felt like I belonged on earth, never mind my human features. For years of my life, growing up, I had never felt normal, except when I was with Byron." Anastasia nodded sympathetically. It was true. Margaux's life had been consumed with abject loneliness, so much so, she had felt compelled to offer her friendship over the mirror. She had been glad when Byron showed up in her life. It was important to keep him there.

"But I don't get it," Romy interrupted. "Why were you guys chasing her all those years and even had her come to me for a regression? What's the hurry?" Arnold nodded gravely. "You could have easily taken her years before. And be gone with her. Why didn't you?"

"Ah, but that was the tricky part." Anastasia said. "There was a reason I had to contact her, to bring her here. It was too important and time was of essence. Now, I could not interfere with your free will, Margaux, all those years you were living on earth, when I found you. I could not interfere with the decisions you made as you lived your life. That was what the Primary Principle was all about. The only way to keep up with you was to keep track of you and help you, indirectly, however frightening and confusing our efforts may have been to you."

"Hence, the eyes she keeps talking about." Arnold remarked drily. "And those strange foreign words."

Romy nodded thoughtfully. "When she came to me for the regression, she spoke about the relentless alien eyes that kept showing up at different places at different times and on this one person she is now romantically involved with, Byron. The eyes scared her more than helped her, unfortunately."

Suddenly, Anastasia froze, lifting her hand in the air. "Please remain silent." She instructed with a firm voice and closed her eyes.

Dolly lifted her head, fully alert.

Margaux, Romy, and Arnold waited in hushed suspense, as the three friends stared at Anastasia, who smiled radiantly and nodded her head briefly, eyes still closed, as if she was speaking to an entity from within her mind. Who was she talking to, now?

Anastasia opened her eyes and turned towards the group. With a beaming smile, she took one of Margaux's hands into hers.

"What?" Margaux asked placing the half-finished tea mug on the table. "What's happening?"

"You will see." Anastasia whispered softly. She turned and waved her hand towards the wall of ponderosa pine. After a series of vibrations, waves, and colors appeared, blending into a convergent eddy in the air, a door soon appeared against the wall.

Slowly, that door creaked open and two solid human figures emerged from the mists behind it. At first they were hard to discern, looking very much like two sinister shadows coming in, before the light of the room became brighter, revealing their true forms.

Margaux gasped in joy. Romy squealed happily, and ran into her husband's arms. Arnold smiled in satisfaction, tipping his head graciously towards Anastasia. There was no denying it. The impossible had indeed been achieved miraculously.

Byron walked through the door hesitantly, followed by the nervous freckled, red-haired Gerald, who was fast examining the room they had just entered. "Oh, but this place is marvelous, absolutely marvelous!" He declared loudly, lifting up and embracing his deliriously happy wife. "Look at me, Romy, I'm no longer maimed." He gently placed his wife down.

"Now, where the hell are we?"

Margaux instantly ran into Byron's open arms and held him tightly, tears brimming inside her eyes. Byron stroked her golden hair and kissed it softly not paying attention to anyone or anything, except for Margaux.

She lifted her head and looked deeply into his eyes. "Oh, my love, my sister brought you back to life! How can I ever thank her!"

Byron gently placed his hand on her tear-stained cheek, his eyes also brimming with tears. "I have no idea what you are talking about, my silly Margaux, but I am indeed very happy to see you too." He placed his lips onto hers, kissing her with a passion born of fire and need. For a time, the two lovers kissed, oblivious to the fact that they were in a crowded room.

Nothing mattered except the two of them now back together.

Arnold slapped Gerald's back. "My God, man, you look like the bookcase never hit your leg. Tell me, did you see what they did to you and Byron back there?"

"No, sorry. They put me to sleep. I missed everything." Gerald shrugged. "The grays are quite mum about the whole process, not even saying a word or two, just going about their business." He placed his hand on Arnold's shoulder and smiled. "It doesn't matter now, Arnold, my friend. A miracle happened. Byron is alive and look, I can walk! Oh, I am beside myself with joy! Come on, let's do a conga line dance! Follow me, mes amis! Yeehah!" Gerald sashayed in the rhythmic fashion reminiscent of a Cuban carnival dance. "Come on, Arnold, you and the others get on behind me!"

Arnold laughed loudly, jerking his finger behind him. "Not likely, my man. Byron's still busy with Margaux."

"Of course." Gerald stopped. He glanced with a smile at the two kissing lovers. What an experience they'd all had in the past day and a half. The five of them and Dolly had been through so much already, it rightfully felt like they were old friends, not day-long acquaintances. He beamed at Byron and Margaux, still oblivious to the world around them. He reached out for Romy's hand. Romy held it tightly.

Gerald turned towards Anastasia and offered his hand. "You did the right thing, ma'am. I only wish I knew what you guys did to him and to me, but apparently you did the right thing. We are so grateful to you. I didn't think I would be able to walk. At least, not for a while. And we certainly didn't think to see Byron back alive. The technology must be quite amazing."

Anastasia graciously bowed her head. "I accept your appreciation, my dear friend. However, please be aware that we do not take this lightly. We do not make it a routine practice to raise the dead, but for this special circumstance, it had been necessary."

"Necessary?" Arnold asked. "How so?"

Anastasia turned towards the kissing couple and beamed in satisfaction. "It was necessary, because he was an important part of her life, just as Margaux is now an important part of my life, and this is what I could do for my sister, what I wanted to do for my sister and her happiness." She turned to Gerald. "And for you too, because we can." Anastasia sighed. "But, my dear friends, and it is a big, big but, it had not been easy getting permission from the One Most High."

"Now I'm more confused than ever," Gerald groaned. "I don't even know how you and Margaux ended up as sisters."

Romy and Arnold laughed. Romy took his arm with enthusiasm. "Come on, Gerald, let's all sit on that sofa. While you and Byron were at the halls of healing, Anastasia had been telling us the story of how they became sisters." She pushed him down on the sofa. "Now relax and let Anastasia fill you in with the story up to now with her mind powers."

"Fill me in with her mind powers? Huh?"

"Yeah, sort of like a regression, but you are being filled with information we already knew." Arnold said. "You need to be up to date with the information, before Anastasia can continue with her story with all of us. Same with Byron."

"And what a story!" Romy exclaimed loudly, twirling around herself, her arms outstretched. She clapped her hands in glee, her eyes shining brightly. "Oh, Gerald, this is such a remarkable story! A first for our QET work! This alone can be an entire book!"

"Assuming anyone believes us." Arnold said drily, rolling up his eyes.

"Ok, ok, ok. Go on, put me under. I'm getting awfully curious." Gerald quickly looked around him, back and forth and up and down and once again all around. "Hey, how did this room happen? Didn't we just come from a place with no walls and no floor with lots of gray and white clouds floating around us?"

Romy laughed. Arnold grinned. Dolly barked.

Byron, Margaux, and Anastasia smiled.

Romy lifted up the teapot and poured the hot water into a mug. "Wait 'til you see your tea!"

Chapter 46

AFTER ANASTASIA PERFORMED A MIND transference of information to Byron and Gerald, the two men joined the others at the sofa.

"All right." Anastasia announced, pouring herself another mug of peppermint tea. "Now, where was I last?"

"Why were the eyes on Byron?" Margaux asked. "What did that mean?"

Anastasia smiled as she sipped the hot tea. "Well, as you all must know by now, it was our ancillary method of trying to get my sister, Margaux, back together with Byron. Each and every time she encountered him. We were hoping the mere presence of what you call those "dark alien eyes" would motivate her to go to him and start a conversation."

"But why?" Romy probed insistently.

Anastasia sighed patiently.

"Our memories were erased." Margaux offered helpfully.

"And then we spent years away from each other." Byron commented sadly, gripping Margaux's hand. He turned towards Anastasia. "Were you responsible for that unusual intervention at my last night attack campaign in Farizal? What happened to me and my buddy then? We lost three days and had our memories erased."

Anastasia slowly placed the tea mug on the table. She paused for a second and surveyed the group. "Let me repeat once again.

The minute I found out that Margaux was my sister, I was stunned and delighted altogether. Of course, I felt this utmost familial need to take care of her and I did throughout her life and that included you, my friend, no matter where you were and who you were with. Unfortunately, my assistants had deemed your bodies viable for the genetic program. We took some DNA from you and your friend."

"I see." Margaux nodded. "Makes sense, but why have those eyes follow me? Why scare me to death Anastasia? Why take me again and again, my time missing, too?"

Anastasia clasped her hands on her lap. She smiled apologetically at Margaux. "I was hoping you would forgive me for what your people might call a transgression of your inalienable rights. For unbeknownst to me, my assistants had been given allowance by the higher powers to track you and abduct you, if only to harvest your eggs and DNA for our genetic program."

"God, you make us sound like mere cattle being rounded up and shepherded about for nefarious reasons." Byron remarked in disgust. "Of course you were wrong to do that." He held Margaux tighter to him. "Why on earth would you do that?"

Anastasia lifted her hand. "Do not upset yourself unnecessarily, my friend. Again, the program had been necessary. We merely intended to use your DNA to improve the human species for, like I said before, you all are surely on the path of self-destruction."

"Once again, that would be accurate." Arnold drawled lazily. "She does have a point."

"I would agree with him." Gerald nodded. "It would seem an act of benevolent intervention. I would probably not hesitate to do so, myself, you know. I really don't blame her."

"Me, neither." Romy agreed. "She was trying to help us all."

"But, but…" Margaux interrupted, sitting upright on the sofa. "How could you possibly harvest my eggs? I have no ovaries, as you must know."

"Oh my poor Margaux." Anastasia responded sadly. "You did have ovaries at first, for how else would you have a child with Byron? Twins, who are now waiting for you."

"Where are our twins?" Byron demanded, grabbing Anastasia's arm.

"All in good time, my dear friend." Anastasia said firmly, lifting her hand in protest. "Your twins are quite safe, I assure you. Please remove yourself from my arm."

"I believe her." Margaux declared, pulling him back onto the sofa. "Let her finish her story first."

Anastasia smoothed the wrinkled folds of her royal-purple toga. She took a deep breath.

"You see, Margaux, for a while you had ovaries and we harvested your eggs for some years, in addition to Byron's sperm." Anastasia smiled. "You both have other children individually, hybrids actually, for we blended your essences with ours and many others."

Byron became furious. "How many are there now? What have you done with them?"

"Hush." Margaux placed her hand on his lap. "We'll talk about that later, Byron. Please let my sister finish."

Byron sighed with resentment. "Go on. I won't interfere."

"Certainly." Anastasia replied graciously. "Well, you see, one day I was told by my assistants about your whereabouts and status, Margaux, and although admittedly while I had no sense of repugnance to your necessary abductions, yours and Byron's, something else happened that only served to emit a sense of horror inside me. I had to act fast."

"Horror?" Margaux asked curiously.

"You had cancer of the ovaries, Margaux. Not many months to live, unless I ordered its removal."

Margaux was stunned. "Cancer?"

Anastasia sighed. "It is an unfortunate byproduct of our mother's familial DNA passed on to you."

"Not another one." Margaux rolled her eyes. "It all makes sense now." She smiled at Anastasia. "I forgive you, Anastasia. You saved my life."

"I agree." Byron relented, kissing Margaux's forehead. "This is one act of alien intervention I have no problem wrapping my head around it. I would have been devastated had she died from this cancer."

"Awesome!" Gerald said in rapt astonishment, placing his empty mug of tea on the table. "Simply out of this world, if you don't mind my saying so. "He turned to Romy. "This indeed could be a book by itself, Romy."

Slowly Anastasia stood up from the sofa, extending her arms. "Please stand up my dear sister and friends." She closed her eyes and waved her hands about the air, humming loudly from her throat.

In an instant, the cozy living room and roaring fireplace slowly converged into the familiar vibrations, waves, and colors, before disappearing into the air. The original space with no walls and no floor ultimately reappeared with the ominous gray mists floating at a short distance.

Dolly whined and hid between Margaux's and Byron's legs.

What was happening now? The couple and their friends all watched Anastasia, who was this time waving both hands vigorously in the air, humming louder from her throat.

The nameless void disappeared in an explosive shimmer of gold, pink, and white colors swooshing around them, before blasting out into space.

A long hallway appeared leading toward an infinite horizon. Bright lights from nowhere completely saturated the hallway, all the way through the diminishing point. Huge Doric columns stood in silent sentinel on both sides of the hallway for miles down the path. The floor comprised of golden oak planks, so smooth and shiny one could actually skate on it with bare feet.

This place was as close to heaven, as ever imagined.

Anastasia graciously beckoned to the five of them. "Come, come, my dear friends and sister, please follow me." Lifting her heavy toga above her ankles, she stepped onto the hallway and began her majestic walk towards the infinity beyond the imposing Doric columns. The heavy toga material trailed behind her like water rippling through a creek.

Byron and Margaux looked at each other for a moment. They grasped each other's hand. Together they followed Anastasia, Dolly obediently at their feet. Their three friends followed suit, keeping pace with the group ahead of them.

Chapter 47

"Wow!" Romy declared staring with astonishment all around the majestic hallway, as she carefully walked along the shiny golden floor, holding Gerald's hand. "It's so beautiful. And yet, so familiar. It's Greek, isn't it?"

"Indeed it is familiar. It is accurately reminiscent of the ancient Greek architecture. Not unlike the Parthenon." Arnold said in agreement, gingerly stepping on the slippery floor. He looked out beyond the hallway. "I would imagine we would find a colossal statue of the goddess Athena at the end of this hallway, who knows."

"Who knows." Gerald nodded, gazing in admiration as he touched the formidable Doric columns, each step of the way. "I wonder why she came up with all this."

"Because, it is a comfortable environment for you all." Anastasia spoke up from the front. "I had felt that such an auspicious meeting for Margaux and Byron with their twins merited beauty in all its surroundings. I looked inside my mind library for such a venue and came up with this. It is beautiful, is it not?"

"Sounds about right." Gerald added. Arnold nodded. "We have such places on earth, you know. Only they are now in ruins."

"Of course." Anastasia responded knowingly. "They were built by my people eons ago. We founded ancient Greece."

"Why did you leave then?" Romy asked bluntly.

"Many reasons too complicated to explain, but basically we were, and still are, explorers of the universe and, therefore, it is difficult for us to stay in one place for long. But some of us did stay behind, shapeshifting our forms to resemble your people. They became watchers of your race." She paused for a second. "There are descendants among your people, even now."

"Amazing." Gerald said. "We can't even tell who these watchers are."

"That is the point, my friend." Anastasia replied.

"Indeed, they are like spies among us." Arnold said. "Who knows how our government and military would react to them."

Anastasia glared at him pointedly. "We are there strictly as observers, my friend, as we have been for thousands of years, nothing more. To interfere in earth's affairs would be in direct violation of the Primary Principle. It would require an event of magnitude proportions to circumvent these hallowed precepts."

Gerald nodded. It was true. And amazing as Anastasia and her people was, the human race was not ready for these otherworldly beings, at least, not yet.

"So how much longer do we have to walk?" Arnold quipped, peering down the lengthy hallway. "I can't see the end of this hallway. It looks terribly endless from here."

"Yes, how much longer?" Byron demanded outright. He was starting to get worried about where they would finally end up. So far they have had to deal with illusions, however pleasant, but still, they were all illusions to him, even Anastasia herself. Once they were on firm ground, preferably on earth with their twins, he would feel better. "There's got to be an end to this hallway. We can't be walking forever."

"Patience, my dear friends, patience." Anastasia responded, picking up her toga dress. She continued the walk in her graceful form. "All in its own time."

"She keeps saying that too." Arnold remarked drily. "This is beginning to feel like some sort of royal procession."

"I hope it's not too long." Gerald stared down the hallway.

Chapter 48

Fifteen minutes later Anastasia raised her hand. "We can stop now that we are close to the point of electromagnetic turbulence." She dropped her voluminous toga dress to the floor and clasped her hands in front of her. She closed her eyes for several seconds and finally nodded with a smile.

"What now?" Byron asked looking ahead and around him. The group was getting tired. There was nothing to be seen in the miles long hallway, except more of the imposing Doric columns and bright lights.

Anastasia gracefully waved her hand in the air. The lights dimmed into a soft incandescent luster. Margaux looked at her sister, quizzically. "What is happening now, Anastasia?"

"Shhhh…" Anastasia softly put her finger on her lips. "Listen… and look…" She pointed quite a distance down the prismatic hallway.

All five looked in anticipation ahead of them. Far ahead of them, a large oval mirror appeared out of the still air between two columns and instantly changed into shimmering, undulating water waves.

"My lord, another wormhole!" Gerald said loudly, staring with wonder at the upsurge of water waves all around the portal, bigger than all of them. There were no edges and yet the water swells were constrained within the parameters, never spilling out.

It was some time, before they all noticed Dolly had gone from the group, running towards the iridescent twirling phenomenon and disappearing into it.

"Dolly, come back!" Margaux shouted in fear. Byron grabbed her arms and held her back. There was no telling what was inside this strange spectacle before them.

"I would imagine she would show up with somebody in tow like she did before," Arnold drawled sarcastically. "I wouldn't worry much."

"Indeed, you are correct." Anastasia responded, nodding graciously. "They are coming, my dears."

All eyes stared at the portal in hushed silence.

In time, three figures appeared breaking through the glistening, rolling waves, not even becoming wet. Dolly was at their feet, happily wagging her tail. There was one tall, resplendent female holding hands with two children, one at each side of her.

Margaux gasped. Byron grimly held his tight grip on her. Romy, Gerald, and Arnold silently watched in awe, their mouths open.

The three figures stopped only a few feet from the group. Dolly sat down beside them. The tall female bowed her head in reverence. Anastasia responded in kind. She turned towards her sister and her lover.

"Margaux and Byron, may I present your twins."

Margaux was beside herself. Her twins. How utterly beautiful they were. Byron relaxed his grip, letting go of her, but Margaux couldn't bring herself to reach out to their twins. Not yet. After so many difficult years in which she had made peace with herself to live a life without a child, she now had two to behold. And they were the exact diminutive replica of herself and Byron. Blonde and dark hair. Blue and brown eyes. Each wearing petite-sized, off-white togas reaching down to their knees. Golden, braided sandals graced their lissome feet.

"Oh my God," was all she could utter, frozen in place.

"Who is this woman with them?" Byron queried Anastasia, as he surveyed the tall, stately, female alien with aristocratic features, most notably her high cheekbones and large, almond-shaped, blue eyes. Her elongated head was elegantly covered by a silken red turban. A heavy, flowing red, empire-waist toga graced her lithesome body.

"Ah, of course, may I also present their surrograce, Maya Puabi."

"Surrograce?"

"What your people on earth might call an au pair. But more than that, it had been necessary to transfer the fetus from Margaux's womb to her body. She is now their assigned protector."

"Not anymore." Byron declared firmly. "We are here to take them back. They rightfully belong to us."

"I am in complete agreement, my dears." Anastasia beckoned to Maya Puabi. The woman bent down to speak to the twins. She let go of their hands.

The twins slowly approached Margaux and Byron, followed by Dolly, wagging her tail. The little girl and boy smiled shyly, showing their dimpled cheeks, which tugged at Margaux's heart. Awestruck, she fell to her knees, followed by Byron on his knees beside her. The twins ran into their open arms.

Dolly joined the hugs, wagging her tail.

"Oh my God, my twins." Margaux groaned, happily hugging them both to her heart. "Oh, my God."

Byron held them all tightly in his embrace, tears flowing down his cheeks. This was beyond his wildest dreams. For some time since his remarkable reunion with Margaux, he had quietly made peace to a life without a family to call his own, for he was unwilling to leave his beloved Margaux. And now with the twins returned to them, they have become a family. It was time to go back to earth.

"Let's go home." Byron declared, lifting himself up from the floor.

"Not so fast, my dears." Anastasia raised her hand. "Not so fast."

"Look!" Romy said as she pointed to the wormhole. "The wormhole is going crazy."

"You're right." Gerald said, seeing the water waves churn some more. He turned to Anastasia. "Are we expecting anyone else?"

Anastasia beamed. "Yes, we are and you will see."

In time, a second group arrived comprised of five figures. All five appeared one by one from within the undulating waves and slowly approached the group. Two of the five were tall, one was mid-sized, and the last two were very small. They all held hands together, as they approached closer and closer to the waiting group of friends. Like the twins, they all wore off-white togas cut at the knees and golden, braided sandals.

But something distinctly separated them from the twins.

"Oh my God, humanoids, but they are like children!" Romy declared surprised and delighted. "Two of them look like teenagers. And, oh, look at the smaller ones. They are quite cute with those big eyes and ears."

"Who are they?" Gerald asked, curiously examining their alien features. They all were slim with impossibly long fingers, arms, and legs, an exaggerated version of the normal human features. Like the surrograce, Maya Puabi, their features included high cheekbones, large, almond-shaped eyes of blue or brown, and an elongated head, but theirs were covered by thick, tousled hair of varying shades of blonde or dark.

"Actually, they are more of your children, Margaux." Anastasia beamed proudly. "Yours and Byron's."

"Forgive me, Anastasia, but how? They all look so different! Nothing like our twins."

"Of course, not, my dears." Anastasia explained. "They are in truth, hybrids, half-human, half-alien. We have successfully created them from your individual essences. They are the pioneers of our experimental genesis program."

Byron was stunned. He actually felt violated. Margaux, however, saw it differently.

"Oh, Anastasia, but they are so beautiful in their own way." Margaux exclaimed. "Tell me, which ones are mine and which ones, Byron's?"

"Kind of hard to tell now." Arnold scratched his head. "So many diverse features and look at their strange hair colors. One of them has gray hair, imagine." Romy and Gerald nodded in agreement. This was truly extraordinary.

Anastasia approached the two, tall humanoids at the front of the group of five. She cupped their faces with her hands lovingly and smiled. "These two are yours, Byron, with two different mothers." Then she pointed behind them. "And the three little ones behind are yours, Margaux, with three different fathers."

"Good grief." Gerald shook his head. "That was fast. Apparently older than the twins. How'd they grow up so fast?"

"Indeed, they do appear older than when you two were first abducted at Loch Tallulah ten years ago. It's as if they were conceived before the twins. How is that even possible?" Arnold remarked scratching his head again.

"I agree." Byron added, becoming perplexed at the timing of it all. It did not make sense to him. "How is that possible?"

Anastasia waved her hand in the air. "Ah, my friends, with us anything is possible. We have the means to accelerate their growth through the use of energies. However, we cannot reveal our methods. You all are not ready for that kind of knowledge, I'm sorry." She turned and faced the group of friends. "I wanted to show you that it was not a waste to have taken you both, especially Margaux. She had very special genetic materials in her DNA, for she is like me, half-alien. And as for Byron, we did find good qualities in your genetic profiling that we had put to good use in developing our hybrids."

"Thanks, I guess." Byron said, lost in thought. The twins were easy. They clearly belonged to Margaux and him. The other five were not so easy. He wasn't even sure how to broach this dilemma of ownership. Anastasia was apparently very powerful in her own right.

"Guys!" Romy piped up excitedly, raising her hand. "All these introductions and such marvelous stories behind them and, yet, we don't even know their names."

"Yes, of course." Margaux looked at her sister. "Have you given them names?"

Anastasia approached the twins standing in front of Margaux and Byron. She bent down to their eye level and smiled at each of them. The twins smiled shyly, both of them leaning closer to their newly-found parents. She cupped her hand on the cheek of the little girl. "This is Mnemosyria, little girl of memories." Then she cupped the cheek of the little boy with the other hand. "And this is Lancelot, little knight of the stars." She looked at Margaux. "All in line with who you are, my dear sister. I know you."

"Mnemosyria and Lancelot." Byron whispered, grinning at Margaux. "Quite fairytale names, but I could get used to it, assuming you like the names."

"Oh, but I love their names." Margaux responded smiling, hugging the twins to her. "They fit our adorable twins born from out of this world."

"And what about the others?" Romy pointed at the group of five hybrid children still huddled together, patiently waiting in silence at a distance.

"No names assigned yet, my dear friends. Only numbers based on the order of their birth." Anastasia stood up and smoothed her toga folds. She clasped her hands and solemnly faced the hybrid group. "We thought it fitting for Margaux and Byron to name them when the time came for their arrival."

"They grew up with numbers?" Gerald asked. "Remarkable. How are they going to adjust to their new names?"

"It will not be a problem at all." Anastasia laughed. "Their minds have evolved to the point where they can make the necessary adjustments, be it their names, or their bodies, or their mind powers, for they are truly half-alien, not unlike myself." She gestured towards the twins. "Mnemosyria and Lancelot, however, are born of a human mother and father, and therefore, it was imperative and appropriate to have their names imprinted upon them at the time of their birth. Fortunately, I know Margaux's proclivity towards a world found only in your fairytales, myths, and legends."

"Oh, but you are so right, Anastasia." Margaux gushed walking up to hug her alien sister. "I couldn't have come up with such beautiful names for my gorgeous twins. Thank you!"

"Oh, but you are most welcome!" Anastasia hugged her sister in delight. A few seconds later, she quickly pushed Margaux back, placing both hands against her temples, grimacing in distress.

Chapter 49

"SILENCE!"

"Huh?" Arnold said. "What's up this time?"

Gerald shrugged. "We'll find out soon enough. In point of fact, I am quite enjoying the surprises she keeps coming up with. More stuff for my book."

"Indeed." Arnold agreed. Romy shushed them both.

All eyes turned towards Anastasia, who had become clearly upset. Small droplets of tears flowed down from her tightly, closed eyes, as she attempted to discern the newly-arrived information from within her powerful mind.

"Ah, but this is terrible, most terrible, terrible news." Anastasia declared, shaking her head. She clutched at her heart. "We have arrived too late, my dear friends. I must take full responsibility."

"Take full responsibility?" Gerald and Arnold stared at each other in confusion. What did she mean? Byron glanced at Romy, who merely shrugged her shoulders. She had no idea either.

"What's wrong, Anastasia?" Margaux asked, concerned at the suffering her sister displayed, unsure what to make of it. She placed her hands on Anastasia's shoulders. "Isn't there anything we can do to help you?"

"Ah, it's but it's happening now, Margaux. We thought there was time. Enough time." She sighed. "Clearly not." She looked up at Margaux. "It's why I had you followed for the past several months and bring you up here to safety."

"Time?" Byron asked, puzzled. All along, he had thought Anastasia was infallible, given the powers she had demonstrated, thus far. "Time for what? What did you mean bring her up here to safety?"

"And us too, apparently." Gerald declared. Arnold and Romy nodded in silence.

"Yes, why, Anastasia?" Margaux urged. She turned her sister around to face her. "What's happening?"

"This." Anastasia released her sister's hands from her shoulders and slowly turned around. She raised her head upwards beyond the endless rise of the columns and hummed loudly, waving her hands wildly in rhythmic motions. Suddenly, several vibrations, waves, and colors appeared and soon manifested solidly into what looked like a giant hologram. In it were images filled with fiery hurls of fire and brimstones and flying explosions of dust and soot, all encompassed by a monstrous, gray mushroom cloud extending upwards for miles.

Everyone gathered behind Anastasia, who stared dejectedly at the holographic image.

Margaux gasped. Byron held her tightly against him, moving her face away from the awful picture. The twins huddled together in fear, sensing the terror in the room.

A blinding explosion of unimaginable strength and proportions had occurred. Worse than a nuclear blast.

On earth.

"Oh, my God!" Romy wailed. "It can't be!" She fell to her knees on the floor in shock and dismay, her hands pressed to her face.

Behind her, both Gerald and Arnold stood paralyzed in utter disbelief, unable to voice a word, much less remove themselves from the awful maelstrom manifested in front of their eyes. Pyroclastic ashes, sulfur rain, roaring, red fire, hot, flowing lava, flying fragments of stones and rocks and the blackness of the darkness all combined to produce a horror in front of their eyes.

In Artemis' Realm.

"Oh my God! Those poor people!" Romy cried out. She ran towards Gerald, both of them holding each other unhappily, as they watched the holographic image together, their emotions wracked with survivor's guilt. Tears flowed from their eyes, as the never-ending apocalyptic fire, brimstone, and lava continued to pour and destroy hundreds of miles of their home landscape. Cities and towns were gone. Lakes and rivers dried up. Forests of trees and flora and fauna were all but demolished and burnt to the ground.

Their home was gone. There was no way to go back. It was too dangerous right now.

Arnold moved closer to the hologram, hands in his pockets, and squinted, searching for that elusive epicenter on the horrific image displayed above him. He turned around to face his friends and Anastasia, his voice choked with tears. "You're right, Anastasia. It's Vulculcan's Folly. It blew ahead of its time."

No one said anything. No one wanted to say anything. All eyes were riveted to the monstrous display of horror hoping for a change. Any kind of change.

In time, the dust settled to the ground on earth. Nothing could be seen for miles around, the bleak landscape lying in utter devastation and ruin.

Anastasia waved her hand upwards in a wide, arcing turn. The giant hologram dematerialized into a mass of vibrations, waves, and colors before they disappeared into the air. Shock still reigned among the group, not sure what to say or do next.

"We can't go back, that's for sure." Gerald announced, breaking the silence. "Our homes are gone."

"It looks that way." Arnold added woefully. He looked at Anastasia and grinned uncomfortably. "I guess you are stuck with us. That is what you meant by bringing all of us here to safety, right?"

Anastasia nodded. She had fully recovered her senses and now resumed command with quiet assertiveness. "That is correct, my friend. And no, I am not entirely stuck with any of you. You all have a choice to return or not. You see, earth is not destroyed, merely severely destructed. There are survivors down there."

"You mean we can rebuild?" Byron asked skeptically. He could hardly believe he had escaped certain death once again. Mario and Calandra, his only family, were gone. There was no reason for him to go back at all, especially now that he had a brand, new family with Margaux, however peculiar it was. He shook his head. "That was major damage down there. I cannot believe there are survivors."

"That is your opinion." Anastasia dismissed his concern. "Of course, there are survivors. By now, we have detected them at various parts of the earth. And of course, you can rebuild, but it will take many millennia to do so. You will have to start from scratch, unfortunately." Anastasia crossed her arms thoughtfully. "Perhaps your species are now ready to accept our presence, no?"

"That's true." Arnold said. "We would have no choice now but to accept your help, whether we like it or not."

"Maybe," Gerald added, hesitation laced in his voice. He stroked his chin thoughtfully. "Maybe not. Personally I wouldn't count on it." Romy nodded in agreement. "We did the research for years. People are still afraid of you. Of extraterrestrials, in general. For years, the government and military had successfully launched a propaganda effort to discredit your people. You are now a scary proposition."

Anastasia lifted her eyebrows. She curved her mouth sarcastically, asserting her strength and power. "Then we will help incognito, of course. There is an alternative plan. We will transport those of you willing to move to other planets, while the earth heals over time. We have done that for the Quashone Indians the last time Vulculcan's Folly blew up 820,000 years ago." Anastasia sighed, as she paced the floor away from the group. She turned to face them. "Actually we caused it to blow up, and we have made penance by transporting the Quashone people to another planet. Then millennia later we returned them to earth, except they were not happy there. They cried out to us many times. So of course, we took them back to that other planet."

"Amazing," Margaux murmured. "That's why they disappeared. So the Quashone legend was true after all. The extraterrestrials caused this awful cataclysm."

"Not this one." Anastasia corrected her sister. "This one was natural and quite expected. Pressure had been building up within Artemis' Realm for several years and had only gotten worse this past year."

Margaux smiled warmly. She took Anastasia's hands into hers. "Never mind all that, Anastasia. I am so grateful you saved me, my love, and my friends from this calamity on earth."

Gerald, Romy, and Arnold nodded in agreement.

Byron approached the two women. "I agree with Margaux. Thank you for saving us, Anastasia. And for giving us back our twins. Not to mention the additional siblings."

Anastasia gripped her sister's hands and took Byron's hand in hers.

"Margaux, Byron, I have a proposition I hope you will both accept. I propose that both you and your family will come with me to my home planet in the Siriana star system. It is my utmost pleasure to bring you all home with me. Dolly, too. My people will all welcome you." Margaux and Byron glanced at each other, smiling. Yes, this was certainly exciting. A new home light years away from the broken earth with their large extended family. It was beyond their wildest imagination.

The five half-alien siblings stood quietly behind the three and Dolly, with Maya Puabi waiting patiently at a distance.

Anastasia released her grip on Margaux's and Byron's hands. She gestured towards Gerald, Romy, and Arnold. "What I'm not certain is what do your friends want to do? Of course, they are more than welcome to come to my home planet with us."

"I will go find out for you." Margaux offered. She walked over to where Romy, Gerald, and Arnold were standing, waiting patiently in silence, uncertain what to do for the moment. She smiled. "I think you guys heard her. What do you want to do?"

Romy looked into Gerald's eyes for a moment. Together they nodded solemnly. They would do this.

"Actually, Margaux, our home is gone down there and we have no family. They are all gone." Romy explained. "Gerald and I are wondering if Anastasia can put us up someplace where we can learn more about other species and the mysteries of the universe. It would be awesome for us. It has been our dream for years." Margaux turned and looked at Anastasia in anticipation. Can this be done?

Anastasia nodded graciously and smiled. She beckoned to Gerald and Romy. "Come. I have just what you need." Anastasia pointed to her left. "Look."

From behind the still-undulating wormhole, four extraterrestrials appeared looking more human than aliens, except for their large, black almond-shaped eyes, pointed ears, elongated heads, and high cheekbones. All four had different hair colors ranging from ash blond, strawberry blonde, brown, and black. They all wore jumpsuit uniforms of flame-retardant, silver material. Each held a sturdy space helmet under their arms.

The extraterrestrial group marched in step toward Anastasia. They proudly stopped in front of her, bowing their heads in deference to their commander.

Gerald and Romy stared at them in fascination. More human-alien hybrids from Anastasia's genetic program. Unlike the five extra siblings of Margaux and Byron's essences, these four appeared fully developed. Feeling peculiar, Gerald and Romy looked down at themselves. The two of them were also wearing the same silver jumpsuit uniforms, helmets appearing under their arms.

They looked at Anastasia puzzled. She gently placed her hands on their shoulders.

"Go with them, my dear friends." Anastasia smiled, leading them towards the waiting alien contingent. "For they are explorers of this vast, infinite universe searching for new knowledge and new species. Do not worry, for they are under my command. Go with them to their starship and you may find just what you are looking for." She paused for a second thoughtfully. "Remember, it is imperative that you open your minds and hearts to what lies in front of you; you must, or it will not happen."

Romy could not contain her happiness. She hugged Anastasia. "Oh, we will, Anastasia! Oh, we will! We always have. Oh, oh, oh thank you so much, Anastasia!" Romy declared with joy. She turned towards her husband. "Oh, my God, Gerald, it's what we've always wanted. What we've always dreamed of. Oh my god! It's actually happening!" She hugged Gerald tightly.

He gave a grateful nod of thanks to Anastasia.

Together Gerald and Romy walked towards Margaux and Byron, both closely surrounded by their seven children and Dolly. Arnold smiled, as he stood by himself a few feet away. It would soon be his turn.

"Oh, Romy, oh, Gerald." Margaux said, hugging her two friends with sadness. "I will miss you both so very much. You have helped me so much. I cannot believe how much we had all gone through these past several hours. It feels like I have known you both forever. You know we have pretty much come full circle."

"Yup." Gerald smiled at Margaux. "From Artemis' Realm in that road trip where we found you lost and hungry many years ago to this remarkable adventure we are going to embark soon. Actually, it's you we have to thank for all this for us. You were the central catalyst, you know. You made our dreams come true."

"I know." Margaux nodded. "I just can't believe all this that's happened. Even now, I'm still absorbing it all."

"I'm sorry there won't be any book to write about." Byron added, smiling. "There's no one to read it on earth, much less publish it."

"Don't be too sure about that, Byron." Gerald grinned mischievously, slapping Byron's shoulder. "Our book may even end up in the Amarnic Records, who knows."

Anastasia nodded thoughtfully.

"Right. Amarnic records. Whatever that is." Byron lifted an eyebrow. What an odd response from Gerald and yet, he did not want to pursue it. He had had enough of the mysteries so far. In point of fact, he was now preparing himself for a life with Margaux and their big family in a strange, new, world light years away from the shattered earth.

He extended his hand. "Good luck, Gerald. To you and your wife. It looks like you both will have a remarkable adventure."

"Many thanks, man." Gerald grasped his hand and shook it firmly. "Good luck, too, Byron, at your new home with your new family. And boy, what a family you have."

Byron looked back at his family and nodded, smiling. "I think so too."

He walked back to stand with Margaux and all of their children, Dolly at their feet.

Gerald and Romy reached out and held hands. Together, they solemnly walked towards Arnold to say their goodbyes.

Arnold hugged them both.

"Are you sure you don't want to come with us?" Gerald repeated. "This is your last chance, you know. Who knows how long we'll be gone."

"I'm sure, Gerald. I'm sure. Now go on both of you." Arnold pushed them ahead. "They're waiting for you."

"Come on, Romy, let the great adventure begin!" Gerald reached out for her hand. She quickly took it and ran with him enthusiastically toward the four aliens waiting patiently for them by the portal.

Halfway, they stopped and turned around. They waved.

"Good bye!"

"Goodbye, Romy, Gerald! Good luck!"

In an instant, the four alien explorers, followed by Romy and Gerald, disappeared into the sloshing surface of the undulating portal.

"Oh, my god, I can't believe they're gone." Margaux said, staring at the spot where her friends had disappeared. "We'll never see them again."

Anastasia walked up to her sister. "That's not true, Margaux. You will see them again. As supreme leader, I give you my promise."

"Oh, that would be wonderful, Anastasia! I have so grown fond of them both."

"And now." Anastasia said, clasping both hands in front of her. "What about your other friend, Arnold. We have many opportunities for one of his superior knowledge, skills, and experience. We know what he can do. He only has to keep an open mind working with us."

All three turned towards Arnold, who stubbornly stared at the floor. Slowly, he looked up at the group, his hands deep in the pockets of his slacks. He did not look happy.

"I just want to go home." He said firmly. "I just want to go back to earth."

"But everything around Artemis' Realm is gone, Arnold. There is nothing there for you. What can you do?" Margaux implored to her friend.

"Margaux, that is not true." Anastasia quickly corrected. "He does have a place to go on earth. I suspect it is with his sister and her family on the other side of the ocean." Arnold nodded. "She needs my help. I'm all she has and she is all I have." He smiled crookedly. "We are also twins, you know."

"Oh, Arnold. I forgot all about Anneliese, your twin. I remember her from that road trip. God, you were both so big and intimidating." Margaux declared. "Did you both ever made the Olympic swimming games?"

"No, we did not make the trials, unfortunately. Life happened. Instead, I enrolled in university and Annaliese married a German politician. She is now a mother of four."

Margaux smiled. "But of course, you must go to your sister. But, seriously, it's a hard life down there now, Arnold, rebuilding the earth. Are you sure you want that life?"

Arnold looked at Margaux sadly. "I cannot abandon my sister any more than Anastasia can abandon you in this time of a horrible tragedy. I really have to go back. I have to help my sister and her family."

Margaux and Byron nodded. It was true, after all. The ties of familial blood were indeed strong among their people. It was how they had managed to survive as a species over eons of time on the dynamic, planet earth.

Anastasia raised her hand in the air. They turned toward her.

"What now?"

"In that case, my dear sister and friends," she pronounced with authoritative gravity. "Now would be a good time for the final truth to come out."

"Final truth?" Margaux asked, puzzled at her announcement. "What final truth? We are twin sisters, aren't we? That was the truth hidden from me all of my life."

Anastasia shook her head firmly. "Not entirely, Margaux. Of course, we are twin sisters, but as you will soon see, I am more like our father, the One Most High, in which case, it was necessary to quickly ferret me away from the arms of our human mother on earth. Even she must not see me."

"What are you talking about?" Byron demanded, grabbing Margaux's hand and pulling her closer to their children. He had had about all the surprises he could take and yet, here was Anastasia announcing another new one.

"It's okay." Arnold reassured them. "It's okay. Go on, Anastasia. Tell us. What is the final truth."

"As I said before, it is time for you all to see me in my true form." Anastasia smiled lovingly at her sister. "For you see, Margaux, like our father, I am also a shapeshifter. It was how I was able to change myself into your form and communicate with you on earth. I did not want to scare you away."

"Scare me away?" Margaux asked puzzled. She gripped Byron's hand harder. "But how?"

Anastasia paused and took in a deep breath. Slowly, she turned around in place, waving her hands in the air in rhythmic motions. By the third revolution, the vibrations, waves, and colors had already consumed her. All of a sudden, Anastasia's human form disappeared. In its place appeared an alien form of truly inexplicable proportions.

Margaux gasped. Byron held her tightly in his arms. Arnold's eyes widened. Even he stepped back from Anastasia, unsure of what would transpire next.

Anastasia's small lips smiled benevolently. Only her voice remained the same, strong and vociferous with an unwavering sense of authority. "Be not afraid, my dear sister and friends. For this is who I really am." She extended her impossibly long arms outwards, as if presenting herself to the world.

"I am of my father, the One Most High."

It was impossible not to stare at Anastasia. Standing tall and proud, her large, triangular-shaped face was bordered at both sides with impossibly high cheekbones, large, clear almond shaped eyes peppered with numerous tiny sky-blue pupils and very long lashes on their rims. In addition, she had long, pointed ears, and an elongated head, crowned by her long, thick, golden hair. The royal-purple toga had disappeared and in its place appeared a velvety-soft, golden unitard, covering the entire length of her extremely long, lissome body, exposing only the equally long, velvety tail that trailed on the floor behind her. Her skin was the color of the ocean—deep cerulean blue.

Arnold grinned. "Why am I not surprised?" He crossed his arms, a hand on his chin. "Of course, she had to be of an insectoid species, albeit with some human traits inherited from her mother." He slowly walked towards and around Anastasia, scrutinizing her body with the admiration and interest of a scientist. "This is indeed remarkable. Except for the color on this skin, I know of only one insect on earth resembling this marvelous entity."

"Don't you dare call her an insect!" Margaux protested loudly, all her protective instincts coming to the fore. "I don't care what Anastasia actually looks like. She is not a circus freak to be stared at. God, she is still my twin sister!"

"My apologies." Arnold bowed his head towards Anastasia. "For the past moment, I had been truly captivated by your remarkable resemblance to the praying mantis, an insect on earth, you know. For all our time on earth, it would seem we and the animals on earth were the only forms to exist, that's how badly self-absorbed we were. The thought of something like you out there is a game changer, indeed. You would be quite a showcase."

"Absolutely not." Margaux demanded, standing her ground, her eyes blazing with anger.

"Good lord, Arnold." Byron intervened, standing with Margaux and glaring at Arnold in disgust. "An insect? You are comparing Margaux's long, lost twin sister to a mere insect on earth? One for show? That's really low of you, you know."

Anastasia laughed melodiously, her voice filling the room with its strong, lilting tones of defiance. She stepped away from her angry sister and her lover. "Margaux, my dear, do not worry. He cannot harm me. I am too powerful for him or for anyone else to 'mess around with.' Besides, your friend is merely being himself, the ever-proficient scientist, supremely excited with the prospect of an unprecedented discovery. I have encountered many like him."

She waved her hand with an air of dismissal. "There is really no need to apologize, for your friend is correct. I am actually of the insectoid race; one that existed since ancient times, long before the human race appeared." She paused for a moment, walking around the room, her head high in the air, her tail gliding up and down and all around in graceful balletic strides. "You see, another ancient race, considerably older than us, created the human species on earth thousands of years ago. Much later, ancient Greece was founded by us, but of course, you know, we have had to shapeshift into a form these primitive people on earth were comfortable with. Time passed. Eventually we left. However, some of us stayed behind to intermingle with them."

"Ah, the demi gods of Greek mythology." Arnold commented, rubbing his chin thoughtfully. "Hercules, Helen of Troy, Theseus, Achilles, Perseus, et cetera, et cetera." He shook his head in disbelief. "And now the so called Watchers among us. Unbelievable."

Anastasia approached Margaux, extending her hands toward her. Unafraid of her newly-discovered, blue-skinned, insectoid sister, a powerful High Priestess, Margaux quickly took her hands into hers. They felt soft and inviting, quite velvety.

"Do you still wish to come to my home planet, Margaux?" Anastasia asked, her voice laced with uncertainty. "As you know by now, all my people look exactly like me."

Margaux gripped Anastasia's hand tighter. "Of course, we want to come home with you, Anastasia." She glanced at Byron, who smiled and nodded. No argument there. She turned to her sister. "But what of your people? Will they accept us as we are? Our children, also? Even Dolly?"

"Most assuredly." Anastasia beamed, her voice teeming with confidence and love. "There is no vice, no iniquity, at my home planet. Our only purpose in life is to search for and understand the greater knowledge the universe has to offer. You will be treated with great respect."

Arnold stepped forward. Byron and Margaux looked at him warily, still feeling protective towards Anastasia.

Arnold glanced at Anastasia and bowed his head solemnly, his voice thick with contrition. "I am quite in deference to your remarkable powers, High Priestess Anastasia. I have no interest in showcasing you, much less studying you like one would a guinea pig." He smiled all around. "I think I am definitely ready to head towards earth. Did you say your people will assist us in rebuilding or relocating, Anastasia?"

Anastasia nodded graciously. "We will still honor our obligation, my friend. We would hope you will assist us when we arrive for your people surely will exhibit resistance towards our efforts to help them. Unfortunately, as Gerald and Romy had pointed out, the current human race is not as open-minded and pure as the Quashone Indians were when we arrived to help them many thousands of years ago."

"I wouldn't disagree with that." Arnold replied. "However, it would be beneficial if your people shapeshifted to look like us. Then I would be able to help at a greater degree. Like I said, we have no choice at this point in time. We desperately need your assistance."

"But of course, my friend." Anastasia bowed her head. "We would be most happy to do so." She pointed towards the dense, undulating wormhole. "There is a shuttle suspended outside of Star Centralia waiting to take you home. Just walk through there."

Halfway down towards the portal, Arnold turned and faced Margaux and Byron, eye to eye. The grim features on his face softened. He smiled and waved. The couple and their children waved back enthusiastically. Dolly barked, wagging her tail excitedly.

"Goodbye, Arnold! Good luck and godspeed! You will need it."

"And how! This has been an incredible experience with you all. I will never forget it. Hell, I will never forget all of you. Goodbye all!"

Unhesitatingly, Arnold entered and disappeared forever into the gateway.

Out in the blackness of the infinite, timeless universe, the supremely massive Star Centralia slowly maneuvered its dark, heavily-fortified, tungsten-molybdenum hull, its multi-colored lights blinking steadily, towards that one tiny, brilliant dot of light 9.3 light years away from the mothership's holding pattern. In instant, it whizzed away at hypersonic speed towards...home.

THE END